DAY OF THE DARK
Stories of Eclipse

DAY OF THE DARK

Stories of Eclipse

EDITED BY
KAYE GEORGE

WILDSIDE PRESS

Published by Wildside Press LLC.
www.wildsidepress.com

CONTENTS

INTRODUCTION

When the idea for this anthology first occurred to me, I was excited right away. I was incredibly lucky that so many excellent short story writers were excited also. My call for submissions netted too many stories, almost all of them print-worthy. I upped the length with the blessings of Wildside Press, who had agreed to publish this volume in time for the total solar eclipse of August 21, 2017.

I'm proud to present this group of stories. They reflect light and dark across the globe, solar and lunar eclipses, and are written across genre lines. There are stories from Finland, Canada, two that take place in Norway and Vienna, and in several places in and off the path of totality.

This is a good cross section to represent a totality of eclipse experiences. I hope you enjoy them as much as I have.

—Kaye George

DARK SIDE OF THE LIGHT

CAROL L. WRIGHT

When Joanne woke up, it was still dark. She rolled over. Sure enough, Eric still wasn't home. She would have been madder about him ruining her big announcement the evening before if she didn't have to rush to the bathroom with an urgent need to pee.

Before she got back under the covers, the nausea hit. The nurse said to keep some crackers on the nightstand to nibble first thing in the morning. She should get some at the store today. *Only another month or so of this.* That was something, at least.

She closed her eyes for what she thought was just a moment or two, then awoke with a start when she realized Eric was there, sitting on the side of the bed in the gathering dawn with a weird smile on his face.

"Hey," she said, lifting herself up on her elbows. "You made it home."

"And I brought you something," Eric said, whipping a huge bundle of flowers from behind his back.

Guilt flowers, Joanne thought.

As if he could read her mind, Eric said, "They're an apology for all the hours I've been putting in at work lately."

She took the flowers and pressed them to her face. "Where did you get them at this hour? What time is it, anyway?"

"About quarter to six. I got them at the all-night grocer. Three bouquets. I spared no expense."

"I'd say you shouldn't have, but considering all the evenings you've left me alone, I'll accept them."

"Sorry, babe. Just a lot going on at work."

"Such as?" she asked, knowing that he couldn't and wouldn't say. Eric's work at NASA was classified, and he took its secrecy very seriously. "I mean," she continued, "it's not like you're about to send up a space shuttle or anything."

Eric worked with CNEOS at the JPL. She hated that the government used acronyms for everything. How was anyone supposed to know what they were doing? *Maybe*, she thought, *that's why they do it.*

"Oh, you know—with the eclipse and all. Hey—I saw the table still set for last night's dinner," he said, changing the subject. "It looks like you went to a lot of trouble. Really sorry, babe."

Joanne went from pleased to pissed. She *had* gone to a lot of trouble. Candles, champagne, her grandmother's good china, and Eric's favorite recipe—all for the big reveal. She had big news, and she wanted to tell him in just the right way.

At least Eric looked really sorry.

"I've decided to take the day off," he said.

"Not to sleep, I hope. If you sleep all day, you'll be jet-lagged for the rest of the week."

"Nah. I caught a cat nap in the lounge. I'm okay. I want to spend the whole day with you." He hesitated. "We can watch the eclipse together."

That will work out well, Joanne reasoned. *Now I'll have the whole day to figure out the best way to make my big announcement. Let me see ...*

As he leaned in for a kiss, his phone chirped. He gave her a quick peck, checked his text, frowned, and stuffed the phone back in his pocket.

She thought about popping the champagne cork to make him a mimosa, and maybe Eggs Benedict. *Ugh.* The thought of eggs sent her stomach roiling.

"C'mon," Eric said. "The sun is rising, and it's going to be another perfect day in Southern California out there." He coughed. "Let's make the most of it. We can do anything you want to do. Maybe something we've put off doing for a long time, and now have the perfect day to do it."

Yeah, Joanne thought. *I have just that kind of thing that I'm busy doing right now.* She grinned at her own cleverness.

"Okay—what's the joke?" Eric said, looking at her sideways.

"Aren't you tired?" she said, hoping to distract him from her grin.

"Sure, a little, but I've been neglecting you. Today, I'm all yours. I don't want to waste a minute of it."

"Well, I was going to do a little online shopping today," Joanne said, drawing out the words. Maybe he would browse with her, and once he saw what she was shopping for, she'd have a perfect way to break the news.

"Online shopping?" His shoulders slumped and he shook his head. Then he glanced up with a look of resolve. "Okay. If that's what will make you happy, feel free. And the sky's the limit. Spend anything you want—a one-day-only offer. Anything you want to order is fine with me."

"Okaaay," Joanne said, wondering what happened to her penny-pinching husband. "It really is what I want to do. Let's browse together."

"You go ahead. While you're shopping, I'll give my mom a call. It's later back East. Then after we're both done, we can do something together."

No, no. That's not the way this is supposed to work at all. But Eric had already pulled out his cell and pressed his mother's speed dial number. He walked away with his phone to his ear.

"But …" she called after him. He was gone. There was no use.

Joanne got dressed and looked in the mirror. Was she imagining it, or were her boobs a little rounder? *There ought to be some compensation for the soreness.* Except for the morning sickness with which she currently had a love/hate relationship, there was no obvious sign of pregnancy. Nothing to indicate that, after seven years of marriage, she and Eric were at last expecting the child they both prayed for but, for unknown reasons, had been unable to conceive.

When her cycle was late, she hadn't wanted to get his hopes up—especially with the long hours he'd been working. Even after the home test, she didn't dare tell him. But yesterday she had finally seen a doctor. She was eight weeks along, and she'd seen the tiny heart beat on the ultrasound. She knew Eric would be over the moon when she told him. Everything had to be perfect.

She went to the kitchen to put the flowers in a vase. When Eric found her there, she looked up at him as brightly as she could.

"How's your mom?"

"Okay. I guess I woke her. I forget she sleeps in now that she's retired."

"You didn't talk long."

"No," he said. "I just told her that I loved her, and she said the same. Sends love to you as well."

Joanne rolled her eyes. "Sure she did." She knew she'd caught him in a lie. His mother had never taken a shine to her, and the long years without producing grandchildren only cemented her dislike. But that didn't matter. Eric had chosen her. Enough said.

Eric took her in his arms. "Well, she would have sent her love if she had any idea how wonderful you are."

"Wow. Flowers and flattery. You ought to pull all-nighters more often if you come home all romantic."

She got the kiss she had been waiting for, and it gave her tingles from her lips to her bare feet.

"So what shall we do this morning?" she asked, pushing her sore breasts slightly away from his chest.

"I thought maybe we could go to the lake. Maybe rent a boat and do a little fishing, and watch the eclipse without a lot of trees in the way."

Fishing. That's his *idea of a perfect day, not mine.* She tried to imagine being out on the lake, in the hot sun, with the boat rocking. Nausea threatened again.

"It's what we did on our first date, remember?" he said.

"No," she said, punching him in the arm. "We went on a party boat at sunset with half the graduating class."

"Well, a bunch of us were fishing off the stern, and I remember a brown-eyed girl, who looked a lot like you, flirting with me."

She laughed. She was flirting. No reason to pretend otherwise. He was a hunk then, and had only improved with age—if your definition of hunk was a nerdy, bespectacled brainiac with a ready smile and a good sense of humor. *Yeah. Definitely a hunk. His kid is going to be as handsome as he is.*

His phone chirped again. He checked the text and frowned.

"Something wrong?"

"Nothing you need to worry about," Eric said, pocketing his cell and pasting on a smile. He stared at the wall for a moment. He seemed so intent on doing something memorable today.

He has no idea how memorable it's going to be, she thought, *if I can just figure out how to tell him. I hate keeping him in the dark.*

"Well, how about I take you out to an early breakfast, and we can figure it out from there," he said.

Her stomach felt a bit better. "Sure. Why not?"

* * * *

On the way to their favorite diner, Eric kept looking at the sky. Joanne stared up through the tinted windshield, but couldn't guess what had captured his attention. So far, it was just a summer sky. The few clouds were high and thin, and the bright morning sun promised another hot day. The earth was parched from a summer dry spell, and the fire danger was high according to the sign outside the firehouse.

"The eclipse hasn't started, has it?"

"No, it won't … uh … start until about nine a.m. It will look almost full here around ten-fifteen."

Joanne remembered seeing a nearly total eclipse years before. Street lights came on and the birds chirped their evening songs. "But you keep looking at the sky. Expecting aliens to invade or something?"

Eric's reaction wasn't what she expected. "Why would you say that?"

"A joke," she said, holding up both hands as if defending herself from attack.

"Sorry I snapped," he said. "I've just got this headache."

"Probably from lack of sleep," Joanne suggested.

After that, she noticed him forcing himself to look anywhere but the sky. *Science nerds can be so weird.*

When they entered the diner, she nearly gagged on the strong stench. "What's that smell? Did they burn the coffee?" she said, covering her nose.

"Smells the same as always," Eric said.

She looked at him to be sure he wasn't joking. Not that she planned to drink the coffee anyway, but the smell took away any appetite she had.

Eric ordered the biggest breakfast the diner offered: French toast, three eggs, hash browns, a grilled blueberry muffin, bacon and sausage. Then he added a stack of pancakes, and in addition to his black coffee, a large orange juice and a hot chocolate with whipped cream.

"I know you like a big breakfast, honey, but don't you think you're overdoing it a bit? You might regret all those calories."

"Nope. From now on, I regret nothing," he said as he poured syrup over nearly the entire mess.

Joanne looked away. She ordered a dry English muffin with a side of peanut butter and a decaf ginger tea. She remembered the nurse saying that protein was supposed to help, but there was no way she could face an egg today.

His cell chirped again. Eric did the same thing he'd been doing all day: checked the text, frowned, then put the phone back in his pocket.

"What's with all the texts?"

"Oh, it's nothing. Just work."

He excused himself to go to the bathroom, leaving Joanne to ponder his odd behavior. He was hiding something. He didn't want to talk about the messages, but it wasn't the same kind of reluctance he usually had about discussing work. Something was different. If it weren't for that kiss this morning, and the flowers, and the ...

Wait! she thought. *These could be the signs of a guilty conscience all right—but not about staying overnight at work. Exactly where was he all night?*

She had heard the tales before. Suddenly a husband gets romantic, but it's because he's been flirting—or worse—with another woman. There were plenty of women at work. Smart women—smarter than her, Joanne knew. Maybe she wasn't intelligent enough to keep him happy.

Could it be? Could he be attracted to someone else? Could he even be having an affair?

Then she thought about the baby. *Maybe if I'd told him already, he wouldn't have been interested in another woman. Maybe things wouldn't have gone this far—however far that is.*

Her mind raced. This was terrible. Would he ask for a divorce? Would their child grow up in a broken home? That was not the fairy tale they had dreamed of.

If she had to raise this child alone, how could she do it? She hadn't had a full-time job since being laid off at Sears. She didn't make enough money to support herself. And even with Eric's government job, they barely had enough for the little luxuries. She'd never be able to make it on child support alone. Where could they live? This was terrible!

Eric returned to the table, and Joanne felt tears fill her eyes.

"What's wrong?" Eric asked, signaling the server for a refill of his coffee.

"You tell me," Joanne said, sticking out her chin. She would be brave. She was strong. She had to be. She was going to be a mother.

Eric looked uncomfortable. "What have you heard?"

"Heard? Nothing. But I'm not a complete idiot, no matter what you might think. I can read the signs."

He glanced out the window. "What signs?"

"All of them," she said, giving him her best attempt at a hairy eyeball.

The goddamn cell chirped again.

"I'm sorry," he said after checking the text. "I have to make a call."

He took his phone and walked away from the table and right out the door. He wanted privacy. It must be *her.*

She decided to follow. He stood just outside with his back to the front door. Cracking the diner door open, she listened to Eric's side of the conversation.

"No, I don't think that's a good idea," he said. A long pause followed. "It might be hard for her to accept, but it's just too late."

Too late for what? To repair our marriage? She felt new tears sting her eyes.

Eric turned, and Joanne let the door close between them. She bolted back to their table in time to prevent the busboy from clearing their plates. Eric still had half of his breakfast to consume.

Her fears confirmed, Joanne rethought the romantic announcement of her pregnancy. *I won't tell him at all. That'll serve him right. I'll move to another state and he'll never meet his child. I won't let that creep anywhere near my baby. How could he do this to me?*

Then she thought about her baby growing up without a father. She knew that wasn't ideal either. *But to grow up with a cheating father—and maybe a floozy stepmother? No. Intolerable.*

It was a few minutes before Eric returned to the table. His breakfast looked soggy and congealed. It was all Joanne could do to keep from sweeping it off the table and into his lap.

"So, what was *that* all about?" she said, hoping her voice dripped with venom.

"Something at work."

That's all the explanation I get? Oh—I guess he's waiting for just the right moment to dump me like a sack of garbage. And to think that I was waiting for the right moment to give him the best news of his life. Well, you can forget that, buster.

"I don't think I want to go out today," Joanne said, folding her napkin. "I have things I need to do at home." *Like find a good lawyer.*

Eric looked up. His eyes betrayed disappointment. "Well, if you'd really rather. I guess we can see the eclipse from there, but it would be better without so many trees around."

"Well, that's what I want."

She refused to look at him, let alone speak to him, on the ride home.

* * * *

"It's still a couple of hours before the eclipse begins. I'm going to call Roger. He probably hasn't left for work yet," Eric said as they entered the house.

Joanne couldn't believe her ears. "Your brother, Roger?" *Couldn't you come up with a better excuse than that? You haven't spoken to your brother in six years, and now you expect me to believe you're going to call him for no reason?*

"Yeah. I just think it's time, you know?"

"Whatever."

Joanne went to their room, and pulled out her own cell. Who did she know who would know a good divorce lawyer? Gloria, of course. She'd been divorced twice and was living comfortably on her former husbands' money. And, fortunately for Joanne, she was an early riser.

"Oh no, honey," Gloria said when she heard why Joanne called.

"No—you don't know a good lawyer?" Joanne asked.

"Oh, of course I do. I know more than one, but I'm just sorry that's something you need. I never would have guessed it of Eric. How long have you two been married?"

"Seven years."

"Oh—well, that's one of the dangerous years."

Gloria gave her three lawyers' names and their phone numbers. "They're the best in town. Make sure you meet with them all so Eric can't get any of them to represent him. Conflict of interest, you know. But make sure you hire the first name. She's the one I use."

"I would never have thought of that. Anything else I need to know?"

"It would be great if you could get proof of infidelity. I hired a PI, but sometimes you can find things on your own, like motel charges on the credit card—that kind of thing."

"Okay. Thanks, Gloria. It sounds like it's going to be expensive."

"Maybe, but I'm living proof that it's worth it in the long run."

After hanging up, Joanne knew where she had to start. She had to get a look at that cell phone and find out who the bimbo was.

Eric joined her in the bedroom looking ashen. "Well, that was tough," he said. "At first, Steph couldn't get Roger to come to the phone. Then when he did, he wouldn't talk. He just said, 'You called. Just tell me what you have to say.'"

"So you really called Roger?"

"Yeah. I said I was." He rubbed his temples. "Got any aspirin?"

"In the medicine cabinet. And what did you expect, calling out of the blue like that?" she snapped, annoyed that he had made her feel sorry for him.

Eric shook his head. "Yeah well, it's done." He looked at his phone and put it in his pocket.

How can I get a look at that phone? Joanne thought about it. There was only one thing that came to mind.

"I've changed my mind. Let's go to the lake."

Eric's face brightened. "Really? Great. I'll pack a cooler."

"Don't forget your bathing suit," Joanne called after him.

"Oh right," he said, returning to the bedroom and pulling it out of a drawer. "I'll be ready in ten minutes. I have special glasses for us to use." He gave her a serious look. "This is going to be fun."

Oh yeah. Tons of fun.

* * * *

The trip took more than half an hour, but Eric didn't waste any time. Moments after arriving, he had stripped down to his swim trunks and t-shirt, locking his clothes in the car. As he spread a blanket on the sand of the nearly deserted beach, Joanne told him she was going to the bath house to change, but instead she went to the parking lot.

His phone was in his pants pocket. She turned it on and was glad, despite his penchant for secrets, that he didn't use the thumbprint recognition lock that came with the phone. She easily guessed his swipe pattern on the number pad—a lower-case "e". She was in.

She scrolled through the texts. The most recent ones were from "Driscoll." She tried to remember if Eric had ever mentioned her. She opened the conversation.

Text from Driscoll at 5:46 a.m.: "Procedure failure confirmed. Sorry."

That doesn't sound too sexy.

Text from Driscoll 6:14 a.m.: "No other options available. Time now very short."

Options for what? Sounds kind of dire.

Text from Driscoll at 6:58 a.m.: "Dr. Steinmetz agrees our assessment. Wants to discuss possible last ditch approach."

Text from Driscoll at 7:10 a.m.: "Please call me."

This was while we were at the diner. It must have been this Driscoll person that he called. What did he say again? Something about it being too late. Too late for what?

Then it hit her. These texts weren't from some girlfriend, nor were they about some illicit attraction. They were talking about something medical. Driscoll must be a nurse or a PA or something who works for this doctor Steinmetz. *Since when has Eric been going to a Doctor Steinmetz?*

She used the phone's browser to check on a doctor by that name in the area. She found several with a variety of specialties, but the only one that seemed to fit the texts was a neurosurgeon.

Oh no! Eric has a brain aneurysm. They tried some procedure, but it didn't work. He's going to die.

Just moments before she was imagining the satisfaction of murdering him, but now, discovering he was dying left her sobbing and gasping for breath.

It all made sense now. Wanting to spend a whole day with her. Calling his mother—and his estranged brother. Wanting to spend time at the lake while he could still enjoy it. The headache. Even eating like there was literally no tomorrow.

And what had she done but make it hard on him to spend one of his last days the way he wanted to.

Why hadn't he told her? They could have gone through this together. She could have helped him. He didn't have to keep her in the dark. But she would act as if she didn't know, since that was how he wanted it.

He didn't even know yet that he was going to be a father. Forget the romantic scene. She had to tell him now.

She locked the car and raced back to the beach, hoping to find Eric on the shore and not somewhere in the lake. He was standing near the water, staring at the sky through some strange dark glasses.

She came up behind him, focusing on where he was looking, straining to figure out what fascinated him so. It looked like the moon was up during the day—only brighter than usual. Almost like a second sun. *Must be some kind of Supermoon or something.* No wonder a science nerd would be interested.

She put her hand on his shoulder. "Darling, come with me. There's something I need to tell you."

Eric took off his glasses and gave her a quizzical look, but followed her to a picnic table in the shade. He blinked several times while his eyes adjusted to the light. They sat opposite each other, and Joanne took his hands in hers.

"I've been trying to find the perfect time to tell you this," she began. "I'm two months pregnant. You're going to be a father."

Eric gasped. "You're … you're pregnant?" He burst into tears. "After all this time you're pregnant now?"

Joanne hadn't seen him cry since before they were married when his father died. "I know. It's a miracle."

And for the first time, she realized that it was more than the fulfillment of their mutual dream. This child was a way for her to hold onto the husband she loved, even after he was gone. She would be sure that the baby learned everything about its father so that it never felt it didn't have a dad.

As soon as Eric gained control of his emotions, he lost it again. It took several tries for him to stop his tears. Joanne waited, wondering whether he would share his sad news with her.

"Do you know if it's a boy or a girl?" he asked.

"No. It's too early to know," she said. "But I hope it's a boy who will grow up to be like you."

Eric struggled to maintain his control. The sun on the beach had grown brighter, and the sand look electrified. Even in the shade it was hot. Eric looked up at the sky, but Joanne held her gaze on him. He looked healthy—well a bit pale from not getting much sun this summer, but still, no one would guess he had an aneurysm.

"Tell me what you're thinking," Joanne prompted, hoping he'd let her in on his dark secret.

"That's classified," he said with a smirk.

"Does that really matter now?"

Eric looked at her and sighed. "Perhaps not," he admitted. "You seem to have an inkling anyway."

Joanne nodded. "Go on."

"Well, my work at the Jet Propulsion Lab is in the Center for Near Earth Object Studies. In a nutshell, we look for things flying around in space in Earth's neighborhood."

Joanne had no idea where he was going with this.

"Most of these objects, comets, asteroids, and the like, are harmless to the Earth, but they can offer us information on the formation of the universe." Eric became more animated as he spoke.

Joanne smiled. *He really loves his work.*

"The gravitational pull of other bodies in space affect orbits of these Near Earth Objects, and if something happens to one of them that changes its gravitational pull, it affects the others as well. Am I going too fast?"

"No. I get it. But I wanted to know about your ... headache."

"I'm getting to that." Eric said. "Our solar system is pretty stable. Our sun is too small to be at risk of ever going nova, and our planets are too far apart to affect each other's orbits."

"So ...?"

"But these 'NEOs' as we call them, we theorize that some don't just stay within our solar system. They travel to other parts of the universe where other forces can affect their trajectories in ways we can't predict. Okay so far?"

"Yes, but what does that have to do ..."

"So, there are lots of comets and asteroids flying around. Some we know about and can predict. Others we can't. When that happens, if it looks like an Earth impact is imminent, we do what we can to avoid a collision, but our science isn't there yet. We can't change physics no matter how many late nights we spend trying to." He looked into Joanne's eyes as if asking, "Do you understand?"

Joanne was flummoxed. She had to take control of this conversation. "What does this have to do with you seeing a doctor?"

"What doctor?"

"Doctor Steinmetz. I saw the name on your phone in a message from somebody named Driscoll."

Eric rolled his eyes. "Larry Driscoll is a colleague. Doctor Steinmetz is in another division at JPL. We consult with her from time to time on these things."

"No, no. This Driscoll performed a procedure and told you there wasn't anything left to do. Then Doctor Steinmetz wanted to talk to you about another possible treatment. You don't have to hide it from me anymore. I saw the texts."

"Okay, but what you don't know ... here, put these on." Eric handed her the glasses. "Now look." Eric pointed at the sky.

Joanne looked up. The moon had doubled in size and brightness. "What's happening to the moon? Is it falling out of the sky?"

"It's not the moon," Eric said. "It's bigger."

Joanne looked from Eric to the object, and back to Eric. "Is it going to hit us?"

Eric looked at his hands.

She stood, not wanting to believe what she now knew to be true. "Is it going to destroy us?" She so wanted to hear that everything was going to be okay, but Eric said nothing. She felt dizzy and sat down. "Why don't people know about this?"

"What's the point? Let people enjoy their day. Go to their eclipse parties. There's nothing they can do to get away from it. Nothing to be gained by sending the public into a panic." He swallowed hard. "Do you really want the last hours of humanity on Earth to be consumed with killing, looting, and suicides?"

"Or maybe prayer," Joanne said.

The heat from the approaching object intensified. It looked larger than the sun.

"It's coming fast, isn't it? We won't be here to see the eclipse." She felt nauseated and knew it wasn't morning sickness.

Eric shrugged. "It doesn't matter anymore."

"But the baby ..." Joanne choked on the words and covered her belly with both hands.

"Will go with us," Eric said. "We'll all go together."

"It's not fair. Just when we were about to have a family, everything ends? It's not right."

"It doesn't matter anymore," he repeated.

"What will it be like?" she asked, her head throbbing.

"The heat will become more intense. We'll all pass out long before impact."

Joanne felt goosebumps despite the rising temperature. "Is this what it means to go into the light?"

Eric thought about his answer. "For us it is. It's what I came here to see."

Leaning on each other, they returned to the beach, staggering across the searing sand to their blanket. It was getting hotter by the second, and too bright to keep their eyes open even with the dark glasses.

They lay beside each other on the blanket, and she felt Eric kiss her. She reached for him, and they embraced as the fireball filled the sky.

Carol L. Wright is a recovering attorney who has spent several years in academia as an adjunct law professor and pre-law advisor. After publishing many articles and a book relating to law and pre-law advising, she turned to writing fiction. She has published several short stories, and is working on a novel-length mystery. She is a founder of the Bethlehem Writers Group, LLC, and a member of Sisters in Crime, SinC Guppies, the Jane Austen Society of North America, and Pennwriters. She is married to her college sweetheart and lives in the Lehigh Valley of Pennsylvania. www.carollwright.com

CHASING THE MOON

LESLIE WHEELER

Madras, Oregon, 9:13 AM, Sunday, August 20, 2017

"Antarctica in 2014. Norway in 2015. Indonesia in 2016." Daphne Yates ticked off the places she and husband Victor had viewed total eclipses of the sun on her smooth, pale, red-tipped fingers. Fingers that had probably never washed a dish, scrubbed a floor, or wiped a baby's behind, Randi Lawrence thought. Her own hands were dry and chapped with bitten-down nails.

"And now here we are in …" Daphne paused and shook out her mane of perfectly styled blond hair. Her gaze took in the kitchen with its clean but cracked linoleum floor, ancient appliances and the dented wood table with mismatched chairs where she and her husband sat. "Madras, Oregon." The peculiar emphasis Daphne placed on the last two words conveyed her low regard for the town.

Randi exchanged glances with her mom, who stood by the stove, flipping another batch of blueberry pancakes. Did Mom also wonder why the Yates had picked Madras as the spot to view the 2017 solar eclipse? After all, there were larger cities with more amenities that lay within the so-called "path of totality." And why had the Yates chosen her family's humble Airbnb over the Madras Chateau Inn & Suites? She wondered even more as Daphne went on about some of the luxury hotels she and her husband had stayed at previously.

Daphne was in the midst of describing the glass-domed lobby with live birch trees growing in the center at their hotel in Norway, when Randi's five-year-old son, Derek, walked into the kitchen and asked, "What's an eclipse?"

"You answer him, Vic." Daphne cast a weary look at her husband. "And plee-zz, keep it short."

Victor Yates turned to the boy with a smile. "Well, Derek, an eclipse is when the moon gets between the sun and the Earth, and the moon covers up the sun." He spoke in the gentle, reassuring voice of Mister Rogers welcoming kids to the neighborhood. Otherwise, Victor bore little resemblance to the late host of the children's TV program. With unruly, salt and pepper hair and heavy, black-framed glasses, he looked like the UC-Berkeley astronomer he was.

"Do you have any more questions?" Victor asked Derek.

The boy stared at him, open-mouthed, as if he couldn't believe this stranger actually wanted to hear from him. Then he launched a barrage of questions. "How does the moon get between the sun and the Earth? What does it look like when the moon covers the sun? How long does it last?"

Victor answered every question Derek lobbed at him in the same gentle, reassuring voice. Warming to the subject, he grew animated. He used words like "umbra" and "corona." Derek listened, captivated, repeating each new word after Victor.

Umbra, corona, Randi echoed silently, as enthralled as her son. And as disappointed as he when Daphne, who had frowned at her manicured nails the entire time Victor was speaking, declared, "Enough! I'm not spending the day sitting around in this kitchen. Let's do something. Take a drive along the coast, see the sights of Portland."

"All right." Victor rose reluctantly. Before leaving, he told Derek, "If you have any more questions, hold onto them until I get back, okay?"

From the kitchen window, Randi and her mom watched the Yates drive away in their BMW.

"It's a wonder he hasn't divorced her," Mom said.

Or done her in, Randi added silently.

As if she guessed Randi's thoughts, Mom said, "Now don't you be getting ideas. Just because he spoke nice to Derek doesn't mean a thing. After tomorrow's eclipse, him and his stuck-up wife will be gone for good."

Gone for good, Randi repeated to herself. *Like the boy in the rock band who'd knocked her up and left the next morning, never to be seen again.*

Hopkinsville, Kentucky, 1:03 PM, the same day

Fred Denton peeled the rubber "Little Green Man" mask off his face. Lord, he was hot. Hungry, too. It was his third day at the "Little Green Men Festival," held every year to celebrate the arrival of extraterrestrials at his wife's granddad's farm on August 21, 1955, and he was ready for a break. Not for the first time, he wished the folks from outer space hadn't picked the steamiest month of the year to land their spaceship in a gully at Elmer "Lucky" Sutton's place.

Even so, Fred was committed to upholding the Green Men tradition. He had been ever since the day, almost thirty years ago, when he'd intervened to stop Tim Murphy from bullying eight-year-old Betsy Sutton with taunts like, "Hey, little green girl, what a big head you have! What floppy, pointed ears! Getta look at those glowing eyes! Wanna go for a ride on my space ship?"

Fred swiped at drops of sweat beading his forehead and trickling down his neck. He lifted the edges of the long black cloak he wore over a green robe and flapped them like wings to create a breeze. That was better. Now he'd get some food.

Fred found a place at a shaded picnic table, took off his green rubber gloves and placed them with his mask on the bench beside him. Then he dug into the two hot dogs and a double order of fries he'd bought at the concession stand. His mother always said he ate like a horse with its head in a trough. Maybe she was right. Only after he'd licked the last of the catsup and mustard off his lips and taken his last swallow of Coke from the jumbo-sized plastic container did he realize his Little Green Man mask was missing.

Fred searched the grass under the bench. He found his gloves, but no mask. Desperate, he asked people around him if they'd seen anyone with his mask. No one had.

Noticing Fred's distress, Officer Charlie Lombardo, grandson of the police chief who'd investigated the 1955 encounter, approached him. "What's up, Fred?"

"Somebody swiped my mask."

"Nah, probably some kid picked it up. He'll lose interest and leave it some place where it'll be found. Or, if he's a good kid, he'll return it to you. You go ahead with your Little Green Man thing and I'll keep an eye out for your mask."

Fred agreed. But just as the Lone Ranger became an ordinary cowboy without his mask, so Fred couldn't truly be a Little Green Man without his. He stuck it out until the festival's evening closing and returned home, downcast but determined. He'd find the person who'd deprived him of his Little Green Manhood, and make him pay!

Nashville, Tennessee, 4:44 PM, the same day

Jesse Ray Richards slipped on a pair of dark glasses before entering Leroy's Place, a dive bar on 2nd Avenue. He tried to steer a straight course to the bar, but kept listing to one side or the other. When he was almost there, he crashed into a table and nearly fell.

"You shit-faced already?" From behind the bar, Leroy the owner greeted Jesse Ray in his raspy smoker's voice.

"Nah." Jesse Ray balanced precariously on a stool.

"Then why the shades?"

"These are protective glasses. I'm trying them out for tomorrow's eclipse."

"Don't look like protectives to me. Ain't no sunlight in here neither. You shit-faced. At the rate you're going, you gonna wind up in a coffin before you hit thirty."

"Cut the sermon, and get me a double straight up," Jesse Ray said. "You'd be hitting the bottle yourself, if you'd been kicked outta your own band."

"So, you've told me a million times before. If you sobered up, maybe they'd take you back."

"No, the bastards wouldn't."

"Start another band."

"Jesse Ray and the Riot Police is the only band for me. It's got my name, for chrissake."

"If that band was so important to you, why'd you do that crazy stuff that got you kicked off?

"What crazy stuff?"

"You don't remember? Jeez, man, your brain's more fried than I thought."

"Give me a minute. It'll come back to me." Jesse Ray closed his eyes and pressed his fingertips on either of his head. "Got it. What's so bad about passing out onstage? I was worn out. We'd been on the road for days. Maybe I shouldn't of got into a fight with that guy in the audience beforehand, but he was hassling us. Besides, that stuff didn't get me off the band."

"Whaddya think did it, then?"

"Jealousy. I was the star. The one everybody came to hear. The one everybody wanted a piece of. The other guys couldn't wait to steal my thunder. But without me, they're nothing."

"Seem to be doing okay."

"Yeah, doing covers."

"Your band was doing covers long before they kicked you out. Heard it was because you hadn't written any new music."

"To hell with 'em. I'm not some kind of machine that cranks out songs. I gotta be in the mood, be inspired."

"What's it take to get you there?"

"That bourbon I asked for would sure help."

"You don't think maybe that's the problem, 'stead of—" Leroy broke off at the creak of the bar door opening. "Uh-oh, here comes trouble."

Jesse Ray stole a glance over his shoulder. Big Bobby stood in the doorway, three hundred pounds of meanness. Jesse Ray hunched over the counter. Maybe if he played dead, Big Bobby would leave him alone.

"That you, Jesse Ray?" Big Bobby bellowed. "And here I was thinkin' you drunk yourself to death." Lumbering to the bar, he placed a hand the size of a baseball mitt on Jesse Ray's shoulder. "Seein' as how you's still livin' an' breathin', how 'bout a song for your old pal, Big Bobby?"

Jesse Ray kept quiet, hoping Big Bobby would tire of the game and find someone else to pick on. Instead, the baseball mitt tightened on his shoulder until his bones were ready to snap. "Sing, boy. Not gonna ask twice."

In a faint, quavering voice, Jesse Ray sang, "Yesterday all my troubles seemed so far away—"

Big Bobby slapped him hard on the cheek. "None of that Beatles shit. I wanna song you wrote special for me."

"Now, Big Bobby," Leroy intervened. "You can't expect Jesse Ray to come up with a song just like that. 'Specially since he's a bit under the weather. I'm sure he'll think of something if you can be patient. While you're waiting, here's a shot an' a beer." Leroy pushed the glasses at Big Bobby, who accepted them grudgingly. Big Bobby tried to settle his bulk onto a stool, but ended up retreating to a nearby table.

After Big Bobby had downed several drinks, Jesse Ray figured he was safe. "I owe you big-time," he told Leroy. "If you hadn't said something, that big, dumb baboon would've clobbered me."

The words were barely out of his mouth when the baseball mitt seized him by the shoulder and yanked him backwards off the stool. His skull cracked on the wooden floor. Everything went black.

Columbia, South Carolina, 7:21 PM, the same day

Hattie Menefee was in the bathroom washing her hands when the phone rang. Drying them hastily, she gripped the two sides of her walker and began the march to the phone in the living room.

Her goal was to make it before the tenth ring when the answering machine kicked in. Otherwise, her son Harold would think she'd grown even more feeble, and insist on having a phone installed in the bathroom as well as every other room in the house. Harold usually called at eight PM, so she got herself in place at a quarter to. But tonight he was early.

His way of testing her? She reached the phone before the tenth ring, but was so breathless she could barely speak at first.

"Everything okay, Mom?" Harold said.

"Fine, just fine."

"How was today's Meal on Wheels? If you're not happy with them, I could—"

"It was fine," Hattie fibbed, though she preferred her own cooking. She accepted this and other services Harold arranged to please him and keep him from nagging her about going into a nursing home.

"How about your meds—are you well stocked? Is the delivery service working all right?"

"Fine, just fine." She wouldn't tell him that the delivery man had been set upon by hoodlums, who'd stolen a month's supply of the pain pills she took for her rheumatoid arthritis. Or that the supplier was out of the drug at the moment.

"Sounds like tomorrow's going to be a big day in Columbia with the solar eclipse and all," Harold said. "I wish I could be there to take you someplace where you'd get a good view, but things have been crazy at the office. I could arrange for a driver to pick you up and ferry you to a good viewing spot, if you'd like."

"I'm fine staying put."

As if to challenge Hattie's assurance that everything was fine, a siren wailed in the street.

"What's that? Some kind of trouble?"

"Just cops on TV," Hattie lied.

"Sure? Two Notch Road isn't the safest—"

"Neighborhood's changed since the last time you were here. Got a Home Depot now, a Holiday Inn, and an Outback Steakhouse."

No need to mention that those businesses were located at the far end of Two Notch Road from where she lived. Or that last year, two kids had been shot and killed a block away from her home.

"Tell you what," Hattie said, warming to the subject, "next time you come, you can take me out for a steak dinner at the Outback."

"You gotta date, Mom!"

Hearing the excitement in his voice, Hattie felt a pang. Harold was a sweet boy and meant well by her. She just wished he understood how important it was to her to be independent and live her life as she saw fit.

The call over, Hattie grabbed her walker and clunked to the window that looked out on the street. Two shadowy figures came together like lovers for a tryst. A quick exchange and they went their separate ways. Hattie was glad Harold wasn't there to see another drug deal go down. Her side of Two Notch Road wasn't safe at night. But tomorrow in the daylight when she took the bus to Martin Luther King Park to watch the eclipse, everything would be fine.

Madras, Oregon, 10:17 AM, Monday, August 21, 2017

Randi Lawrence couldn't believe what she was seeing. Or whom she was seeing it with. For over an hour, she, Mom, Derek and Victor Yates had watched in awe as the moon's shadow moved over the mountains to the west. Over Mount Hood, crowned with snow even in August, and over the Three Sisters, nicknamed Faith, Hope, and Charity, also snow-capped. In a few minutes, it would arrive at the spot where they stood at the City-County Airport.

Last night, after Derek and Mom had gone to bed, Randi had dozed in front of the TV in the living room. The sound of a car pulling into the driveway woke her. Eager to avoid snotty Daphne, she headed for the stairs. Halfway up, a voice called her name. Victor Yates stood in doorway, his face haggard and his salt-and-pepper hair wilder than ever.

"Don't go," he said in a voice that was ragged instead of reassuring.

Randi hurried down the stairs. "What is it? Where's your wife?"

"Gone. I left her at the Portland airport earlier this evening."

"Why?" Randi blurted, even though she knew it was none of her business.

"Let's go into the kitchen and I'll explain."

Seated opposite Randi at the dented kitchen table, Victor told her that his marriage had been in trouble for some time. He and his wife wanted different things. He preferred the simple life. Daphne craved glamour and excitement. He was happy living in a modest bungalow in Berkeley. She wanted a McMansion in Sausalito or Marin County. He was content to work in obscurity. She wanted him to become another Carl Sagan. He wanted children. She did not. She was furious he'd brought her here for the eclipse, instead of a posh big city hotel.

"She told me she was leaving me, and demanded I drive her to the airport immediately. I think she was surprised I took her at her word. In the past when she threatened to leave, I tried to appease her. This time, I drove her to the airport, got her luggage out of the trunk and left her on the curb, screaming curses." Victor paused to a run hand through his hair. "I know that sounds cruel, but I've had it."

Randi wasn't sure how to respond. "I'm sorry," she said at last.

"Don't be. It's for the best." Victor stared thoughtfully into space. Then he got up, yawned and stretched. "Time to catch a few winks before we watch the eclipse."

"We?" Randi repeated.

"Yes." Victor smiled for the first time that night. "With Derek and your mom, of course."

* * * *

Now, Randi, Derek, Victor and Mom huddled on the tarmac, while the moon's shadow drew closer and closer. As darkness enveloped them, turning day into night, Derek, who stood on one side of Randi with Victor on the other, took her hand and squeezed it. "Pass along," he whispered. "Like at school." Randi took Victor's hand and squeezed, he squeezed Mom's hand, and they passed the squeeze back and forth for the duration of the eclipse.

In those three minutes, Randi felt they were a family. And even if she and Victor went their different ways, she would always treasure the moments spent together in the wondrous shadow of the moon.

Hopkinsville, Kentucky, 1: 09 PM, the same day

Do criminals return to the scene of the crime? Fred Denton thought so. He showed up at the fairgrounds where the Little Green Men Festival was being held bright and early the next morning. But to no avail. Discouraged, he decided to focus on the partial eclipse that was just beginning. He put on his protective glasses, and was about to train his gaze upward when a flash of green caught his eye.

A man wearing a Darth Vader costume stood to one side of the Music Stand where a local gospel group was performing. He waved a green mask teasingly at Fred before disappearing behind the bandstand. Fred gave chase. When the man suddenly leaped onto the stage with the startled musicians, Fred followed. He tripped on a tangle of electrical cords and fell.

Untangling himself and scrambling to his feet, Fred spotted his quarry near the entrance to a huge inflatable UFO. He dashed toward it, zigzagging around kids wearing green outfits with antennas for the Little Aliens Costume Contest later in the day, and adults bearing trays of green drinks and "Alien Stew." Liquid sloshed and antennas bobbed crazily.

Seconds before Fred arrived at the UFO, Darth Vader dove inside. Fred went after him. He grabbed at Darth's bouncing figure, but the Dark Lord eluded him and bounced out of the UFO. Fred tried to follow, but was met with a rushing tide of screaming kids coming in.

Torpedoing through them, Fred sprawled onto the grass. He picked himself up and glanced around. The eclipse was only minutes away from totality. If he didn't find Darth soon, he risked losing him for good. But the Dark Lord was nowhere to be seen.

Fred was ready to give up when a figure emerged from behind a concession booth and raced toward the 38-foot metal flying saucer that was a prominent fixture of the festival. Fred took off after the figure and chased it around the saucer. Round and round the men went. Then, in a burst of energy worthy of the football player he'd been, Fred overtook Darth, tackled and brought him to the ground, even as the last rays of light gave way to total darkness.

Fred lay, panting, on top of Darth. When the darkness began to lift, he ripped off the man's mask. His antagonist was none other than his wife's old tormentor, Tim Murphy. "Still up to your old tricks, eh, Tim?" Fred said. "I've a good mind to …" He shook a fist in Murphy's face.

A hand on his shoulder restrained him. "I'm in charge here," Officer Lombardo said. Fred rolled off Murphy and levered himself up. "He's the guy who swiped my Little Green Man Mask."

"That so?" Lombardo demanded.

"Yeah. Whatcha gonna do about it?" Murphy challenged.

"Tim Murphy," Lombardo intoned solemnly, "in the name of the law, I arrest you for the theft of a Little Green Man Mask, impersonating Darth Vader, and disturbing the peace during a solar eclipse."

"You can't do that," Murphy whined.

"Oh, yes, I can!" Clapping a pair of handcuffs on Murphy, Lombardo hauled him to his feet. Fred grinned. He had his Little Green Man Mask back, and he could just imagine the headlines on tomorrow's paper: **Little Green Man Triumphs Over Dark Lord during Total Solar Eclipse.**

Nashville, Tennessee, 1:17 PM, the same day

Wind whipped Jesse Ray's face and tore at his hair, while a band of demented demons beat drums in his brain. Groaning, he opened his eyes to find himself zooming down the highway in a red early-model convertible that was equal parts chrome and rust, and the length and width of a king-size mattress.

"Wass going on? What're we doing in this junker?" Jesse Ray asked Leroy, who sat behind the wheel.

"Don't you be calling my Chevy Impala land yacht a junker," Leroy scolded.

"Sorry. Didn't know you had a car."

"Lots 'bout me you don't know," Leroy replied cryptically.

"Okay. But do you mind telling me where we're going?"

"We be driving on beautiful Briley Parkway headed for the Grand Ole Opry," Leroy said in his best tour guide voice.

"The Grand Ole Opry—why?"

"Because, my man, while you was out cold after Big Bobby knocked you off the stool, I got to thinkin' 'bout how you oughta get out more if you's ever gonna find your inspiration someplace other than the bottle."

"Yeah, well, the Opry ain't gonna do it. It'll just make me feel worse being around all those successful dudes. Besides, I can't afford a ticket."

"You don't need one. The show we gonna see is free. Outdoors, too."

"Who's performing?"

"This little group called Sun, Moon, an' Earth."

"If you mean the eclipse, I don't have the right glasses to—"

"Now you do." Leroy tossed a small plastic package into Jesse Ray's lap.

* * * *

Jesse Ray couldn't remember when anything had moved him so much. As the moon slowly covered up the sun until it became a black disc, surrounded by a wispy glow, he felt something stir deep within him. He was sorry when the moon moved on and ordinary daylight replaced the eerie twilight of the eclipse. It was like a wonderful dream he didn't want to end. A confidence he hadn't felt in a long time filled him. Music played in his head. He began to hum.

"What's that you humming? Leroy asked.

"A new song."

"What's it called?"

"'Chasing the Moon.'"

Columbia, South Carolina, 2:14 PM, the same day

When the bus reached the stop for Martin Luther King Park, Hattie Menefee rose slowly from her seat near the front. She hobbled toward the door with her rolling walker folded under her arm.

"Let me help you, ma'am." The bus driver sprang from his seat, took her walker, and was down the steps in a flash. Hattie accepted his proffered hand and eased herself down, one step at a time. At the bottom, she gripped the walker he'd unfolded for her and thanked him. Would a white driver have shown her the same courtesy? She wasn't sure. At least now she didn't have to sit in the back of the bus.

An open space in the midst of busy city streets, the park was crowded on the afternoon of the solar eclipse. Hattie saw college students, families with small children, and teenagers travelling in packs. Black folks mingled with whites, though that hadn't always been so. She remembered a time when the park had been for whites only, when it was called Valley Park instead of Martin Luther King Park.

It was good to be out among other people, but it was also tiring. The small children racing about made Hattie feel all of her eighty-seven years. So much energy! "Slow down," she wanted to say to them. "You got your whole lives before you."

She had a different message for the group of black youths sharing a joint in a far corner of the baseball field. "It's not too late to turn your lives around and make something of yourselves." But the words went unspoken, as Hattie pushed on, fighting fatigue, achy joints and a leaky heart to reach the place where she would lay herself down.

She arrived at the Stone of Hope moments before the eclipse became total. In the remaining light, she folded up her walker and settled on the bench around the fountain. In the middle of the water, a stone shaped like a globe perched on top of an uncapped pyramid.

Hattie didn't need to read the inscription carved on the monument stone in front, which came from Martin Luther King's "I have a Dream" speech. She already knew the words by heart: "With this faith we will be able to hew out of the mountain of despair, a stone of hope."

Hattie felt pain, but also release. And when the darkness came for her, she was not afraid. It gathered her up like the sweet chariot in the gospel song, carrying her home—over the edge of the continent, across the ocean to Africa, where the red ball of the sun was setting.

An award-winning author of books about American history and biographies, Leslie Wheeler is the author of three Miranda Lewis "living history" mysteries. Her short stories have appeared in a number of anthologies published by Level Best Books, where she served as a co-editor/publisher for six years. She is a member of Mystery Writers of America and Sisters in Crime, serving as Speakers Bureau Coordinator of the New England chapter. She's also a founding member of the New England Crime Bake Committee, and chairs the Crime Bake-sponsored Al Blanchard Award Committee.

THE PATH OF TOTALITY

KATHERINE TOMLINSON

To say the astronomy community was anticipating the August 21, 2017 solar eclipse with the excitement of a child waiting for Christmas morning was an understatement. The event would be the first total solar eclipse visible in the continental U.S. since 1979, and everyone who was anyone in the astronomy community intended to be somewhere along the path of totality stretching across United States from Oregon to Georgia and South Carolina.

Stanford University physicist Dr. Ashok "Drash" Chhabra, the movie-star handsome author of the wildly popular book, *Darkness at Noon: Myth, Math, and Solar Eclipses*, was everywhere as 2017 dawned, his enthusiasm and love for his topic infectious as he made guest appearances on a stream of morning infotainment shows and sat down with dozens of late-night news explainers.

"The shadow will last nearly two minutes along the path of totality, and it will be nearly as dark as night," Drash said, and he was so charismatic that people wanted to hear more. He told viewers and listeners he was especially excited that the August eclipse would be an "American event."

"This is the first eclipse to pass over the United States in the 21st century," he said as he handed out cheap "eclipse glasses" with smoked lenses to studio audiences from Alabama to the Yukon.

Not everyone Drash talked to was as excited as he was. Griff Marlowe, the weatherman of a small Indiana television station, surprised the scientist with his hostile attitude and pointed questioning during what was supposed to be a brief and light-hearted segment on a morning news show that normally focused on local farm reports and high school basketball.

"Dr. Chhabra, can you explain to me why the shadow is only falling over the United States?" Griff asked, mispronouncing Drash's last name so badly it sounded like he was having a coughing fit.

When Drash attempted to explain the math and science behind the path of totality, Griff cut him off. "I think we can all agree that something's going on," he said.

"Nothing is going on," Drash said.

"Really?" Griff said. "What makes you such an expert? Where did you get your degree in astrology?"

"Astronomy," Drash corrected. "My doctorate is from Oxford."

"Oxford," Griff repeated, nodding his head sadly, "so your degree isn't from an American school?"

And as Drash wondered if he'd wandered into an elaborate practical joke arranged by his colleagues at Notre Dame, the broadcast went to commercial.

"We're out of time," Griff announced as the show came back from the break, "but I'd like to thank Dr. Chupacabra for being here today to talk about the eclipse and what we can do to prevent it."

* * * *

Back in his office at Stanford, Drash laughed about the encounter while his colleagues took to teasing him with the new nickname, "Chupacabra." At that point, Drash wasn't too worried about the conspiracy nuts. They'd been out in force during the series of so-called "blood moon" eclipses in 2016, events heralded as the harbinger of the apocalypse by a segment of the scientifically challenged populace. And before that, he'd dealt with comet-conspiracists who saw signs and evil portents in everything from the appearance of Comet McNaught in 2007 to the predicted return of Halley's comet in 2062.

Drash's colleague G. Taylor Wells, who chaired the Astrophysics department at McGill University, was not as sanguine, however. "Remember what happened to Galileo," he said darkly.

"I'm no Galileo," Drash said.

"Exactly," Greg responded. "If they did that to Galileo, what are they going to do to you?"

"You worry too much," Drash told his friend, but he didn't mention the conversation to his wife, who thought Canadians were more sensible than Americans.

Drash and Greg were co-hosting a "North American Eclipse Party" for their students and fellow eclipse enthusiasts and were looking forward to geeking out in each other's company, which they hadn't done since Drash's bachelor party. The event was scheduled for Madras, Oregon where the totality was expected to last for more than two minutes. Two hundred of what Drash jokingly called "shadow-seekers" had already sent in their deposits to secure rooms at five motels in Madras and there'd been so much interest that Drash had reached out to motels in nearby Culver and Metolius to see if they had any available rooms. The event was shaping up to be the scientific shindig of the year, with plans to study the motion and dynamics of the eclipse as well as measuring the temperature of the solar corona. Drash mentioned the party every time he spoke, encouraging people to join in the fun.

In May, an altfax blogger named Jerrin Plage took issue with the plan to measure the temperature of the corona. "Why are tax dollars being spent to measure the temperature of a Mexican beer?" he asked his readers, using a photo of a sweating bottle of Corona to draw readers to his post. "Everyone knows the proper temperature to store beer is at 50 degrees Fahrenheit." A lot of the people who left comments on that post disagreed with that temperature, but no one questioned Plage's statement that tax dollars were being wasted in such a frivolous manner.

Plage's blog didn't have much reach but when Maribeth Grimes, a Twitter influencer from Plano, Texas (@VigilantVagina) suggested the eclipse was a manmade event, the idea started getting some traction.

Grimes, who positioned herself as the "the conservative voice for the millennial woman," was sneeringly referred to as "the Tea Party Twat" by her detractors, but she had quietly carved out a niche among women who thought Ann Coulter's politics were too left-leaning. In the approaching eclipse, she saw an opportunity to stake out an issue and make it her own. She coined the phrase, "Don't Be Left in the Dark," and designed t-shirts she sold through her Vigilant Vagina site.

In May, presidential advisor Grayson Monck spotted a story about Grimes on the Drudge Report and realized that she was on to something. Monck, whose liberal arts degree came from a notorious party school in Florida, was eager to connect the dots Maribeth had so carefully laid out. And even though Monck was infamously averse to any science that wasn't faith-based, he embraced Maribeth's "common sense" assessment of the upcoming "eclipse situation."

"Something's going on, people," he said, parroting her words but sounding much more authoritative. (Maribeth had all the smug self-righteousness of a county clerk denying gay couples a marriage license because of her religious beliefs, but when she spoke in public, her voice tended to sound squeaky and somewhat comical.)

Monck's contribution to the notion that the coming eclipse was preventable was that he married that concept to a theory that Drash had planned it as the prelude to a massive radical Islamist attack.

He'd singled out Drash as a target because the scientist had become a pop culture figure and inspired dozens of memes that Monck considered subversive, if not downright seditious.

He didn't like that his grandson had started using Drash's catch-phrase—*Because, science!*—to sass his mother, who had home-schooled him since he was a toddler and couldn't figure out where he was getting all his information about godless evolution.

Monck called on Stanford to expel Drash on the grounds that he was an illegal immigrant and possible terrorist, ignoring Drash's protests that his family had been in the United States for three generations. "Then go back to whatever Muslim hellhole you came from," Monck said, responding to Drash's protests on Twitter, apparently not realizing that the predominant faith in Punjab, where Drash's great-grandparents were born, is Sikhism and that Drash himself was a Presbyterian, just like the president.

When Stanford refused to fire Drash, Monck turned up the heat, calling a press conference in June in what he called "an attempt to divert disaster and expose a massive cover-up by a compromised institution in the pay of foreign governments."

"It's 'Operation Jade Helm' all over again," he said in answer to a question from a reporter from the *Washington Times Weekly*, one of the few media outlets that still had access to White House pressers.

"The terrorists are going to move in under cover of darkness, take out all the patriots, and when the lights come back, it'll all be over but the shouting."

"But the totality is only supposed to last for two minutes," objected a reporter from *Teen Vogue*. "That's not much time to take over the country."

"Who says it's only going to last two minutes?" Monck fired back.

The reporter looked startled. "Everyone," she said. "Science."

Monck pounced on her answer. "And you believe everything science tells you?"

No one heard her answer because the reporter from the *Washington Times* asked a follow-up question.

Things got so bad for Drash he all but disappeared from social media. He created a new gmail account to communicate with friends and family so that their emails wouldn't get lost in the tsunami of hate that was being directed at him.

People who'd planned to come to the North American Eclipse Party began to reverse their RSVPs.

Drash's wife begged him to cancel the event.

"Not everyone is ignorant," he told her and he redoubled his attempts to explain to the public at large what was about to happen. Scientists from all over the world signed petitions and published open letters and sent him messages, but those efforts only solidified Monck's resolve. He continued to call for investigations into Drash's professional and personal life.

In July, Drash booked a spot on an early-morning chat show with a perky hostess who had once been Miss Arkansas. She greeted him warmly in the Green Room and offered him juice and muffins. "I'm so glad you could take time from your busy schedule to visit us here," she said on air, and then followed her welcome with a compliment. "I understand you're considered the world's greatest eclipse expert."

"I wouldn't say that," Drash said, "although I do have a coffee mug with those very words on it." The former Miss Arkansas laughed at that and patted him on his arm flirtatiously.

"You're being too modest," she said, leaning forward, close enough that he could smell the scent of the Marlboro Light she'd inhaled minutes before in her dressing room.

"Tell me, how long have you known about this eclipse?" she asked.

Drash thought it was a weird question to ask, but he energetically launched into his answer. "Well," he said, "we've been able to predict eclipses for thousands of years, but modern eclipse math began in the 19th century with William Bessell. He wasn't actually a scientist, but thanks to him and his mathematical model, we can literally predict when eclipses will occur for thousands of years into the future."

"So, you've known about this event for a thousand years," the host said, putting a little question mark into her voice and tilting her head to the right.

"Maybe not a thousand years," he said, "but for a pretty long while."

"So, what are you planning to do about it?" she asked.

"Do?" Drash asked.

"To stop it," she clarified.

"Nothing," he said. "I can't do anything to stop it."

"You must be pleased your plan has taken on a life of its own?"

"What plan?" he asked. "There is no plan."

"You're being disingenuous Dr. Chhabra," the host said with a smile. "Can you deny that, in the past, eclipses have been responsible for horrific acts of violence? In 1321, a hundred and sixty Jews were burned at the stake in France during an eclipse. In an eclipse in 1986, the Lake Nios volcano in Cameroon erupted, killing nearly two thousand people. Are you saying that was a coincidence?"

"We aren't living in the fourteenth century anymore," Drash said, thinking, *at least I'm not.*

The host smiled a "gotcha" smile. "And do you deny that the marshals moved in on Randy Weaver's cabin in Idaho under the cover of an eclipse?"

After a moment Drash asked, "When did that happen?"

"In 1995," she answered.

"There weren't any eclipses visible in North America in 1995," Drash said, hoping he was right. She didn't look convinced so he tried another tack.

"Eclipses aren't like comet strikes," he said. "They're totally benign occurrences."

"Really?" she said, raising her beautifully arched eyebrows. "You call plunging half the world into darkness in the middle of the day a good thing? I'd hate to hear what you call a bad thing."

"I'm not doing it," Drash said, exasperated. "It's a celestial event."

"Caused by what?" she shot back.

And that's when he lost his temper. "Because … science," he said, not quite shouting.

To give her credit, the host had game. Rather than simply cut his microphone, she'd pivoted to riff on his answer. "Okay, so maybe I don't understand the science," she said, putting air quotes around the word "science" and flipping her artfully styled blond hair behind one bony shoulder. "But tell me, what is the purpose of this eclipse? Why here? Why now?"

"There is no why," he said.

"And yet you have told us you've known this eclipse would happen …" she made a show of consulting her notes, "… for thousands of years."

"Yes," Drash said.

"So why does no one seem to know why this eclipse is happening? Why are you the only harbinger of doom? Is it simply because this is an event of your own making?"

And that's when Drash made his fatal mistake. "Let's say, for the sake of argument, that I am responsible for the eclipse," he said, and it didn't matter what else he said after that because almost before the words were out of his mouth, the clip of him saying, "I am responsible for the eclipse" had been uploaded on YouTube where it was viewed more than a million times in the next two hours, provoking anti-eclipse rallies all across the United States. Monck returned to the fray tweeting the hashtag #BeAfraidoftheDark and repeating his dire predictions about what might happen "when the lights go out."

Other scientists spoke up in Drash's defense, pointing out that Monck had absolutely zero scientific training and was therefore uniquely unqualified to pontificate about physics. The response from the twitter-verse was a resounding, "We don't care," and one troll using the handle

@scienceisstupidAF seemed to speak for everyone when he commented, "You don't need to be no rocket scientwist to know what is going on."

A week before the eclipse, it got really nasty.

"Why is this man not in prison?" a Dallas-based shock jock asked his morning drive-time audience.

Posts clamoring for Drash's arrest circulated on Facebook.

The office of Drash's congresswoman was flooded with phone calls from angry constituents demanding his incarceration. "Why is this so-called doctor talking about the eclipse like it's a done deal?" asked a botoxed commentator on an off-network news show.

Drash's wife was terrified. Their home address had been posted on several websites and they didn't have a security system. Reporters laid siege to their condo and followed her whenever she left to run an errand. People left burning bags of dog shit on their front steps, and heaved bricks and stones through their front windows.

Drash moved his wife to a nearby hotel and began sleeping on a couch in his office.

Protestors showed up on the Stanford campus in numbers too large for the Stanford University Department of Safety to contain. Alarmed colleagues spoke out on Drash's behalf, sending out press releases, recording sound bites, and generally attempting to hold back the flood of hysteria that was sweeping the nation. Greg Wells got into a fist fight with a television pundit who suggested on air that Drash had faked the 1969 moon landing, the explosion at Chernobyl, and Hurricane Katrina. As staffers rushed to separate the two, the pundit shouted, "The truth is out there. Just Google it."

Disgusted, Greg flew to Oregon three days before the eclipse to make last-minute arrangements with the local event organizers as Drash contemplated the pros and cons of skipping the party and just flying to Reykjavik until the eclipse was over.

By then, there was a full-scale panic. Bottled water, toilet paper, ammunition and, oddly, sunscreen sold out in cities across the country. When a "man on the street" interviewer asked a woman why she'd filled her cart with tubes of SPF 23 Coppertone when the eclipse was supposed to black out the sun, she replied simply that she believed the opposite was going to happen.

"The sun is going to go supernova and fry us all," she said. "The eclipse is just a cover story."

Riots broke out all over the San Francisco area and Drash finally decided it was too dangerous to even attempt to drive to the airport. He called Greg Wells to tell him that he wasn't coming to Oregon.

"That's okay," Greg told him. "No one else is coming either."

There was a long silence between them and then Drash said, "If they're acting like this now, what are they going to do when it gets dark?"

"How much damage can they do in two minutes?" his colleague responded.

On the day of the eclipse, Drash woke early to monitor the equipment on boats off the western coast of the continent where the sun would rise while totally eclipsed. Few people had ever witnessed such a thing and he'd been told it was an eerie sight to see. At 10:15 a.m. Pacific Daylight Time, the eclipse path made landfall, leaving a little sliver of Oregon in total darkness for a minute and fifty-eight seconds.

At almost the same moment, riots blew up in the streets of Oakland, Portland, and Seattle—three cities that were nowhere near the path of totality.

Drash watched everything unfold on the tiny screen of a little TV he kept in his office, and grew more and more depressed with each passing moment.

Even as the shadow moved across the nation, leaving brilliant sunny skies in its wake, the riots continued, On Instagram, pictures of people protesting the eclipse soon dominated the app's "Top Post" list.

As the day wore on, Drash wanted nothing so much as to go home, so at 7:57 p.m., as the sun was setting, he packed up his laptop and his phone and headed for his car.

He didn't notice the two women standing next to a cream-colored Mitsubishi Eclipse.

He didn't notice them but they saw him and recognized him instantly as the immigrant Muslim astronomer who had predicted the onset of the apocalypse and not been able to deliver it.

"It's him," the taller woman said as she gripped a socket wrench in her right hand.

The second woman said nothing but tapped the tire iron she carried against her left thigh, felt the reassuring weight of it empowering her.

They hung back as they saw Drash greet Jamal Jenkins, a mathematician and Iraq war veteran who'd just returned from guarding the water protectors at Standing Rock. The two men exchanged a few words and then Jamal embraced the other scientist and headed to his own car.

Drash was just unlocking the door of his Prius when the women stepped up behind him.

It was Elizabeth who struck first, bashing her wrench over Drash's head so hard she thought the metal might bend against the bone.

Kate followed up with a blow from the tire iron that sent Drash to the ground.

As he curled himself in a fetal ball, the two women continued to beat him.

Drash heard something crunch and thought at first it was his glasses breaking. A moment later, an electric current of pain told him it was his face shattering.

"Please, please," he begged as he was swallowed by the darkness.

When it was over, Kate threw up, leaving DNA evidence all over the crime scene, but by the time Drash's body was found, a rare August rain had washed much of the vomit and blood away.

A security camera in the parking lot caught the license plate of Elizabeth's car as she and Kate drove away. The two were arrested two days later. They claimed they'd acted on God's orders and lawyered up.

Elizabeth's husband reached out to Grayson Monck for help, telling the presidential advisor that in addition to being inspired by God, his wife had been spurred to action by Monck's many public statements about how dangerous Drash was.

Monck's administrative aide told the man that if he ever repeated the accusation that Elizabeth's deranged actions were motivated by admiration of him, he would sue.

Kate copped a plea and received a three-year sentence, reduced to four months and a thousand hours of community service. Greg Wells testified at Elizabeth's sentencing hearing and afterwards was swamped by reporters who were impressed by his eloquent plea for a return to rationality. "Science doesn't care what you believe," he said, quoting a meme he'd seen somewhere. "Science is not a liberal conspiracy."

He accepted a job as a science commentator for a major American network but before he could take up his new duties, he was killed while buying a round of sourdough bread in the departures lounge of San Francisco International Airport. Three other travelers were killed in the attack and four more were wounded. The shooter died at the scene, along with his victims, but the investigation showed that he had ties to ISIS. The police found a heavily annotated copy of Drash Chhabra's book, *Darkness at Noon*, on his bookshelf next to a well-thumbed copy of the *Qur'an* and several dog-eared issues of *Rumiyah* magazine, and that discovery that kicked off a fresh round of speculation about the late scientist's role in the August, 2017 eclipse. There was enough of an outcry to get Elizabeth a new trial.

Maribeth Grimes paid for her lawyer in return for exclusive interviews she broadcast on her Vigilant Vagina podcast.

Elizabeth's supporters showed up in the courtroom wearing t-shirts with an image of the Statue of Liberty's torch and the slogan, "Out of darkness, light." The jury was unable to come to a verdict—seven of the jurors had college degrees and could not be convinced that Elizabeth's fears of a scientific coup d'état were justified—and so the judge dismissed the case. Elizabeth moved to Texas to work with Maribeth Grimes full time and the two women landed a book deal from a publisher specializing in what Maribeth called "the truth about what's going on." She and her co-author had a falling-out over creative differences, however, and the manuscript was never delivered.

Drash's widow moved to Toronto and began the process of becoming a Canadian citizen. She signed the lease on a Sunnybrook condo on July 2, 2019, just as another solar eclipse was sweeping across parts of Chile and Argentina. The Buenos Aires paper *Crónica* published a picture of city crowds waiting for the event with their eclipse glasses on, but otherwise, the event passed without comment.

Katherine Tomlinson is a former reporter who prefers making things up. Her short fiction has been published in numerous anthologies. "Water Sports" was nominated for a Pushcart Prize in 2011. Her serial novel, *NoHo Noir*, was published on the AOL site patch.com. In addition to writing crime fiction and horror under her own name, she writes fantasy and science fiction as "Kat Parrish." Her essays have appeared in *Pearls of Wisdom from Grandma, What Was I Thinking?* and in *Disarm*, the gun control anthology. She lives in the Pacific Northwest. Follow her on Twitter @storyauthority.

BLOOD MOON

PAUL D. MARKS

Late in the day. I'm tired. Alone and lonely—two different things.
Surrounded by ten million people and no one to talk to. No one I
wanna talk to.

I stare out the window of my little apartment building, two stories,
six units, all of them suffocated by the manufactured early dusk from the
gleaming new office towers across the alley. Towers that mean this city's
on the move. Reaching for the sky. Some BS like that. It gets dark here
an hour before it does the next block over. These old mini apartment
buildings, all someone's dreamy idea of quaint in the near past, have
outlived their time and probably won't avoid the wrecking ball much
longer. Every day they disappear into the darkness of daylight as the
street is swallowed in the early gloom of the towering buildings.

I've lived in my second floor apartment over a year now and still
don't know my neighbors more than a passing nod's worth. Sometimes I
think they're only shadows on the pavement, nothing more than walking
body outlines.

Is it just me?

* * * *

Day fades to night. You wouldn't be able to see a thing because of
the total eclipse of the moon if not for the glow of the streetlamps, the
sting of car headlights and the reflected *glory* of the city coming from a
window here and there. You'd think that would be enough to light up the
night, but it's not. Before the moon goes dark, it turns red—becomes a
blood moon. And that's fine with me—blood moon. In fact it's perfect,
couldn't be more appropriate.

When there is no moon it's different, dark and somber. I can tell the
difference in the tone of the night. So can you if you just look around.
The lights of the city without the moon to back them up blind me, and
all I can think of is that I want to kill. Take a life. Is that so strange these
days?

Maybe, maybe not. A lot of people want to kill, I'm sure as hell not the first or only. Some actually go out and do it. Will I? Can I?

People say strange things happen when the moon is full. Everything from the murder rate increasing to werewolves roaming the streets. Crime flies when you're having a good time. People think it has something to do with the pull of the moon causing some kind of madness.

But what about moonless nights? What about the most moonless night of all, the night of a total eclipse? I don't think it's any different during an eclipse. Except for me. I live for the dark.

I need to ditch this cramped hole. Bedroom, living room, kitchen. But it's on the west side of L.A.—the good part of town. The part where people can afford burglar bars, alarms and security patrols to keep the wolves at bay. I'm choking on my own desperation. I have to get out. But go where? A club? Restaurant. Get mugged coming or going. So I sit, the TV droning in the background. *Taxi Driver* streaming from Netflix.

Beethoven's *Moonlight Sonata* drifts from the apartment next to mine. Pretty girl. She plays it on her piano every night. Lonely music, especially the first movement. Music playing in the background of an Edward Hopper painting. I want to talk to her. Ask her to a movie or a bar. Can't. I tried talking to a woman on the street today. She clammed up, looked at me like I was a stalker. Every man's a predator today.

The haunting music is as broken as the night. As lost and broken as the Dreams I had when I first came to the City of Angels. It's been said before and I won't be the last to say it, people come West to reinvent themselves. To start over. They come for redemption and its opposite. They come for Hollywood, for the pot of gold at the end of the rainbow.

I sold my soul to the dealer. No, not that dealer. The one who sells you visions of Hollywood and palm trees and sidewalks paved with Dreams. I came here with a plan. So many of us do. And now I can't even pay the rent anymore.

I've sold those Dreams down the river. I've sold my soul. What else is there?

And now my isolation creeps in through the cracks in the walls, the pores of my skin, the fissures in my life. It spreads like a Rorschach blot of blood on a paper towel.

* * * *

"Are you a member of the club, *sir*?" the man in the blue blazer with the crest on it asks. The *sir* a sneer, the crest a shield.

The doorman at the hipster heaven doesn't like my look either.

The jerk that cut me off on the freeway today, who I honked at and who flipped *me* off.

The cretin on the other end of the telephone line trying to sell me something from his scripted BS. Today solar panels. Tomorrow cemetery plots. Insurance. Time shares. Gym memberships. Newspaper subscriptions—like anyone reads those anymore. They sell you the good life, the hot life, the easy life, if I just surrender. And they have it all in their computers. They capture my life—do they steal my spirit like those primitives who thought that if you photographed them you'd steal their souls? Only this is for real—they *are* stealing my soul.

Pols who want my vote, left and right, right and wrong. And who I never hear from except for the week before an election. Yeah, they could give a damn if I breathe or die.

Spammers. Hackers. Phishers.

Tech help who can't help. Who won't help. Who are too stupid to help. Who you can't understand and who just don't give a damn.

Store clerks talking to other clerks or their boyfriends or girlfriends or texting them. The hell that there's a customer waiting in line.

Movie stars with eighth grade educations telling me what a fool I am.

Bible Thumpers and Hipster Wanna-bes.

I looked in the obituaries today, something I never do. I hardly ever look at a newspaper anymore. For some reason I picked one up and when I opened it I turned straight to the obituaries. My eyes landed on one obit in particular, Megan Birch. Megan. Someone I hadn't thought about in years. But someone that I did spend plenty of time thinking about and being with. We dated back in the day when we both had Big Dreams, too big to accommodate our relationship. So we went our separate ways. Every once in a while she'd call or I'd call her. We'd get together. Always thinking maybe some day we'd get together permanently, after we'd established our lives. And now she was dead. Breast cancer. So what's the point. What the hell's the fucking point? But it didn't matter, I was already planning my *party* for tonight. Her death just makes me all the more certain.

Does it matter? Any of it? Everyone's a celeb. Walking around with cell phones, snapping selfies, making *stars* of themselves with their own YouTube channels. Oozing attitude—everything is attitude. *On* all the time. Watching movies, listening to music, but mostly just looking at pictures of themselves. Everyone plugged into that giant sucking machine, but isolated and closed off. The constant drone in the background, the hum that lulls you to sleep.

And I can't sleep without its hypnotic pulse fluttering in the background.

I want to be a star. Everyone's in showbiz. Everyone's a star. But I still can't see the stars in the sky.

Art fails.

False gods everywhere.

I'm not a member of the club. So I am alone.

Maybe I'd do better out in the middle of nowhere, the badlands. The high and lonesome. Lonesome dogies. Cowboys, cowpokes. They knew what they were here for. Do I?

Bury me not on the lone prairie—but no prairies, lone or otherwise around here.

Help me.

* * * *

Door slam.

Thumping. Screams—muffled by papier-mâché walls as real and solid as those on a movie set.

The young woman who lives downstairs, attacked. One year ago today.

Her boyfriend comes home. The bad guy takes off. I join the chase. Might give me a chance to stomp someone.

Footsteps running.

Three sets.

We chase the guy down the alley. The boyfriend has a bat. I have my .357.

The cops can't be bothered.

I find out later, dude broke in. Beat her face black and blue.

She died from her injuries. Dude's partying somewhere else with someone else.

Ah, Los Angeles.

L.A.

The Big Orange. Lotus Land.

La La Land.

* * * *

And me, I sit and stare out the window into the darkness of the night, lit only by a single streetlamp that casts its amber but empty glow on shapeless forms without any color. My view, the apartment house next door. A bleak wall of decay. A new building, already falling apart. A new building where the builders couldn't bother to line up the drain pipe with the drain outlet. Rain water sloshes down the side of the building, amplifying the crack in the new stucco, splitting the wall, separating it. Stucco, the *sine qua non* of L.A. architecture.

A seagull wanders by. A little off the beaten path this far inland. Lost.

The sky is falling, or is it just the fallout of a thousand AKs tearing the negative silence?

* * * *

School shootings, riots, protests, civil unrest. All in a day's work.

Twenty-eight people killed in La La Land last weekend. Not bad. Not as good as it gets, but not bad. If I go out and blast a couple more it won't make any difference. No one gives a damn anyway. I know I don't. Cops'll probably give me a medal like Travis got in *Taxi Driver*. Hell, everybody's famous for something these days, even if it's nothing. And everybody's guaranteed their fifteen minutes or fifteen seconds in our super-heated society. Wanna-bes everywhere. Wanna-be singers. Wanna-be actors. Wanna-be SuperStars. Wanna-be Mass Murderers. They get their fifteen minutes. Why shouldn't I get mine? Especially when Up is Down and In is Out.

I don't know life anymore. Only filmic reality, video games, virtual reality. Streaming visions of murderous cyber hookers and knifing animatronic drug dealers. Cell phones, selfies. Internet. If it's on the screen, large or small, it's real. If I'm in a thousand arm-length pictures, it's real. If I'm on the web, online, plugged in, it's real.

Time slows. Dreams die. Nothing can fill the empty hole. I want to do something like Travis Bickle, make a statement, good or bad, it doesn't matter. I just want to matter.

And Bickle is only Camus' Meursault, a stranger in a yellow Checker cab, on the rain-slicked, neon-soaked streets of NYC, instead of Meursault in the sunlight and silence of the hot-as-fire sand in the blazing Algiers sun. But if Bickle is Meursault, then who is Meursault? And who am I?

I am Bickle. I am Meursault.

There were things I believed in at one time. The usual things. But one by one they let me down. And maybe I let myself down. Or maybe I just wasn't good enough. But where would I go? What would I do? I'm already at the end of the continent. The end where people go to start over. To go further west would be like walking the plank, falling off the edge of the continent, plunging into the Pacific with the tiniest of splashes, never to be heard from again. To go home means returning with my tail between my legs. It means defeat. Failure. I told you so. It means a life as a normal person while straining at the straitjacket. No constraints for me. You reach a point where you just don't care anymore, one way or another, come and get me, or don't.

The cylinder spins freely, freshly oiled.

Is the world absurd or is it just me? Is everything upside down or am I just the square peg in the round hole? I mean if a guy drives a Beamer and lives in a nice McMansion in the good part of town he must be respectable, right? Doesn't matter that he made his coin selling H to kids cracked out of their minds. Selling kids to men, who crawl out from under rocks on Hollywood Boulevard—Dream Central. He's a good guy. Good neighbor. He has the right labels on his clothes, his watch, his cars. Meanwhile, I can barely pay the bills each month. Maybe I'm in the wrong biz.

Is it me? Hard to say.

* * * *

Hard and round, it looks like a suppository from hell—a suppository that will alleviate all your troubles. Heavy, it hefts well. 158 grain. Not a silver bullet, that's for sure. But it gleams silver under the bright light and that's all that matters—what it looks like under the lights.

Now I lay me down to sleep.

The Big Sleep.

If I should die before I wake—

If I should wake before I die.

Silence screams.

The brightness of the night blinds me.

I look out the window. Waiting for the first person to walk by.

I stare out the window. Waiting.

Life is waiting. A waiting game.

I can wait no longer.

Quiet outside now. Quiet for the city at night. Does it know what's coming?

Only the low rush of cars in the distance.

No stars. No moon. Can't blame it on the full moon. Blame it on the eclipse.

Blame fate. Blame God. Blame the Mexicans or the blacks or the Jews. They're always good for a scapegoat. Blame anyone you like. Sure as hell don't want to blame it on myself. Just pass a law—that'll solve all our problems.

My skin crawls, lacerated by the heat. Sweat dribbles down my back. Balmy L.A.

Everyone comes here. Party Land, USA. No one ever works, judging by the traffic at all times of day and night. No one has to. But everyone's a star in their own movie. I want to be the star of mine.

The streets are choking. The parks turning brown and red with the blood of gang bangers. The rats kill each other for a piece of bread.

The hills are on fire. Santa Anas crease your skin with hell-bent crimson anger, making you insane—or is that just another goddamn excuse?

Everyone fighting for their piece of the pie. Everyone looking for a way out.

It's just no fun anymore. No damn fun.

And whose fault is it? Mine, of course. Blame me.

Oh say can you see.

Footsteps echo outside. Whose? It doesn't matter. I stare out the front window. On the street below a cold-steel Hopper wedge of light illuminates a spot on the sidewalk beyond the roofline of the first floor apartment. Moths besiege the light, not knowing it's the siren call to their untimely deaths. Headlights from a passing car sweep the street, like the brighter-than-daylight lights at a Hollywood premier. Fitting.

The footsteps get closer. Louder.

I wait.

And wait.

Like those people waiting to get out of Casablanca, I wait … and wait … and wait.

Here they come. Louder.

I shove the screen off the window. It crashes to the sidewalk below. No one cares. They don't respond to car alarms, house alarms, yells or cries for help. Why the fuck should I care?

Why?

God, I'll make you a deal. You stop me by midnight and I'll put the gun down.

We all have choices, don't we? Free will. I don't have to do this. I can put the gun away. Nobody would even know how close they came. Either way, what difference does it make? It's a choice, a decision I've made. Why? And how did I get here? Does it really matter? Another random act of violence in a city full of them. You know what they say, one death is a tragedy, a million a statistic. So if one more is added to the queue his death is a tragedy to his family, his girlfriend, but to society it's just another statistic. Another nameless nobody to add to the list.

Will I actually go through with it? Can I? And what becomes of me if I do?

It's almost midnight now. No word from God. Is there ever any word?

Midnight. And the moon is blood red. Perfect.

Cock the hammer. Click.

The footsteps quicken, crunching leaves underfoot.

A man. Unsuspecting. Maybe coming home from working late or heading out for a date.

Maybe I know him. Maybe not.

It doesn't matter.

I heft the gun. The grip feels good in my hand.

Should I?

Why not? No one cares. No one gives a damn. Least of all me.

Here he comes.

I want to see his face.

Goddammit! Turn into the light. I want to see your face.

Your eyes.

Don't be anonymous.

He moves under the street lamp. A salmon glow surrounds him, while a hard shadow slices across his face. He hardly looks human. But I want him to. I don't want to kill a fiend. I want to kill a man.

I have to kill a man. I'll be a hero.

He drops something. His keys. Bends over to pick them up.

Who is he? Someone's husband. Boyfriend. A thief. Son, lover, doctor, lawyer, Indian chief. What's he wearing? Hard to tell. Looks like jeans and a long sleeved shirt. L.A. casual.

I hold the revolver out. Straight arm it, just like I've seen them do on TV and in the movies over and over again.

He stands up, face in the lamp light. Not handsome, not ugly. Just average. A regular guy, no longer an anonymous, faceless person. An innocent—is anyone really innocent? There's a small cut on his cheek like he cut himself shaving. Perfect.

Ready.

Aim.

Fire.

It sounds so dramatic, doesn't it?

The shot echoes loudly. A shot heard 'round the world? Unlikely.

Strangely, I feel nothing.

The body falls. Will anyone notice or will they just step around him? Will they do any more than pull out their cell phones and video him? Will there be anything to say he was here other than a small stain on the pavement? And even that will fade over time.

I am a hero.

Is it an existential act or just the action of a mad dog? Dog bites man, par for the course. Man bites dog, unusual to say the least. Man shoots man, par for the course.

Now I am become Death, the destroyer of worlds.

I turn the gun on myself. I don't fire. Why should I?

Paul D. Marks is the author of the Shamus Award-Winning mystery-thriller *White Heat*. *Publishers Weekly* calls *White Heat* a "taut crime yarn." His story "Ghosts of Bunker Hill" was voted #1 in the 2016 *Ellery Queen* Readers Poll. "Howling at the Moon" (*EQMM* 11/14) was short-listed for both the 2015 Anthony and Macavity Awards. *Midwest Review* calls his novella *Vortex* "… a nonstop staccato action noir." His story "Deserted Cities of the Heart" appears in Akashic's *St. Louis Noir*. And his story "Twelve Angry Days" appears in the May-June, 2017 issue of *Alfred Hitchcock's Mystery Magazine*. www.PaulDMarks.com

TORGNYR THE BASTARD, SPEAKER OF LAW

SUZANNE BERUBE RORHUS

"You do not actually have to hire someone to speak for you," Torgnyr the Bastard said. He hefted the small pile of cut silver and coins in his hand. A nice profit if he accepted this client. "Any man can speak to the king."

Maurice the Christian shrugged eloquently. "I am not comfortable enough in your language to speak in front of the entire assembly," he said. "And in the Frankish lands, such as me would never speak to a king. I do not dare."

"I dare," his wife interrupted. "This barbarian king has no right to exile us because we are Christians. We have not broken your laws. We own land here."

Torgnyr studied the woman with distaste. Claudine wore a red gown as if she herself were a queen. Her hair was fastened on top of her head in an elaborate arrangement and she wore a large gold cross around her neck. "If you speak in your husband's place, m'lady, you will undercut your husband's authority. This will not help your case." He poured the silver onto the table, pushing it into a neat pile with his forefinger.

A girl of perhaps seven summers entered through the open doorway of the Christians' longhouse, crossing the dim room to the fireplace where the adults sat. She stopped on catching sight of Torgnyr. The child burst into tears and hurried to her mother's side, burying her head in Claudine's ample skirts.

Torgnyr sighed. One of the many disadvantages of being known as the ugliest man in the Norse lands was this propensity for frightening small children. He turned his attention back to Maurice. "The decision is yours."

"How does this work?" Maurice asked. He glanced at his wife and sobbing daughter. "Claudine, take Christina outside, please. I cannot hear myself think."

"The girl is named Christina?" Torgnyr asked. "Would her life in the Norse lands not be easier if she were not named after her religion?"

"Does the Norse religion not advocate tolerance for others? We were told your gods are not jealous," Maurice said.

"There are those who would say that the same cannot be said of your Christian god," Torgnyr said as diplomatically as he could manage. "I believe that is the basis for the king's objection. He is afraid if Christians establish a foothold here, they will attempt to force our people to convert. The Christians have been known to create terror in other lands."

"We are simply here to farm the land I inherited from my aunt's husband. We are not causing anyone terror. If you barbarians want to worship your false gods, I will not stop you."

"Perhaps it *would* be best if I spoke on your behalf. I doubt the king will take kindly to having Odin called a 'false god'." Torgnyr raked a hand through his long, curly red hair. "What exactly did the king's man say to you?"

"No one contacted us directly. I have only heard from my neighbors that the king is planning to confiscate Christian lands. One neighbor offered us half what the land is worth and said we should take the money and be grateful. Another said the king would declare us outlaws. What is this?"

Torgnyr made a face. "Outlawing is worse than exile. Outlaw means you are outside the law. A man can kill you without fear of the law's consequence."

Maurice wrung his hands. "How can I protect my family? My youngest son was born here—does that count for nothing? How can this happen? We have broken no laws!"

"King Eirik the Victorious is newly selected. His father was criticized for not doing enough to protect our people from invaders and so this king is determined to appear strong. If you wish me to speak for you, I will meet with the king before all the men arrive for the assembly. I can try to persuade the king but I cannot control him."

Maurice slid the pile of silver across the table. "Do so. Do this for me and I will give you my daughter's hand in marriage."

Torgnyr glanced at the girl. She still hid behind her mother but her face, wet with tears and snot, peered over her mother's shoulder. When their eyes met, the girl stuck her tongue out at him and crossed her eyes.

"That will not be necessary," he said to Maurice. He stood and swept the silver into his palm. "I will see you at the assembly."

* * * *

The king's stronghold was only another day's ride from the village where the Christians lived. Torgnyr arrived the day before the assembly to find preparations in full swing. Before speaking to the king, Torgnyr decided to visit with his friend Wahid. He met the Arab at the Law Stone where the assembly would soon take place. Wahid was directing men as they set up tents to create a temporary village to house those who would gather for the assembly. When Wahid spied Torgnyr, he gave his men a few more directions then scrabbled over the stones to join him.

"Welcome, brother!" he said with a slight bow. He grasped Torgnyr on each shoulder then hugged him tightly. "It has been too long since I have seen you. Come, let us take some refreshments while these men finish their work."

Torgnyr allowed himself to be led to Wahid's tent. The interior was quiet compared to the noise of the workers outside. He sank gratefully onto a cushion and accepted a mug of water. No ale from this friend, unfortunately.

"Are you ready for your big moment tomorrow?" Wahid asked, a teasing twinkle in his eye. "Not afraid you will forget your recitation?"

Torgnyr scoffed. "My father banged the law into the heads of my brother and myself from birth. I couldn't forget the miserable thing if I wanted."

Every year, the king of the Eastern Norse lands gathered all the freemen in his kingdom for a large assembly where the men voted on laws and decided the fate of accused lawbreakers. For the king's Speaker of Law, the first day of the assembly featured him in the starring role. Torgnyr's job was to recite from memory one third of the kingdom's laws so that all could hear and know the law. This year he was to recite the middle portion and despite his brave words to Wahid, he had been practicing furiously.

"Have you heard King Eirik speak about Christians in the kingdom?" he asked his friend.

Wahid chuckled. "I'd hate to be one of them these days," he said. "The king has declared them dangerous. I believe he plans to propose outlawing Christianity and requiring all Christians to be removed."

"That is not in accordance with our laws," Torgnyr protested. "A man has to break a law in order to be exiled or executed."

"New king, new laws." Wahid shrugged. "I'm sure he will create a law that Christians will break."

Wahid changed the subject. "I have heard of an interesting astronomical event that is to occur soon. Shall I tell you about it?"

"I will come later to discuss the stars with you," Torgnyr said. "Perhaps I had best speak to the king now, before he goes so far as to propose a new law. He will be more willing to change his mind if it is done in private."

* * * *

King Eirik welcomed him, ushering him into his tent with a hearty slap on the back. "Good to see you!" he boomed. "How is your father doing? And your clever younger brother?"

"They are well, thank you for asking," Torgnyr said.

Torgnyr's father, named Torgnyr the Great, had been Speaker of Law for King Eirik's father. He was now retired and living on his farm two days north of the king's stronghold. In his stead, Torgnyr the Bastard served as Speaker of Law for the current king. His half brother, also named Torgnyr, was the son of Torgnyr the Great and his wife Marit and so was known as Torgnyr Torgnyrson. Torgnyr's own mother, an Irish serving girl on his father's farm, had died giving birth to her bastard son. According to his father, Torgnyr had inherited his unfortunate looks from her.

He would just as soon not discuss his family's well-being at the moment. "I have been asked to speak to you on behalf of a Christian family," he began.

"Do you accept commissions from Christians now?" the king asked. He laughed and nudged Torgnyr. "You will accept work from anyone as long as his silver is pure, will you not?"

Torgnyr fought to control his temper. "Please hear me out. I believe these Christians make a good case. They have not broken our laws."

"The Christians are a threat to our way of life. They occupy good land, Norse land, meant for Norse men. They enter an area then spread their filthy religion to their neighbors, by force if necessary. Look around you. The world is changing and we have to protect ourselves. My father's cousin in the Danish lands has become Christian. The Germanic people in the south have become Christian. The Saxons and the Franks have been Christian for hundreds of years. If we become Christian, we will lose our way of life. How is a man to go a-Viking if he is a Christian? The gold is all kept in the monasteries. If we are Christians, the one-god will not allow us to take this gold. And it belongs to us because we are the strongest!"

"I don't want the Christians to take over from the Norse gods either," Torgnyr said. "But when we are in our kingdom, we have to follow our laws. If not, we will have civil unrest."

"I am the king," Eirik said. "I will decide the laws."

"The law is king," Torgnyr corrected. "And the law decides the king."

Eirik rose, fist clenched. Torgnyr scrambled to his feet. The king towered over him menacingly.

"Perhaps it is time for that tradition to die. I know what is best for my people. They are like children. They need the firm hand of a father to keep them from harm. I am that father and I am responsible for protecting them from themselves."

"We are men, not boys. We will decide what is best for us." Torgnyr stalked out of the king's tent before he could be thrown out.

* * * *

The morning of the assembly dawned clear and cool. Torgnyr commanded the crowd's attention. "Silence!" he boomed. He had not been named "Thor's Noise" for nothing. His voice, unusually powerful and now amplified by the sheer cliff wall behind him, resonated through the crowd. Startled into obedience, the men swiveled to stare at him.

He allowed time for those who had never met him to stare. He knew his face caught people off guard. His green eyes bulged in their sockets, giving him a constantly surprised mien, and a scar slit his upper lip, dividing it into two unequal parts and making his smile indistinguishable from his snarl.

"I will recite the law now," Torgnyr told the crowd. "You will listen and abide by our laws. Tomorrow we will vote on new laws and then we will judge crimes. If you have a crime to present, have your witnesses ready."

For the rest of the morning and into the afternoon, Torgnyr recited. The rhythms flowed from his lips as sagas from the mouth of a skald. By the time he finished, he was nearly as exhausted as his audience.

The gathered men broke into small groups as they prepared to head to their tents for the night. Torgnyr hopped down from the Law Stone and reached for the mug of water offered by Wahid.

"Thanks. This was thirsty work." He drained the mug and handed it back to Wahid. "After I wash my face, I am going to join some others for ale. Will you join us?"

Wahid clapped his back. "I will not, thank you. I dislike the vulgarity on display when the men are drunk. Have dinner with me first and I can tell you about the astronomical event I mentioned. I think you will find it interesting."

Before Torgnyr could reply, the king sprang to the Law Stone and banged his shield with his sword. "One moment, my friends, before we close for the day," he said.

Torgnyr and Wahid exchanged glances and moved closer to the platform.

"We have an important new law to discuss tomorrow," Eirik continued. "I will outline it tonight and you can discuss it over your ale this evening. How many of you wish to be Christians?"

Only one hand rose. Maurice. Torgnyr shook his head at the Frank, motioning for him to lower his hand.

"Exactly," Eirik said. "And yet the Christians will not tolerate other religions. If we allow this cult to take root in our society, we will all find ourselves worshipping the Pope rather than the gods of our fathers. The law I will propose is a simple one: keep the Norse lands for the Norse men. All Christians will be outlawed, effective immediately. Those who see the wisdom of this, stop by my tent tonight and have an ale on me. We must celebrate the return of our land to its former greatness!"

The crowd hooted and banged shields as they jostled towards the king's tent. Torgnyr turned to Wahid. "I guess I drink alone tonight. I will join you for dinner after all."

* * * *

"What shall I say?" Torgnyr asked. He'd brought his own ale to Wahid's tent and now sat in an alcohol-fueled depression. "The king will be allowed to pass his law because most men are not affected. Only a Christian will care."

He took another sip of his ale. "I should warn Maurice to sell his land tonight for half its value and leave with his family. There is no place for him here."

Wahid looked at his friend. "You are eager to give up? I admit I am no fan of the Christians, considering the devastation they have wrecked upon the Arabic lands. But do you think the king will stop at outlawing Christians? He enjoys the taste of power on his tongue. Once the Christians are gone, the Arabs and the Jews will be next. After that, who knows? Perhaps the red-headed such as you will be outlawed. You are half-Irish, are you not? The Norse lands are to be for the Norse men, not the half-Irish."

"King Eirik is forsaking the rule of law," Torgnyr said. "He would take away our masculinity and make us as boys again, subject to the will of a strong father."

"That might be what you say to the people," Wahid conceded. "No Norse man likes to be seen as a child. That might be your only hope."

"Let us talk of something else. What is this star event that has you so excited?"

"Ah!" Wahid said, rubbing his hands in delight. "Neither you nor I have ever seen such a thing in our lifetimes! The sun will be consumed by the moon in two days' time."

Torgnyr, caught in the act of drinking, spit out his ale. "Hah!" he exclaimed. He wiped his chin. "You are funny tonight. Do you believe that old legend about the wolf Skoll chasing and eating the god Sol? Nonsense. If there is one thing I have learned to count on, it is the invariability of the sun."

"I jest not, my friend. The moon will swallow the sun an hour or so after noon two days hence. For several minutes, the sun will be completely gone from the midday sky."

Torgnyr studied his friend. "You believe this, do you?"

Wahid shot him a quelling look. "Of course. It is not a question of belief. The mathematics do not lie."

"What should we do? We must create a great deal of noise to frighten away Skoll. The men must be ready."

"Noise or not, the sun will reappear where it had been before. Can you not use this information somehow during the assembly?"

The idea had merit and Torgnyr returned to his own tent to ponder the possibilities.

* * * *

When the men assembled in the morning in front of the Law Stone, Torgnyr sought out Maurice. When he finally found the man, alone at the back of the crowd, he saw that during the night someone had taken the opportunity to pulp the man's face.

"Who did this to you?" he asked Maurice, ignoring the unfriendly looks of the men nearby.

Maurice looked around at the armed men waiting impatiently for the assembly to begin. "No one."

"You did this to yourself? Don't be a fool. The persons who did this to you must be brought to justice."

"There will be no justice for a foreigner here," Maurice said. "Perhaps I should simply abandon my farm and escape with my family while I still have my life."

Torgnyr was torn. Should he advise the man to flee and protect his family? Or to stay put and trust in the rule of law?

"Who would take your lands if you left?" he asked.

Maurice looked startled. "Either the king or my neighbors, I suppose," he said. "The man on my eastern border has offered several times to buy the land for a pittance."

Torgnyr eyed the Frank closely. "And is this the same man who beat you? We can fight him in the courts. He is greedy and he cannot be allowed to steal another's land by force. And neither can the king."

Their conversation was interrupted by the king's arrival on the Law Stone. As expected, he proposed his law barring Christians from the kingdom. "The Christian one-god is a threat to our people," he declared. "I propose a law making his worship illegal. Once this law is passed, we will try the case of Maurice the Christian. He is guilty of breaking this law and must be outlawed."

Torgnyr joined the king on the platform. "You would declare a man guilty of violating a law that does not yet exist? This is backwards. First we create the law, then the crime occurs, then comes the trial and punishment."

The king waved this inconsequential issue aside. "Do you think he will stop being Christian as soon as the law is passed? No need to wait. I demand that we now vote on this law. Those who are not my enemies, vote 'aye'."

"Not so fast! We will open the floor to debate! This is the people's law, not the king's order."

Eirik narrowed his eyes. "You overstep your place, lawman. I am king here."

"And we are men here. We are capable of choosing to accept or reject Christianity. We do not need to be protected from the one-god by our king."

It took two hours of rancorous debate, but in the end, Torgnyr persuaded the men to overrule the law. "No one, king or freeman, can outlaw someone based on his religion and seize his land without just cause," he declared.

King Eirik drew his sword. "You are outlawed, lawman. This law is not overruled. I am king, not you and not 'law'." The men erupted into clamor again, some pledging their loyalty to the king's bold statement, others shouting threats. Both sides shouted and banged their shields with battle axes, knives, or swords.

Torgnyr faced the king. He opened his arms so that all could see he was unarmed. Eirik's sword hovered near his breastbone. He paused, allowing the spectators to settle down.

"You are king because we have chosen you," he said, his voice icily calm. "You are king at our will. But remember this: above you, the law is our king. By our laws, we can strip you of your power and behead you where you stand." He turned to the crowd. "Will we be men, ruled by the laws we create? Or will we live as the slaves, thralls to the whim of one man?"

The crowd pressed closer as they argued the point. Though some were willing to allow Eirik his way in all things, most were too independent to submit themselves so fully to another's rule.

Torgnyr remembered his conversation with Wahid. "Attention!" he shouted, eventually making himself heard. "We must not fight among ourselves. Let us let the gods decide. Tomorrow when we begin the day's assembly, we will try the cases before the Thing. After we decide the guilt or innocence of the accused, we will ask the gods for a sign. If the gods can communicate with us before the assembly ends tomorrow, we will know that they do not wish us to throw away our laws and only submit ourselves to the king. If they do not give us a sign, we will have to decide this issue ourselves."

* * * *

"I'm counting heavily on this astronomical event of yours," he confessed to Wahid that night.

"It will happen tomorrow," Wahid said placidly. He sat on a cushion, peeling an apple. "The orbits of the sun and moon will intersect tomorrow. The moon will pass in front of the sun and the sun will disappear. Such an event is called an '*ekleipsis*' by the Greeks, meaning the sun has abandoned the people."

Torgnyr squirmed on his cushion. He hated to ask this next question, realizing it made him look like a fool, but he could not help himself. "And the sun will then come back?"

Wahid smiled tolerantly. "It will indeed, but not before many a man is frightened."

"Very well. I'll use it. I hate to use signs of the supernatural in place of logic, but I believe this king is immune to appeals of logic."

"And what will you do next?" Wahid asked.

"What do you mean?"

"You and King Eirik will never have the close relationship that your father enjoyed with Eirik's father. He will not listen to you and he might even grow to hate you if he believes you have tricked him."

Torgnyr shrugged. "I have thought about going to the Western Norse lands to visit my cousin. He is in the household of the king of Tønsberg. Perhaps Torgnyr Torgnyrson will have better luck with Eirik the Victorious than I."

Wahid eyed his friend. "Perhaps you will permit me to join you on this journey? Even if the king allows Christians to remain, I do not feel safe here as an Arab."

"Will the king permit you to leave? He values your education and counsel. He might insist that you remain."

"Which is why I was going to suggest that we keep our plans secret for the moment," Wahid said.

The final day of the Thing dawned with the glory of early Fall. Birds in the trees sang, heedless of the coming winter. The air was chilled but not cold and the sun shone warmly on the ground in front of the Law Stone. Torgnyr turned his face upwards to enjoy the sun's warmth.

He believed Wahid, he really did. Still, the thought of losing the sun forever left a knot in his stomach.

"You'll be back soon, right?" he murmured, eyes still closed.

"Look at that idiot," a voice boomed by his ear.

Torgnyr opened his eyes to see Claudine and Maurice staring at him.

"He's talking to the sun," Claudine declared. She nudged her husband. "I told you I should speak for us rather than this simple Norse donkey."

Ignoring her, Torgnyr addressed Maurice. "Are you ready for today's trial? No matter what happens, I want you to remain calm. Come, let us men go and discuss strategy."

Claudine shot him a look of hatred but Torgnyr led Maurice away.

* * * *

"Where is your sign from the gods, lawman?" the king demanded. He had presented his "evidence" concerning the evil intentions of the Christian family and had listened impatiently to Torgnyr's rebuttal. It was abundantly clear that the king's mind was made up. Logic or no, he needed to be seen as protecting his people and so the outsiders had to go.

Torgnyr looked at Wahid next to him on the Law Stone. The Arab nodded slightly. "The sign will come soon," Torgnyr declared, hoping that he wasn't making a fool of himself. Despite his appearance, he did not relish the role of jester.

Torgnyr motioned for Maurice to join the group on the Law Stone. With the king, Wahid, himself, and now Maurice up there, the stone's top was crowded. Torgnyr shifted slightly to avoid slipping off the edge, making room for Maurice to stand between him and Wahid. The two advisors each held one of Maurice's hands. The Frank appeared very uncomfortable but Torgnyr ignored this.

"I call upon Thor, god of thunder, to stand together with the Christian and Arab gods. Give us a sign that we must stand together. Show us that we must not throw a man and his family into exile based on his religion." His voice, strong on a normal day, now boomed over the heads of the men gathered for the assembly.

The king scoffed. He stood, arms crossed over his chest, gazing at the trio with their arms raised. "Am I supposed to be impressed?" he asked. "Where is this sign of yours?"

Torgnyr judged that this was the best opportunity to plead his client's entire case. "King Eirik. If the gods send us a sign, will you buy the Christian's land from him at twice its value?"

"You must take me for a fool. Your 'sign from the gods' will be a bird pooping or a leaf falling. I will take the Christian's land for the kingdom for free once he is exiled for his crime."

"His crime of following his religion?" Torgnyr asked.

"Don't be naïve. His crime of bringing his religion into our community for the purpose of forcing us to convert."

"I will let the assembly decide if a sign is 'worthy'," Torgnyr offered. "If your subjects decide that they have seen a clear sign, will you buy the land at twice its price? If there is no sign, I will exile myself from this kingdom forever."

"I'll take that deal, lawman. You are not the Speaker of Law that your father was. In fact, if the gods send us this sign, I'll pay three times the land price."

Torgnyr fought to control his excitement. His commission on the sale of the land would fund his exile quite nicely. And the king, in front of his subjects, could not go back on his word. No Norse man would allow a cheat to be king. Torgnyr dried his sweaty hands on his tunic and clasped Maurice's hand again. "The deal is made," he declared.

Wahid used his free hand to point upward. A tiny dark spot nibbled at the edge of the sun. "Is that enough of a sign, King Eirik?" he asked.

Eirik looked upwards and frowned. "No, of course not. That's just …" he searched for the right word, "… just a cloud in front of the sun."

Torgnyr forbore mentioning the day was cloudless. If the Arab was right, the sign would grow.

All the men turned, hands shielding their eyes as they stared at the sun.

The shadow grew, encroaching further into the sun. Torgnyr had the urge to vomit. Without the sun, all life on Earth would die. He would die.

After ten minutes, the birds stopped singing, as if they, too, were confused by the sun's abandonment.

"It's Ragnarok!" a man shouted. "It's the end of the world! The wolves will eat the sun and the moon and the gods will battle for us all!" The man banged his axe against his shield to frighten the wolves. The other men did the same until all two hundred were shouting and banging.

The acrid smell next to him told him that Maurice had wet his pants.

"Is this enough of a sign?" Torgnyr shouted over the din. The king merely gaped at him, too dazed to even bang his shield.

"King Eirik! Is this a sign?"

The spell broken, the king nodded and pulled his sword, banging it against his shield as loudly as he could.

Torgnyr watched the sky. It was dark as night now and the only noise was that of the shields. The shadow over the sun was studded with small beads of light which provided the only illumination.

The shadow moved further and the sun took the appearance of a golden ring with a gem on top. The ring then disappeared, leaving only a reddish glow.

Too frightened to watch, Torgnyr turned away. The men were silent now, their protests against the wolves forgotten in their awe. Shadowy bands of light and dark dappled the cliff and the rocky terrain, moving across the land like waves in the harbor.

"Is this a sign, King Eirik?" Torgnyr asked into the silence.

"Oh yes," the king said. His face was pale and sweaty.

As they continued to watch, the shadow moved across the sun further. A half-circle of light appeared at the edge, nearly blinding the watchers with its brilliance.

"Hurrah!" The men burst into laughter and jubilation. They resumed banging their shields to encourage the wolves' retreat.

The king turned to Maurice. He had the look of a man sober after years of being drunk. "Tell me more about this one-god of yours," he said.

"No, Sire, I will not. I will not commit a crime by imposing my beliefs on you."

Torgnyr looked at his client with new respect. He hadn't figured the man had courage enough to speak to the king so boldly. He tugged on Maurice's sleeve. "Come. We have much to do. You must pack up your family and prepare to leave. As soon as you collect the land price for your farm, Wahid and I will escort you to your new home."

Suzanne Berube Rorhus attended the Squaw Valley Community of Writers and is an active member of Mystery Writers of America and International Thriller Writers. Her published short fiction has appeared in *Ellery Queen Mystery Magazine*, the anthologies *Memphis Noir*, *Flash and Bang*, and *Moon Shot*, and in various online and print publications, including *Norwegian American Weekly*. In addition to writing, she is starting law school in the fall.

AN ECLIPSE OF HEARTS

DEE MCKINNEY

"AAAAH! AAAAAH!"

Screams were nothing new to Dr. Enid Seward. She heard them both in the ER as a part-time hospitalist and when she scratched off an organ thief, child eater, or other bona fide supernatural critter with a satisfying thwack. *Whoever said childbirth was the most precious moment in a woman's life*, thought Enid, *needed more drugs*.

Enid assisted her best friend Lara with a patient who showed up at the hospital dilated to ten centimeters. The women wouldn't focus. No time to get her upstairs, Enid and Lara propped up the soon-to-be mom on the edge of an exam bed and let nature take its rapid course. They'd been through the "I can't do this" and "Please knock me out" moments. Problem was, this kid was on exit mode, hand first. Enid weighed options.

"Ms. Owens, I need to cut an episiotomy. Okay?"

"Bitch! You're going to *cut* me?" wailed the woman.

"I prefer not, but in this case, it's the safest option for the baby. Everything's going fine. Can you trust us?" Enid looked at Lara, who squeezed Ms. Owen's hand.

"Okay, okay, just get it over with! Get this thing out!"

Enid injected lidocaine and made the smallest incision she could. In under a minute, the baby's right arm and head emerged, with the left arm in normal position. Enid sighed in relief and got a gush of amniotic fluid all over her scrub pants as a thank you for helping deliver a healthy eight-pound boy.

An hour later, she'd showered and changed, flopping down beside Lara on one of the couches in the lounge. "Oh … my … god. How many was that? In the past twenty-four hours or so?"

"A baker's dozen," said Lara, rebraiding her glossy black hair which frizzed from hours of work and sweat with no break. "Aren't you grateful I trained as both a nurse and midwife? I mean, how long has it been since you attended a birth?"

Enid thought. "Six years? Seven? I didn't like OB. Too much cutesy for me. Jumping into helicopters with an organ container and wearing sweatpants is more my style."

"Aw, you're such a grumpus. I love helping new moms."

"I know, and you're good at it. I'm not. Thanks for being there," said Enid.

"It was fun, but kind of weird, this sharp uptick in ER babies since last night. Full moon?" asked Lara.

Enid made it her business to know moon phases and other astronomical events, thanks to her "other" job, the one that had nothing to do with medicine. She pulled up an app on her mobile. "Sort of. In fact, tonight is a penumbral lunar eclipse."

"A what?"

"Well, a lunar eclipse happens when the moon is full. It lines up with the sun, with Earth in the middle. The Earth's shadow falls on the moon. That's what makes an eclipse. It's called penumbral when just the outer shadow of Earth falls on the moon's face. It's subtle. Most people think it's just an ordinary full moon."

Lara stared. "You know some of the oddest things."

"Yeah. So, thirteen babies? That's what's odd." Enid looked at the clock. "Shift ends in ten. It's my turn to bring coffee. The usual double double?"

"We may need a triple triple if another thirteen pregnant women show up," said Lara.

* * * *

Charting complete, Enid snuggled in her pea coat and walked the mile to her condo. The penumbral moon illuminated the greater Vancouver skyline. Lara's numbers were right, and spookier still, most of the thirteens births had some sort of anomaly. Hand by the face, foot in the mouth, face up, a full caul, and even a long umbilical cord that could've caused a serious problem. Lara's experience kept everyone safe. All the babies and moms were fine. Still, Enid felt the tingle in her bones. Jokes about full moons and Valentine's Day next week aside, she knew someone or something was messing with the city and her people. This sudden population explosion needed research.

At home, Enid pulled a red silk braided cord from around her neck. She fit its dangling skeleton key into the steamer trunk in her garage. This was the eternal problem—how to find specific information from a hundred years of Seward family journals. Her father had been in the process of cataloging them when he died, and they remained disorganized because his sole heir was a workaholic. Enid grabbed a large stack and returned to her living room, spreading them out across the coffee table. Too many to cover in the thirty-six hours until her next shift. She pulled out her mobile and dialed.

"Hello?"

"Hi, Allie. It's Enid."

"Not on a date with Dr. Brian McKenzie and his Scottish terrier?" Allie asked.

"You drive me nuts. You know that?" Enid growled at her mentor. They may have mended their fractured friendship in the last year, but Allie's know-it-all attitude still set Enid on edge.

"I do. You're just so adorable together."

Enid knew one thing that would get Allie's mind off her former student's percolating romance with Brian. "Thirteen babies delivered in about twenty-six hours. All in the ER, none pre-registered with OB. Penumbral moon. Seward family journals."

"I'll be there in fifteen minutes," said Allie, hanging up.

As Enid organized the books by dates, Allie let herself in and rushed to pull off her long cardigan. She pulled on her tortoiseshell reading glasses and reached for the nearest book without even a greeting.

"Hello to you, too. Not on call tonight at the morgue?" Enid asked.

"Oh, no. I told them they had to cut back a bit on the schedule, even if I am just a part-timer," Allie said, pushing her silver hair behind her ears. "The new mortgage helper makes quite a difference in my bank account. He's a sweet boy. Helps with the yard and such. Nice to have someone downstairs in the apartment again. So, tell me about the case."

"I'm not sure we have a case, but this felt off to me. Not worth bothering the RCMP and Constable Edgefield since I don't see evidence of any crime," Enid said. "Just a hunch."

"I love that you're trusting your instincts. At last!"

"Yeah, dandy. Okay, so in just over a day, we had thirteen deliveries in the ER, most of them crowning when the moms waddled in the door. Out of the blue. No correlation with higher deliveries or pre-registrations in regular OB. Moms and babies are fine, though I didn't see any co-parents or relatives with them. Something quirky about each birth, though. I had a boy with a hand up by the head, plus the first intact caul I've ever seen."

"No indications for a C-section?"

"No time. Good thing Lara was on shift with me because I'm out of practice. It could've been a nightmare, but aside from two episiotomies and a few small tears, no complications we couldn't handle," said Enid. "I checked the charts. All thirteen were single moms. None listed a father."

"What ages?" Allie asked.

"Not what statistics would predict. Twenty-five to thirty years old, healthy."

"Mental state?"

"Fine. Happy. When I clocked out, they were all on the OB floor doing well."

Allie gnawed her lip. Enid recognized it as her mentor's thinking face. "Certain creatures have reputations for seducing women. You know about vamp—"

"No!" said Enid. "We don't use the V word! Ever! Dead things don't create life. That's basic biology, professor. Plus, I'm not tempting fate. End of story."

"So, let's hit the books."

Enid pulled up her lunar app and looked for 20ᵗʰ century penumbral eclipses. "See if you find anything for March 1904."

Allie flipped through the closest journals and pulled one out. "Spring 1904. Worth a look."

Enid opened it and read Dr. Jack Seward's words aloud.

31 March, 1904

I've scarce had a solid meal, much less time to see Edith and the children. I know she is exhausted with the three of them on her own, and I would gladly arrange for Miss Baker or Miss Tyner from the village to help. They, however, are at the hospital working day and night. I have sent a telegram to Jonathan in hopes that Mina might take the train and come for a short visit. The daffodils are in bloom, and perhaps Mina might entice Edith and the children outside.

So, we are a hospital for sick children, yet what do we do when seven women arrive at our door, alone and friendless, in need of a doctor and midwife? We took them all in, without question, of course. The doorbell tolled every three hours or so, starting last night at sunset. Where did they come from? That is quite the oddity. Two of the women are local, unmarried, yet of good repute. They hid their conditions well. Another three were travelers, journeying to visit family for Easter week. The last two, well, I have not inquired. My colleague said this was an April Fool's Day prank after a mere nine hours of work. He is not so amused now, over a day later. Unless contagious, sick children regularly stay in one ward. We curtained off partitions in haste to allow some modesty for the women patients. Some have visited each other in a cheerful manner.

Perhaps because of my wife's difficulty in birthing our youngest son, I feared the worst. Yet all seven ladies are in fine health, and their children alike, three boys and four girls. It is not in my general purview to note such things, nor to pry, but the mothers are remarkable in appearance. One might name them beauties in the fashion of Elizabeth

Bennet—fresh, dewy complexions, rosy limbs, and of good nature. They needed no wet nurses.

Curious yet respectful of their provenance, I spoke with the fourth lady to give birth, Miss Katharine Franor. She nursed her daughter, quite at her ease. She was en route to Winchester when she stopped for assistance. A woman that late in pregnancy should not have been away from home.

"Madam, you may of course stay here until you mend and are ready to travel. Might I inquire if there is someone I could telegraph for you? A friend or your, ah, husband?"

She laughed in that happy way new mothers do as she rocked the baby. "You're most kind, Dr. Seward. I have a sister who expects me, and it would be so thoughtful of you to let her know I am well. In fact, I hope to take the Saturday train to arrive in time for Easter."

"But that is day after tomorrow!" I exclaimed.

"Oh, but I feel wonderful! Surely my health is good?"

"It is, Miss Franor," I reassured her. "Have you chosen a name for your beautiful daughter?"

She stroked the baby's tiny red curls. "She's such a bright wee thing. What do you think of a flower name, doctor? Perhaps Daisy? Or Violet? I shall have to think on it."

A shadow passed the door, and young Miss Molly Baker waited for me. "Those are lovely," I said. "If you need anything, please just call. One of the nursing sisters is just outside."

Molly Baker has been a blessing since she came here as a servant. Now, she runs the day-to-day affairs and is apprenticing as a nurse. More than once, I've found her wise for her years. If she chose to speak, my time would be well spent listening.

"May we talk in private, Dr. Seward?"

I escorted her to my office and poured cold tea. "What an odd night, day, and night this has been, my dear Molly!" I drank my cup in a single sip. We had worked together so often in such odd circumstances, she asked that I address her thus when not with patients. Besides, my own children think of her as an older sister, and she was so helpful to Edith during her difficult lying in.

"Yes, sir, you could say that. Have our new mothers said aught to you of their condition?"

I pondered this. I meant to ask Miss Franor, but somehow, I could not bring myself to press her for details. "No. Have any spoken to you?"

"No, sir, not a one, though you know I'm one for the talking. They've not said a bit about their circumstances," replied Molly. I heard worry in her voice.

"Surely you don't think this relates to a creature seeking to harm the children?" I said, thinking back to an occasion a few years earlier. "If so, we must take immediate precautions."

"Not harm, sir, at least, no intent of such. But back home, we weren't far from the North Sea. Lots of good English folk in those parts have the red hair."

"So they do. Pray tell what you mean. Most of these children had no hair at all, not a remarkable characteristic in newborns."

She tugged at her apron. "Two did, a right thick mane of it. Red, too. Could be 'tis the ulda, sir."

"The what?"

Molly sighed. "They came with the raiders from Norway and them parts. Half of Britain has Viking blood, you know that, Dr. Seward." I nodded for her to continue. "Well, the ulda are a handsome folk. The women are beautiful, as are the men, though long in the nose. The ulda have a reputation, you see, for, well, granting the gift of children to those who want 'em."

"Good lord! Are you telling me that some sort of Nordic fairy enchanted these women and, er, did ill by them?" I stood and paced by my desk.

"No, I don't think that's it at all. They don't mean harm. I heard tell that some folk who are lonely light a fire during the shadowed moon. What do you call it?"

"An eclipse," I said.

"Yes, I couldn't remember the name. Perhaps there was one nine or ten months ago. I wouldn't say the ulda is a fiend or monstrous, though I'd be wary of it myself," Molly explained, sitting her cup down.

I thought about the women. "Do you think our patients are any danger to themselves or their babies?"

"No, sir, I'd say not. 'Tis just, well, odd things do seem to come your way, don't they, Dr. Seward?" Molly was a shrewd lass.

"I find your knowledge sound, dear girl. We shall make sure the mothers and babies are well before sending them home." I motioned to the door. "Get yourself some rest. I believe Edith plans to invite you for Easter dinner on Sunday, and Lucius, Helena, and Robert will tire you out with their games."

Viking fertility fairies? I know much sadder and more terrifying creatures walk the earth. This time, I believe I shall let the sun rise and set without interfering in this peculiar chain of events.

* * * *

Allie laughed until tears ran down her plump cheeks. "Oh, that's just too much. Swedish love magic! Stellen Skarsgård visiting lonely English women and getting them with child! Maybe there's an Abba soundtrack."

Enid closed the book and gnawed her thumbnail. "Allie, this isn't funny! We don't need some rapist running around the city, enchanting hapless women and getting them pregnant. Who the heck is Stellen Skarsgård? Wait, he's that nutty astronomer in the Thor movies."

"That's not quite how I remember him," Allie sniffed. "Are you sure it wasn't consensual? Didn't the journal say the *ulda* meant no harm?"

"That's Molly's take. Jack didn't pursue it because work and raising three children overwhelmed him, not to mention the monster-hunting hobby on the side."

"Or perhaps he saw no need to harm a creature that these women may have called upon by their own choice."

"They're like the women we saw. None of them talked about their situations or the fathers. Like, they couldn't. Memory problems? Or a condition? It sounds like coercion of some kind. Believe me, if there's an *ulda* in Vancouver, we're going to find it and settle this," said Enid. She rifled through her kitchen drawers and pulled out a chef's knife, a heavy wood French rolling pin, and a prescription pad. "You can borrow one of my jackets. We're heading to Grouse Mountain after a quick stop at the pharmacy."

"Because why?"

Enid's green eyes narrowed. "Forests, a penumbral eclipse, and lots of romance on the ski slopes. I'm luring this thing in for a chat." She tore off a signed prescription from her pad.

* * * *

Allie drove as Enid smeared high-dose estrogen cream on her own neck and wrists, then dabbed some behind Allie's ears.

"Among your wacky plans for stalking things that lurk in the night, this is about the silliest one ever," said the older woman. "Ugh, Enid, that's off-label use!"

"I'll smell luscious to an *ulda*. Right?"

"I suppose." Allie parked and presented her season pass as they boarded the gondola to the peak. No one took a second look at Enid's backpack. As they exited the gate at the mountain top, the guide said, "Closing in about ninety minutes, ladies. Don't get stuck up there."

"We just want to get a few short runs in," said Enid. "Couldn't resist the clear skies and that moon."

"Sure is a pretty night for it," the guide agreed.

Passing the lodge, Enid headed for the top of the Grouse Grind. She had no intention of trekking at night. It provided an excellent cover of heavy evergreens, a thick canopy of firs and spruce. She could think of no better place within a short drive that had a more Scandinavian-like climate.

Enid pulled out her rolling pin from the backpack, tucking it under her jacket. Then she waited. Allie leaned against a tree, casting glances around as if she were afraid of getting caught. The moon was so bright, it cut through the branches, casting spindles of shadow on the ground.

Enid checked her watch. They didn't have much time. To her surprise, she heard the crunch of snow and saw Brian, six feet of solid, handsome male with dark auburn hair, walking over from the lodge. Enid groaned. Skiing with her would-be boyfriend sounded fun, but not while she messed with an *ulda*. For all she knew, Molly Baker's story had big holes. The creature might have eaten potential rival suitors. Enid heard Allie gasp and dreaded the ribbing on their drive home.

"Brian, hey. Didn't know you were coming up here tonight," Enid said.

"It's him! Who would've thought we'd meet Stellen Skarsgård at Grouse Mountain?" Allie jumped up and down like a kid.

Brian looked at Allie and smiled. Enid's hackles went up. "Wait a damn minute. Brian, where's John Hamish?"

"Uh, I left him at home. Too cold out here," he said.

"Wrong answer! Scotties live to roll in the snow. Plus, no dogs allowed on the Grind! Brian would know that!" shouted Enid. "Give it up, *ulda*. Or ..."

"You're lonely," said Brian. "You're a widow. You've thought about me before."

"I ..." Enid felt mired in the snow, Brian's voice steady and soothing.

"It's okay. We've been putting this off a while, and I'm done waiting. Aren't you?"

Enid stepped toward Brian when a huge snowball blasted his head.

"Oops! I meant that for her. I want your autograph!" said Allie. "I mean, what are the chances of this? I just love your work." Caked snow fell from Allie's gloves as she gazed in rapture. For a moment, Enid no longer saw Brian. His form flickered into the mature yet handsome Swedish actor Allie adored. Enid shook herself, and the movie star was gone. In his place stood a red-haired, pale, skinny man in green jeans and a Nordic navy and white sweater. The *ulda* stared at Allie. *Not bad looking, despite the deviated septum,* Enid thought, *but he's no Brian McKenzie. Or Stellen Skarsgård.*

Enid wasn't sure she had the physical strength to knock the *ulda* down, but she pulled out the rolling pin and leapt for its throat. To her surprise, the shape shifter had a light frame, almost as if its bones were hollow like a bird's. Thanks to weekly judo, Enid pinned the *ulda* against the nearest Sitka spruce, her hands on the rolling pin across its neck.

"Don't hurt it!" shouted Allie.

Enid pushed the wood across the *ulda*'s windpipe as its long, thin fingers clawed her hands to get free. "Okay, lover boy. Talk. Or else I cut off more than your airway."

The *ulda* nodded. Enid gave the wooden rolling pin another shove for good measure. The creature slid to the ground, back against the rough tree bark.

"I wasn't going to harm you," croaked the *ulda*, rubbing its throat. It had a sing-song accent. Enid couldn't tell its eye color in the tree-filtered light. "Your scent. Both, but you most." It pointed to Enid. "The call felt so strong."

She threw the tube of estrogen ointment at him. "It wasn't what you think."

"I can see that now." The *ulda* coughed. "Who was I to know you used a love balm? You came to the woods in an eclipse. I have to answer when someone makes the sign."

"Did the other women in the city call as well?" asked Allie. The *ulda* nodded. "You're tied to some sort of lunar cycle, I'm guessing?" It stared at her and shrugged.

"You forced them into relations with you? Bearing your children?" snarled Enid.

"No! That's against the law."

"What law?"

"The law of the forests," the *ulda* said. "The rules of our kind. We come when asked, and should we do ill to the callers, we wither and die. Like the ash and oak leaves in autumn."

"Scandinavians built the first structures here," Allie remarked. "I can see why he'd be attracted to the place."

Enid studied the *ulda*. "Are you always male? Do they forget you when you leave?"

It shook its head. "Sometimes I'm female. Depends on the one who wants my presence. Even in huge settlements like this, people feel alone. I sense it, and if the moon is right, I go to them. A few remember. Most recall a romantic interlude, a happy one."

"That explains the baby boom," said Allie, "since there was a minor eclipse about ten months ago. Plus, the red hair. It tends to skip generations. Not all its offspring would have it."

"Right, assuming genetics apply with this thing."

"The ones with my hair color tend to be extraordinary," said the creature with pride. "Artistic and such. Not all get the gift."

Weighing options, Enid circled the *ulda*. The creature had a childlike frailness to it that invoked her sympathy. Yet she couldn't trust it. That wasn't in the Seward nature. "Okay, look here. You've got to put some limits on your, um, passionate activities. You make an oath that you'll only answer three calls in any eclipse. Then, we'll let you go."

"Let it have four," said Allie. "Be a sport." Enid rolled her eyes.

"Four's a good number," nodded the *ulda*. "I will promise this."

"Well, swear on something. What do you consider special or important?"

The *ulda* pondered the question. "You have a tree that grows here. Pretty, with pointed leaves. Everyone loves it. I see it all over the city."

"The big leaf maple," said Enid. "*Acer macrophyllum*." She foraged around the top of the trail, digging through fallen leaves now turning loamy. After a few minutes, she found one, torn but still amber gold. "Swear on that."

The *ulda* took it from her. Enid thought she saw the leaf sparkle with a green flash. "I promise I will not spread my fertile seed or open my womb to any more than four humans who call whenever the moon is shaded." It looked at Enid. "Good enough, child of *draugr* banes? I know who you are now. Much like your ancestors, protecting the innocent and slaying fiends."

Enid could translate the word "vampire" in most languages. She liked the sound of the Norse kenning for someone who hunted monsters. *Draugr* bane—it fit. "Aren't you clever. All right, you're free to go. Do me a favor, though, and take these along." She tossed the *ulda* a Durex box. "For all the lonely people who don't want to continue your line." The *ulda* gave her a grin. Enid caught a flicker of Brian in its face, and then the creature disappeared. Over the loudspeaker, a Grouse Mountain employee announced the last gondolas would be leaving in ten minutes.

As they made their way to the line of waiting skiers, Allie gave her a look. "You didn't see Michael. You saw Brian. Does this mean you're ready to move on?"

Enid stared at the waiting couples and families. "Yes. It's taken a while. The Seward journals changed me. I'm still deciding if that's a good thing. If Brian's part of the new me, then I'm ready. I think." She breathed. "Fine, I want a relationship. I can say that and not flashback to Michael every time I touch Brian. Happy now?"

Allie put an arm around Enid's shoulders. "You showed mercy to a creature that was, in essence, harmless. You brought children into the world. You found yet another fascinating tale from your great-grandfather. Plus, I'm happy that you want Brian in your life. I'd call this night a win."

Enid didn't tell her that she'd recorded the names of the new moms in her own personal journals for long-term follow-up. No need to worry

Allie. "You're right. I also educated a Scandinavian fairy on birth control. Don't forget that part."

Allie giggled as they climbed aboard the gondola. Enid looked back to the crest of the mountain, catching the flutter of an owl across the eclipsed moon. Yep, there were far worse ways for a *draugr* bane to spend her evening than getting a close-up of Stellen Skarsgård's horny doppelganger in a snowy forest.

Dee McKinney is a full-time history professor and part-time writer who would love to see those roles flip. Dr. Enid Seward also appears in a novel she's querying, the first in a series. She lives with her husband, teenage son, and six dogs in rural Georgia. She is proud to be a Guppy, a SinC, and an associate member in the Crime Writers of Canada.

THE BAKER'S BOY:
A YOUNG HAYDN STORY

NUPUR TUSTIN

"When day turns to night, the world will be turned upside down."
The crone's throaty cackle penetrated Haydn's consciousness as he walked through St. Michael's square to his quarters in the Michaelerhaus.

He glanced up from the letter he was reading. The precise hour at which the sun would be overshadowed, plunging all of Vienna into darkness, had yet to arrive. But his own world had already been overturned.

It was bad enough that the bookseller to whom he'd taken a set of his minuets had rejected them. "They will never sell, boy," he had assured Haydn, casting no more than a cursory glance at the music.

It was even worse that all his hopes of cutting a dashing figure before his family were crushed. The position of first violinist he had counted on as all but his, was irretrievably lost; squandered on a man scarcely deserving of the honor, but far better connected than Haydn himself could claim to be.

And now his father's letter informed him that his brother Michael, five years younger than he, had already eclipsed him. The Bishop of Grosswardein had taken Michael into his employ; promising a salary of no less than two hundred gulden a year.

What could a man not do with such a sum? It was beyond Haydn's wildest imaginings. He had until now counted himself fortunate to receive a meal and lessons as the opera composer Nicola Porpora's musical valet.

"Can the good Lord have intended you to be a composer, Sepperl?" his father gently enquired in his letter. "Such ill luck dogs you in your pursuits, my boy, can it not be possible your true calling lies with the Church? Your talents would not go unappreciated there. Why, Pfarrer Reinhard assures me the position of organist at St. Catherine's is yours, if you will but have it."

It was a better proposition than joining a monastery as his mother had once suggested. A secure position, yet the thought of taking it plunged Haydn into despair. It would mean giving up all ambition of becoming a composer such as Hasse or Mattheson or even Gluck.

He suppressed a sigh, and glanced up again. The crone, a bent, haggard old woman, was still sitting on the steps of St. Michael's Church, calling out to passersby.

"Beware the darkness that comes." She brought out a yellowing shred of linen from her basket. "There is no power against it, but through the Grace that comes from keeping a piece of the Lord's Shroud nearby.

"Come one, come all. There is a piece for everyone. Five kreutzers will cast your woes from you."

Would it really? Haydn wondered. He felt in his pocket. A few coins jingled within. Just enough for a hearty bowl of beef soup with potato dumplings that would fill his stomach. Or for a piece of cloth that … Well, who knew what it could do?

It was money he could ill-afford to spend. But he had tried every other avenue, and failed. What harm could there be in trying one more?

A crowd had formed before the wrinkled old woman. Haydn stepped forward, taking his place behind poor Hans, the baker's boy.

"I see dark times in your future," the crone said to the idiot baker's boy when it was his turn. "This piece of sacred cloth will dispel it, never fear."

She turned to Haydn. "The wheel is turning; he who is down must go up," she intoned, pressing a coarse bit of linen into his palm. Would that it were true!

* * * *

The day passed uneventfully enough. Vienna was briefly plunged into darkness. But that was all.

No Prussians thundered in through the gates, ready to take the city captive and unseat Their Imperial Majesties, Maria Theresa and her consort Francis of Lorraine. The fortune tellers crowding St. Michael's square had been predicting the dire event for months, selling relics and crosses to ward off the evil.

But then neither did Prince Eugene's Kapellmeister send word of having reversed his decision against Haydn's appointment. Even so, the small piece of shroud did much toward restoring his good humor and his faith. And that night when he went to bed, he laid it carefully on the wine crate that served him as a nightstand.

He arose, as always, on the ninth peal of the Angelus, eager to read a portion of Mattheson's *Vollkommene Capellmeister* before going down to Porpora's apartment. If there were time, he would sit at his harpsichord, and work out an idea for a divertimento he had. Maybe that would fare better than his minuets.

He had just buttoned his shirt and washed his face when an uproar from the streets caught his attention. He turned toward the small window, surprised. What commotion was so loud as to penetrate the thick walls of his damp, miserable attic in the Michaelerhaus?

Filled with a strange apprehension, he leaned out the small window. What calamity could have befallen the world today? A sea of people thronged the square below. His eye followed their movement, caught sight of a solitary police guard, then paused on the closed door of Master Bettler's shop.

Had some evil befallen Hans, the baker's lad? Haydn clutched the shroud tightly in his fist. He had not thought much of the old crone's words, but now they rang unpleasantly in his ears.

The door to the baker's shop opened just then. Two police guards emerged into the gray dawn, laboring under the weight of the gurney they carried forth.

"Make way!" the first man standing guard outside shouted, swinging his truncheon this way and that to carve a path among the crowd.

Heedless of his own safety, Haydn leaned farther out, straining to see. Whatever lay on the makeshift bed was almost entirely covered in coarse white linen. But from the mounds the sheet formed, it was clear a body lay under it.

A corpse, the thought flashed through his brain as he hastily pulled himself back in.

Dear God! Was Hans dead?

As if in response to his question, the door to the baker's shop opened again. Two more guards stepped out, dragging a struggling figure between them.

"I didn't do it. I swear it, I did not!" The baker's lad thrashed around as he protested his innocence. One of the guards cuffed him a blow that sent his head lolling back.

Haydn, staring down into the other's gray eyes, wide with terror, thought the despair they held would haunt him until he went to his grave. What had Hans done? Risen up against Master Bettler?

Haydn did not believe it. Hans, no more than a year or two older than Haydn's fourteen-year-old youngest brother Johann, was a harmless lad. Too much of a simpleton, Haydn thought, to kill his master.

Besides for all that Master Bettler berated the lad for his stupidity, cuffing his ears for the frequent mistakes the idiot boy unwittingly made, the baker was the only man willing to employ the half-witted boy.

"They will lead the poor lad to the gallows," he muttered to himself as Hans still protested his innocence.

"Master Bettler was like a father to me. I would never hurt him."

His tone and his eyes strongly proclaimed his innocence. But when Haydn saw his blood-besmirched apron, his misgivings returned. Could such a vast quantity of blood be explained away? If so, surely the police guards, more experienced in such matters, would have done it already?

But he could not settle the question so easily in his own mind. It seemed important to do so, however. What protection had the shroud afforded Hans, if it had not prevented him from killing his master? And, if he had not done the deed, why had it not saved him from the gallows?

His own fate, Haydn felt, was bound up with that of the lad's. If the shroud had no power to save Hans, it would be powerless to reverse his own fortunes. His fingers tightened around the bit of cloth. *No, no, surely, that was not possible?*

* * * *

He found Porpora, an hour later, in a foul mood, pacing the floor in his nightgown. "Where have you been, then? There is no bread for my breakfast. The baker seems to have managed to get himself killed before making his deliveries."

"Yes, I know," Haydn replied instantly, only to realize a mere second later that Porpora expected him to have already made provisions for the morning meal. "I can procure a loaf or two, I am sure, from Master Mueller in the Kohlmarkt."

"What good does it do to go now?" Porpora grumbled, his shrunken cheeks looking more pinched than ever. "Our first pupil arrives in a few minutes. I shall have to teach on an empty stomach, I suppose."

The day wore on. Pupils came and went. Haydn, unable to rid himself of the image of Hans's eyes, could barely concentrate. It did not show in his playing, or so he thought until the departure of the last pupil when Porpora hurled his stick at him, and called him a blockhead.

"Do you think I tolerate your presence to admire your beauty?" The insult left Haydn unfazed. He had a pock-marked face, a nose too pronounced, like a rugged promontory, but his musical skills more than made up for all that.

But he was mortified by Porpora's next words. "All day today," the great singer scolded, "you have either lagged behind the singer or raced so far ahead, we have had to rush through the lyrics to catch up with you. What were you thinking?"

Haydn hung his head. "I was not, I fear. The untoward event of the morning seems to have stricken my mind." He sought out Porpora's eyes. "I cannot but think they lead an innocent lad to the gallows. What justice is there in this world if a thing like that can happen?" Try as he might, he was unable to keep the despair out of his voice.

But instead of scoffing at him, Porpora's features softened. "The only justice there is, is the one that we fight for, Sepperl. Sitting by and hanging your head in despair will get you nowhere."

Haydn frowned, puzzling over his master's remarks. What could he, a young man barely able to keep himself alive, do to help Hans? He hadn't even been able to prevail upon Prince Eugene's Kapellmeister to hire him.

Before he could say anything more, Porpora flung a few coins down on the clavier. "Be off with you, then! Get me a loaf or two of bread and half a pound of meat. I am starving."

* * * *

By the time he crossed the square, arriving near the door of Master Bettler's bakery, Haydn had gleaned a little more of what had happened. The baker had been stabbed in the early hours of the morning while he had been busy baking his bread.

Hans had found him barely alive, or so he said, when he arrived that morning at the first peal of the Angelus. Master Bettler, lying in a pool of his own blood near a pan of freshly baked bread, had died in his assistant's arms.

There was nothing to say this was not the case. But it was equally probable that Hans had killed the baker, and been discovered before he could make his own escape.

A police guard was still posted by the bakery door. Frau Bettler stood before him in her Sunday finery, trying in vain to convince him to let her in.

"Are the bags of flour and the loaves within to rot, then? We have lost good money this morning from all the deliveries my husband failed to make. What purpose can it serve to close the bakery?"

"I cannot tell, Frau Bettler. But those are my orders. No one can go in."

Haydn walked slowly past. Why Frau Bettler thought she would be able to sell any of her husband's loaves of bread, he didn't know. Word of his gruesome death, barely a few feet from his own oven, seemed to have already spread around the city.

Even if the loaves were not spattered with the dead man's blood, who would want them? God alone knew what evil humors rose from a corpse.

The thought made Haydn's empty stomach churn. On the other hand, why stand guard over the bakery? Were there really people who wouldn't hesitate to go in and steal a loaf or two? The Bürgermeister thought so, no doubt.

He purchased his loaves of bread from Master Mueller in the Kohlmarkt, then entered the butcher's shop next door. The butcher was nowhere to be seen, so Haydn prepared to wait. Ten minutes went past. Porpora must be impatiently awaiting his return.

Haydn rapped loudly on the countertop. "Master Goss? Are you within?"

"Coming," a voice called from within, followed almost immediately by a burly man in a bloody apron.

"You have not been waiting long, I hope, Master Sepperl," he said, wiping his hands on a bloodied towel. "Frau Lichtenberger's maid sent for two freshly slaughtered pigs at midday. I have just finished preparing the meat. It is bloody work, I can tell you that."

"So, I see," Haydn responded, compelled, he knew not why, to scrutinize the butcher's person. Blood was sprayed all over his hair and face. Splotches of it ran down his apron, too. The butcher seemed to notice his gaze, for he glanced ruefully down.

"There is no preventing that. The blood gushes forth like a fountain as soon as the blade plunges in."

"Gushes forth?" Haydn repeated, staring at the upside-down, teardrop-shaped stains sprayed on the butcher's apron. An image of Hans's apron formed in his mind, far different in appearance from the butcher's. There had been a single large patch of blood smeared on the front of it, around the waist, and going up toward the boy's chest.

Had Hans been telling the truth, after all?

He glanced up at the butcher. "Are your aprons so sprayed every time you slaughter an animal, Master Goss?"

The butcher nodded. "Every time, I fear, Master Sepperl. I usually wear a black apron, so it matters not. But no amount of scrubbing will take the stains out of this white one. I shall have to discard it."

* * * *

With his purchases under one arm, the butcher's blood-soiled apron under the other, Haydn hurried back to Porpora's apartment. He had eaten nothing since midday yesterday, but his hunger was all but forgotten in the excitement of the discovery he'd made.

Here was a way to save Hans from the gallows. He should never have doubted the good Lord. The butcher's apron, soiled from the blood spurting out of a dying animal, looked nothing like the bloodied apron Hans had been wearing.

Did that not confirm Hans was no murderer? He had the butcher's apron to prove it. And if that did not help, Master Goss was quite willing to slaughter another pig before the police guards and the Bürgermeister.

The demonstration would show the pattern of stains likely to form on whoever had wielded the knife against Master Bettler. The murderer had undoubtedly been covered in a spray of blood just like the butcher.

Porpora was reading when Haydn returned. He looked up briefly, but if he noticed the bloodied apron under his valet's arm, he showed no sign of it.

Haydn quickly prepared the midday meal: slicing one of the loaves of bread, setting out the butter, chopping the meat up, and frying it with some onions and salt. A rude meal, but Porpora, long accustomed to his rudimentary culinary efforts, tolerated it well enough.

After the meal, Porpora prepared to leave for his afternoon walk.

"You may have the rest of the day off," he said to Haydn, wrapping himself in a thick, woolen cloak despite the warmth of the day. "You will want it, I suppose, to help your friend. Although what purpose Herr Goss's apron can serve, I know not, unless you mean to tell the police guards it was the butcher who killed the baker."

* * * *

Haydn was quite sure the butcher had done no such thing. But who had? Frau Bettler, the baker's wife?

She had seemed more distressed by the loss of money and flour her husband's death had occasioned than by his untimely demise. Not surprising, Haydn supposed, given that the baker, not an unattractive man, by any means, was said to have a wandering eye.

Then there was the matter of Frau Bettler's dress. A stylish gown of dove-grey silk he had seen her wear to church on Sunday. Why wear it in the middle of the week?

The more he thought about it, the more likely it seemed that Frau Bettler had committed the evil deed. The blue linen dress she usually wore was, no doubt, so spattered with her husband's blood, she had been forced to rid herself of it.

But the police guard, still standing in front of the baker's shop, thought little of the apron—"Are we to knock on every door in the city, asking to examine people's garments?"—and still less of Haydn's theory.

"Nonsense! Someone would have seen Frau Bettler running through the streets all covered in blood. Why, there are police guards who patrol the streets all night. Very little escapes their notice."

"She could've slipped out of her dress," Haydn persisted.

"What! And roamed the streets in her shift? Someone would have seen that for sure."

Haydn sighed. A woman in a state of undress would be even more noticeable than one covered in blood.

He was about to give up when he noticed Porpora at the other end of the square, still wrapped in his cloak, deep in conversation with a beautiful, young woman, similarly wrapped. He had little time to wonder why. The garment itself attracted his attention.

He turned back to the guard. "Do you see that woman?"

"I do indeed," was the reply. "But I would set my sights far lower, my friend. She is much too pretty for the likes of you."

"It was her cloak I was interested in." Haydn explained. "The garment covers a woman so completely, she could be as naked as the day she was born under it, and no one would know it. And it was cold last night."

"I suppose it is possible," the guard admitted sourly. "But that tells us nothing about which woman committed the deed. Mere suppositions will not persuade the Inspector to let the baker's lad go."

Haydn scratched his chin. He was quite sure it was Frau Bettler who had killed her husband. But if an apron covered in pig's blood and a theory about a cloak did little to prove Hans' innocence, it did still less to prove Frau Bettler's guilt.

"Now, if you could find her dress covered in blood," the police guard's gruff voice broke in upon Haydn's ponderings. The words brought an inspired thought.

"I think I can!" he announced. "But I will need your help."

* * * *

Late that night, Haydn stood concealed behind the entrance of the Michaelerhaus, his eyes trained on the bakery shop across the dark square. The door stood invitingly ajar. The police guard who had stood sentry all day was gone. But a bell in Haydn's pocket would summon the man should the need arise.

He had waited thus, shivering in the cold, for nearly an hour. The piece of shroud he had purchased was folded in his palm. He knew not how long he would have to wait, but he did not think his plan would come to naught after all.

He was beginning to doze off when a soft creaking sound aroused him. He stared across the street. The shop door, open just a little while back, was now closed. Was someone within? He thought he discerned a dim light through the crack at the bottom.

He sprinted across the square, his fingers closed over the bell to muffle its jangling. The bakery windows were too high for him to see through. He tried the door, pushing it open, and peered in. Finding no one within, he stepped inside.

A candle stood on the empty countertop, casting a dim glow on the dark stone floor. In the wall directly behind it was a curtained doorway.

It was where the ovens were, no doubt. He lifted the end of the countertop, went behind it, and thrust the curtain aside. The ovens were stoked, a welcoming warmth arising from them.

A tall, slim woman, wrapped in a cloak, stood with her back to him. As Haydn watched, she reached up to a shelf set into the wall, removed the flour barrel, and withdrew the tightly rolled up bundle concealed behind it.

From within her cloak, she brought out a large pair of scissors, and proceeded to unfurl the bundle—a lavender-blue dress, its waist and white yoke heavily spattered with teardrop-shaped blood stains. Just as her fingers, curled into the scissor loops, pried the blades apart, Haydn stepped forward.

"Stop!" he called, ringing his bell at the same time. The woman froze, her hands went to her ears to shut out the shrill clanging of his bell, then she slowly spun around.

But it was not Frau Bettler.

For a single startled moment, they stared at each other, Haydn recognizing the young woman who had been walking with Porpora that afternoon. Before either one of them could break the silence, the guards drawn by the sound of his bell had swarmed into the shop.

Haydn found his voice at last. "What reason could you have for killing Master Bettler?" he asked as the guards restrained the woman.

Her chin jutted stubbornly out, but she remained silent.

* * * *

"I suppose I have you to thank for losing a good singer," Porpora greeted Haydn the next morning, but he didn't seem particularly annoyed at the turn of events.

"Was she one of your pupils?" Haydn asked. He had never seen her before yesterday.

"Of course not. Maria had no need of lessons. She had the voice of an angel. I heard her singing in the square on one of my walks, and offered to procure her a position at the Kärntnertortheater. What made her kill the baker?"

"She was in love with Master Bettler. Had been his mistress for some time," Haydn replied, recounting the details he had managed to glean from the guard he had befriended. "But he apparently wanted nothing more to do with her."

"Why not?" Porpora demanded. "She was better looking than that horse-featured wife of his."

Haydn fingered his shroud, and smiled. "Do you recall the old hag who sat on the steps of the Michaelerkirche selling pieces of the Lord's Shroud?"

Porpora looked puzzled. "What has she to do with anything?"

"It seems Master Bettler bought a piece of the shroud from her, and was told that a 'woman would be the death of him.' He took that to mean his wife would murder him for his philandering, so he made haste to break it off with his mistress."

Haydn's smile widened at the irony of it all. "Thus bringing about the very fate the old crone had warned against."

But the shroud had helped Hans just as she had promised it would. And who knew, perhaps his own fortunes would turn, too. He may have been overlooked as first violinist; but perhaps he would someday be Kapellmeister.

"Stop daydreaming, Sepperl!" Porpora's voice broke gruffly into Haydn's thoughts. "We have a long day ahead of us."

A former journalist, Nupur Tustin relies upon a Ph.D. in Communication and an M.A. in English to orchestrate fictional mayhem; and a Weber Upright to compose music. Her short stories have appeared in *Mystery Weekly* and *Heater Magazine*. A 200-word story, "Voices," was a finalist in the prestigious Golden Donut contest organized by the Writers' Police Academy in 2015. "The Baker's Boy," Tustin's first Joseph Haydn short story, introduces her Haydn Mystery series. Readers intrigued by the young Haydn's detecting skills are directed to *A Minor Deception*, the first chronicle of his adventures as a mature man. Haydn Series: ntustin. com

BLACK MONDAY

CHÉRI VAUSÉ

The images brushed behind my eyes like ghosts. She was always there, a *femme fantôme* conjured up by my paranoia, by my belief that she was coming back to end me. This last week I spent in the hospital only proved to me that Lulu wasn't finished, that I wasn't paranoid enough, even though the doctor and the cops told me otherwise. Yet, in Lulu's brutal simplicity, I understood her thinking, I got what she wanted to do. She wanted to die, but didn't want to go alone. In her homeless mind, the eclipse was the perfect setting for the killing. The darkness, the distraction, the out-sized miracle of it. She always held a silent contempt for life, for the beauty of the world, the universe. I tried to tell the cops, but they didn't believe me. Maybe I am crazy, but I believe her.

August 21 arrived with a hammer. It banged on my head until I opened my eyes. I hoped I could just sleep through it, but the sun was persistent. When I tried to move, my insides cork-screwed. I scrabbled through a few pill bottles on my night stand, until I found one that rattled. Rolling over to the edge of the bed on my uninjured side, I stared at the label. Through the blur, I could make out a V and an I. My friend, Vicodin. Two little pills were kissing at the bottom of the orange plastic container. Squinting a few times, my dry eyes toured the stand for anything that might be wet. Kentucky's finest extended an invitation to the ball. I accepted. We danced. The pills slid down easy, the whiskey killing the buzzer going off in my head.

All that was left was the sound of traffic outside my bedroom window, which was odd. I live on a dead end road. My only neighbors are some sagebrush, Chorro cactus, and a few gnarled mesquite trees, including the ghosts of the Mescaleros and Comanches, but that's it. I managed to make it to a sitting position and peeked through the curtains. A dozen or more pickups, a couple of campers, and various four-wheel drive SUVs, were all log-jammed at the end of my dirt road. It looked like the entire population of Terlingua, Texas decided to view the eclipse from my little knoll in the Comanche Mountains. I glanced at my clock. 8:05. The solar eclipse wasn't scheduled to debut until 11:31.

The pills were meandering around in my empty stomach, still undecided about taking effect, but I was sick of being in bed. The climb out began to twist my insides like a wet dishrag. Every slash of Lulu's knife shouted at me, reminding me of how stupid I was to let that crazy bitch into my life. When I was just about at my limit, I finally landed on my feet. So far, so good.

By the time I made it to my shower, I wasn't sure bathing was such a good idea. My left arm was in a cast, and the doctor said not to get the bandages wet, so … After about fifteen minutes of the struggle with my shower head, and drowning my bathroom in several inches of hot water, I lowered my stitched body to the edge of the tub. My heart was clawing at my chest to get out, and my legs were numb. Another panic attack. I grabbed a towel and smothered my face. It took a few moments, but my heart began to slow.

The honking of the eclipse entourage finally stopped. My new neighbors must have found their perfect spot. I could hear the snap of beer cans and bottle tops flipping off. If Texans knew anything, they knew how to party, and an eclipse of the sun was reason enough to throw a big one. The air was filling with the smell of charring meat over mesquite and charcoal. I had visions of a slab next to a giant slice of a Texas sweet and a whole jalapeño. My eyes watered just thinking about it. Not to be outdone, my stomach decided to weigh in with a symphony of squeaks and gurgles, reminding me my last meal ended up in a pink liver shaped plastic container.

Lulu decided to show up at that moment, her knife poised in her fist. My heart pounded against my chest, and I couldn't catch my breath. It was insane that you could know something was an illusion, and still react to it. Crazy.

The panic finally passed, but I knew that I needed help, and I was man enough to admit it. I stepped into a pair of shorts, snagged my cell, then fished through the numbers until I found Molly's.

"Robert?" the voice answered. "I was just about to drive to Alpine to visit—"

"I'm at home."

"You're out, but—"

"I got the Good Housekeeping Seal of Approval last night."

"How did you get home from the hospital?"

"Jayce."

"I thought he was out of town for two months."

Hesitating, I weighed my options and decided to tell the truth. "I hitched."

"Why did you lie?"

"I … I didn't want you to worry."

"Is there anything I can do to help?"

I knew in that moment that I had finally made a good decision in my life. She was the right one to call.

"I'm okay …" I could feel my resolve melting like the fat on the barbecuing meat outside my house, and I started to blubber like a girl. "I'm sorry," I managed to choke out.

"I'll be right over," she said.

That dull quiet on the line felt full of promise. She was coming, the one woman who never tried to get something from me. But Lulu wasn't finished. This attack came tearing at me, causing my heart to flail like a dying fish in my chest. The room began to disappear into tiny flashing dots, and winked out.

* * * *

"Robert, wake up."

It was a voice I recognized, but I couldn't quite climb out of that deep pit I was in. Then, I heard her soft voice wafting toward me, and the cool feel of a hand on my cheek. I opened my eyes.

"There you are." Molly was kneeling beside me, her bright, blue eyes gazing at me with concern. "Wouldn't you rather be in bed than on the floor?" She smiled.

I stared at her, understanding the joke, but my mind didn't seem to be connected to my mouth. "Uh huh," I think I finally grunted.

"I can't lift you, so you'll have to help."

After a few failed attempts, I finally made it to my feet. She helped me to the side of my bed, the sweat pouring off my forehead and upper lip. She pulled the covers back and I hoisted my legs onto the bed with difficulty. Then, she covered them over, and began stuffing pillows behind my back, her hair brushing my arm and shoulder.

"There ya go. Comfy?"

I nodded my dumb head. All I could think of was running my fingers through that thick, silky mane of brown hair just once, and we'd make love the rest of the day. Then, I'd be happy to die. I moved my hand up to touch it, but she stepped out of reach. She had been the only good thing in my life, and I had managed to—

"Do you have a prescription that should be filled?"

I nodded again.

She read the labels on the prescription bottles on the stand. "All these are for Lulu." She frowned. "I think this is it, but the date … It's the only one with your name on it." She looked confused, as she held it out to me to read. It was the Vicodin. "Did you take any today?"

I shook my head no.

"Well, I'll call it in. First, I think you should eat. Whiskey is not a meal." She was eyeing the bottle standing proud amid the orange pill containers.

"I know," I croaked.

"You're back." She smiled that wonderful disarming grin of hers. "Hungry?"

I nodded.

She twirled from the room, leaving the faint scent of her perfume behind. I had nothing to do except listen to her in the kitchen, guessing what she was up to. She was on the phone reading the prescription number on the label, her voice hesitant. The microwave whirred, and the toaster clicked. My name was mentioned, then hers, and I could hear her chant her cell number. The refrigerator door opened. I knew she wouldn't find much in there. I hadn't been shopping since before Lulu tried to kill me.

My heart flipped and my legs numbed. Not again.

"You look awfully pale," Molly said. I could see her between the flashing dots, standing in the doorway. "Don't you pass out on me again, mister."

I think I nodded my head.

"Good. This is all I could find."

My sight returned, and I could see the tray in her hands: a glass of water, a cup of hot chocolate, and a plate with two slices of buttered toast with melting peanut butter on the top.

"You haven't a thing in the house to cook. Even the mold on the cheese has mold." She chuckled, stretching out a hand to touch my cheek. "I know it's not much, but at least I know you'll eat this."

Hot chocolate and peanut butter were my favorite snack foods.

She proceeded to eye each label of the pill bottles, then separated one from the rest. All the others she slid into the trash can.

"This is Percocet." She held the bottle up and set it next to the glass of water. "It's Lulu's prescription, but if you're in terrible pain while I'm gone, take one. Only one. But, I advise you to wait until the doctor calls to hear what he recommends. Okay?" She stepped over to my dresser, scooped up her purse, and turned back to look at me. "You really do need someone to look after you, don't ya?"

I started to open my mouth, but nothing came out.

"Your doctor is in surgery. As soon as he's out, he'll call."

She examined me for a moment, a compassionate look washing over her face. Slowly, she turned and left the room. I could hear the front screen door slam, and a couple of kids laughing and screeching. Molly laughed, too. I love her laugh. I glanced at the clock. It was after nine thirty. Lulu had less than two hours to show up in the flesh.

Molly didn't live far from my house, but I was afraid I would be in a coma by the time she returned, because the Vicodin was gaining ground. I crammed the toast in my mouth and washed it down with the hot cocoa. Nestling between the sheets, I surrendered to the effects. It was quiet and dark in that space.

* * * *

I wasn't sure how long I wallowed there before I felt something touch me. I startled awake. Terrified I'd see Lulu standing over me, plunging her knife into my chest over and over, I panicked, my insides jerking to attention.

"Hey, it's me. Relax." Molly was standing by my bed holding a tray. "I let you sleep for a while. You looked so peaceful."

I pushed myself up with my good arm, and she set the tray on my lap.

"Eat the soup while it's hot," she said. There was that smile again. Why couldn't I have seen how great she was before I messed up with Lulu?

"Thanks," I managed to say. "It looks great."

There was a moment of discomfort between us, and she flushed red. I'm sure it was because of her husband Chad, her attraction to me making her feel guilty. I hated that I was still hurting her, even when I didn't mean to.

11:15 flashed. We were creeping ever closer to the witching moment. I ate my soup and sandwich, while Molly busied herself in the kitchen cooking. I set the tray aside, and tried not to use my stomach muscles getting up. I was getting better at it, and managed to stand without feeling like I was going to pass out. Once I was on my feet, I marched into the kitchen. If I needed anything to heal, it was Molly's forgiveness for cheating on her.

"Molly." I swallowed. "I love you. Can you ever forgive me for hurting you? For Lulu? For—" I couldn't say anything else. My throat slammed shut.

"Robert. I forgave you a long time ago." There was a certain tone to her voice, and the word *but* dangled somewhere at the end of her words. She hesitated. I could tell she didn't want to hurt me, either. "We'll always be friends, but," there it was, "you can't talk about loving me anymore."

It hadn't occurred to me that she might really love Chad. I stepped closer to her, and she didn't move. Placing my good hand on her shoulder, I moved closer. She allowed me to put my arm around her. I kissed the top of her head, and she let it slip back so her face was tilted up to mine. I slid my arm over to her other shoulder and pulled her closer, lowering my lips to hers. We kissed. At first, it was just friendly, but then our bodies were touching, our mouths opened, and our tongues met. I could feel her body melt into me, the kiss a full-blown tongue exploratory. All I wanted was to carry her to my bed, to make love to her, but she pushed me away.

"I'm married, Bobby. Those days are over."

I wasn't going to let her get away with that, "those days are over," nonsense. She touched her tongue to mine. I knew what that meant. That was an invitation for me to take her.

"I want you back."

"I couldn't hurt Chad. Besides, he's in Afghanistan, unable to defend himself. He doesn't deserve that."

"I don't care about Chad."

"Well, I do."

"You kissed me back. There was no mistaking that."

Her resolve was melting as quickly as mine had when we were on the phone. I could see it in her eyes.

"God help me, because I do love you," she said. "But Bobby, it can't be—"

"Then what was that kiss all about?" I said, cutting her off.

She stared at me, her face angry, but more at herself than me. "The habit of years of kissing you, the fact I'm lonesome for my husband … And … Oh, I don't know." She threw her hands into the air. "It was a mistake, all right. A mistake."

Her retort begged the question, "Was I a mistake?"

She waited for a long time to answer, but she said in a low voice, "Yes." Her eyes dropped to the floor, her cheeks flushing red.

There it was. She couldn't have done a better job than Lulu had. Turning her back to me, she began to chop green onions on my cutting board. I moved behind her, pinned her to the counter with my body, and slipped my good arm around her again.

"We were not a mistake."

"Stop, Bobby."

"Let me love you," I said. "I want to love you, so much."

"No, Bobby. It's not right."

"I need to get back on track. You always anchored me."

I tried to wrap my fractured arm around her, but the cast … I pulled on her shoulder so she was facing me again, but the damned cast hooked on a drawer knob. Frustrated, I fumbled around until it broke free. I could feel my skin tear. Somehow, my arms found their way around her, but she pushed me away, gently but firmly.

"No, Bobby." I reached for her, but she held her hands out in front of her, pushing me back. "I said, no. Chad's your best friend. You don't want to hurt him in this way. And I certainly don't. I love him." A shocked look moved over her face. "Oh, my god, Bobby."

I looked down. Blood was trickling down my chest everywhere. "I just tore some of my stitches, that's all."

"Let me fix that." She pushed at me, and we padded into the bathroom. "Sit," she demanded.

I dutifully followed her instructions, and she removed each bandage, examining my stitches. She opened the medicine cabinet and pulled out some gauze to clean my wounds. Dabbing away, she'd pause, and make her assessment, until she determined the extent of my injuries.

"Put your hand over this." She had me hold the gauze in place. "You have any super glue?"

"It's in the …" My voice trailed off, as I pointed in the direction of the kitchen.

She left me seated on the toilet, while she disappeared in search of the glue. Drawers were opened then shut. I could tell she was still angry with herself. I didn't care. I was determined to get her into bed with me.

"Found it."

She rushed in through the doorway, and set to work. Her fingers felt cool, intelligent, and delicate against my skin. She sealed every opened gash with a line of glue, holding it between her fingers until each dried.

"There," she said, taking a step back to examine her work. "That looks like the last one. That should hold until you see your doctor. Which is?"

I just sat on the toilet staring at her, feeling lost, and torn, like my stitches. "I can't help but want you back," I said, hoping my words wouldn't fall inert against her heart.

"Where did you think all of this would be going?" She had that look of disappointed melancholy etched on her face. "Did you think if you played on my sympathies that we would get back together?"

"Maybe … Yes." I raised my chin up. "Yes, I did. We were good together."

"Good together?" Tears trailed down her face. "You and I remember a very different relationship. You always did what you wanted, never considering my feelings."

"There were good times. You have to admit that."

"No, Bobby. Chad was there when you were whoring around with Lulu, with the others. He was there when you humiliated me, time after time. He was there. Won't you even consider him? He's your best friend."

I grabbed her arm as she started to leave. "Chad can take care of himself, but I need you." I forced her to face me. "I'm sorry. I'll never make that mistake again. Lulu is out of my life, now. Can't we start over?"

"If it had been once, or even twice, I might believe you, forgive you. But you were with her for six months. Six months, and in our bed. And what about the other women? You think I've forgotten about all of them? The nights you were out drinking?" Her lower lip trembled, and she pulled away. "I'll put your dinner in the oven, and then I'm going home."

"Can't you stay for the eclipse? I'm afraid to be alone during the eclipse. Lulu—" My throat slammed shut.

She sighed, then said, "All right, for the eclipse. But after, I'm going home where I belong."

The sting of those last words hurt worse than my knife wounds. She didn't belong to me anymore. I stood, and plodded into my bedroom, and slid on my sandals, while she returned to the kitchen.

"Would you like some lemonade?" she said in a raised voice.

"That would be nice."

"I'll bring a glass out to you. It's already started."

I checked my watch. She was right. It was 11:45. I grabbed my sunglasses, and wandered through the sliding doors to my side patio. A couple recognized me and waved, but had a puzzled look on their face.

"Accident," I said.

A few more couples wandered past and said, "What happened to you?"

Once again, I replied, "Accident." They looked at me curiously, but smiled and raised their bottles of beer in a salute. I slipped on my sunglasses, and lowered my stitched and super-glued body to the lounger.

When I laid my head back, I could feel something was wrong, something was terribly wrong. Turning my head, I saw Lulu sneaking in through the back gate. She marched over to me, leering. I felt a shock of terror rush through me, but she turned and wandered into the house. My heart slammed into my chest, and I tried to leap up from the lounger, but I managed to fall on the ground and skin my elbow and knee. I picked myself up, feeling my skin tear, but I didn't care. Limping into the kitchen, I saw Molly placing my dinner in the oven with mitts on her hands. She started to say something when I put my finger on my lips.

"Lulu's in the house," I mouthed. "Get out." Molly started to protest, but I insisted, "Now."

She tiptoed her way into the living room, and out the front door. Through the window, I watched her rush toward a group of guys I knew. They played pool every Friday night at the Aces 'n' Eights bar on the edge of town—where I met Lulu. She was standing surrounded by them, looking pale and terrified, while she spoke on the phone to someone. Probably the sheriff. I glanced over at the cutting board where Molly had cut up a bunch of vegetables for a salad. The knife was too small. I grabbed the butcher knife from the wooden block.

I'm not sure what happened next, but I felt dizzy and nauseous, as everything grew dark around me. A sharp pain stabbed through my side. I spun around to see Lulu with a sardonic smile stretched across her face, her hand covered in my blood. I jabbed at her, but my aim must have been off. Her knife kept flashing before me, plunging in and out. The room was growing black, as the moon moved in front of the sun. The eclipse. When I took a step, my foot slipped out from under me and I hit the tile, my foot coated in my blood pooling on the floor. Lulu walked away. Outside, the crowd was *ooing* and *ahing*, and all I could think about was missing the eclipse with Molly. The darkness coated my world like dust, and I felt cold, so cold. And it was a blistering August day ...

* * * *

The sheriff's deputies swarmed over the small house. Cameras flashed in the kitchen of Robert Jeffery Madison. Molly stood in the living room, weeping, and the young men from the Aces 'n' Eights pool team were gathered around her looking helpless.

"Mrs. Molly French?" the sheriff asked, as he moved toward her.

She wiped her face with her hands, and cleared her throat. "Yes," she said in a small cracked voice.

"Were you aware Mr. Madison escaped from the hospital this morning?"

"Why did you use the word, escape?"

"Because he was under guard." She started to interrupt him, but he said, "The deputy left his post for a moment. That's when Mr. Madison sneaked out."

"I don't understand."

"Maybe the doctor can explain this better."

Molly looked defiant. "You explain it to me, now."

"We found Ms. Lulu Garcia's body yesterday," the sheriff said. "The coroner said she'd been dead a little over a week."

Molly's mouth dropped open, and she stared at the sheriff in disbelief. Swallowing, she managed to say, "Then, who attacked Robert?"

"Only his fingerprints were found on the knife."

"What are you saying?"

"The psychiatrist said that he stabbed himself. The angle of the wounds all show that."

Molly stumbled back a few steps, while she watched two men carry the zipped body bag out through the screen door toward an ambulance. A crowd had gathered, and necks were craned to get a clearer view. A skirling wind began to blow across the Comanche Mountains, and clouds rushed in, sharpening the moment into a fine edge. A small ding sounded in the kitchen, as the timer she set for Robert's dinner went off. Molly had the oddest feeling that she escaped something, but didn't know what it was.

After teaching theology for more than twenty-five years, Chéri Vausé decided to change careers and write novels, specifically, the noir mystery. Her background is never far from her, as she enjoys adding a touch of mysticism in every story. With all her children grown, she now lives on a small ranch in Central Texas with her husband and two dogs and four ducks.

I'LL BE A SUNBEAM

M.K. WALLER

Sun of my soul, Thou Savior dear,
It is not night if Thou be near;
Oh, may no earthborn cloud arise
To hide Thee from Thy servant's eyes.

Our voices, my quicksilver soprano and Joe McDowell's rich tenor, rose, commingling, filling the empty sanctuary. This was the most pleasant hour of my week—when I left my job at the library to meet Joe for noontime duet practice at the Kilburn Community Church. With me at the piano and Joe standing beside me turning pages, we made the rafters ring.

For most of the year, both of us went back to work after practice. But in summer, Joe, a history teacher at the high school, rarely had any pressing business, and he got into the habit of walking me back to work. Then he started coming into my office to sit and visit. On those days, I told staff we were discussing collection development and left them to supervise patrons. I also closed the blinds between my office and the reading room. Joe was on the library board, so no one questioned my story, but if they'd seen him lounging in his chair with his hands behind his head, they might have gotten the wrong idea. In a small town, a single woman in a position of trust must avoid even the appearance of evil.

That Monday, after I'd secured the office against prying eyes, Joe started talking about old times.

"Do you remember how we used to spend summer afternoons on the river out at Paradise Bluff? Going down those old wooden stairs, lying on the gravel bar, splashing around in the water?"

I picked up a book from a stack on my desk and stuck a label on its spine. "I remember. I'd lie in the sun all afternoon, and when I got home, Mama would say, 'Marva Lu, just look what you've done to yourself. You are burned to a crisp. You're going to *ruin* your alabaster skin.' She always worried that sunbathing would ruin my alabaster skin."

"Well, honey, you sure didn't ruin it. It's still as white as the keys on a new Steinway."

"How sweet of you to say so." I wasn't sure I liked being compared to a piano, but a compliment is a compliment, and I hadn't gotten many of those lately.

"And the picnics. Your mama's fried chicken and my mama's potato salad."

It was really our cook Lola's fried chicken. Mama just claimed it.

"The good old days." He turned his eyes up to the ceiling and sighed.

"Oh, I remember it all. Fried chicken, sunbathing, you grabbing me and holding me under the water till I almost drowned before you let me go." I put clear tape over the spine label and picked up another book. "What I don't remember is anybody actually swimming."

"We had too much fun doing other things. I wasn't a strong swimmer anyway. But I loved playing in the water. And just being with y'all."

I personally believed what he loved most was Bonita and her bikini. My sister Bonita was the youngest in the crowd, but she developed early. Mama absolutely forbade her to wear anything but her blue gingham one-piece, and as long as Mama was taking us out to Paradise Bluff, that's what she wore. But when I turned fifteen and got my driver's license, I started driving us out there. And every day, as soon as we got to the Mobil station on Main Street, Bonita would set up a howl, and nothing would do but we had to stop so she could slip into the restroom and change. Joe goofed around with me, but when Bonita was wearing that bikini—there wasn't enough cotton in it to stop up an aspirin bottle—he only had eyes for her.

Joe leaned forward and rested his elbows on his knees. He had a faraway look in his eye. "I haven't been out there in years. It's kind of sad, you grow up and get responsibilities, seems like you to forget the simple pleasures of youth."

"Um-hmm, sad." Watching him leave with that silly smile on his face, I knew he was thinking about Bonita's little red bikini.

It was high time I did something about that.

* * * *

After Joe left, I got busy decorating the bulletin board with a special display in honor of the upcoming solar eclipse. North Texas wasn't in the direct path, but research informed me that even though we wouldn't see totality, it would get dark enough to be worth watching. At my urging, the city council had declared Monday the 21st an official holiday.

I assembled materials—dust jackets from *The Sun Also Rises*, *Raisin in the Sun*, *House of the Rising Sun*, *The Sun King*—and copies of some old sheet music I found in Mama's piano bench—"Sun of My Soul," which Joe and I were going to sing on Sunday, "Wait Till the Sun Shines, Nellie," "You Are My Sunshine," even "Jesus Wants Me for a Sunbeam," which I intended to teach my kindergarten Sunday school class. It would be a most attractive display.

The best thing about doing bulletin boards is it requires no thought. While your hands stick pins into corkboard, your mind is free to wander.

While I arranged dust jackets, my mind wandered to Joe. I'd never been interested in him romantically, but I'd always liked him. He was good looking in a boyish way—sandy hair neatly trimmed, green eyes, and you could tell from his trim physique that he wasn't just sitting around letting himself go to pot.

Joe couldn't tell, because as a traditional librarian, I kept myself properly under wraps, but I hadn't let myself deteriorate either. I'd been taking belly dance lessons for years, and I looked pretty darned good in a bikini. The bottom drawer of my bureau was full of them.

Last spring they were in my suitcase, packed for a trip to Aruba, from which I intended never to return. But then my plan went awry—and that was *such* a shame, because Mama had been acting as nutty as a pecan bottom at thrashing time, driving that Corvette like a bat out of Bandera, people running for cover whenever they saw her coming down the street, and we were just waiting for the day when she mowed down an innocent pedestrian, and *somebody* had to take matters in hand, and Lord knows I *tried*—well, anyway, I didn't get to Aruba, certainly not on the pittance they paid me at the library.

Taking those bikinis out of the suitcase was a terrible letdown. I was depressed for weeks afterward. But I didn't give up. I was stuck here in Kilburn for a while longer, but I kept up my belly dance lessons as if nothing had happened. I was going to devise another plan for getting what I wanted. At present, however, I was considering how to make the best use of my time here.

I was tacking up a copy of Agatha Christie's *Evil Under the Sun* when it came to me that Joe would make an excellent project.

* * * *

To have a private conversation, the best place in town was the Dairy Queen across the corner from the library. Teenagers had deserted it in favor of the new Sonic out on the highway, and the only people at the DQ at noon were senior citizens, who had to shout at each other across the table. If you didn't mind the shouting, you could discuss anything you wanted and no one would hear.

In fact, the Dairy Queen was where my siblings and I met last spring when I told them about what I had in store for Mama.

Today's topic wasn't nearly so serious, but it was sensitive, so the next day I asked Beryl Dixon to meet me at the DQ. First thing, of course, we had to observe the amenities, such as her asking, "How's your crazy mama getting along, has she taken her shotgun to any more of the neighbors?" and, "Has Squeaky Vardaman forgiven your mama for running over his old daddy with her Corvette?" I had no desire to be reminded of that fiasco, but if I wanted her help, I had to do my part. After she squeezed enough information out of me to satisfy her curiosity, I edged gracefully into the subject I wanted to talk about.

I asked, casually, "Are you excited about the eclipse?"

"What eclipse?" she said.

Honestly, the woman never looked at a newspaper. "The solar eclipse that's happening next Monday. *You* know—when the moon comes between Earth and the sun?" I waited for a response. None came. "When it's going to get dark in the middle of the day."

"Oh, *that*. The kids told me about it. They're going to watch it from Jaycee Ord's back yard."

"That'll be fun for them." I paused for effect. "I'm going to watch from Paradise Bluff."

She broke out into a big smile. "I haven't been out there since high school."

"You and I could go together. It won't get completely dark, because we're not in the path, but it'll be dark enough. We can go early and have a picnic while we wait."

She pulled a pad and a pen from her purse and started a list. When she got to toothpicks, I broke in. "Let's invite somebody to go with us."

"How about Bonita? She's a lot of fun. On our class trip to the art museum, she was a *hoot*."

"Hoot" wasn't what Mama called it. The principal phoned from Fort Worth and said that Bonita and a couple of the boys had gotten loose and managed to get hold of some liquor and made such a ruckus that the Fort Worth police hauled them off to jail. The police chief reamed them out and let them go, but when the school bus pulled up in front of the school the next day, Mama was there waiting. I don't know exactly what happened, but the next year, after the senior trip, the sponsors voted Bonita the title of "Best Behaved Girl." We'd expected Beryl to get the award, because she was a lady at all times, but I guess Bonita's conduct was so unexpected, the teachers were shocked into celebrating it. Beryl was named "Most Thoughtful."

Twenty years later, Beryl was still a saint. Now she was worrying that if we asked too many people, we might run out of food, but if we asked only a few, there'd be hurt feelings.

"Let's keep it small," I said. "How about Joe McDowell?"

She wrinkled her nose. "I don't know him all that well. He was a lot older than me."

I jumped in before she observed Joe and I were the same age. "He and my brother Frank were buddies in Boy Scouts, so he was at our house a lot. He's real nice."

She put pen to paper. "Okay, we'll ask Joe and his wife."

I had this covered. "His wife's in Phoenix, has been since last Wednesday. Her mother had major surgery, and she'll be gone at least a month. Joe told one of my clerks. By now, he'd probably be grateful for a home-cooked meal."

"All righty, then. It'll be me and Bobby, and you ask Joe—"

"You ask him," I said.

"But I don't know him—"

"It'll look better coming from you. You have a husband. If I ask him and it gets around, people will say I'm trying to be a homewrecker. You know that an unmarried woman must be above reproach. If you ask him and then it gets out, you can say he's going with you and Bobby, and they won't think a thing of it." I paused. "Really, with Joe's wife away, it's best nobody but you know I'm in the party."

"You are so right." She flipped her pad closed and tucked it into her purse. "People around here do nothing but gossip."

I wondered if she knew they were gossiping about her and Bobby.

* * * *

On the way home, I stopped by Mama's house. Since the police sent her home after she ran her Corvette over old Judge Vardaman—she owned the bank, so the law wasn't about to touch her—she had to be watched at all times. We couldn't find a soul willing to stay with her for two hours, much less twenty-four, so Frank and Bonita and I rotated weekends, and Lonnie moved in from the ranch to live with her. That triggered a minor eruption, because he brought all his stray cats with him, and Mama said she was not going to have those animals clawing her upholstery and coughing up hairballs on her Persian rug. But Lonnie was her favorite, so she finally agreed he could bring them.

But even Lonnie couldn't watch her all the time. Last month she decided Mrs. Pancoast's sheets hanging on the laundry line were ghosts and got her shotgun and nearly blew the woman's head off. For the second time. And for the second time, we had to send Mrs. Pancoast to that spa in New Mexico till she regained her equilibrium.

When I arrived at Mama's that day, Lonnie met me on the front porch. "She's at it again, Marva Lu," he said. "She's in the dining room, having a dinner party."

"Having a dinner party" was what Mama called it.

"Who's the guest this week? Harry Truman?" President Truman came to dinner at least twice a month. The fact that he'd been dead for over forty years didn't stop him.

Dinner parties upset Lonnie. As far as I was concerned, as long as Mama wasn't shooting up Mrs. Pancoast's bed linens, she could invite the whole Supreme Court.

Lonnie nodded. "Yeah, it's Harry Truman, but this time he didn't bring General MacArthur. It's worse than that. He brought Mamie Eisenhower. Mama says they're up to some hanky-panky and she's going to call the White House and tell Ike."

If only we'd been able to take care of Mama before she ran over old Judge Vardaman.

I closed my eyes. All I could see was the sunny, sandy beach at Aruba, so I opened them again.

"I hate to do this to you, Lonnie, but I'm too tired to dress for dinner and make polite conversation with empty chairs. I'm going home. Tell them I'm sorry, but I had to go back to work. An emergency cataloging thing." I patted his hand. "And disable the phone." I had enough trouble without having to explain Mama to the FBI.

* * * *

My original plan was to picnic and watch the eclipse from the top of Paradise Bluff. But then I thought of a new twist. The eclipse would provide an excellent opportunity to knock Bonita's bikini out of Joe's head. After the sun came out again, we could go down to the river and swim. I called Beryl.

"Wear your bathing suit under your clothes," I said. There was no place to change out there—it was the same as when I was a girl, only deserted, since the kids found a new place to make out, or whatever they called it now. "And don't forget to tell Joe."

On Sunday, I arranged for Mama's cook—a different one, not Lola, who cooked when I was a girl—to fry some chicken and make deviled eggs. I laid out my clothes—khaki shorts and a navy blouse and, to go under them, a purple bikini—and put a towel and sunscreen in a tote bag.

Everything was just fine until Beryl phoned and said Bobby wouldn't be going with us. He had to stay home and paint the kitchen.

"Good grief, Beryl," I said. "Tell him he can paint the kitchen Tuesday or Wednesday or Saturday, or next year, for that matter."

"No way. I've begged him for ages to paint it, and he finally said he would do it tomorrow, and I'm not about to ask him to put it off. He might never be in the mood again."

Nothing I said could budge her.

Bobby's paint job threw a big monkey wrench into the works. Bobby and Beryl were supposed to keep each other busy while I got Joe off to myself. With a threesome, that would be practically impossible. But I could make a start.

Joe would see me in my bikini. Beryl wouldn't look nearly as good. All those years of belly dance lessons would pay off, and the image of Bonita's bikini would fade into nothingness. After tomorrow, I would have no trouble getting him out to Paradise Bluff all by myself.

* * * *

I drove out to the Bluff Monday morning. The graveled area where we used to park was overgrown with grass and weeds. I drove on up-river several hundred yards and hid my car behind a stand of willows. I wanted to surprise Joe.

With plenty of time to spare, I walked around the old place. It had changed more than I expected. The railing at the edge of the Bluff was rusted. The stairs leading down to the river were rickety. Trumpet vine wound around the railings and tendrils snaked across the steps. This wasn't going to work. There used to be an alternate route. Downstream, where the incline wasn't so steep, there was a path. We might be able to negotiate it. Or maybe not.

But even if we couldn't swim, the day could still be a success. When Beryl wasn't listening, I would suggest to Joe that we make it our project to shore up the stairs, clear the brush, get the old swimming hole back in shape. He would go along. He was like Beryl—thoughtful.

After checking things out, I got the basket and quilts out of the car and carried them to a little clearing that was perfect for picnicking. I spread the quilts and sat down. From this perspective, Paradise Bluff was still a beautiful place. I lay back. The August sun beat down, but in the shade of the cottonwoods it was pleasant. A light breeze came up and rustled the leaves, and the sun sifting through dappled the ground and danced as they quivered. Lying there, looking up at the sky, I almost forgot why I was here. Joe didn't seem nearly so important.

I closed my eyes and sang to myself.

Jesus wants me for a sunbeam,
To shine for Him each day;
In every way try to please Him,
At home, at school, at play.

For the first time in years, I thought about nature. Why did we treat it so shabbily? Why, just last spring, I, myself, was all set to do it harm. I was going to give Mama one of those sleeping pills that lets you get up and drive while you're asleep, and then Frank and I were going to load her into her Corvette and drive her out here and push the car over Paradise Bluff. It seemed like a good idea at the time—Mama had become such a liability, seeing ghosts, shooting at sheets, careening around the Courthouse Square in that car, and with her out of the way, Frank and Bonita and Lonnie and I could divide up her estate, and I would have enough money to head for Aruba and never come back. It was a good plan and would have worked, too, if Lonnie hadn't slipped up and let Mama get into the driver's seat and back over old Judge Vardaman. And then the police sent her home. It was a big let-down.

But now, I could see the damage I would have done to this lovely place, spilling oil and gasoline and other toxins into the river. I was ashamed I'd ever devised the plan. I was still determined to solve the Mama problem, of course, because I had to get my hands on my inheritance so I could head for Aruba. But there was surely a more ecologically sound way to do it. And this time I wouldn't ask my siblings to help. Because Lonnie told me if he got wind that I was plotting something else, he would go straight to the sheriff. Lonnie always had a soft spot for Mama.

I heard a car coming and looked at my watch. Beryl was right on time. I hoped to goodness Joe was with her. I wouldn't have put it past him to stay behind and help Bobby paint the kitchen.

One car door slammed and then another. I walked forward until I could see the top of the Bluff and then stepped behind a tree and peeked around the trunk. Joe and Beryl appeared at the edge of the Bluff. I stepped out, but before I could call to them, they turned to face each other. Then Joe wrapped his arms around Beryl and pulled her close and kissed her, and she just stood there and kissed him back.

This wasn't what I planned.

When they finally separated, I shouted, "Hello," and waved. "Come on over. I've put some quilts down. From here we can see the river."

They jumped away from each other like the guilty things they were. Instead of coming straight to the clearing, they went to Beryl's car and returned carrying a basket of provisions and an ice chest. I pretended I hadn't seen a thing.

Nevertheless, the next hour was filled with tension. Joe hardly looked at me. Every so often, his cheeks would turn pink; it was obvious he was thinking about what I'd witnessed. A couple of times I caught his eye and gave him a sympathetic smile, to show him I didn't blame him for the indiscretion. Beryl, on the other hand, chattered away, as if she thought filling every minute with noise would make me forget. I behaved with my usual grace. I didn't want to embarrass Joe more than he already was, and I wasn't about to let Beryl know what I was thinking.

Because Beryl was the one at fault. The rumors about her and Bobby were obviously true. She was on the prowl. As soon as I mentioned asking Joe to join us for the eclipse, and told her his wife was out of town, she started scheming. Bobby painting the kitchen—that wasn't *his* idea, and that story about begging him—she *nagged* him until he couldn't take any more, she gave him an *ultimatum*—paint it *today* or *else*. Beryl made sure Bobby stayed home so she could get her claws into Joe. That kiss—it wasn't *Joe's* idea. She threw her arms around him, pulled him down, kissed him, and he was too shocked to resist.

Beryl had done everything she could to spoil my perfect day.

We were relaxing, drinking lemonade, when suddenly the leaves stopped rustling. The breeze died down. It grew so still, just like before a tornado hits. The air took on a golden glow.

"It's starting," I said.

We grabbed our eclipse glasses and moved downriver, out of the trees, to the Bluff's highest point. As we stood there, silent, the light grew dimmer and dimmer. The trees across the river turned into silhouettes against the darkened sky.

"I have an idea," I said. "Let's go down the stairs a piece, so we can see the sky reflected in the river."

As soon as I said "stairs," Beryl was off at a trot. I followed, and Joe fell in behind me. At the very top, the stairs felt relatively stable. But about three steps down, my foot caught on a tendril of trumpet vine. Lurching forward, I fell against Beryl. I righted myself, but Beryl lost her balance and started to fall. She turned, grabbed at the handrail, but lost her grip. There was no way I could save her.

But, somehow, Joe reached around me and got hold of her, tried to pull her back. That was his fatal mistake. Beryl panicked, reached for him, and, just as she had earlier that day, pulled him down toward her. It looked like she was trying to kiss him again. But instead, she pushed him into the railing. It broke under his weight. Tearing himself from Beryl's embrace, he fell. His scream, mingled with hers, echoed up and down the river.

Joe was not supposed to fall.

Beryl wouldn't stop screaming, of course, but I managed to get her to the clearing and gave her one of the sleeping pills I'd carried in my purse ever since the night Mama ran over old Judge Vardaman. Then I got out my phone to call the sheriff. It crossed my mind, briefly, that I could drag Beryl back to the stairs and dispose of her as well. But on second thought, that seemed like gilding the lily. I needed her to back up my story about Joe's accident.

While Beryl snored, I pondered. This had not been the best year of my life. No matter how well I organized things, the wrong person always died. It was downright demoralizing.

But like Mama told me when I was a little girl—when you fall off your horse, slap the dust off your Levis and get right back in the saddle.

It was a shame about Joe. But I never intended for him to be permanent. Just a temporary distraction until I could get to those Speedo-clad hunks on the beach at Aruba.

I closed my eyes, listened to the quiet, waited as the sun's rays grew brighter, and leaves began to rustle, and birds began to sing.

For now, I would be content to stay in Kilburn, work in the library, teach Sunday school, sing duets at church. Although without Joe, they would be solos. I would avoid even the appearance of evil. In the end, I would figure out how to get rid of Mama. Until then, I would try to be like Beryl: Most Thoughtful.

I leaned back against the trunk of a cottonwood, waited for the sheriff, and sang softly to myself.

A sunbeam, a sunbeam,
Jesus wants me for a sunbeam;
A sunbeam, a sunbeam,
I'll be a sunbeam for Him

M.K. Waller is a former teacher, former librarian, former paralegal, and former pianist at several small churches desperate for someone who could find middle C. A native of Central Texas, she grew up in Fentress, a small farming town on the banks of the San Marcos River; memories of that time and place inform much of her work. Her short stories and memoir appear in Austin Mystery Writers' *Murder on Wheels* (Wildside), *Mysterical-E*, Texas Mountain Trail Writers' *Chaos West of the Pecos*; and Story Circle Network's *True Words Anthology* and *Journal*. She blogs at Telling the Truth, Mainly: kathywaller1.com

OCEAN'S FIFTY

LAURA OLES

Most people look at me and make judgments pretty quickly. I get it.

Why would any middle-aged man want to waste what's left of his life cooking in a food truck? If he'd just worked harder and gone to college, he wouldn't have to do this. But looks are deceiving, and I'm fine with the judging. They don't know any better. I was respectable once, and trust me, respectable is overrated.

After hustling in a sales job for most of my life in Denver, I realized I was sick to death of answering to people half my age whose management experience could be attributed to coaching a little league softball team. The harsh winters didn't help, either, and I found myself dreaming of spending my days on the beach doing some sort of job where flip-flops and shorts would be standard business attire. So, enough dreaming. I quit my job, moved out of my apartment and headed south, finally stopping in Port Aransas, Texas.

In reality, I probably should have stayed longer, saved more, but I've never been a practical person anyway. I worked in sales for as long as I could and tried to make it interesting so I felt less trapped. But something about it always felt false, restrained, like I was an imposter. I like to play some things a bit fast and loose, which got me in trouble several times at the day job, but then again, I got results so they usually didn't mind turning a blind eye as long as the money kept coming in. A scold and a wink, that's how it went.

I know how the world works.

The world likes results.

Besides, I'm not one of those guys who boldly crosses lines and does immoral things; I like to do the right thing. That lets me sleep at night. I'd say that most of the people in this world are wired the same way. Not strict rule followers, not flagrant rule breakers, but somewhere in the middle. The worst thing I can cop to right now is running a mostly cash business. I don't mind telling you that there's no way I'm giving the government what they think they should get from what I've earned hustling in this food truck every day.

I've lived here a couple of years now and already feel like a local. Port Aransas is a small place, a few thousand people living here, tens of thousands who visit during the summer and holiday months. The food is great, the fishing better, and the views the best. And the people? The people are what keep me opening up shop each day. I'm a lot like a bartender; I learn a little bit about my customers' lives each time they visit.

We're in the throes of full throttle summer here in South Texas, getting towards the end of August and the heat can be stifling. Any breeze that comes by offers little relief; it's more like being dusted in the face with a hair dryer. The one thing I'm looking forward to is that the total solar eclipse is coming soon, and I'm anxious to see what the afternoon sky will look like when the moon inserts itself between the sun and the Earth. I've always been fascinated by these events; the idea that the moon can block the sun's rays and cast a shadow on our home planet is remarkable. We get to witness our world from a larger perspective, and I like being reminded that we're only a tiny part of this thing we call the universe.

But first, work. I like to have myself prepped and ready by eleven, and where I'm located, in Fisherman's Wharf, that means steady traffic will be coming for lunch soon, especially this time of year. I get my stations prepped, all my ingredients chopped fresh, and I'm ready to go. I have an inside connection for the best tortillas on the island and don't bother trying to make them, because Marta's the master. I'd rather pay her for them.

"Here you go, darling," Marta says, her barely five-foot self reaching up to my window to hand me a plain white plastic bag, the foil-wrapped tortillas peeking through the opaque material. "I threw in a few extra in case you need a snack."

I put them off to the side and then hand her the cash. "Thanks, love," I tell her. "Big day today?"

She shakes her head. "Not really. Lots of deliveries in the morning and then I'm taking the afternoon off."

"Big date?"

She smiles at me. "Maybe." She waves and walks off, slowly disappearing into a growing crowd of visitors. I don't know how much she sells each day but she must make a small fortune to drive that Range Rover.

I start to see a few regulars make their way to me. A couple of tourists, I'm guessing, in between. Frank is up first.

"You want the usual?" I ask Frank, "or you want to branch out a bit this time?"

"How can I pick anything else when the fish tacos are so good?" he says. I take his money and get started on his order. I double up the corn tortillas at the base and go heavy on the grilled fish, light on the slaw and on the sauce. Frank likes it that way. I fold up the Styrofoam container and hand it to him with plastic utensils wrapped in a napkin.

I have a small line forming, and I knock them out one at a time, smiling, making jokes, making sure to garnish each plate well, a touch of pineapple and strawberry on the side. Out of the corner of my eye, I see him, waiting for the line to thin out. I pretend not to notice him and he pretends he isn't waiting for everyone to leave. He stands on the sidewalk, smoking a cigarette, watching two guys set up their gear, opening folding chairs and organizing bait buckets and poles.

My crowd clears and I focus my attention on clean up, getting ready. He walks towards me and smiles.

"How's it going, Joe?" he asks. "Looks like a nice opening crowd there."

"Not bad for a Thursday," I reply. "You hungry, Barry?"

He nods. "Fish tacos, please." He looks around casually, but I know he never looks around casually. There's always a reason. He tilts his head towards the closest pier. "You happen to notice anything unusual?"

I lean closer out the window. "You talking about the Wallace brothers?"

He nods. "They're mixing up their meeting times, and I can't have my guys standing out here full time waiting to bust them."

"Yeah, they've moved to meeting around four o'clock. They're usually out here for about a half hour, and they're doing drops in that trash can over by 213."

He glances over his shoulder in the general direction and then looks at me. "If we can't bust them with the drugs on them, we can at least get them from the trash can. Get it out of circulation. Probably just annoy them more than anything but at least it's something."

I can tell he wants to say something else but he hesitates, so I make it easier on him.

"You need help with something else?"

"Mmhmm, but you aren't going to like this one."

"What do you mean?"

"It's about Marta."

The shock on my face is too easy to read. "What you mean? She's good people, Barry."

He nods. "I don't disagree, but lots of good people do bad things sometimes. You know this from the work we do together."

I cut the conversation short by getting started on his second order while he stands by the window, his back to me, studying the people gathering to fish, to skip school, to skip work, to enjoy a day on the beach. I package up his food, extra fruit on the side because I know he has a sweet tooth. I hand it to him and he hands me cash.

"Thanks, buddy. See you soon."

He walks away and I check the cash. A hundred bucks for a ten-dollar plate, which means I just netted ninety for ten minutes' work as a confidential informant. The CI work has been solid, pays well, and I'm helping local law enforcement clean up small pockets of bad dealings.

But Marta is different.

Marta's a friend.

Marta's not for sale.

* * * *

"Good morning, Joe," Marta says, hoisting a large bag of wrapped tortillas towards me as I lean out of my food truck. Her spirit seems heavier today, the usual lilt in her voice is absent and she seems tired, as though she stayed up too late or has something on her mind. I suppose I don't know her well enough to know the difference between the two. I fish for an answer.

"You feeling okay today? You seem a little ... less like yourself today." I try not to add too much to the question, a trick I learned in sales. Never finish a sentence for another person because they might just agree with you rather than telling the truth.

She shrugs. "I'm okay, Joe, just have a little problem I'm trying to work out."

"Something I can help you with?" I ask, hoping she'll take me up on my offer. Marta's very attractive. Did I mention that?

"I don't know, Joe. I think I have to figure this one out by myself. It's a pretty big problem."

"Hold on," I tell her, as I move to the side out of view to pour her a cup of coffee. Two sugars and cream, just how she likes it. I hand it to her and she smiles. Her mood lifts a bit.

"Why don't you come by and let me cook you dinner tonight?" I ask. I lean forward out of the window of my truck. "No funny business, you know. Just two friends, watching the waves under the nighttime sky."

"You want to sit outside and observe darkness?" she asks.

I nod.

"Most people like to sit by the water during the day … because you can see it." Her grin tells me she's poking fun at my idea.

"This area is really beautiful at night," I tell her. "So, you in?"

"Well, it seems to fit my mood right now, so why not?"

"Come by and I'll make us dinner and we can sit over by marker 220." She nods, holds her coffee in the air as a thank you, turns and walks away.

I give it even money that she shows.

* * * *

One thing I love about summer is how late the sun sets. It's great for business because people stay around to fish longer, chat longer and eat later. Today's been a good day, almost a record day for sales, although Uncle Sam will think I'm just getting by with this little food truck venture. I go ahead and prep two plates for a late dinner with Marta, figuring I'll just eat hers if she doesn't show. I've been so busy cooking that I never cooked for myself, and the scraps I stole in between dishes didn't hold me over. I'm starving, and at this point, I don't even care if I get stood up.

Okay, I care a little bit.

I make two signature plates and wrap them in foil to keep the heat inside. It's almost ten o'clock and still no Marta. I don't even have her cell phone number. I'm about to crack open the meal I cooked for us when I see the headlights of her car pull into a lot across the way. I can see her from a distance, walking towards me. She gives me a half-hearted wave.

"I didn't think you'd show," I tell her, only half kidding. "I was about to eat without you."

"I know, I'm sorry. This thing really has me wrapped in knots."

I grab the two Styrofoam containers with our food inside and nod towards the side exit of my truck. "Let's go sit out here and eat."

I carry both containers and lead her to one of my favorite places to sit and watch the water. It's a corner cove with a gorgeous rock formation, and when the waves hit, it feels magical, serene. There's a bench nearby—lots of people love this location, but with the darkness, we now have no company—and I motion to Marta to sit. I hand her a plate and she opens it, admires the food, likely to stoke my ego, which I'm fine with, and then begins eating.

"Your tortillas are amazing," she jokes. I give her a grimace and she laughs.

"I'm kidding, Joe. It's all really good. I see why your food truck is the busiest one out here."

"Thanks, hon. I like it. It's a good life."

She nods but says nothing. We're well into our meal before I prompt her.

"So, you want to talk about it?" I ask.

She uses her fork to move the cabbage slaw around in the container. "I don't know, Joe. What I'm dealing with is pretty big, and there's nothing you can do about it."

"How do you know I'm not some fantastically connected undercover mastermind who can solve any problem?"

"Working out of a food truck?" she deadpans.

"It's a fantastic cover story, isn't it?"

She sighs, closes the cover to her food container and looks at me. Her expression is a serious one.

"Joe, the short answer is that I owe some people some money, and I don't want to get into the details because it's best you don't know. I was actually trying to help my brother and now I'm on the hook, and it's bad."

"Like how much?" I ask.

"I don't want to tell you."

"You can tell me, Marta. Who am I going to tell?" I immediately think of Detective Barry and push the thought out of my head.

"I need fifty ... thousand."

I almost choke on the last bite of my food. "That's a big number, Marta."

She nods. "It sounds even worse when I say it out loud."

I point to her car. "Can you sell the Range Rover? That's gotta be worth some money."

She shakes her head. "It's a lease, Joe. I can't get anything back for it. Right now, it's just another debt I owe."

"How long would you need the money for?" I ask.

"I don't know," she says. "I could probably pay it off in a few months if I have time to work more and maybe sell some other stuff. I just don't have that kind of time."

"I can lend it to you," I say before really thinking about the consequences of the words that just spilled out of my mouth. I actually can, I have that much plus a bit more in savings, and my expenses are crazy low living here. Add my cash business and CI work, I could float her for a year if she needed it.

"Oh, Joe, I couldn't possibly borrow that kind of money from you," she says. "I mean, I don't know for sure when I could pay you back. I shouldn't have even told you about this."

I put my hand on hers, not in a romantic way. I'm genuinely worried about her. "Marta, what happens if you don't get this money soon?"

She looks me right in the eye. "Bad things, Joe. Really bad things."

I give her a pat, and say, "I'll have it for you tomorrow."

She jumps to hug me, our food containers falling to the floor, slices of colorful slaw decorating the pavement by our bench. She squeezes me so tight that I almost can't breathe. In her desperation, she's much stronger than she looks. We sit for a moment, hugging, and then I release her. I can tell from her reaction that whatever she's involved in, it might be every bit as bad as Detective Barry said. And I don't want to know the details.

We sit on the bench for hours, barely speaking, watching the quiet wonder of the night sky and the ocean waves. I consider that Marta is her own strange universe, so many mysteries and contradictions inside. The darkness is beautiful and a bit disturbing, much like the woman sitting next to me.

* * * *

I'm at work a bit early today, seeing as how I had to get to the bank, withdraw a huge chunk of my life savings, and carry it in my backpack. I'm almost nauseated with this kind of money on me. What if I get robbed? Am I sending out a signal that I'm carrying a brick of cash on me? I'm sweating and it isn't because of the summer heat. Giving this money to Marta will almost be a relief, and I realize what an odd thing that is to feel.

Marta shows up a little earlier today, delivery in hand, a smile on her face. She seems back to being her old self. I like seeing her this way.

"Good morning," she says, her smile bright. "How are you today?"

"I'm good," I reply, a grin on my face and a pit in my stomach. I take the bag from her and then hand her a Styrofoam container, wrapped in a plastic bag, with my life savings hidden inside.

"Here's that special order you asked for today," I say. "Be careful not to drop it."

She takes it from me and exhales what I can only see as relief. She holds her hand out for me, and I reach through my window and give her a squeeze. "You have no idea how grateful I am for this," she says. "I promise to pay you back, twelve months, tops."

I nod, a mixture of angst and pride settling in. How could I not help her when I'm just sitting on that money anyway? Maybe I can pick up some extra CI work to help refill my coffers.

I watch her walk away, still nervous but also thankful that I had the ability to help a friend so desperately in need. Besides, if her life was in danger and something happened to her, I'd never forgive myself.

I spent my money to settle my conscience.

I think it was a good trade.

* * * *

I'm back in my food truck, getting here early again simply because I'm hoping Marta will show up soon. I want to know she's safe and that she has what she needs. I keep looking out the window, but no sign of her yet. I check my watch and it's now past ten o'clock. I'm going to need my tortillas soon for the day's orders.

It's August 21st, the day of the total solar eclipse, although for us islanders, we will only see a partial. It doesn't matter; I'm looking forwa rd to it all the same, almost as much as seeing Marta today.

I down two cups of coffee, check my prep stations far more times than necessary, and wait. Being anxious and stuck in a food truck is tough. I can't even pace. I can only sit with my anxiety. It's lousy company.

I see a young woman step out of a car in the area where Marta normally parks. I watch her as she reaches inside her vehicle and pulls out a plastic bag. She walks towards me, tilting her head to one side to keep her long blond hair from covering her face, the wind gusts picking up as she comes closer.

"Are you Joe?" she asks. I wonder if she can sense my disappointment.

"That's me," I say, offering a smile I don't really feel like extending. "Where's Marta?"

"She had to take care of some things today so she asked me to make the delivery. I'm Janine."

"Nice to meet you," I say, taking the bag from her. "You think Marta will be back tomorrow?"

She shrugs her shoulders. "Maybe. She didn't say. She just asked me to cover deliveries today." She turns and leaves, offering her goodbye in the form of a wave she throws over her shoulder.

I take the bag and open it. On top of the foil wrapped discs are a red carnation and a simple note that says, "Thank you, Joe. You're a lifesaver."

The disappointment I felt fades, replaced by a sense of knowing that I did the right thing, even if I don't understand the situation. I can see a crowd gathering so I get my mind straight on the work.

My lunch rush hits and I keep busy, which is good because I need the distraction. It's now close to 12:30 and the sky is darkening, the bright sunlight gradually edged out by the moon as she inserts herself between the sun and the Earth. I keep peeking out my window to catch glimpses of the changing atmosphere, and now just past one o'clock, the world outside my truck feels a bit more somber.

I see Detective Barry roll up in his casual but not casual way, waiting until I have no line at my window. He's predictable that way.

"How you doing, Barry?" I ask. "The usual today?"

He nods. "Of course." He gestures to the sky. "Boy, that eclipse is really something isn't it? I wonder how many people here understand what they're seeing."

"I don't know," is all I offer. "It's pretty remarkable, isn't it?"

"That it is." He looks around before he speaks. "So, you know that thing I talked about a few days ago? With Marta?"

I nod, offering not one thing that I know.

"I need to know when you saw her the last time and if there's anything she said that seems … unusual."

Like 50K unusual?

He must see something on my face because he pushes me. "I know you like her, but you don't know her like you think you do, okay? You need to tell me what you know."

"Why, Barry? So you can put her in jail?"

"Look, I can't tell you much right now, but trust me, it's for the best that you tell me what you know."

"Marta's a good woman, okay? She's fixing whatever problem she's got going on. It'll be fine."

Barry studies my face. I sometimes forget that he's actually trained in interrogations. "Please tell me that you aren't involved in anything."

I hold my hand up. "No way. I have no idea what she's into. I just …"

Barry takes his cap off and rubs his forehead. "You didn't give her any money did you? Please tell me you didn't."

I can feel the blood draining from my face. Can he see how white it is now? He must because he says, "Joe, you did, didn't you?"

I stammer. "She said her life was in danger, Barry …"

"How much did you give her?"

The nausea is back and I don't want to tell him. I'm feeling light-headed now and I want to sit down, but I can't. I lean on my window and take a few deep breaths.

"I might have given her some money. As a loan."

"How much, Joe?

"Fifty," I say, not wanting to utter 'thousand' at the end of it.

"Are you out of your mind?" Barry says, his voice louder than normal. "You realize you aren't going to see her again, right?"

I shake my head. "You're wrong about that, Barry."

"When did you give her the money?"

"Yesterday."

Barry rubs his eyes with his forefinger. "I knew I should have come back here sooner. I thought we had more time."

"What do you mean?"

He ignores my question and answers with one of his own. "Did you see her today?"

I shake my head. "No, she had another girl, Janine, do the delivery."

His expression tells me that he thinks I'm a gullible idiot. I'm starting to think he's right.

"She said she had gotten into trouble because of something her brother had done and she needed the money to fix it."

Barry sighs the kind of sigh a parent gives when a child offers a stupid reason for stupid behavior. "Marta doesn't have a brother."

Now I feel panic, my money gone, freely given away because I thought I was doing the right thing. Turns out I was just another mark.

"Skip the food today, Joe. I need to get back and see if we can track her down. I'll let you know if I hear anything, and you damn well better call me if she shows up or contacts you."

"Of course," is all I can muster.

Detective Barry leaves me alone to tend to my customers, pondering the reality that I will likely never see my money, or Marta, ever again. The sky is darker now, the solar eclipse at its peak coverage, the sky sending a signal that I made a mistake when I gave Marta my savings. I believe the universe speaks to us, and this time, she's telling me I was wrong.

My motivation to work is different now. I chose this life because it's what I wanted. It was my freedom. Now it's what I need to do. I no longer have a choice. I'm not broke but I'm close, and I'm going to need to keep working so I can pay my bills. My food truck feels smaller now, more stifling, much like the cubicle life I had left behind.

Laura Oles is a photo industry journalist who spent twenty years covering tech and trends before turning to crime fiction. She is a Writers' League of Texas and Killer Nashville Claymore finalist and her short story "Buon Viaggio" appears in *Murder on Wheels*, which won the Silver Falchion for Best Anthology in 2016. Her debut novel, *Daughters of Bad Men*, will be published by Red Adept Publishing in 2017. Laura is a member of Sisters in Crime, Austin Mystery Writers, and Writers' League of Texas.

THE DEVIL'S STANDTABLE

MELISSA H. BLAINE

I took one look at the busy parking lot for the Devil's Standtable trailhead and began to mentally calculate the odds that I would be staked, screamed at, or offered as a sacrifice to the disappearing sun. The screaming started before I even had the car in park, which left me hoping that the staking and sacrificing would wait until after the solar eclipse.

My chances of death started with my partner, and I use that term loosely. Walter Lockwood was busy stuffing cupcakes iced with red frosting and tiny sprinkles into his ghostly white face. The frosting had stained Walter's fangs, making him look like he'd drained some poor soul in a back alley. The fangs, of course, were fake and underneath the makeup, his face was a shade lighter than mine. The disguise was convincing though. The man in the car next to us screamed and drove away in a squeal of tires, and when a nearby mother spotted Walter, she gave a small squeak and gathered her three children under her arms like a mother hen, herding them away from us. Why Walter, a decent wizard in his own right, chose to disguise himself as a vampire was a bit of a mystery, although I suspected that Walter was just insecure. The supernatural and human psyches aren't always so different.

The lot teemed with cars and people, most of whom had been keeping a close eye on the sky until we arrived. I wiped a trickle of sweat from my forehead, gathered my unruly black hair in a makeshift bun, and did my own assessment of the sun through my solar eclipse glasses. My eyes narrowed when I realized the moon was already sneaking over the edge of the sun. I'd been waiting for August 21, 2017 for what seemed like ages. The date circled on the calendar like some women mark their wedding dates. As an astronomy buff, this was on my bucket list to see. I just hadn't planned on working while it happened.

We were already a half hour late for a mysterious meeting with Agent Oto, who'd called yesterday to ask us for a rendezvous. On our way, Walter had insisted we stop at a bakery in Carbondale for his daily ration of cupcakes. From there, we had headed south on 51, wound our way over to Makanda, and drove straight into the heart of Giant City State Park.

Walter was oblivious to all the commotion, as usual. "Come on, Pops."

I sighed inwardly at his use of my despised nickname. I'd asked him at least a thousand times to call me Poppy, but it never seemed to sink in. My first badge had even sported "Pops Inca" when I'd received it, thanks to Walter's haphazard completion of my paperwork. As the token human in the Department of Prophecies (DOP), the first in close to a hundred years, I had a tiny amount of pull. The head of the department had interceded quickly. I think he was afraid that his now-required human agent might quit and leave him to explain why to the U.S. Office of Interspecies Cooperation. It was bad enough that I'd been relegated to the bottom tier of federal agencies. I wasn't also going to wear a badge that made me sound like a white-haired old man.

"What exactly did Agent Oto need us for?" I asked.

Walter fished in his pocket and handed a folded piece of white paper back to me. Opening it, I read:

Near the Devil's table, between the Devil's backbones, blood shall seep to the earth. As the moon blots out the sun, the powerful reckoning shall be birthed.

I raised an eyebrow. If Oto wanted help with this, it didn't sound like he wanted a friendly chat. It sounded like he wanted us to help him stop a monster. Of course, Oto could be wrong too. Prophecies are squirrely things. They present one possible future, but only one. Thousands of prophecies don't come true because something in history edges it away. They're also ambiguous enough that it's always a guess whether you're on target or not. Sure, we were at a place called the Devil's Standtable, but the reference in the prophecy could be to this place or to a table cursed by a demon in Idaho.

As agents in the DOP, we monitored prophecies and tried to decipher what they meant, but we also edged history toward or away from what the prophecies foretold. That brought a whole bunch of politics into the mix, as no one ever agreed on which direction a prophecy should go. Even the ominous tone of this one could be good or bad. Depending on who you were, that powerful reckoning might be welcome or it might be your descent into hell.

"Why exactly did Oto call us for this?" I gave the sky a sideways glance, noting that the moon was already eating up a good sized crescent shape out of the sun.

"Oto and I used to be partners back in the day. He's worried that some new group called Human Only is planning something around the prophecy. I guess they've got some underground network set up to collect prophecies. And then they try to interfere with them. They want to kill off non-humans," Walter said.

"Besides Oto knows that I'm better than anyone else he can get to help," he continued. I rolled my eyes at his back. Walter wasn't a bad guy. He was kind of like a little old grandmother who sets you up on blind dates. The motives might be good, but the results were a complete and utter disaster.

He turned to look back at me. "Did I tell you that Oto and I were once here? Well, not exactly here, just a little to the west. It was back in '73. We were rookies. Oto had about six months on me, but we were both pretty green."

Waiting for me to catch up, Walter gazed off into the trees, as if he was watching a film reel of the events. "We got sent down here on a prophecy about a river creature. We searched high and low and couldn't find anything that remotely fit, until the night before we were getting ready to leave. Stories started coming in about what the locals called the Big Muddy Monster. Seven feet tall that thing was, hairy and covered in mud. It bit Oto in the ass when we were taking it down."

He chuckled, an unnatural, forced sound, and then glanced around as if he was coming out from under a spell. I followed him under a narrow waterfall. The calming sound of the water would have had more of an effect if I hadn't noticed a yellow and black snake with a large head slither under one of the rock slabs. If a rattlesnake bit me out here, Walter would probably try to use his nonexistent survival skills to try to save me.

I scampered over the rocks as quickly as I could, trying not to think of slithery things lurking underneath. My feet had just hit the dirt again when the sound of a gunshot echoed through the trees and bounced off the rock bluff. Walter whirled around, his brows furrowed. Our eyes met and without a word, we sprinted up the trail, our feet pounding over the path.

A rock bluff towered over me. Next to it stood the standtable, which looked like a giant pulpit. It had a narrow pedestal rising from the ground, with a large flat rock balanced on top. At some point in time, the standtable must have been part of the bluff next to it, but now a gap of four to five feet separated the two. The lingering sunlight warmed the yellow, cream, and gray sandstone on the base. I couldn't help wonder if it would soon be covered in blood.

I couldn't see what was over the top of the main bluff, but it looked like a flat plateau, a bigger version of the rock that formed the top of the standtable. The sandstone had been worn rough by thousands of years of rain, wind, and sun, making the wall jagged. Walter and I raced to it. I picked a handhold and started climbing up, my fingers bending at the tips to grasp whatever bit of leverage I could find.

The challenge of climbing didn't occupy my mind enough to forget that a killer might lurk above me. To distract myself, I tried to work my way through the prophecy. Oto must have thought "near the Devil's table" referred to the standtable, but there were several "Devil's back-bones" scattered around the country. Colorado had one, Maryland had a county park with the name, maybe one in Indiana, and one near here in Illinois, along with probably a dozen or so colloquial uses of the term here and there. Of course, this one was on the path of the solar eclipse and the greatest duration of the eclipse's totality would be close, but still, Oto might have been completely wrong in pegging the prophecy to this location.

I shifted my body and made a grab for a handhold just out of my reach. My fingers ached as they clawed at the rock. Above me, I could hear voices, but they floated off on the wind. It was like trying to listen to a conversation across the room over the hum of a crowded bar. The eclipse had to be getting close. If I didn't get to the top soon, I wasn't going to have a chance to do much of anything about the prophecy.

As I hoisted myself over the edge to the top of the bluff, it was instantly clear that Walter and I had climbed our way into a hornet's nest. To my right, a woman with a belly the size of a beach ball lay on the smooth stone of the standtable. By the sounds of her moans, it appeared that little beach ball was about to make an entrance.

Straight ahead of me, a light-haired man sprawled on his stomach, blood pooling around his head. His right hand clutched something metal. It took me a second or two to realize it was a badge. I heard Walter give a short gasp as he came to the same realization. Agent Oto wasn't going to be any help in this fight.

Standing over Oto was a young, stocky guy in his mid-30s, and by the way he kept glancing back at the woman, I guessed that he might also be the beach ball's daddy. But the laboring woman wasn't his only concern. He held a handgun on a group of three people, two men and a woman, who were pointing their own guns right back at him. The group of three had a camouflage pattern painted on their faces in greens, grays, and tans. They stood to my left, leaving Walter and me in the middle of a standoff.

Walter and I slowly stood, pulled our guns, and began inching away from each other. Everyone seemed to be human, which leveled the playing field for me. But it hampered Walter. It was illegal for agents to use magic against humans. Nobody seemed to notice us, but I didn't think it would last. Above us the sky grew darker. I could have sworn I heard a clap of thunder in the distance. If Oto had been right that this was the spot for the prophecy, it seemed likely that the rising power could be the incoming beach ball.

I caught Walter's eye, but it was already too late to set any plan in motion. One of the hunters turned his gun toward us.

"We got more government goons." His voice was gravelly and rough.

"Well, keep your eye on them then, Darnell. Just try not to shoot another one of them; we don't need the whole government coming after us. Maxim, go cover the vampire." The woman's voice was exasperated and her dark eyes flashed with annoyance. She motioned for Maxim, a tall overly muscled guy, to move toward Walter, while she kept her gun trained on the guy standing over Oto. Clearly, she was the woman in charge.

"Shut up, Rosie. I can do my job. You just keep your eye on that knocked up bitch. We didn't drag her and the hillbilly all the way here for you to screw this up." Darnell had a blond five o'clock shadow on his chin. He moved closer to me while his buddy inched toward Walter. Everyone had a gun pointed at them except for the poor woman groaning in pain on the Devil's Standtable.

Here's the thing: I had no clue what the end result of this prophecy was going to be. Make the wrong choice and maybe the kid grew up to be the next Hitler. Make the right choice and maybe I'd save the world. The only thing I knew was that Rosie, Darnell, and Maxim were responsible for Oto's death. So, I took a chance and shuffled over to the daddy-to-be. Walter seemed to be thinking the same thing. It wasn't long before it was three on three, the last line of defense standing between guns and the laboring woman.

"Billy!" the pregnant woman cried and the stocky man left my side. I heard footsteps thud against wood as Billy crossed the makeshift bridge I had seen linking the bluff to the standtable. His voice was gentle as he reassured the woman he called Abby.

Rosie, Darnell, and Maxim moved forward, stepping over and around Oto's lifeless body. Walter and I fell back, outnumbered without Billy's gun. My foot scuffed against the rock and pebbles skittered off the ledge, falling between the bluff and the standtable. We needed to think of something quickly or we'd soon be following the stones down. Sweat trailed down my face, stinging my eyes. I heard Billy, from a distance, urge the woman to push as the sky grew darker and darker.

The eclipse had to be near totality. My mind whirled, grasping at escape plans and abandoning them just as quickly. Even if I could get to safety, I couldn't leave a woman in labor to three people with guns. It was clear that the terrible trio wanted to either take the baby or kill it.

Walter backed up another foot and stumbled, dropping his gun. It bounced off the rock and into the chasm. Now it was three on one.

In the distance, fireworks thundered in the darkness, just as the air was filled by the cry of a newborn.

My reaction was almost involuntary. I turned to the sound, forgetting about the terrible trio and their guns. Forgetting about Oto's prone body. Forgetting about the danger that we were in. Over the woman's head, a perfect circle of light surrounded the moon.

Rosie rushed past me to the wood plank and started to cross from the bluff to the standtable. She moved cautiously, but quickly, in the ways of someone who had practiced similar movements before. She was halfway across when the deepest, most primeval growl shook the rocks around us.

I whipped my head around. Standing behind Darnell and Maxim was a large ape-like creature. Brown, shaggy hair covered its body and its eyes were black pools. It dwarfed the two men as it swiped a broad hand at them, knocking Darnell to the ground. The sweat on my neck turned cold in an instant. I aimed my gun at the creature, but didn't shoot. As a glimmer of sun cut through the darkness, I lowered the gun to my side. The creature met my eyes, turned, and loped down the bluff. Within a couple of seconds, it was gone.

Rosie yelled at Darnell and Maxim and the three raced across the bluff after the bigfoot, abandoning the new parents and baby. As I watched them go, Walter came to stand beside me.

"You okay, Pops?" Walter's face had sweat trails through his make-up. "How'd that thing get here? It looked like a cousin to the Big Muddy Monster that Oto and I took down."

I didn't say anything. I just gave my head a tilt toward the ground in front of us.

"Oto's gone!" Walter began scanning the top of the bluff that we were on, turning this way and that, looking for Oto's body. "Did that thing take him?"

"That thing *was* Oto," I said. "His body was gone as soon as it showed up, and I saw Oto's badge in its hand."

"That's not ..." Walter began.

"You said the Big Muddy Monster bit Oto, right? Back in '73? What if the monster is really a kind of were-ape?"

"But, why wouldn't Oto have changed before now? And he was dead."

I shrugged. "Bigfoot wouldn't be the first were-change that requires trauma for the turn. Or maybe whatever the bite contained wasn't strong enough to change Oto until now. Neither one of us checked him. He could have been alive."

"Is he part of the prophecy? It said blood would be spilled at the Devil's Standtable, but he was over here."

"The prophecy said 'near the Devil's Standtable,' and this seems near. His blood seeped to the earth from the gunshot, and he was reborn in a sense." I said. "It could be either one, but my money's on the new Big Muddy Monster. The Human Only trio thinks it's him, too. They took off after him and left the kid. Whatever their plan is, they're probably hoping they can catch Oto and use him instead."

Walter stared at the stain of blood where Oto's body had been. "I'd better go report this." He walked to the edge of the bluff and started climbing down. His head had just dipped out of sight when Abby, Billy, and the new baby, now wrapped in Billy's t-shirt, walked over the makeshift bridge and onto the bluff.

"So, my baby's not the great power?" Abby's face furrowed in confusion.

"I don't think so, ma'am," I said.

"But we drove all the way from Montana. Those people gave me medicine to have the baby and I did, right on time. Just like they wanted. They owe us." Her voice trailed off. Billy came up behind her and led her toward the edge. He lowered her and the baby down with some ropes that must have been on the standtable, and then descended himself.

I was alone at the top of the bluff. The sky grew brighter as I sat on the warm stone. The eclipse totality was over, but the moon still had to finish its trek across the sun. I pulled out my solar eclipse glasses and turned my face up to the emerging light. I already knew what was happening back at the car. Walter would call the local law enforcement and the bigwigs from the Department of Prophecy. They'd show up and Walter would tell them how he had felt Oto was in trouble and dragged me here kicking and screaming to help him. He'd puff out his chest and spin a tale about how he had disabled the guns of four people, helped a woman give birth, and discovered that the Big Muddy Monster was a were-ape. There'd be fist bumps and slaps on the back. In a few weeks, he'd probably get a medal and his name would christen the new were-ape species. He'd make me bring him coffee while he ate my share of the morning's cupcakes.

I sat and watched the end of an eclipse.

Melissa H. Blaine spent hours exploring the trails of Giant City State Park and surrounding areas while earning a master's degree in Sociology at Southern Illinois University-Carbondale. Now living in Michigan, she enjoys visiting cemeteries, hiking her dog, and tracking down local legends. You can learn more about Melissa and her current projects at melissahblaine.com.

DATE NIGHT

CARI DUBIEL

I hate being alone. The house feels so empty. And I keep hearing this noise downstairs.

Squeak.

Just loud enough to be disturbing. Just loud enough to mean something is wrong.

Fuzzy, familiar shapes hulk around me in our bedroom. I huddle in the center of the bed, blankets pulled over me even in the sweltering heat. There is no light, not even moonlight. The sky is dark with a new moon.

I can't sleep. I listen. I hear it again.

I toss the sheets over the side, vault out of bed, crouch beside it. Since I know how to regulate my own breathing, I do it. My knees shake, my feet bend. Pain shoots up behind my thighs.

The noise comes again—the squeak. Shoes that don't know the cracks and crevices of our floors. Or, I suppose, shoes that don't remember.

Someone is in the house.

* * * *

The eclipse was not that exciting. From what Trevor said, I thought it was going to be this wild and crazy thing. It was a little weird, mostly because of what it made me do. I felt almost possessed. But I'm getting ahead of myself.

I leaned against the front door, tracing a pattern on the wood porch with the tip of my toe. I was on the phone with Trevor's mother. "And the baby's okay?" She had picked them up that morning so Trevor and I could have a date night. That wasn't happening now.

She wasn't even listening. Like mother, like son. "The eclipse is starting," she breathed. "My God, Grace."

Darkness crossed the sky. My foot jumped, ricocheting off the wooden porch. "The baby, Karen. He's okay?"

"Both kids are fine," she reported. "Brandon is asleep. Lily is out here with me."

"I'll let you go then," I said curtly, pressing the button to end the call.

People had traveled miles and miles to our little town in Indiana to see this thing happen. A total solar eclipse, a rare astronomical event. To my husband, Trevor, it was such a big deal that he'd broken his promise to come home early and spend time with me.

He is a physicist. He does all these science things I don't understand, things with quantum whatsits and atoms. These are the kinds of conversations we have:

Him: *What would you do if I could time travel?*

Me: (shrug) *What would you do?*

Him: *I'd have to find you. Wherever you were. At that time.*

Me: *I don't believe it. I don't believe it could happen.*

Him: *But if it could? Would you believe me?*

Me: (shrug)

"I've got to work late today," he told me, on the phone after the kids had already left. "We don't know when we'll have this opportunity again." So he should have told me weeks ago. He should have planned for it. It would have been nice. But there was nothing I could do about it now, and looked as if I would be alone for a while.

I stood on the porch, watching people emerge from their homes. All of them—at least, the people who are home during the work day—were hushed as they watched the sky.

I stepped into the grass and executed a few *pliés*. The stretch of my legs felt good. Loose and limber, like muscles I hadn't used were coming awake after far too long. I pirouetted a few times, holding my head upright and keeping my eye on a fixed point in the distance. As the sun disappeared, I danced in an eerie, lightless world.

That was the weird part. It was like my dancer's body had taken over, like I'd lost control of the mom-self, the house person—I refused to call myself a housewife.

And I loved it.

The grass felt cool under my bare feet even though the air was warm. The neighborhood was full of a sparking, unnatural energy. I took a deep breath and leaped into a *jeté*. Still, no one noticed me.

After what seemed like hours later, but was probably only minutes, the moon finished crossing the sun. The murmur in the street died down. Aside from the fact that my children were gone, and that I had danced again for a few fleeting moments, everything went back to normal.

* * * *

My ear against the door, I strain to make sense of the noises—the infinitesimal cracks in the silence.

I wish we had a security system.

I contemplate the idea of being murdered. If I die, I'll never get to see my children grow up. I'm so grateful they're not here tonight, by this fluke chance. Still, I nearly choke at the thought. Anytime I've entertained that thought, it takes my breath away. I don't know where my daughter's sharp wit will take her one day. My baby is so small that I can only see rays of his growing personality. I can't imagine not being with them.

All this is churning in my head.

Could it be Trevor? But Trevor wouldn't be sneaky. He'd turn on all the lights and clomp around like I wasn't here at all.

No, this intruder doesn't want me to know he's here. At least, not yet. And my phone is downstairs, plugged in on the kitchen island. This man—or woman, I suppose—has probably already noticed my phone. He knows I have no way of contacting anyone for help.

Do I wait? Do I climb out the window? Do I leave, pretend I don't know he's there?

My hands shake. I listen for the hitch in my breath. I want to slow down. I want to make up my mind.

It has to be the guy from before.

* * * *

I made myself a cup of tea and sat in the kitchen. Without Trevor or the kids, there were some things I could get done around the house. But I wanted to sit and think about it for a few minutes. Make a nice to-do list, crossing off the items as I went along. There is a certain satisfaction in that.

My phone rang as I started to write. "It didn't work," Trevor fretted. I could almost see him wringing his hands, pacing across his lab.

"So come home."

His reply came too fast. "We won't have another chance like this for a year."

"That's what you said earlier." I didn't insist he come home, even after he forgot to tell me I scheduled our date night for the most important date of the year for his research. He could have said something weeks ago, and he chose this morning to tell me. After I'd already packed the kids' things and made arrangements with his mother.

"I have to stay." He was awestruck, it seemed, by his own work. "I have to find out what went wrong with the timestream."

"It can't wait until tomorrow?" I didn't know why I bothered asking.

"We can still go out to dinner," he said. "We'll have time tonight."

The quiet was deafening. No screaming. No little hands scrabbling at my jeans, demanding milk, to be picked up, something to eat, needing so much. Now no one needed anything from me, and I was the one who needed. The one who ached for companionship, human words other than the nonsense of childhood babbling. I wanted my best friend back, the man who cared about my interests, my inner life, anything at all but work.

A flicker of movement caught my eye outside the kitchen window, where a patch of forest borders our property. I set down my pen.

It was definitely a person, walking back and forth across the length of our border, looking right at me.

I didn't recognize him—I could tell he was an older man, gray hair and beard, but he was too far away for me to distinguish his features. He saw me and began to walk towards the house.

I panicked. Should I call the police? Alert a neighbor? Do something …

Then I heard thunder. A ripple of loud noise I could not identify.

Then I realized I heard shots, a handful of them, rising in quick succession.

An illegal hunter? Thank God my children were away. I hoped no one was hurt.

I picked up my pen. Stillness returned, as if nothing had happened. I hesitated, started to write something, and put down my pen again.

I used to be the kind of person who walked towards a challenge. I was a dancer. I tortured my body, beating it till it bled, withholding food from it until it was whittled away to bone. If I conquered a role, it was on to the next. Harder, faster, better.

Now I was a coward, but I chose this life. I chose to let Trevor do his thing so I could step back. So my body could rest. But it hasn't forgiven me yet.

I stood up, asked my body to propel me forward. Maybe it was weak now that it had tasted dance again. Maybe it remembered those times. How good they were, how dangerous. Pain can be seductive.

I walked to the edge of the woods, inspected the property line. I didn't have to look for long. The person I saw was gone, leaving no trace. The shout of the bullet left no evidence. I was alone again.

* * * *

I can't stop thinking about what is going to happen to me.

The person who was out there, the person who was firing shots, that person is armed. That person is here for me.

I stand up, pulling myself out of the bent and pretzeled position near the floor. I am suddenly angry. My heart cranks. Who is Trevor to leave me like this? What kind of a husband leaves his wife alone in the house?

This is my fault. I have let him paint me into this corner, let him make me into the person I am now. Sad and scared and useless, hiding behind a door that can't protect me. The person I used to be was fierce and independent, always gunning for the next role or promotion, a shining star. God. The metaphor is so obvious you could slap me with it. I've been eclipsed.

But the sun comes out. It always comes back out.

I open the door and hurl myself into the hallway.

* * * *

"Are you coming home?" It was all I could do to wait until five to call Trevor. He didn't answer at first. *Maybe he's in the car,* I thought. *Maybe he doesn't want to pick up since he's driving.* Wishful thinking. He did pick up when I called the second time.

He sighed. "I'm at the lab for the duration." Pause. "Sweetie."

I had finished the tasks on my to-do list and was sitting on the deck. Clouds rolled across the sky. I was sure the astronomy community was pleased that the weather waited until the eclipse was finished. It sounded like the physics community wasn't as happy. My sigh matched his. "How long is that?"

"Could be overnight."

I gritted my teeth. "I'm scared," I told him. "There was a guy in the woods earlier."

"Probably some yahoo hunter."

In the middle of summer?

"Now, Grace, I have to go. I'll call you before I leave. Go pick up a nice dinner. Don't cook anything. Just relax."

"The kids will be home in the morning." I sounded like a mouse. A squeaky mouse.

"It'll be nice to see them." Trevor trailed off. A beep sounded in my ear, signaling the end of the call.

It was all I could do not to cry then, but I decided to make the best of it. I poured a glass of red wine, ran a bubble bath. Turned the tap all the way to scalding. I listened to the rush of the water and stretched my long legs out.

* * * *

"Who's there?" I throw on all the lights as I charge downstairs.

There is no response to my call, and I brace myself for a volley of shots, a knife to my neck, whatever attack the intruder wants to lead off with. I can almost smell his sour breath against my skin.

Swallowing, I shoot through the kitchen and grab my phone off the charger. Ha! I've got him now. I can call 9-1-1.

Do I need to?

The rush of blood to my face and limbs subsides. Well. Perhaps I was worried about nothing. I tiptoe to the front door and throw the dead-bolt. There. I never should have left it open anyway.

But I didn't leave it open. I locked it before I went upstairs for my sad bath with a glass of wine.

Shit.

"You wouldn't have heard me break in. I still have a key."

I whirl at the sound of Trevor's voice. "Oh God, you scared me so much!" I run and leap into his arms, and he pulls me to him, hugging me more tightly than he has in … Well, I can't remember. When was the last time? At night, if I reach for him, he turns away. Says he has to sleep, so he can be rested for the lab in the morning.

I pull back and hold him at arm's length. "So did you finish your experiment? Finally?"

He peers at me. With a growing dread, I examine his face. Something is not quite right about the man I just embraced. I shudder, involuntarily, and he notices. "We did. Finally." There is a hint of gravel in his voice, as if he's aged overnight. More wrinkles surround his eyes, the corners of his mouth. His beard and temples are gray.

"Who are you?" But I don't actually need an answer.

"I wanted to see you," he says. "Since we never did have our date night. I wanted to make it up to you."

"You didn't have to scare me like that." *Shoes that don't remember our cracks and crevices.* "Well, I suppose you would have scared me no matter what."

He nods. "Trevor won't be home until dawn. Got a beer?"

* * * *

This Trevor is forty-five. He is the "older" man I saw in the woods. Apparently, time travel produces loud sounds.

His version of Grace left him two years after today. Two more years of waiting for him to change. Two more years of struggling in silence.

"What is she doing now?" I am having a beer too, although I probably shouldn't after all the wine from earlier. My head spins with a carbonated buzz.

He shrugs. "She left me for a widower. His kids played soccer with Lily."

I can imagine it. I can almost picture the phantom interloper. Maybe I've even met him already. Maybe his wife's alive now. Handsome, wounded, as lonely as I am. Trevor would be happy to let us go. "Will that happen? Now?" I don't know anything about physics, about Trevor's experiments. I never believed that any of this was possible. Maybe he could get an atom to move back in space and time, but never a person.

He shrugs again, tips back his bottle. "I've altered the timeline. A new one will split off in place of mine, most likely. But the eclipse is a fixed point in time. So it's over between me and my Grace, anyway." He spins the bottle, sloshing the liquid inside. "Things could be different for you."

Should they be? I examine his face again. Older, he is handsome, having grown into his long body. He has filled out, with some muscle. He is sexy. Not the man I married—this man is worn by the world—this man has regrets.

I feel profoundly sorry for him.

"I wanted to see you dance again," he says. He sets the bottle down. "I don't expect anything from you. But I'd like it."

Does he know? Did I tell him I danced that night? That day, really? Or does he remember when we first got together, how he'd go to my performances and wait for me backstage with roses? I gape at him.

He smiles. "I know this is hard to digest."

I shake my head. "Don't patronize me, Trevor. I'm not stupid."

"I know. Oh, I know. I never should have underestimated you."

"No." I slam my bottle down and cross to the dining room. I push the table aside and strike the first pose in a wild sequence. It's one I learned years ago, and I shouldn't attempt it, and it comes back all too easy. I am a firebird, on the stage again, lost in the moment.

When I am done I whip my hair back and glare at him. "Does she dance?"

He doesn't answer. He just pushes his bar stool aside and reaches for me.

Later, I feel a bit guilty as he leaves me at the door. His hand feels so right in mine. "Thank you," he says. "Like I said, I didn't expect ..."

"I know." I put my finger to my lips. "Will you come back?"

He shakes his head. "You never know."

"Thank you," I tell him, leaning in for a kiss.

I head upstairs and crawl into bed, sweaty and spinning. I need to get some sleep. The kids will be home in a few hours. As I slide into the dark, I wonder … will there be an alternate timeline? Or has Trevor always come back? Will I marry that widower in spite of myself?

* * * *

A few hours later, sun streams in through the bedroom window. I yawn, stretch. My Trevor is not home yet, or at least that's what I think until I find him downstairs, surveying the mess. "What happened here?" He arches an eyebrow.

"Oh." I flush. "I was dancing."

He is exhausted, and he'll go to bed and sleep all day while I entertain the kids. He might even go back to the lab. But right now, his eyes light up. "How wonderful, Grace," he says.

We don't hug or kiss. Guilt flickers at the edges of my mind and then is gone. We stare and smile, goofy, at one another, infinite opportunities spreading before us.

Cari Dubiel is a librarian and writer in Northeast Ohio. She is finishing a five-year term as Library Liaison to the national board of Sisters in Crime. Her short stories have been published in two anthologies and two online magazines.

AWAITING THE HOUR

JOSEPH S. WALKER

Although he was awake most of the night, obsessively checking and rechecking weather reports, Monday morning found Matthew feeling wired with energy he couldn't contain or direct.

How do you behave on the day you've waited decades for?

Without really thinking about it he went to the closet in the spare bedroom where he'd hung his old suits when he retired, each sheathed in its plastic dry cleaner bag. It felt right to present himself formally for the occasion. He chose the light blue and adorned it with a yellow tie and matching pocket square. He'd lost weight, and he had to cinch his old belt in two extra notches, but when he looked in the mirror he was satisfied with what he saw. His hands might tremble slightly, but they had not forgotten how to make a neatly executed knot. Matthew nodded to himself. On his way out of the bedroom he raised his hand and briefly touched Alex's face in the picture hanging near the door. Today was for him.

There were hours yet to fill. He sat on the porch for a time, nursing a cup of coffee and watching the familiar neighborhood stir itself awake. Over the years this had become a sleepy little corner of town. Most of the children had grown and left. Matthew raised his hand politely as the parents left behind passed by on morning walks or drove off to work. He knew their faces, even if he had grown uncertain of names. The truth was that he felt little association with them. When he and Alex had moved in all those years ago, there had been a distinct frostiness. Two men living together was still a novelty in those days, particularly in Kentucky. By the time the neighbors decided that they were, after all, just two more guys mowing the lawn and taking out the garbage, the chance for real connection had passed.

He was in the kitchen rinsing out the coffee cup when he heard his front door open and close. He turned off the water and cocked his head. There was a murmuring voice, the creak of shifting weight. Someone was in the house. Still carrying the dishtowel, Matthew walked around the corner.

There were two of them, standing just inside the front door, hovering like they were trying to decide where to sit. The man was wearing khaki shorts and a white t-shirt, his blond hair hanging shaggily to his shoulders. The woman was in jeans and a halter top with dark hair cut almost to her skull. Both had tattoos on their arms and Matthew was looking at these when he realized the man was holding a gun, a revolver with a two inch barrel.

For a moment they all looked at each other. The man made a move as if to raise the gun, seemed to think better of it.

"Do you remember me?" he asked. *Old man* hung in the air. He hadn't said it, but he might as well have.

"No," said Matthew.

"I was here last year with the crew that redid your roof."

Matthew nodded as if this explained something. "What do you want?"

The man chewed his lip. "Is there anybody else here?"

"No."

"Sit down," the man said.

Matthew pulled out a chair and sat at the dining room table. He began folding the dish towel.

The man nudged the woman. "Look around," he said. "Make sure he's telling the truth."

The woman looked at Matthew. "Sorry, mister," she said. She moved off toward the bedrooms.

Matthew put the folded towel on the table and rested his hands on either side of it as the man came and sat across from him.

A thought struck the man and he leaned back in the chair and yelled over his shoulder. "Close the curtains!"

There was a rattling noise from the other room as curtain rings slid into place, and the light in the hallway got slightly dimmer. It startled Matthew more than the couple had, or even the gun. He knew from the sound exactly where the woman was standing, exactly how hard she had pulled. You get to know the sounds of your own home, each as distinct as a different bird's call, and you know without looking what door has been opened or closed, what faucet is running, where someone is walking. Then you go a few years without hearing any of those sounds, because there's nobody to make them but you. When you hear them again your mind will do strange things. For a fraction of a heartbeat, when he heard the curtains, Matthew felt Alex's presence. Remembering that he was gone was a punch of grief behind his ribs.

"You're all gussied up," the man said. "You going somewhere? Is somebody coming here?"

"No," Matthew said.

"Listen," the man said. He put the hand with the gun on the table. "We're not here to make any trouble. If you don't give me any reason to hurt you I won't. But lying is a reason."

Matthew nodded. "I'm not lying to you, young man."

The man stared at him for a long minute. The woman came back through the room and walked into the kitchen and closed the drapes. Matthew listened as she opened the basement door and went down and almost immediately came back up. She leaned against the wall. "Just storage in the basement. There's nobody else here."

Matthew looked at her. "My name is Matthew Shaw, young lady. What's yours?"

"Don't answer that," the man said immediately.

Matthew looked back at him. "I take it you're planning to be here a while. I have to have something to call you."

"Sir and ma'am will do fine."

Matthew shrugged. "What do you want?"

The man chewed his lip again. "The car out front is yours?"

"It is. I'll give you the keys."

"Got any cash?"

"Very little in the house. A few hundred dollars, maybe."

"We'll come back to that."

"Hey, Bonnie and Clyde," the woman said.

They both looked at her. "What?" the man asked.

"He can call me Bonnie and you Clyde. That fits, don't it?"

Matthew couldn't help himself. "You know what happened to them, don't you?"

She looked interested. "No, I never saw that movie. What happens?"

"They die," Matthew said. "Gunned down like dogs." He and Alex had gone to the movie on one of their first dates, just a few months after Matthew got back to the states. Neither of them would have used the word *date* at the time, of course. Things were so much more difficult then, all the wary circling until you were sure you both wanted the same thing. Today, Matthew knew, you could just walk through the world telling everybody you met exactly what you wanted.

"Whatever," Clyde said. "Everybody fucking dies." He seemed to reach a decision. "Here's the deal, Matt." Again Matthew heard the *old man*. "We need to be out of sight for a little while. So we're just going to hole up here until nightfall and then we'll take your car and your money and it will all be over with. You'll have an exciting story to tell at the bingo hall."

Matthew picked up the towel, opened it, and began to refold it. "I'm too old to bullshit," he said. "What you mean is that you're going to keep me around today in case it turns out you need a hostage. Then tonight you're going to kill me and take whatever you want."

"Aw, no!" Bonnie cried out. She moved beside Matthew's chair and put her hand on his shoulder. "We wouldn't hurt you, mister, honest."

"Sure," Clyde said. "We'll just tie you up when we leave. Get a little more of a head start."

It was simpler to pretend to believe him. "Fine. You won't have any trouble out of me." He leaned forward. "Except one thing. I need to be out in the backyard at twenty past one. Just for five minutes."

Clyde snorted. "What the fuck? That when your neighbor comes out to water her rosebushes or something? No fucking way. We're all staying inside."

Matthew shook his head. "You can kill me tonight. I don't give a damn. But I need those five minutes."

"Forget it."

Matthew held his gaze. "You refuse an old man this one thing?"

Clyde grinned, mocking. "Yeah, old man," he said. "I refuse."

Matthew nodded slowly. "Okay, then," he said.

Let it not be said he hadn't given the boy a chance.

* * * *

They moved out into the living room. Clyde had Matthew sit in a recliner in the corner farthest from the front door. Bonnie lounged on the couch. Clyde sat beside her at first but he was too jumpy to stay in one place. He drifted around the room, sometimes peering around the edges of the curtains, asking Matthew when the mail was delivered and if cops ever cruised down the street. Matthew's answers were terse but polite.

Bonnie dozed off for twenty minutes, waking when Clyde stomped past her again. "Whyn't you watch TV?" she moaned, stretching. "You're driving me nuts."

"TV puts me to sleep," Clyde said. "We'll watch the news at 11:30, though." He had stopped in front of a framed picture on the wall near a built-in bookcase. "This you?"

"That's what they tell me," Matthew said. The man in the picture seemed impossibly young to him now, many years younger than Clyde. He was wearing fatigues, grinning as he sat at the gunner's port in a Huey and gave a thumbs-up. The photo was on a black velvet backdrop, surrounded by a cluster of medals. Matthew hated the display. It felt like bragging, bragging about something he didn't want to remember at all. It was Alex who insisted on putting it together and hanging it where anyone who visited the house would see.

It's part of you, he had said. *And I won't have you denying any part of yourself.*

Clyde had moved on to the next picture on the wall: Matthew and Alex in their matching tuxes on the beach at Cape Cod. "Hey man, what's this?"

Matthew's throat was dry. "My wedding."

Clyde barked out a laugh. "Get this, Lizzie. We got the world's oldest fruit with us."

"Who's Lizzie, *Clyde*?" the woman said.

Clyde grimaced. He turned to Matthew. "You were a fruit when you were in Vietnam?"

"Yes."

"Well, where's this guy now? Your *husband*?"

Matthew held his gaze. "He died."

Clyde grunted and turned away.

"I'm sorry to hear that, mister," Bonnie said drowsily from her nest on the couch. Matthew nodded at her tightly.

Clyde hunched his shoulders and leaned against the wall, looking at the front window and chewing his lip. Matthew had seen the look on his face before, on soldiers before battle, on cops at the marches Alex had asked him to go to. It was the look of a man wondering what he was capable of doing.

* * * *

When Bonnie got restless Clyde sent her to search the house. Matthew told her where to find the small amount of cash he kept on hand but Clyde said she should search anyway, and bring anything of value she could find. "And make sure he doesn't have a gun."

The two men sat in the living room, listening to her rummage through the bedrooms and office. Clyde's right foot bounced up and down and he shifted the gun from hand to hand. He had not put it down or even slipped it in a pocket since Matthew had been watching him. It was a small gun but even a tiny weight gets burdensome with time.

"You don't have to stare at me," he said. Matthew shrugged and let his gaze drift to the ceiling.

"I don't know what made me think of this place," Clyde said. Matthew couldn't tell if he was trying to chat or just talking to fill the silence. "I mean, I noticed it was a real quiet neighborhood when we were doing your roof last year."

Matthew had long since gotten comfortable with silence. He didn't say anything.

"You're retired, right?" Clyde leaned back on the couch, his foot still bouncing. "What did you do?"

Matthew sighed. "I was an accountant."

"Man, I couldn't hack that. All those fucking numbers. Weren't you bored out of your skull?"

"I don't mind numbers."

Clyde gestured with the gun. "What about your *husband*?" He was incapable of saying the word without making it sound like something that tasted bad. "What did he do?"

Matthew didn't want to talk about Alex. "Dentist."

"No fucking kidding. Jesus, the most boring gay couple in the world."

There was nothing to say to that. Maybe it was true. Matthew didn't think it sounded like such a bad thing to be. So he was surprised to hear himself talking again. "Alex wasn't boring. His real love was astronomy."

"What, you mean horoscopes?"

Matthew shook his head. "That's astrology. It's bullshit. I mean the real science. Planets, stars, galaxies. We took vacations to the world's great telescopes."

Clyde snorted. "Oh yeah, I take it back. Sounds fucking fascinating."

Bonnie came back into the living room before Matthew had to think of an answer to that. One of the pillowcases from Matthew's bed dangled from her right hand. She handed Clyde a little stack of bills and he glanced at it and tucked it in his breast pocket without counting it. Bonnie perched on the edge of the couch and dumped the pillowcase out onto the coffee table. The small chest with Alex's collection of silver dollars. A couple of watches and some cufflinks. Matthew's laptop computer and the cell phone he rarely bothered to charge. Prescription drug bottles from the bathroom. She poured it all out as casually as a child emptying out a toy chest and Matthew winced as the items bounced and skittered, scratching up the surface of the table.

"There's not much here," she said. "Didn't see no gun."

Clyde grunted and scrounged through the pile. He picked up the drug bottles and tucked one—the painkillers, Matthew assumed—in his pocket.

"Shove it back in the bag," he said. "Might be a few bucks in there."

The most expensive thing in the house was the telescope mounted on its tripod in the office. Matthew wasn't surprised that she'd paid it no attention. He wouldn't have looked twice at it either before meeting Alex, before going out on hillsides with him and listening to him talk about the first time he'd seen Jupiter's moons with his own eyes. Some doors have to be opened for you.

* * * *

At 11:30 Clyde had Matthew turn on the local news. The three of them sat and watched the familiar cycle—traffic accidents, local politics, sports, weather. Matthew had never lived in or visited a town with interesting local news. The inevitable lighter story at the end of the half hour was about the eclipse that would be visible in the area that afternoon.

As the program went on Clyde grew more and more agitated, eventually pacing back and forth in the small space between the couch and the coffee table. When a soap opera started Matthew flicked off the set.

"Fuck!" Clyde exclaimed. He flopped down on the sofa and stared at the set in wonder. "I really thought we'd be on there, babe."

"What exactly did you do?" Matthew asked.

Clyde looked at him slyly.

Matthew shrugged. "Tell me or don't. I can't imagine what it will change."

Bonnie nudged Clyde's shoulder. "Oh, just tell him."

Clyde looked down at his gun. "Killed my parole officer."

Matthew cocked his head. "Yes, I would think that would be on the news."

"Maybe they haven't found him yet," said Bonnie.

Clyde nodded, looked up at Matthew, half grinning. "See, I robbed this gas station last night? And then he had to pick this damned morning to come around for one of his surprise visits. Fucker was always trying to nail me. Well, I couldn't have him finding a bunch of cash I couldn't account for."

"So you shot him," said Matthew. "And just left him in your house?"

"Yeah," Clyde said. "Then we took off, but I figured they'd be looking for my car, so we ditched that and just started riding a bus around. And we were a couple blocks away when I remembered working on your place."

"And you decided to hole up until nightfall," Matthew said.

"Well, yeah," Clyde said. He looked at the gun again, uncertainly.

Matthew closed his eyes. He was dealing with the world's dumbest criminal, and the time he had to do something about it was running out.

Clyde was apparently tired of explaining himself. "I'm getting hungry. What kind of food you got around this place?"

"Basic stuff," Matthew said. "Pasta. Fish sticks."

"Fish sticks," Clyde said. "Jesus, I haven't had a fish stick since grade school." He pushed Bonnie's shoulder. "Go make us all some fish sticks, babe."

She pushed back at him. "How long you known me, *babe*? I don't do kitchens. Make him cook for us."

"Sure," Matthew said. "I can make us lunch."

"Fine," Clyde said. "But you go with him, make sure he doesn't sneak out the back or call anybody."

Matthew stood up from the chair, trying to make standing look harder than it really was. He had been starting to think he was going to have to bait Clyde close to the chair. Being upright was a step in the right direction. He started to shuffle toward the kitchen.

"Hey," Clyde said. "Toss me the clicker before you go. Maybe some other channel has it."

Matthew reached back, picked up the remote and flipped it onto the couch. Clyde picked it up and switched the set back on, settling back against the cushion as he began to flip. He paid no mind as Matthew and Bonnie walked to the kitchen.

Once there she jumped up on the counter and crossed her legs. "Don't expect any help from me, mister," she said. "My mom spent half her life trying to get me to cook. I fucking hate kitchens."

"I don't need any help," Matthew said. He turned on the oven to preheat and turned the knob for one of the front burners as high as it would go. He got a baking sheet from the drawer under the oven, a box of fish sticks from the freezer, and a pouch of linguini and set them on the counter. "Tell me something. How much did he get from the gas station?"

Bonnie was chewing on a nail. "Like a hundred and fifty bucks. Everybody just uses their cards these days."

"So for that he killed a man."

Bonnie shrugged. "If he goes back up it'll be for at least fifteen years. He's no good at doing time."

Matthew started to open the food. Since Alex had died he'd been doing time of a sort himself. Waiting.

"Can't believe it's only lunchtime," Bonnie said. "It's gonna be forever before he wants to leave. Hey, you got any soda?"

"Diet Coke."

"Lemme have one."

He got a can from the refrigerator and passed it to her. Clyde bellowed from the living room. "Nothing on the other channels either. Everything okay in there?"

"Fine!" Bonnie yelled back. She stuck her tongue out in Clyde's direction and winked at Matthew. He smiled at her weakly and arranged the fish sticks on the baking sheet.

"He can be a pain, I know," she said. "Hey, tell me on the level. Why did you want to be outside at one?"

"Twenty after one," Matthew said automatically. He glanced at the clock on the wall. Fifty-seven minutes from now. He got the big pot from under the sink and put it under the faucet to fill. "I need to be out there to see the eclipse."

"Oh yeah, I heard about that," she said. She took a swig from the can. "It's supposed to be some big deal."

"It's the first eclipse in centuries to cross the entire American continent," Matthew said. "It will be the last total solar eclipse in America in my lifetime, and quite likely in yours." He took the full pot of water and set it on the hot burner. "The vast majority of people will never see one."

"So what's it gonna look like?"

Matthew crossed his arms and watched the stove. "It will look like a black disc sliding over the sun," he said. "If you're in the path of totality, it will cover the sun completely for a moment, and you'll be able to look directly at the solar corona. Then it will slide off the other side. The whole thing will last just a few minutes."

"Huh," she said. "And are we in the, what'd you say, path of totality?"

"We are," Matthew said. He kept his voice carefully controlled. "We are in it very precisely, as a matter of fact. That's why we bought this house forty years ago."

"Say what?"

"Alex took the long view," Matthew said. He was no longer talking to Bonnie, not really. "He plotted out the exact course the eclipse would take and found us a house damn near right on the center line. He said we would watch it together in our old age."

The water in the pot was beginning to bubble slightly.

"He didn't know he wouldn't be here," Matthew said. "He liked to talk about how on the day of the eclipse we'd be out in the backyard with our filtered glasses on, and the shadow would be racing toward us, all the way from Oregon, coming faster than the speed of sound."

The oven beeped, indicating that it was done preheating. The water in the pot was bubbling fiercely now.

"It should really be him here," Matthew said. "It was his dream."

"Hey," said Bonnie. "Shouldn't you be putting them noodles in?"

"But I'm here," Matthew said. He stepped forward, grasped the handle of the pot, and turned to fling the boiling water in Bonnie's face, past the arms she was raising too late to stop him.

There was a sickening hiss that was immediately lost in her screams. His own hand was burned from the handle but he ignored it. He dropped the pan and stepped forward again. Bonnie was off the counter and falling to the floor, screaming hysterically, and he could hear Clyde yelling and feel the floor registering fast-approaching steps. Matthew reached over the convulsing girl and pulled the biggest knife from the rack on the counter where she had been sitting.

Too slow, he was thinking.

He was still turning back to face the corner of the room as Clyde came around it, his mouth twisted in rage and surprise, the gun held straight out in front of him. Matthew saw the muzzle flash and felt something punch him hard in his right side, and then his left hand closed over Clyde's gun hand, pushing it off to the side, and the knife was coming up. He felt the shock of the gun going off twice more travel up his arm and then the knife was past Clyde's defensive arm and for a moment Matthew was back in basic, fifty years ago, learning about the things that a determined man can do with a blade.

The next thing he was aware of was being on the floor, with Clyde underneath him and an enormous dull pain from his right hip to his shoulder. He rolled away from the younger man and, with some difficulty, sat up. It was impossibly quiet. The knife was in Clyde's chest and a pool of blood was spreading out beneath him. He looked at Bonnie and saw that one of Clyde's panicked shots had caught her in the back of the head. It was a mess, but he'd seen worse.

He explored himself. The bullet had caught him high on the right side. The entry wound wasn't bleeding much. He couldn't tell if there was an exit wound. Breathing was tough, so he was guessing Clyde had done some damage to his lung. His hand was blistering where he'd grabbed the pot handle. Overall he didn't think he was going to die. At least not immediately, and in—he looked at the clock—forty-four minutes he wouldn't give a damn anyway.

Remembering something, he leaned forward. It sent a twist of agony through his side but he found the bottle of pills Clyde had shoved in his pocket. He transferred them to his own. He couldn't take any yet. He wasn't going to risk falling asleep.

It took him a solid ten minutes to get his feet securely under him. Much of his blue suit was now dark with blood, most of it Clyde's, but there was no time to do anything about that. He pulled his belt out of its loops and used it to secure a clean dishtowel over the entry wound.

On his way to the back door he got a cold can of soda and held it in his burned hand. No time for anything else. He'd been listening for sirens or cries outside but heard nothing. There was nobody around in the middle of the day on a Monday to hear a brief scream and a few muffled pops.

He stumbled down the three steps to the backyard. For a moment he thought he'd gotten the time wrong after all and it was starting, but then he realized the darkness creeping in at the edge of his vision was his alone, not the world's. He shook his head and willed it away. The big two-person lounger was waiting in the middle of the yard. On the cast-iron table beside it were two pairs of dark glasses and another picture, the two of them at the solar observatory in Arizona.

It seemed to take much longer than it should have to reach the chair. He half collapsed into it, remembering to put the glasses on before he looked up. There wasn't a cloud in the sky and the sun was whole and round and perfect. He was on time.

"Alex," he said out loud.

Afterwards there would be time, plenty of time to take the pills, to call the police, to go to the hospital, to answer questions. Or perhaps there wouldn't. Matthew was no longer thinking of Bonnie and Clyde. He was thinking of *Bonnie and Clyde*, the first tentative touch of hand to hand, all the years that followed. He was on time.

Above him, a section of the sun's perfect unbroken circle bulged inward and broke, and as the world grew dim the great black circle made its steady progression into place.

Joseph S. Walker is a teacher living in Indiana. He is a member of the Mystery Writers of America and his work has previously appeared in *Alfred Hitchcock's Mystery Magazine*, *The First Line*, and other venues. The first story in his Cinnamon crime series, "Cinnamon's Solace," is currently available on Amazon, and will soon be followed by the full-length novel *Cinnamon's Shadow*.

A GOLDEN ECLIPSE

DEBRA H. GOLDSTEIN

"I'll make one more call, then we'll have you give it a try," Joe Martin said.

Agent Lana Bradford nodded at Joe, her unaccustomed ponytail bobbing. Hopefully, this was the only thing she hadn't considered in prepping for her first undercover assignment. She trained her eyes back on Joe punching numbers into his phone.

"It's Joe Martin, Three A Travel. This is not a sales call. I'm responding to your recent Winter Travel Show request for information about viewing the North America eclipse."

Sitting beside him, Lana forced her lips upward when he made an okay sign with his hand and flashed her a wide-toothed grin. Fixated by the gold-capped upper tooth centering his smile, she tried not to stare at him.

"Yes, ma'am." He peered through his reading glasses at a script. "With it being over forty years since a total solar eclipse passed over the continental United States, August 21, 2017 is definitely going to be a special time for Americans to find a spot between Oregon and South Carolina to experience this spectacle. That's why we're providing safety information about looking at an eclipse and, if you like, information about the different existing viewing opportunities. You do realize that depending upon where one chooses to watch from is the difference between having a second or two minutes and thirty-eight seconds to see the moon pass between the sun and the Earth?"

Putting down his script, he consulted the separate list of names he used to make his calls. "Between you and me, Mrs. ... Maple, thanks to my wife booking a discounted Three A package last month, we're going to be sitting pretty on a hotel veranda in St. Louis, Missouri for one of the longer exposures."

Lana observed how he paused and listened intently. "I agree," he said, again smiling in Lana's direction. "She's giving me a once-in-a-lifetime gift. Considering how low the prices are right now, you can do the same thing for your husband. Do you think he'd be more interested in seeing the eclipse as part of a rafting trip down the Salmon River or from an observation mountaintop, hotel veranda, or campground site?"

She couldn't hear Mrs. Maple's response, but because he flipped his script to its back page, she was certain this part of his spiel would concentrate on what hotel accommodations were available. Once Joe started speaking again, Lana tuned him out and glanced around the one room office.

Four women, who she assumed were housewives who also had answered his ad for part-time telemarketers, sat across the room. Their metal six-foot table was identical to the one where Joe and she sat. Both tabletops were covered with white paper cloths too short to drop more than an inch or two over their sides. Each of the blue-jean clad women wore a headset and were engrossed in conversations.

The only other thing in the room was a bare card table dedicated to a coffee pot and its fixings. When Lana saw dust swirl above the table in the sunshine coming through the room's one window, she realized there weren't any window treatments. She made a mental note to avoid the coffee as she listened to ascertain where Joe was in his pitch.

After sitting through his full con repeatedly that morning, she knew how the conversation would go. He'd recommend a hotel that met the mark's price range, charge a partial deposit to her credit card, obtain an email to send her a receipt, and combine his thank you with advising her to use protective eyewear or view the eclipse indirectly.

The only problem with the transaction, as Lana well knew, was that the partial deposit never reached the hotel or campsite. Rather, it found its way directly into Joe Martin's personal overseas banking account. The mark wouldn't be any wiser until she and her husband showed up at the booked location clutching their worthless receipt.

As he repeated the credit card number, Lana leaned forward, trying to look attentive while her mind wandered. His looks didn't hold any attraction for her. His gold tooth was a good match for his padded girth and thinning hair. From its faded orange, she figured he'd probably been a true redhead thirty years ago. She wondered what type of scams he pulled back then?

There was no question in Lana's mind that he'd been a grifter for most of his life, but he'd only hit the Bureau's radar two years earlier when he made the mistake of swindling the director's mother-in-law. Even then, Martin or whatever name he'd used, had pulled the magazine con off so well he'd been long gone before anyone realized she'd been scammed.

Burner phones, rerouted e-mails and servers, and usually working alone made tracing him difficult. In fact, if it hadn't been for a case with a much bigger wire transfer takedown that somehow had accidently recorded one of his transactions, the Bureau would never have gotten the break that led them to this telemarketing eclipse vacation scheme.

Hence, her assignment to infiltrate his operation by responding to his ad in the neighborhood trading post for part-time telemarketers. She'd shown up with her hair pulled back in a pony-tail, no make-up, and a story about wanting to make a little extra spending money working while her children were in school. Apparently, he'd bought it because he hired her. Now, it was only a matter of time until the team took him down.

In her mind, Lana started to make a list of crimes he could be charged with. She stopped abruptly when she realized Joe was talking to her.

"Do you think you've got the idea now?"

She nodded. "Call the names in the order they're on the list. When the person comes on the line, make sure they understand this isn't a sales call but simply the information they specifically requested at the travel show, and then slide into the sales pitch using the script."

He grinned. Lana tried not to stare at his gold tooth, but it was hard. It certainly wasn't dulled by any coffee stains. She remembered reading somewhere that one should never get a gold front tooth as it was too soft to chew on, but that obviously was not a problem for Joe Martin. "I do have a question."

"Yes?

"During the time I've been observing you, you've made twelve calls but only had three takers. Is that the average success rate I should expect?"

"Using this list, I'd say that's about right." He placed his hand on the folded data list. "These folks expressed an interest in solar eclipse information, so they or someone in their family are more liable to nibble at our once in a lifetime discounted, if you buy now, opportunity."

He pointed across the room. "Once you end up over there, your cold call success odds are more like one in fifteen."

She followed his gaze to where the four housewives sat. They all were still engaged in telephone conversations. "They've been here longer, so why give me this list?"

"Easier for you to get your feet wet. Besides, I get the feeling that with a little help from me, you can be a superstar."

Lana wasn't sure how to interpret his comment, but opted to take it at face value. She hoped her features conveyed an earnest expression—even if it was because she was thinking of arresting him rather than swindling gullible eclipse lovers. "You're right," she said. "I'm definitely willing to work. After all, more calls, more sales, more commission."

When he didn't respond to her economic analysis, she decided flattery might get her more information than dwelling on profit. "I still can't imagine how you realized there was a niche for your travel agency to specialize in eclipses. The way you think out of the box is impressive."

She was glad to see the line of his jaw soften. She hoped her words had hit a sweet spot.

"Booking vacation spots has gone on forever," Joe said. "You can Google anything. Rock climbing, ghost hunting, or in this case, viewing the North American eclipse, and you'll find someone has created a travel package for it. My goal is for Three A Travel to get its piece of the action. With the upcoming eclipse, our options to sell are endless."

Lana raised an eyebrow. "But you just said you only want a share of the business? With so many eclipse options, do you want us to push one type or geographic area more?"

"No." Joe picked up one of the scripts. He pulled the cover sheet, a picture of an eclipse, off and held it so she could see the rectangular shape of the paper. "There are a lot of miles between Oregon and South Carolina. That means there are an infinite number of vantage points for vendors to book people into. Think of this piece of paper as all of those possible places."

He tore a corner off the page and handed it to her. She looked at the paper resting in her palm as Joe said, "I'm not greedy. I just want to get that corner of the business. Within our agency's limits, that's more than enough for us."

Lana pointed at the print-out of names. "But you obviously are beating the odds by having a list like that. Did you have to steal it?"

Joe threw back his head and laughed. "What do you think I am? A crook? Anyone can buy lists of anything and everything you want from various list houses. These names all were gathered at the Winter Travel Show by a company that sells high-end sunglasses. It offered to email safe eclipse viewing instructions to anyone who left a name and address in its fishbowl. Not only did the company send each of these folks a paragraph about eclipse viewing, but also its current eyeglasses catalog. Then, it sold the collected names to a clearing house. I bought the list for ten cents a name."

Lana felt her cheeks flushing. "I'm sorry if I came across as accusing you of doing something wrong. I had no idea …."

"It's okay." Joe raised his hand to hush her. "Hey, lunch break in five," he yelled across the room. Lana glanced at her watch. It wasn't quite 11:30. She'd debated giving the team the signal to raid the room before his call to Mrs. Maple, but had decided one more recorded con would be another nail in his coffin. Calling the team in now would mean they'd miss the four other housewives.

That would be a definite problem. Lana hoped the fear generated by being arrested would translate into each part-time telemarketer being more than willing to testify to the nature of the calls they'd been making—especially after the defense of good faith was suggested to them. No, she decided, she wouldn't give the signal until everyone was back from lunch and resumed working.

Lana stood to leave with the others.

"Wait," Joe said, motioning her to sit back down. "We'll go a little later. Without them here, it will be a quieter for you to make your first calls. Ready?"

Lana nodded, wondering how long she could stall to avoid accidentally making a sale.

"Actually, I have one more question."

"Shoot."

She wished she could. "A few times in the script, you mentioned eclipse viewing instructions, but I never heard you give any. What page in the script are those on?"

"They're not in the script. That's how the eyeglass manufacturer got them to sign up. If it should come up during your phone call, either offer to email them the information again or gloss over it if they're buying a travel package. If you get pressed, adlib."

She pushed a loose strand of chestnut hair back behind her ear, confused why he hadn't bothered to cover that angle in the script. Surely someone would want more detailed info than the paragraph they'd received. "Adlib?"

"Think of it this way. You know a solar eclipse is when the moon passes between the sun and the Earth, blocking light from reaching Earth. The entire process can take a couple of hours, but the actual visible total eclipse can last from a hundredth of a second to a few minutes, depending upon where you are viewing it from. All you have to tell them is that there's no danger to the eye during the total phase of the solar eclipse, but the problem is most people don't recognize which phase of the eclipse is occurring. That's why it's important they have protective eyewear or use an indirect observation technique. At that point, end the call."

He handed her his headset. "Your turn now. I have a feeling you'll be the one to eclipse my sales record."

She took the headset and pulled the contact list closer to her. She lightly ran her finger down the page until it rested on the name below Mrs. Maple. There was no turning back now. She dialed the number.

The phone began to ring. After the third ring, she heard both a click and her own intake of breath as an answering machine message began. Lana glanced at Joe. He motioned for her to hang up. Relieved, she did.

Joe handed her a pen. "Put a notation next to the name, so we know it needs to be called again."

She did as he said and then looked up at him again. "Next name?"

"Yeah."

Lana dialed, hoping for another answering machine. No such luck, a man answered. Three words into her script, she heard a reverberating bang when he slammed the phone down. "Guess he's one of those who believes phone solicitors are all swindlers. My mother always does."

Joe didn't say anything, so Lana marked the name off the call list and proceeded to the next one. This time, a woman answered.

Without any effort, Lana quickly engaged in a give and take that fell right into the script. As she flipped to the page with available campsites, Lana felt a surge of adrenalin, until she remembered she didn't really want to make this sale. With Joe sitting at the table listening to everything she said, she tried to think of a way to avoid closing the deal, but it was going too well. Apparently, the old saying about 'a sucker being born every minute,' was accurate.

Based upon the script, it was time to take the charge number. There would be more paperwork, but the Bureau would simply have to refund the money later.

While the woman went to get her charge card, Lana excitedly turned to Joe. In doing so, she accidently let her hand hang up the phone. "Oh, no," Lana said. "I didn't mean to do that. I'll call her right back."

She fumbled with the phone, headset, and list of names and numbers. Joe put his hand over hers. With his other hand, he took the headset from her. "It's okay. We all make mistakes, even me."

"But I can fix this one. Just give me the phone."

"Relax. You've got the idea now. Go have lunch and this afternoon, things will be much easier." He glanced at his watch. "Everyone will be back from lunch at one. Why don't you do the same?"

Lana got up. Joe stared at her, but didn't move.

"Aren't you coming?"

"No," he said. "I have a few things to clean up and get ready for this afternoon's session. I'll grab something when I'm done. Believe me, you'll be golden in no time."

Even though he was smiling at her, his gold tooth flashing, Lana didn't think she should dawdle. She gathered up her things, left quickly and ducked into the first ladies room. This undercover stuff wasn't too bad. She felt good about how things had gone so far and knew she'd be over the top when she reported to the director that the team had reeled in its catch.

Lana called her team. Once they agreed to make the raid at 1:15, it was only a matter of killing time until she returned to the office suite just before one. The four housewives stood outside the door chatting. A sign proclaimed the office closed.

"Mr. Martin's not back, yet, but we're early," one said. Lana joined them. Through small talk she confirmed each had responded to the part-time telemarketer ad in the neighborhood trading post. A few minutes after one, when the same woman commented, "I hope he gets back soon. I pick up my kids at three," Lana felt the hairs on the back of her neck tingle.

Something wasn't right. She reached for the doorknob, a bad feeling burning in the pit of her stomach. The knob turned. The door was unlocked.

Following her, the other women crowded into the empty room. Except for the coffee pot and something on the table where Lana and Joe Martin had sat, the tabletops had been cleared. There was no sign of the phones, lists, and scripts. Ignoring the chatter of the other telemarketers complaining about being stiffed and the arrival of her team, Lana walked to the table to see what wasn't important enough for Joe to have taken with him.

It was the beautiful eclipse picture page he'd pulled from his script minus its torn corner. Martin's gold crown sat where the piece was missing.

Judge Debra H. Goldstein is the author of *Should Have Played Poker: a Carrie Martin and the Mah Jongg Players Mystery* (Five Star, 2016) and the 2012 IPPY Award winning *Maze in Blue*, a mystery set on the University of Michigan's campus. Her short stories and essays have been published in numerous periodicals and anthologies, including *Alfred Hitchcock Mystery Magazine*, *Mardi Gras Murder* and *The Killer Wore Cranberry: a Fourth Meal of Mayhem*. Debra serves on the national Sisters in Crime, Guppy Chapter and Alabama Writers Conclave boards, and is a MWA member. She lives in Birmingham, Alabama.

PICTURE PERFECT

LD MASTERSON

Joe Harmon never went anywhere without a camera. Not a smartphone camera or a little pocket digital either, but a full size DSLR with full-frame CMOS, 30.4MP resolution, and a continuous shooting speed of 8 frames per second. And, of course, a couple of his favorite lenses so he was always ready to capture that perfect shot. Photography was his joy.

He was President of the MAPC, the Mayfair Amateur Photography Club, a group of local photographers who met monthly to discuss techniques and the latest equipment, and to share the best of their work from that month. They even held a contest, with a little traveling trophy, for the best photo of the month. Sometimes the choice was based on the subject, sometimes on composition or creativity, but there was one constant … the trophy almost always went home with Joe.

Until Sam Rice.

Sam Rice had been a thorn in Joe's side since Sam had moved to Mayfair three years ago. He was one of those guys who bullied his way in everywhere. Buddying up to all of Joe's friends. Showing up at softball with a cooler of beer to share. Volunteering with the kids' soccer program. He'd even finagled an invitation to join Joe's Lodge. But when they invited him to become a member of the MAPC … that was the final straw. They were serious photographers. Amateurs, yes, but serious. Joe had seen Sam's camera. It was a museum piece. He didn't belong.

Then Sam won one of their monthly contests, then another, and another. Now the trophy almost always went home with Sam.

Joe hated Sam Rice.

* * * *

"Joe, where are you going?" Claire's voice stopped him as he passed through the kitchen, camera bag over his shoulder.

"Over to Swain's Pond. I want to take a few pictures. The light is really good this morning." He glanced at his wife, then away, shifting the bag strap impatiently. Claire didn't share his love of photography.

She was always complaining about the money he spent on cameras and equipment, and how she had to cut coupons and watch for sales just to buy groceries. And she nagged him to death about things she wanted done around the house.

"The light will be good this afternoon, too, I'm sure. Come on, honey, you promised me you were going fix the latch on the screen door today."

"I'll do it next weekend."

"Joe Harmon, you and I both know there will be nothing done in this town next weekend except getting ready for that eclipse."

That was true. On Monday, August 21, 2017 a total solar eclipse was going to travel across the United States, and Mayfair, Kentucky was directly in its path. Center line. A photographer's dream come true. Joe had ordered two new filters and a state-of-the-art lens for the occasion. Of course, he hadn't mentioned that to Claire.

"Then I'll do it the week after."

"It won't take that long. If you could just—"

"Damn it, Claire. Stop nagging. I'll get it done when I get it done."

He pushed his way out the screen door which slapped shut and bounced open again. Joe stopped and pushed it closed. *There. You just have to close it gently. The latch can wait.*

* * * *

During the following week, photographers and sightseers swarmed all over Mayfair, as they had every other city and town along the eclipse's path. Hotels and motels were full and many enterprising residents had rented out their spare bedrooms, their kids' bedrooms, or even their own.

Joe strolled down his driveway to retrieve the Sunday paper that damn Lewis kid never managed to throw all the way to the porch. The sky was clear and would be for the next several days according to the latest forecast. Perfect. He stood there in his summer robe and slippers and watched the traffic on his usually quiet street. Ah well, he couldn't blame them. And they wouldn't be in his way. His tripod was set up and ready on the small balcony outside his bedroom. He'd done several test shots already, using the coordinates he'd checked and double checked on numerous websites. The position was perfect to give him an unobstructed view. This was going to be his greatest photo shoot ever.

"Hey, Joe." Sam Rice's voice broke into Joe's thoughts.

Sam was on the sidewalk, jogging lightly in place, flaunting his physique in shorts and one of those compression tees, darkened with sweat. Joe worked up a friendly smile and walked over to meet him.

"Sam. Having your morning run, I see."

"Yeah, though it was a bit of a challenge this morning with all the traffic."

Joe made a show of checking out the traffic. "The eclipse has really brought them in. Can't blame them, I guess. If we weren't in the path, I'd have traveled across the country to see it." He gave Sam a sideways glance. "Wouldn't you?"

"Oh hell, I'm right here and I'm going to miss it."

Joe jerked his head around in disbelief. "What?"

"Bummer, huh? We're installing a new mainframe and no one gets to take the afternoon off. Our corporate offices aren't impressed by rare natural phenomena."

"So you're not going to shoot it? No pictures." Was this the best news ever or the worst?

"Oh, I'm going to try. I'm setting my camera up on the roof of my carport and using a timer. Hopefully I'll get something." His lack of concern irked Joe.

"So, will you make it to the MAPC meeting tomorrow night? You know, we're all going to bring our eclipse pictures, see who got what."

"Yeah, I'll be there. Might be a little late. I'll swing by the house, grab my camera, and we can all see what I got together." His grin was warm and unconcerned. "Gotta keep going. See you tomorrow night."

Sam moved off and Joe walked slowly up his driveway, wrestling with his thoughts. Sam was going to miss the eclipse. He was using a timer. Joe would definitely beat him this time. But where was the satisfaction in that? To beat the shots of an unattended camera. Especially the one Sam Rice used. It would be meaningless. The others would see it as if Sam hadn't shot at all. It would be … Joe stopped as a horrifying thought struck him. What if Sam won? What if whatever pictures he got with his ancient camera on an unattended tripod shooting on a timer were still better than Joe's? No. That wouldn't happen. It couldn't happen.

He wouldn't let it happen.

Joe stared at the newspaper in his hand. Delivered to his driveway by the teenager Kyle Lewis.

* * * *

It was close to noon on Monday when Kyle Lewis let himself into Sam Rice's small back yard and made his way to the rear of the empty carport. The scent of honeysuckle hung thick in the air and someone had a grill going nearby. Mr. Harmon had promised him there'd be no one home and Kyle sure hoped that was true. He'd seen Mr. Rice working out at Murphy's Gym and Kyle didn't want to come up on his bad side.

He circled the open-sided carport. No ladder, but it wouldn't be hard to climb the supports. A quick glance around and he scrambled to the top. There was the camera, sitting on the tripod, just like Mr. Harmon said. Mr. Harmon said it was a joke, between him and Mr. Rice, 'cause they were friends. Kyle hoped so, but wasn't sure Mr. Rice was gonna find it very funny. He'd heard everybody talking, and taking pictures of this eclipse was a big deal. He'd tried to tell Mr. Harmon no, but the money was enough to get his car running again, and he was getting damn tired of delivering those newspapers on his old bike.

The mount on the top of the tripod was pretty much like Mr. Harmon described it. He loosened the first screw, adjusted the camera thirty degrees to the left, and re-tightened it. Then he loosened the elevation screw to raise the camera angle twenty degrees.

A door slammed nearby. Kyle dropped flat onto his stomach. Crap. Did that come from the Rice house or the one next door? Kyle decided discretion was indeed the better part of valor, did a quick belly crawl to the rear of the structure, and swung himself over the side.

* * * *

Joe sat on his balcony on a small white wrought iron chair. The tiny balcony used to hold a pair of chairs and a matching table, just big enough for a pair of mugs. When they'd first moved in, he and Claire would sit out there in the morning, talking and enjoying their coffee together. But he'd moved the table and the second chair to the ground level patio to make room for his tripod when he was trying to get a picture of the hawk that was scaring the birds away from Claire's feeders. That was ... three, maybe four years ago. He never got around to bringing the other chair and the table back.

He'd been out there for over an hour, checking and re-checking his settings, exposure, coordinates. It was almost time now. The camera's filter was in place and he had his own protective glasses ready.

The moon inched its way in front of the sun, taking that first small bite, and Joe began taking his shots, checking the framing as he went. He could take his time here. Pictures at this stage were of lower interest and these were mostly test shots. It would be well over an hour to the total eclipse.

Slowly the sun became a crescent, becoming narrower and narrower as the moon covered its face. "Oh wow," he breathed. Then, louder, "Claire. Claire, it's happening. You need to get out here."

No answer.

"Claire." Where was she? He thought she was in the house, waiting. Something like this, she'd want to see it with him. Wouldn't she? Had he asked her?

The sky started to darken and everything around him took on an eerie edge. The air turned cool. Joe forgot about Claire and turned all his attention to his shots.

* * * *

Kyle Lewis scrambled up the side support of Sam Rice's carport. This was a two-part job and he had to make sure he finished it. He'd messed up a little on part one, leaving the camera resting on the level plate of the tripod base instead of pointed up as Mr. Harmon had wanted, but either way, Mr. Rice didn't get any pictures of the eclipse. Kyle quickly returned the camera to its original position and tightened the screws. That was part of the joke. Mr. Harmon said it was important that Mr. Rice not know what had been done. Well, that was okay by Kyle. He didn't want him to know what had been done or by whom.

* * * *

Joe looked at the images on his monitor and it was all he could do to sit still in his chair. They were better than he could possibly have imagined. Beautiful. Incredible. His choice of filters and exposures had been perfect. These were by far the best photographs he had ever taken.

"Claire," he called. No answer. Blast. He wanted her to see these. He wanted *someone* to see them.

"Claire." She must have gone out. Didn't even stay and watch the eclipse with him. He tried to work up a little righteous indignation but he felt too good. He hadn't even needed Kyle Lewis and his little *joke*. Nothing Sam Rice could have taken could beat these. Tonight Joe would regain the respect and recognition he deserved.

* * * *

The air at Mayfair Amateur Photography Club meeting was charged with excitement. All twelve of the original members were there when Joe arrived. There was no sign of Sam but then, he said he might be late. That was fine with Joe. It was nice to enjoy his friends without Sam Rice sucking up all the attention in the room. Yeah, that was it, what bugged him about Sam. The man always managed to be the center of attention.

"Hey, Joe."

Several of them called greetings as he entered the VFW hall where they met. The big flat screen was already on and connected to the club's laptop. Each of them would load their photos, either directly from their camera or from a flash drive and view them together on the screen. Joe had spent the afternoon selecting the best of his shots to share. He was certain the others had done the same.

"Bar's open, Joe. Want a beer?"

That was Warren Ross. Branch Manager of the Mayfair Credit Union, where Joe did all his banking. He was a good banker but a lousy photographer. Right up there with smartphone selfies.

"Thanks, Warren."

"Did you get some good stuff?" Theo Parvlokas. Cop. Not bad with a camera but no patience. Probably came with the job.

"Yeah. I think so." Joe could afford to be modest. His photos would speak for him today.

"Where's Sam? Isn't he coming?" Andy Bookman. Joe's insurance agent. He was the one who put Sam up for membership in the club. Without even discussing it with Joe first.

Joe forced himself not to scowl. "He'll be late. Said not to wait on him." As if Sam Rice had any say in when they started. But they'd probably want to wait just to be polite. "Are we all set? Whose turn is it to go first?"

They started with Warren. His photos were, as expected, flat, pedestrian, and often over or under exposed. Each picture was discussed. What worked, what didn't, what he could have done differently. Joe enjoyed this part of the meeting. He knew the others appreciated his advice and it made him feel good to help. Especially tonight. Sam Rice's opinions were definitely *not* missed.

The next batch were better. Alan Fleece, a deacon in Joe's church. His wife sang in the choir with Claire. He was a decent photographer but Joe knew the pictures he brought tonight would blow these away.

One after another, they presented their pictures to the group. Some were really quite good.

"You know," he said to them, "we had a great opportunity today and I think we truly made the most of it."

There were words of agreement and some self-congratulations.

Now it was his turn. Joe cued up his first picture and took the remote.

"Hey, everyone. Sorry I'm late."

Sam Rice burst into the room and all attention turned to him. Joe ground his teeth and set the remote aside. He wasn't going to waste even one picture while the others were greeting Sam, getting him a beer, asking about his day, telling him how glad they were that he made it.

"Did you get some good shots?" Warren asked him.

"Didn't Joe tell you?" Sam looked over at Joe who waved his hand, giving the floor to Sam. "I have no idea. I had to work today so I set my camera on a timer to see if I could get anything that way." He held up his camera. "Haven't even looked at it yet. I thought I'd do it here and give you guys a good laugh."

There's was a round of laughter and some encouragement for him to load it up.

"Who's up now?' Sam asked.

"I was just getting started," Joe told him.

"Great. Let's look at yours. I know they'll be a hell of a lot better than these."

Joe hesitated. He was sure Sam was right, considering he would have shot after shot of empty sky. But Joe wanted them walking out of there talking about his work and if they saw Sam's fiasco last, that would be the topic of the evening. "No, let's load yours. I'm sure we're all curious to see what you got. I'll go last." He withdrew his flash drive and moved away from the laptop.

Sam stepped up and plugged his camera cable into the laptop's USB port.

"Okay. Now this was on autofocus so it should have stayed on maximum distance unless a bird flew by or something. I'll set it to auto-advance so we can flip right through these. Tell me to stop if you see something worth looking at."

The first shots were a total blur, but not the sky Joe was expecting. Then a dark shape began to appear and the others began to call out comments amid general laughter.

"Hey, Sam. That doesn't look like an eclipse to me."

"Yeah, I think your positioning was a little off, buddy."

The shape became clearer … it was the side of a building.

"Definitely not an eclipse."

"Hell, Sam, that's your house. I think you were set up a little low."

"No offense, Sam, but I've already seen your house. It not that photogenic."

The camera came into focus and revealed an image clearly visible through a second story window. A couple in bed, obviously having sex. Sam moved to pick up the remote but Theo beat him to it.

"No way, Sam, this is just getting good."

"Woo, Sammy boy. Now we know why you weren't taking pictures."

"Oh yeah. Look at that body. I would have skipped a total eclipse for that, too."

Joe clenched his fists in silent rage and looked away from the screen. Again, Sam had made himself the center of attention. After this, no one would care about Joe's pictures. The whole night had become about Sam screwing some bimbo.

"Oh, nice move there."

"I'm not sure that's even legal in this state."

"Hey, isn't that ..."

"Oh my God, it's ..."

"Holy shit."

Joe realized the room had grown quiet. He turned his gaze back to the screen.

* * * *

The Mayfair Amateur Photography Club didn't vote on a best picture that night. There was no need. Every man there knew the most memorable picture was the one Sam—with some inadvertent help—had taken through his own bedroom window ... a beautifully framed shot of Sam Rice having sex with Joe Harmon's wife.

LD Masterson lived on both coasts before becoming landlocked in Ohio. After twenty years managing computers for the American Red Cross, she now divides her time between writing and enjoying her grandchildren. Her short stories have been published in several anthologies and magazines and she's currently working on her second novel. LD is a member of Mystery Writers of America, Sisters in Crime, and the Western Ohio Writers' Association. Catch her at: ldmasterson-author.blogspot.com or ldmasterson.com

THE DARKEST HOUR

KAYE GEORGE

I think it was on a Saturday afternoon when Tom got the bright idea to rent out our spare room for the eclipse. I wish I'd just killed him then. I can see now that my desire totally eclipsed my judgment.

"Look at the path!" He waved a printout in front of me so that I couldn't see it. "It's coming right over our house. People will pay to stay here. We can rake it in."

When I grabbed the paper from him, I saw that the solar eclipse was going to be total where we lived, south of Knoxville, but it wasn't going to be total for the maximum amount of time.

"People are going to want to go south, where it lasts longer, Tom." I had to call him "Tom" to keep from calling him "Idiot." Tom had gotten a lot of hare-brained ideas during our four years of marriage, and this looked like it was going to be another one.

"No, they'll pay to stay here. I know they will."

I didn't ask who "they" were. If I kept quiet, he might forget about his scheme and let it die. I hoped it would get dropped like his idea to rent out our half-acre back yard as a paddock. How lovely it would have been to smell horse droppings from the kitchen window on a spring day. I hoped he would forget about it like he forgot about his plan to lead tours of Knoxville—after buying a fifteen-passenger van that a local church was getting rid of. The van sat in the back yard, useless since it didn't run. I hoped the idea would wither on the vine like the grape arbor he planted at the end of the back yard, planning on making, bottling, and selling his own wine before he learned how many years grape vines have to mature before they produce grapes. That is, if they don't die first, like his did.

Tom was good at what he did. He sold insurance. He provided a comfortable living for us. I worked at the local drug store part time, not because we needed more income, but because I wanted something to do while I was trying—still—to get pregnant. Every month I shed a tear or two when that awful red smear showed up, telling me I had failed again at conceiving a bundle of joy.

He was not, however, good at much of anything else. When we moved into the two story house, he decided it needed a wall removed to make the living space more open. I grew alarmed and called in a structural engineer before he got it completely down. Good thing, too. It was a load-bearing wall and the ceiling would have caved in if he'd finished. It cost quite a bit to rebuild the damage he did.

Another time he thought we needed a more modern toilet in the master bath. Apparently, he hadn't turned the water off completely before he pulled the old one. The flood made it necessary to replace the floor, the bottom molding, and the cabinet for the sink, plus have a lot of work done in the deluged crawl space. We still had occasional rodent problems, probably because they thought they could get water under our house.

The worst may have been the spacious balcony he built outside our bedroom. It was cantilevered, mostly because he liked that word, I thought. However, I was afraid to stand on it after my first foray. It wobbled and swayed under my weight for a moment before I stepped back into the bedroom.

"It's fine," he said, spreading his arms to indicate how marvelous his balcony was. "It won't come down. It's physics. And leverage."

That never convinced me to spend time there.

So, in comparison, renting out a room didn't seem like it would do that much harm.

He decided to use Angie's List rather than Craig's, since he wanted people who weren't local to see it.

Unnecessary Expense Number One.

We were flooded with applicants. Since we only had one guest room, we had to turn down about a hundred and fifty people.

"How about this one, honey?" he said.

They gave their ages as 65 and 75 and the younger one used a walker. "Do you think they might have trouble with the stairs?"

"Yeah, you're right, Arden. I don't want any heart attacks in the house." He scrolled down to another one. "These two guys?"

"Are you serious? They're eighteen and nineteen. And they named their frat as a reference on their app. They'll invite their buddies and party until our house is destroyed."

We combed through dozens of them.

"Maybe," I said, "desirable people have friends and relatives that will put them up."

"These two look harmless."

He showed me a gay couple. One of the guys liked to paint, he said in the comments. I'd always kind of wanted to learn to do that. I'd never told Tom about my secret dream. He would think it a waste of time, not practical. I envisioned me forming a friendship with them and learning on the sly. It would be fun. "Let's have them. I think they'd be good."

He ignored me.

"Here's one!" He clicked on a response from a normal-looking young couple, about our age.

"They look fine." I took a closer look. The guy looked large and truculent. Rather fascinating. The brunette woman was petite and gorgeous, model material. "What all do they say?"

Of course, Tom hadn't thought to ask any pertinent questions about lifestyle, neatness-level, or substance abuse.

"Just that they don't know anyone in this area. They live not too far north of here, moved from California a year ago."

"Okay, let's rent to them." I wanted to get this decision done.

"Oh, and they have a baby."

I couldn't answer right away. My feelings warred inside me. I loved babies, but we'd been trying for so long to have one. I was beginning to think we never would. Did I want to have one in the house? Would it make me feel worse? It would only be a few days. Two, three at the most. I gave a mental shrug and nodded at him.

"It's weeks until the eclipse." He didn't notice the grim look that went with my acquiescence. "I'll be able to get the yard in good shape by then."

I thought he meant trim the bushes and mow the lawn, but no. He came home the next day with a new grill.

"Do we need a new grill?" There was nothing at all wrong with ours. I knew that since I was the one who usually used it.

"We need a bigger one, so we can serve our guests. Look, it has five burners!"

"Why does a grill need burners? It's not a stove."

"It can use propane, wood, or charcoal. Or all of them at once."

"Tom, we don't need this. How much did it cost?"

When he didn't answer me, I knew the answer. Too much.

Unnecessary Expense Number Two.

I never did find a receipt for it. He must have paid for it from his business account because I couldn't find a record anywhere. I could only imagine—thousands, I was pretty sure. I seethed whenever the sun glinted off that big stainless steel thing, hunkering in the corner of the patio.

A couple of weeks later it was lawn furniture. I knew ours wasn't in the best of shape, but Holy Helios, we didn't need this stuff.

"How many guests are you expecting? I thought it was a couple with a baby. Are they bringing relatives?"

He lifted one shoulder. "You never know when we might want to throw a party, now that we have the grill."

Was he trying to impress the gorgeous brunette?

It was delivered by a store van. First they hauled out a glass topped table and six chairs, then they dragged what looked like living room furniture. An ell-shaped cushioned couch, low coffee table, and several ottoman-like seats, also cushioned.

"The patio looks crowded, Tom. This stuff doesn't all fit here."

"Sure it does. We can move this big pot." He heaved my large pot of geraniums and daisies onto the lawn.

I seethed.

Unnecessary Expense Number Three. Did that count as three strikes, making one out?

When I realized my foot was tapping double-time on the patio, my teeth were grinding, and my fists were so tight my palms were hurting from my nails, I had to say something. "Put that pot back onto the patio. Right now. I worked hard to grow those flowers and the pot will kill the grass there."

Maybe the reference to harm that might befall his lawn was what convinced him, but by the end of my short tirade he had moved from truculent to reluctant, but compliant. The pot came back to the patio, although awfully near to the barbeque.

I busied myself tidying and freshening the guest room over the next few days. The time was drawing near. I found a crib in a garage sale and it came with crib sheets and a waterproof pad. Would they bring a blanket for the baby? It would be August, so they wouldn't need heavy blankets, or any, really. But I put a baby blanket on the crib and a darling lightweight coverlet I found at Beyond Baths on the bed.

Tom appeared in the doorway. "What are you doing?"

"Look." I gestured around the room at the newly made bed, the crib in the corner, the second-hand dresser I'd picked up at a resale shop and polished to a shine. I'd sewed gingham curtains that picked up the colors in the quilt and hung some framed art prints of Monet and Van Gogh. "Doesn't it look nice? I think I'd love to stay here myself."

"Did you buy all this stuff? How much did it cost?"

"A fraction of what you've spent so far."

I was fuming and didn't speak to Tom for about three days, slamming his meals down in front of him and eating at the counter myself. The vision of him being snake-bitten, poisoned, and eventually dying painfully, brought about by my last comment to him, comforted me somewhat.

During those three days, I asked myself over and over, why had I married him? What had I seen in him? Did he have good qualities, besides holding a job? Did we have anything in common? I resolved to see a lawyer now and explore leaving him after this eclipse fiasco was over.

It was a few days before I got in to see the one my divorced cousin recommended, but I was still worked up when I went in. I had, by then, started speaking to Tom again, but only a word here and there, usually *yes* or *no*.

The meeting at the lawyer's office started out badly and got worse.

"Have a seat," he said, a corpulent, scruffy sort of guy with a bad shave. He would have looked better if he hadn't bothered and had gone for the scruffy look. Instead, it looked like he needed a new blade in his razor. And a new suit. Maybe a cleaner shirt that smelled better.

He motioned me to a chair before his battered wooden desk.

"So you're here about a divorce?"

Since he was a divorce attorney, that should have been obvious.

I asked what my options were. Divorce, separation, and staying married, he said.

Thanks, Captain Obvious. "I'd like to know what the expenses would be."

He drummed a pen on his blotter and talked around my question until I was ready to leave.

The figure he finally named for the no-fault was higher than I could have imagined. I wouldn't be able to save that much from my drug store salary. It didn't take me long to thank him and leave.

I walked around the streets outside his downtown office for about an hour, considering my options. There were ways of leaving. There was divorce. There was moving out. And there was another way. I was the beneficiary on his rather substantial company life insurance policy. After all, he sold the stuff. If he were to, well, die, I would be fine.

I started daydreaming. Without Tom in the house, I could redo the master bedroom, put in a larger, deeper tub, maybe one with little shelves all around.

The more I thought about life without Tom, but with his insurance money, the more I smiled at home. Maybe he took my random, spontaneous smiling to mean I was happy. He warmed up and started being extra solicitous. He even took me to the steak place we used to go when we were first married. He apologized for all the money he'd spent and admitted he'd gone overboard.

"It'll be fun having someone here to appreciate the place, won't it? Then we can enjoy it after they leave."

He stayed in and watched my favorite TV show with me two nights in a row, even gave me neck rubs. It was starting to work. I remembered what I had seen in him when we first met. He had lovely dark, wavy hair and deep, bedroom eyes to go with it. And his hands were gentle and sensitive when he touched me.

The day of the arrival of our guests came, two days before the eclipse, Saturday the 19th. They showed up in the late afternoon, driving their huge SUV up the driveway.

We were sitting on the front porch. Tom hurried down the steps to meet them and I followed. The man hopped out and shook Tom's hand.

"Hi. Baxter. And this is Melanie." He was a huge man, at least six five, and solidly built. He waved toward his wife, who was just as pretty as her picture. She got out on the other side and stuck her head inside the car to unbuckle the baby.

"Glad to meet you," Tom said with a big grin.

"We're glad you're here safe," I said, smiling at them, too. "We're Tom and Arden."

It was grins all around, except for the baby, who began squalling as soon as Melanie lifted her out of the car.

"And this is Sadie," said Baxter, ignoring the fact that Sadie was upset at the sight of us.

Melanie sat on the porch rocker soothing the baby and Tom helped Baxter with their luggage, bumping them up the stairs. They had quite a few suitcases for three days. Some had to be put in the hallway since they didn't all fit into the room.

When they came down Baxter went to his wife to try to comfort the still sobbing Sadie. He patted the baby's tiny back with his huge paw.

The baby was finally settling into a case of adorable hiccups.

"May I?" I asked, stretching my arms toward Sadie.

As I held her and rocked, I couldn't tear my eyes from her tiny, pudgy face. So expressive, so flawless.

"What's that?" Melanie shrieked, pointing to the front yard.

Tom squinted where she was pointing. "It's a rat. We've had some trouble with rodents. I'll have to put out more arsenic." He turned to me. "Do we have any more?"

"It should be in the shed," I said, softly, so I wouldn't disturb the baby.

"But they're not in the house, are they?" Melanie chewed her lower lip.

Tom assured her they never had been. I guess he didn't count the crawl space.

Tom leaned close to me and said, "They seem like nice people."

"They're not too good with the poor baby," I whispered back. She had calmed the instant I picked her up. I seemed to have a knack.

Baxter took her after a few minutes. I went into the kitchen and brought out lemonade, which they accepted, draining the glasses and asking for refills.

When they finished, they trooped upstairs. Sadie's hiccups were gone, but she was making tiny fussy noises now.

Tom and I sat on the porch enjoying the quiet for a few moments until they came back down.

"When is dinner?" Baxter asked, looming over us.

Tom looked at me, I have no idea why.

"We don't furnish dinner," I said.

They both looked surprised. I turned away, tired of them already.

"Well, do you have a list of local restaurants?" Melanie asked, her voice thin and whiny. The words "at least" were implied.

I fished my phone out of my pocket and brought up a list, which they could just as easily have done. "Do any of these look good?" I asked handed my phone to Melanie.

"Are there any that you recommend to your guests?" Baxter asked.

A light went off in my head—they thought we rented out our room all the time.

Tom laughed. "This is a one-off for us, just for the eclipse. We've never rented out the room before. But we can do a barbeque tomorrow night if you want to."

Melanie brightened. "That sounds good. What time will we eat?"

Tom shrugged and gave me a glance. "Six? Does that sound good?"

That was our usual dinner time. I supposed it would be all right.

Baxter looked pained. "That's a little late for us. What with getting Sadie to bed and all. Could it be earlier?"

"Five thirty?" I countered.

"How about five." Melanie ignored me and gave Tom a definite flirty look, tilting her head and batting her lashes.

Tom grinned back at her. "Five it is."

Of course, after they left to scout out a place to eat that night, Tom ran to the premium grocery store and got five of the most expensive tenderloin fillets they had.

Unnecessary Expense Number Four. I asked myself if we were starting on the first strike of the second out, or if this was a Final Four sort of strike.

"You got five steaks?" I unpacked his grocery bag in the kitchen, wondering if he'd invited the butcher, or maybe the checkout lady.

"You never know how hungry people will be." He stood in the doorway, fidgeting. "Look, I have to run some errands. I'll be right back."

Before I could ask him where he was going, he ran out the back door, started up the Honda, and drove off.

In a couple of hours, Baxter came back in a taxi with a wailing Sadie. He jiggled her as he plodded from the driveway toward the house. He looked weary. Maybe he was tired of that baby crying all the time.

"Are you okay?" I asked.

His eyes squinted as he looked up at me. He mounted the porch steps. "We think Sadie is sick. Melanie stopped at an emergency place to try to get some medicine for her."

Maybe the baby was ill. "Oh, I'm sorry she doesn't feel well. Is there anything I can do?" I wanted to hold her again, but he turned away.

"I think we just need to take a rest. Melanie should be here soon."

He trudged upstairs, holding the baby awkwardly. I sat on the porch and rocked. I had nothing to do. Tom and I always ordered pizza on Saturday night, so I wouldn't be preparing dinner. The sun, that glowing orb that would disappear on Monday for a couple of minutes, was heading toward the horizon. I must have dozed, because when I raised my head up it was dark. The Honda was still gone. I was a bit alarmed. When I called him and got no answer, I texted: *Are you OK?*

Nothing. Dead silence.

I went inside and heard Baxter walking around upstairs, his footsteps slow and heavy. I went up to check on them. He opened the door to my knock and I asked if Sadie was feeling better.

"No. She acts like she's in pain. And Melanie's not back yet," he said through gritted teeth. "I don't know what the hell is taking her so long. She knows I don't like to be left alone with the baby."

That gave me a dark, sick feeling. Tom wasn't back either. I remembered that flirty look Melanie had given him. Had I seen a reaction from Tom? I thought I had noticed a flare of jealousy from Baxter. Were they together somewhere right now, too busy to respond to calls and texts?

Then I saw the baby, lying in the crib. She had wadded up the coverlet with her pudgy fist and stuffed it in her mouth, chewing on it. I was afraid she might bite off a piece and choke, so I went to her and eased the cover from her mouth. And smelled a poopy baby. I fanned my face. What an odor, from such a tiny being!

"Looks like she needs changing." Baxter bit out the words. "Will you please leave us so I can clean her up?"

What a rude man. I slammed the door as I left.

Tom and Melanie were coming in the front door together as I stomped down the first two stairs. Her eyes were glowing and Tom was giving her a toothy grin. I stood very still and my body turned cold. They didn't see me as they drew close, embraced, and kissed. I crossed my arms in front of me like a shield. She tossed her hair and started to run up the stairs.

"Did you get some medicine for Sadie?" I blocked her way, ice dripping from my words.

"Oh." She stopped and had the good grace to blush.

I looked down at Tom, but he had already gone into the kitchen.

"I couldn't find anything. I think she's teething anyway. She'll be okay."

How could she be so unconcerned about her own baby? "Where did you try?"

"Just everywhere. Excuse me." She brushed past me, ran up the rest of the flight and into the guest room, the first room at the top of the stairs.

I lingered midway down, not wanting to confront Tom in the kitchen. I crept down to the foyer and out the front door to resume my seat on the rocker. A core of coldness inside me grew hot, my anger building until my head felt ready to explode and my ears rang like a clanging carillon. The strain of wanting a baby more than I ever had, plus my unfaithful husband, churned inside me, wanting to explode like a super nova.

Restless, I walked around to the back yard and stopped. Was that Melanie by the shed? Maybe she and Baxter had quarreled too. I left her to have her privacy and returned to the porch. Eventually, Tom stuck his head out the door. "Oh, there you are. I've been looking for you. Want to order a pizza now?"

I couldn't have eaten anything for fear I would throw it up. My stomach roiled like the Titanic as it was sinking. "I already ate."

He came up beside me and ruffled my hair. "You always have room for pizza, right?"

I slapped his hand away.

He sat in the chair next to me. "So what should we do tonight? TV?"

"Where have you been all this time?"

"Errands."

"Where? You didn't bring anything home."

"Couldn't find what I needed." He stared straight ahead.

I studied his face. "Funny. That's exactly what Melanie said."

He whipped around toward me. "Huh? What do you mean?"

"She went to get some medicine for the baby and spent the longest time not finding what she needed."

He looked away again.

I shivered, even though the evening air was warm. "It's almost like you two went to the same place," I said softly.

He grunted.

I got up and went inside. Could I rescue my fragile marriage? Did I want to?

A wave of calm coolness washed over me. I thought I knew the answer to that.

* * * *

Sunday was strained. We had the barbeque. Tom cooked outside on his new grill, even though rain sprinkled on and off while he cooked. Melanie made it her mission to bring Tom a second, then a third beer and stayed out drinking with him, companionably, under an umbrella.

When the rain stopped, the air was muggy and sticky, as it often is in August in Knoxville. We ate inside since the new furniture was wet. I could feel steam rising inside my head to match that rising from the patio tiles as the sun warmed them. For once, Sadie was smiling and happy, banging a spoon on my polished mahogany table with gusto. Such a cute kid.

I caught the looks Tom and Melanie exchanged. They seemed as steamy as my head and the patio. I wondered what would happen after tomorrow.

Baxter and Melanie both declined dessert, a blueberry cobbler I had made from scratch. Still fuming, I dropped a plate onto a glass rinsing the dishes to load the dishwasher, and they both shattered.

"Here, let me clean that up," Tom said, coming in as I was sweeping the shards from the floor.

Maybe a guilty husband could turn out to be a good thing. Maybe he would be super helpful to make up for his indiscretion. I left the room and sat in the darkened, quiet den while he swept, thinking about my options. I hadn't yet come to any definite conclusion.

Would there be an opportunity to take care of my problem during the eclipse? How dark would it get? Could I get away with something, unseen, during the total part of the total eclipse? My iPad was sitting on the end table, so I did a search. It seemed it would be very dark, like the dead of night, at the height of the eclipse, which would last a little over a minute here in the village of Farragut. So, I pondered, what could be accomplished in a minute that would make me a grieving widow? Or a widow, anyway.

* * * *

The big day came. I had mixed a pitcher of margaritas and carried them upstairs. They all agreed that it would be nice, even romantic, to view the eclipse from our bedroom balcony. Baxter had run out for more diapers and wasn't back yet. Sadie was napping on our bed, close by, as the sun started to disappear. We all looked silly in our eclipse glasses, but I had to admit that it was exciting watching the moon move in front of the sun and slowly eat away at it. The air grew cool and a slight breeze came up. I heard Baxter's car drive up. I stepped into the bedroom, ostensibly to refill my glass. I gazed upon the perfect little face of Sadie, wishing she were mine, teething, spitting up, poop, and whatever else she came with.

I flicked off the bedroom lights so there would be utter darkness at the moment of maximum eclipse.

Baxter thundered up the stairs. "Am I late? Did I miss it?"

Melanie walked in off the balcony. "You're just in time, dear." With her back to us, she poured a glass from the pitcher and handed it to him. "Here, I fixed you a drink."

"Don't forget your dark glasses," I called as he grabbed the drink and put one foot onto the balcony. He transferred his weight, ready for the next step, when I heard a groan, then a creak, then splintering and the balcony gave way and crashed down. It took Tom and Melanie with it, but I felt Baxter manage to step back into the bedroom in time.

At that moment, the sun disappeared and darkness reigned.

We were both silent, unable to see anything, hearing the clatter of the wood and the metal chairs, and the screams of Tom and Melanie. The brief screams stopped abruptly. Another breeze, cooler now, sprang up.

I heard Baxter gulp down his drink, then silence for another moment, then his heavy footfalls started for the stairs.

Sadie awoke and cooed in the darkness.

I felt for the dresser and set my drink down. Making my way to the bed, I patted Sadie on her diapered bottom.

Baxter's footsteps faltered, he let out a gurgling sound, and crashed to the floor.

I jumped up and turned on the lights. Baxter's large body lay writhing on the floor, in agony. I remembered seeing Melanie by the shed, where we stored the arsenic. I had meant for all three of them to fall. Only two had, but it seemed Melanie had finished the job for me.

I dialed 9-1-1, told them someone was ill at my house and there had also been an accident. It was only a few minutes before I heard the sirens in the distance. They neared while I picked Sadie up and cuddled her. I nuzzled the top of her head. She smelled wonderful.

It was eventually determined that the balcony incident, which killed both Tom and Melanie, was an accident.

However, I was arrested for poisoning Baxter and lost possession of the precious baby. I had gotten away with killing Tom and Melanie. Eventually, though, I was convicted of the one crime I didn't do that day. My desire for that baby eclipsed my judgment.

Kaye George, national-bestselling and multiple-award-winning author, writes four series: Imogene Duckworthy; Cressa Carraway Musical Mysteries; People of the Wind (Neanderthal), and as Janet Cantrell, the Fat Cat series. She's working on a new cozy series for Lyrical Press. You can find her short stories in anthologies and magazines and her collection, *A Patchwork of Stories*. She reviews for *Suspense Magazine*. She lives in Knoxville, TN.

BABY KILLER

MARGARET S. HAMILTON

Mandy Malone woke, tangled in sweaty sheets, hearing the chant "Baby Killer, Baby Killer." In her nightmare, the trees had whispered the phrase. The words became louder. "Baby Killer, Baby Killer." Was someone outside? The upstairs windows were open to the cool night air. Motion-activated floodlights flicked on and off. Could it be the crazy cat lady? She'd never come during the night.

Mandy wrapped her arms around her pregnant belly. She and her husband, Andy, loved their first-born, gender not revealed, nicknamed "Jumbo." What felt like a baby elephant fired off several kicks. A future soccer player. Pulling herself to her feet, Mandy grabbed her phone and stumbled downstairs.

In the kitchen, she flicked on the electric kettle and unwrapped a chamomile tea bag. Thumbing through her phone, Mandy checked for a message from Andy. Nothing. He had left Jericho, Ohio the previous day on a camping trip to Tennessee with his astronomer buddies, determined to experience the path of totality—the moon completely covering the sun—during the solar eclipse. Out of cell range, of course. Mandy sighed. Andy had landed a tenure-track position at the local college and was determined to share his eclipse experience with his students, including videos.

Munching on a handful of crackers, Mandy sank into a lounge chair in the sunroom adjoining the kitchen. The sky grew lighter, the air oppressive ahead of an approaching band of thunderstorms. A blurred streak flashed by. Sitting up, Mandy scanned the backyard. The feral cat they called Bobbie, large and tawny with a white underbelly and short, black-tipped tail, usually returned to her litter around daybreak. Animal control had advised Mandy that feral cats were a problem in the college campus area and not to feed or approach the cat.

* * * *

Later that morning, after her routine check-up, Mandy paused to send a text to Andy: *Jumbo ok, 3 more weeks*, before she left the town medical center. The voice in her head resumed its chant. "Baby Killer. Baby Killer." Cradling her huge belly, Mandy sagged to a nearby bench. Not again. She put her hands over her ears and started to cry. Was she hallucinating? None of her birthing class friends had the problem.

The chanting grew louder. "Baby Killer. Baby Killer." With difficulty, Mandy shifted to look behind the bench. She wasn't hearing things. It was Florence Kennedy, the crazy cat lady, wearing her usual cat print muumuu and carrying an umbrella. When Florence had discovered that Mandy lived in her former family home, she had started following Mandy on her daily walks, muttering that eclipses killed babies.

Florence brandished her umbrella at Mandy and continued her chant. "Baby Killer, Baby Killer."

Thunder rumbled in the sky and Mandy saw the first cracks of lightning. She'd walked to the doctor's office, anxious to complete her daily hour of exercise before the storm. Grasping the arm of the bench, Mandy rolled sideways and pulled herself up. She had a coffee date with a birthing class friend in fifteen minutes.

Ella Gunderson drove up in her rusty Suburban and ran down the window. "Mandy, glad I caught you before the storm. Climb in."

Mandy stepped on the running board and heaved herself into the front seat. Panting, she pulled her seatbelt straps above and below her belly, and clicked the buckle.

Ella handed her a tissue. "Everything all right?"

Mandy dabbed her face and blew her nose. "With the baby, sure. Three more weeks, at least." Mandy gestured toward Florence. "She says I'm a baby killer."

Ella clambered out and confronted Florence. "Are you harassing Mandy again?"

Florence blinked. "She's a baby killer."

"No, she isn't. Stop upsetting her."

"The eclipse is coming. Babies die," Florence said.

"Solar eclipses do not kill babies. Not my baby and not Mandy's baby."

Florence opened her umbrella and wandered away, followed by a scraggly calico cat.

Ella reached into a cooler in the back seat and handed Mandy a can of decaf iced tea. "The kids are at the library collecting their summer reading awards. Instead of getting coffee, we can chat on the way to pick them up."

Mandy sipped her tea. "Four kids in school all day for the first time. What will you do with yourself?"

Ella laughed. "Number five's gonna be a breeze. I'm back teaching after the new year, with Mom as my daycare backup. This baby's definitely a team effort. The kids read stories to my belly every night."

The storm broke, the rain falling in torrents during their five-minute drive. "Storm bands are moving through," Ella said. "Headed northeast. Andy will have good weather for the eclipse in Tennessee, and so should we."

"I wish I hadn't told him to go," Mandy said. "I had nightmares last night."

Ella glanced at her. "Eclipse nightmares?"

Mandy nodded and closed her eyes.

At the library, the Gunderson kids climbed aboard, each carrying a new paperback book.

Kirsten, the oldest, unfolded a piece of paper. "Mom and Mandy, the library has a special solar eclipse exhibit. The kids took forever picking out their books, so I made some notes." She scanned the page. "Do you know not to hold a knife during the eclipse? And not to touch your belly? It will give the baby a birthmark. And don't watch the eclipse. The baby will have a cleft palate."

"All superstitions. Ignore them," Ella said. "Mandy and I will be inside the library during the eclipse. I promise I'll sit in a chair and take a nap. You kids can watch with the special welder's glasses Dad ordered."

Kirsten continued to read her notes. "Do you know about red panties with a safety pin? It's the modern version of old Aztec and Mayan beliefs, when pregnant women wore a red string and an arrowhead to prevent birth defects."

Ella and Mandy exchanged smiles. "We're covered in that department," Mandy said.

Ella's twin boys shrieked with laughter. "Are we finished talking about underwear?" one of them asked.

"Yeah, is it lunchtime yet?" the other one tuned in.

"Kirsty, read me my book," their younger sister said.

As Ella pulled into Mandy's driveway, a large cat darted across the yard. "Mandy, is that your cat? It must be close to twenty pounds," Ella said.

"She's a feral cat. We call her Bobbie," Mandy said.

"You're not feeding her?" Ella asked.

"No way."

Florence Kennedy walked around the corner of the house, carrying an empty plastic bag. As she approached the passenger side of the car, Mandy ran down the window.

"You haven't fed Kitty," Florence said. "She's hungry cuz she's nursing. I left her food on the back stoop."

Ella climbed out of the van. "You shouldn't leave cat food outside. It attracts raccoons and skunks. You know that."

Florence started to snivel. "I have to take care of my kitties." She pointed at Mandy. "She won't do it."

Mandy pulled out her phone and handed Ella her house keys. "Why don't you guys grab a popsicle while I phone the police to take Florence home?"

"I am home," Florence said. "This is my house."

Ella shooed her kids inside the bungalow.

Mandy watched Florence wander around the front yard, calling for the cats she'd owned over the years. She had seen photos of the Sears bungalow, a reeking, flea-infested wreck, before the college had purchased it. Now rebuilt, it nestled in a shady grove planted with ferns and pink impatiens, hanging baskets of fuchsias on the porch. Perfect for raising a family.

Officer Bethany Schmidt pulled up in her police SUV. "Florence, what are you doing here? I'll give you a lift home."

Florence backed away, shaking her head. "No ... no, this is my house. For me and my kitties. My baby lives here, too."

Mandy knew Florence had dementia, with no family to care for her. After a competency hearing, she had been moved into a local assisted-living facility. Florence was otherwise healthy, and frequently managed to wander off. The police watched out for Florence and drove her back to her new home when they found her roaming around town.

But this was the first Mandy had heard of Florence having a child.

Officer Schmidt assisted her into the front seat of the SUV and fastened Florence's seatbelt. "You can ride in the front seat, but don't touch any of the buttons on the dashboard or console."

Mandy bit her lip, trying not to laugh. She'd heard that Florence delighted in turning on the siren and flashing lights. She walked around the car to have a private word with the police officer.

"There's a feral cat living in the woods. Florence left food for it."

"I'll alert animal control," Officer Schmidt said. "A male bobcat was spotted this week in the college bird sanctuary. Your so-called feral cat might be its mate."

"But the sanctuary's fenced to keep the coyotes out," Mandy said.

"Bobcats have been known to climb trees." She turned her ignition key. "Any chance you can stay with a friend until your husband gets back?"

"I guess so."

"One more thing I need to share," Officer Schmidt said. "Chief wants to put a lid on talk about babies dying during the eclipse." She frowned. "We still have an open case from the 1998 solar eclipse, when a pregnant woman disappeared and was never found. The local paper agreed not to re-publish the story, and we asked the library to pull the original newspapers from their exhibit."

"How awful," Mandy said. "Ella's daughter, Kirsten, saw the exhibit this morning."

"Could you and your pregnant friends stick together, all in one place, during the eclipse?" Officer Schmidt asked.

"I'll get the word out on social media. We'll have a get-together in the library."

The bright blue Jericho Senior Center van pulled up. A woman wearing scrubs and rubber clogs got out and approached Officer Schmidt's side of the police SUV. "Did you find Florence? We suspected she might be here."

"I'll drive Florence back," Officer Schmidt said. "I need to review your security procedures."

"It won't happen again," the woman said. She walked around the car and grabbed Florence's door handle.

Officer Schmidt clicked the door locks. "We'll see you back at the Senior Center."

"Have it your way." The woman in scrubs stormed back to the van and sped away.

* * * *

Pulling open the glass storm door, Mandy stepped into the bungalow main floor great room. With additional support beams, the room extended the length of the house to the kitchen. She admired her favorite feature, the original oak mantle over the fireplace, its ornate carvings surrounding a mirror sanded and stained to their original beauty.

Mandy found Ella in the sunroom lying in a lounge chair, Kirsten reading to her sister, the boys sitting on the back stoop eating popsicles. She slumped into a rocking chair.

"Mandy, you're exhausted," Ella said. "Did you get any sleep last night?"

Mandy yawned and nodded. "Some. I had dreams about the trees whispering 'Baby Killer.' I thought it was a nightmare, but when I woke, the motion-detector floodlights flicked on and off."

"It might have been Florence." Ella sat up. "I want you to pack a bag. You're staying with us until Andy gets back. No more nonsense about baby killers." She opened the door to the back stoop and picked up a plant saucer filled with cat food.

"Officer Schmidt thinks we've got a bobcat in the woods," Mandy said.

"All the more reason not to stay here."

* * * *

Mandy and Ella dropped the kids and a babysitter at the local pool, and headed for the Town Clerk's office. Eagle Scouts had created a comprehensive database of birth, marriage, and death certificates. The women discovered that Florence Mary Kennedy had been born in Jericho in 1934. Mandy jotted down the names of Florence's parents.

"Florence said she had a baby," Mandy said.

"Dementia," Ella said.

Mandy shook her head. "I think she's telling the truth." They checked, but found no birth certificate for Florence's child.

Ella found death certificates for Florence's parents in the mid-nineties. "Florence was on her own for over twenty years, with only her cats for company."

Mandy stood up and yawned. "We need to elevate our legs. Let's go back to your house and research eclipses."

They stretched out on Ella's queen-sized bed, their ankles propped on the low headboard. Mandy scrolled through her tablet. "Solar eclipse in 1954, when Florence was twenty." She turned her head. "What do you think? She could have had a baby during the eclipse and lost it."

Ella opened one eye. "Or she kept cats instead." She closed it. "We've got an hour till the kids are dropped off. Let's make the most of it."

* * * *

Eclipse Day, August twenty-first, dawned crisp and cool, a whiff of fall in the air. Before school started the next day, it seemed to Mandy that all of Jericho was assembled on the Town Green for lunch, games, and eclipse viewing. Grills for hotdogs and hamburgers lined one end of the Green, picnic tables with red checkered cloths scattered under the towering maple trees. The high school jazz band played in the gazebo as shrieking children raced in circles.

Kirsten and her middle school friends had organized children's games on the barricaded streets around the Green: cornhole, jump rope, and four square. Frisbees flew through the air, impromptu soccer scrimmages and stickball games nearby.

Mandy and Ella joined a group of birthing class friends, the self-proclaimed Red Panties Society, in the library adjacent to the Green. They would watch the festivities from the comfort of upholstered chairs. Mandy texted Andy another update. Out of cell range and missing all the fun.

Mandy saw Florence pass by, accompanied by a woman in blue hospital scrubs. They headed up a side street toward her bungalow. Pulling herself upright, she texted Ella.

Ella read the text, announced, "Kid crisis," and beckoned to Mandy to follow her.

As the eclipse started, Ella sped through the quiet streets to Mandy's bungalow. The birds roosted in the trees, singing their twilight songs. The gentle breeze stopped. Mandy shivered. The temperature had dropped ten degrees in the past hour. The sky grew darker.

"Got your keys?" Ella asked.

Mandy pulled them out of her purse. She and Ella walked along the edge of the woods to the back of the house, their shadows an odd shape on the grass. Mandy willed herself not to look at the disappearing sun. Rounding the corner of the house, they tiptoed up the back steps. They found the back door ajar, a key in the deadbolt. With Mandy in the lead, they pushed open the door and slipped into the laundry room. Mandy paused to send Officer Schmidt a quick text.

Mandy could hear voices from the living room, Florence's characteristic mumble and a more strident female voice, probably that of the woman in scrubs.

A cat mewed at her feet. Mandy gasped and put a hand over her mouth, her heart pounding. Only the scraggly calico cat, not the bobcat. Ella shooed the cat through the kitchen door. Twitching its ears, the cat headed for the living room.

"There you are," Florence cooed. "Find a nice birdy for breakfast?" The cat yowled in reply.

The sky grew darker. Only a few remnants of sun remained as the moon's shadow crept across it. Jericho would have a ninety-one percent eclipse, not totality.

In the dim light, Mandy and Ella crept through the kitchen doorway and hid in a corner of the dining area, next to a tall bookcase.

The woman with Florence clicked on a lamp as the calico cat leaped up on the mantle.

"That's where Papa put my papers," Florence said. "The papers about my baby." She shuffled to the mantle and poked at the ornate carvings.

"This is getting us nowhere," the woman in scrubs said. She pulled a pocket flashlight out of her pocket and jabbed at the carving. The cat hissed and clawed her.

"Ow," she shrieked and brandished the flashlight. "Florence, where are the papers?"

Florence continued to poke around the mirror. One side of its frame fell off, revealing a small compartment.

"That's more like it," the woman in scrubs said. She reached inside and pulled out a piece of paper and what looked like an old photo. Walking over to the lamp, she quickly scanned them. "Let's see. Florence Mary Kennedy, father not named, had a baby boy, stillborn. Signed by Jane Adams, Midwife."

She looked at Florence, who cuddled her cat. "Your baby was born dead, on June 30th, 1954."

"The eclipse killed my baby. I told her," Florence said.

The woman examined the black-and-white photo, turning it over to read the inscription on the back. "Thank you for giving us your beautiful baby boy. He is our greatest joy."

Florence buried her face in the cat's fur. "Eclipses kill babies."

"You had a son, Florence. You told me you had a daughter. Your son was put up for adoption." She handed Florence the photo. The sky lightened, and the birds started chirping. Mandy heard a car door slam in the driveway.

"Who's that?" the woman asked. "You said the people who live here were away."

Mandy heard someone slip in the back door. She sighed with relief. Officer Schmidt. Beckoning her into the dining area, Mandy and Ella, one at a time, maneuvered their oversized bodies back into the kitchen.

Officer Schmidt flicked on the dining area chandelier and continued to the front of the house. "Find what you were looking for?" She held up a door key. "Where did you get the deadbolt key?"

The woman in scrubs went on the offensive. "It's all Florence's doing. She wanted the documents her father hid in a compartment over the fireplace."

Mandy walked back into the dining area. "We overheard everything. Florence had a son. The baby's father wasn't named. We didn't find the birth certificate in the town records."

"That's got nothing to do with me," the woman said.

"As a matter of fact, it does," Officer Schmidt said. "The Department finally received your out-of-state background information. Deborah

Clark, you're wanted in New Jersey for stealing from elderly patients by posing as their daughter or niece. Still at it, are you, hoping to find evidence of Florence's child?"

"Florence asked me to help her," the woman said.

"I doubt that Florence took the key," Mandy said. "Did you steal it or have a duplicate made?" She took a deep breath. "No wonder I heard voices whispering in the windows. Was that you, too, trying to scare me into leaving the house?" Mandy walked toward Deborah Clark.

"What was your plan?" Mandy asked. "To pretend to be Florence's long lost child? It's a little late for that. The proceeds from the sale of her house were put in a trust to pay for her care."

Deborah Clark turned and headed for the front door. She yanked the knob, but the deadbolt held fast.

Officer Schmidt snapped handcuffs on her wrists. "I'll stick around till my backup arrives to take Florence home."

"I'll lock the back door and sit with Florence on the front porch for a few minutes," Mandy said.

Florence poked at the hidden compartment in the fireplace before she made her way to the porch. Sitting in a rocking chair, the calico cat on her lap, she gently touched the photo of her son.

"What was your son's name?" Mandy asked.

"William, the same as his daddy." She smiled. "Billy was my sweetheart, but Mama and Papa didn't like him."

"You're not a baby killer, are you?" Mandy asked.

Florence cuddled the cat. "No baby killers at this house."

"Florence, do you remember the solar eclipse in 1998? Your parents had recently died."

Florence closed her eyes. "Eclipses kill babies." She whispered, "Eclipses kill mommies, too."

"Your mama?" Mandy asked.

"The mommy who looked like you. A man chased the mommy into the woods. The mommy didn't come back." She held up a pendant on a chain. "I found the mommy's necklace."

Ella cleared her throat. "What's she talking about?"

A tear trickled down Mandy's cheek. "An open case from 1998, when a pregnant woman disappeared. Officer Schmidt will need to request a cadaver dog in addition to animal control."

Her phone pinged with a text message from Andy. *Got video of eclipse. On my way home. Can't find my house key.*

She texted a reply. *Key found, mystery solved, Jumbo fine.*

Margaret S. Hamilton has published short stories in *Mysterical-E, Kings River Life*, and the Darkhouse *Destination: Mystery!* Anthology. She was a finalist in the 2016 *Southern Writers Magazine* short story contest. Margaret writes a monthly blog for *Writers Who Kill* and is a member of Sisters in Crime and Mystery Writers of America. She is completing her debut contemporary cozy novel, *Curtains for the Corpse*, which is set in the fictional Jericho, Ohio. Margaret lives in Cincinnati. www.margaretshamilton.wordpress.com

FLYING GIRL

TONI GOODYEAR

The bear was coming toward her. Callie couldn't see him, but she knew it all right. She knew from Flying Girl that bears in the forest made the kind of noises she was hearing now—crashing through woods, tree branches fiercely snapping—the kind of coming-for-you noises that sweet deer, with their soft brown eyes and their way of floating like feathers or leaping with joy like eleven lords never made.

Flying Girl said not to worry, that if you leave bears alone they'll leave you alone. But now, caught as she was on this narrow, muddy mountain path, with a great falling-off to one side and the bear's forest on the other, Callie didn't know how to do that—she didn't know where a person should go to leave a bear alone.

Her chest felt like someone had curled a hard fist inside her, and her hands shook like they had a few weeks ago when she'd had to stand up before her second grade class and tell them how she planned to spend this summer. And even though Flying Girl of the Cherokee wasn't afraid of bears, she knew that she, Callie Scott Randolph of Evansville, Indiana, *was* afraid.

Very much afraid.

She tucked her hands under the shoulder straps of her small backpack and moved faster, scuttling along the trail as silently as she could, her new hiking boots feeling tight, not like her old sneakers. She hoped the bear couldn't hear her. Did bears have special hearing, like owls, or could they, like bats, discover where someone was by listening to their echo? She didn't think so, but she quickened her pace until she was half running, head down, picking her way over roots and rocks as quickly as she dared. She didn't want to fall now, not when she needed to find a place to leave this bear alone.

The trail continued to climb and Callie scurried upward with it. In a few places, jumbles of larger rocks adjoined the trail on the forest side opposite the fall-off. Her father said the mountain had once been higher, that chunks of it had broken off and rushed downhill like someone going too fast on a sled, but these someones were strong enough to knock down trees and carve new spaces in the woods. Callie loved climbing on rocks; she'd always been a good climber—a "natural athlete" was what her father had called her, his chest puffed out, that time she'd won first prize at the Field Day climbing wall.

The thrashing and snapping sounded even closer now. Would the bear stop to eat berries or leaves? She swallowed hard and moved faster, wishing it to be so. Twice she slipped and felt the sting of a branch or sharp stone against a bare knee. The cuts and scratches stung, but she did not stop.

Around a bend, off the path, she spied a flat slab of stone that looked like a tabletop—a roof with a rocky floor beneath. Two great trees, now great red logs, had fallen on the tabletop, making it look more like a cave of wood than of rock. She headed straight to it, wriggled out of her backpack and threw it in ahead of her. The shelter was roomy; if she wanted to, she could stretch her body out flat, from the opening to the back wall, with space to spare. But the entrance was wide and the roof was high—enough, she realized, to let in any bear that found her. She tried not to think about that. Her job was to hide.

She slid as far back under the roof as she could, until she was settled against the back wall, and drew her backpack to her. She started to take out her little book. Maybe Flying Girl said something else about bears that Callie had forgotten, something important that she could use now. But it wasn't a time to read books. She knew very well what Flying Girl would tell her—that now was a time to be as still as a lizard, as brave as a mountain lion, and as small as a beetle.

She hunched her shoulders and tried not to cry as she listened for the sounds of bear on the wind.

* * * *

"Don't go far, stay where we can hear you," had been the last thing her mother had told her.

And Callie had done that. Or tried to.

They had stopped early for the day at what her parents called their "backcountry campsite," a small circle of blackened stones in a small patch of ground among the trees. Her father had said they were lucky there was no one else here to want it or he might have to fight them for it. He'd put up his fists and laughed when he said that, the deep, fun laugh Callie loved so much. She knew he was joking; her father hated fighting.

Last she'd seen, her parents had been setting up a small tarp on ropes, a lean-to where the three of them could huddle if it rained. "Tents are heavy, and the way to honor the Earth is off the beaten path," her mother had said.

Callie never understood why some trails were "beaten" and others not, but she already understood from Flying Girl that walking in ways different from others and learning how to honor the Earth was what her parents wanted to teach her. Every summer for as long as she could remember they had packed up the jeep and brought her to new places to hike and camp. Last year the dark and mysterious Black Mountains, so silent they made her want to whisper. This year the Great Smoky Mountains with their deep, green forests and blue-gray sky.

She had gotten permission to go scouting for mushrooms while her father gathered kindling and her mother laid three pairs of shorts still wet from the morning's rain showers out to dry. Callie had her pocket camera to take pictures for her Earth Book, pictures of the fairytale 'shrooms that poked up so unexpectedly from the forest floor—the great colonies of orange buttons that grew on fallen logs, and the spotted red toadstool which was the most beautiful of all mushrooms but which she must never touch because it was poison.

She didn't know when she'd stopped hearing the sounds of her parents and the camp, or how long it had been since the last "Marco" call to which she had shouted "Polo" to let them know she was okay and not too far away. She'd had good luck on her mushroom hunt and had taken good pictures, she remembered that.

And when she got back to the campsite her parents were gone.

Gone.

Only the tarp strung on rope and the clothes laid out to dry. No fire smoldering. No backpacks.

"Marco," she called loudly, again and again. But no "Polo" came back to greet her.

Good campers, Callie knew, "left no trace." Her parents would never leave her, and they would never leave a campsite like this. Unless—for some reason—they couldn't help it.

Though the day was warm, her stomach quivered the way it had the first time she went ice skating on the neighborhood pond. Something bad had to have happened while she was gone. Something bad that made them have to go away—in a hurry.

She thought suddenly of that strange-looking man they'd met the day before, back at the last shelter. He had worn a dirty orange hunting hat and two windbreakers despite it being summer. She'd named him Jacket Man. His beard and long hair were scruffy, and he carried a raggedy cloth sack. Her parents had simply nodded a polite "Good day" to him, hadn't smiled and chatted like they usually did with the other hikers. Then her father had quickly steered her by the shoulders on down the trail.

"Why was that man wearing two jackets?" she'd asked after they'd gone a ways and their pace had slowed.

"There are all kinds of people, Callie. I think that one may be a bit down on his luck."

Her father had spoken softly, but his voice was hard. She guessed that being down on one's luck was not a good thing.

She'd thought no more about Jacket Man. They had kept moving along their planned trail on the way to something called the Dome, a place that her mother said was the top of the mountain. She never saw Jacket Man again.

Later, huddling alone in the camp site, wondering where her parents could be, she had lifted a hand to her forehead to brush her hair from her eyes and recoiled in pain. Her head hurt. When she took her hand away there was a dab of blood on her fingers. She looked at it in surprise. How, when, had she hurt herself?

She took her small mirror from her backpack, the one she used to help her comb her hair when they were camping. There were scratches on her forehead and cheek, and a bruise on the right side of her dirty face. It occurred to her now that she had pains in other places that had nothing to do with taking pictures of mushrooms. She ran a hand under the leg of her shorts and down the backside of her thigh. Hurts were there too, scrapes rough beneath her fingers, like she had slid down a garden wall.

Something else was confusing. It was already later in the day than it should have been. Had she been so busy hunting mushrooms that she'd lost track of time? Had she been gone so long? She checked the watch her mother had given her for her birthday, a soft, braided wristband of bright colors made by the Navajo, something like Flying Girl, though a Cherokee, might also wear, with a small clock face with clear and simple numbers and a little button that made it light in the dark. Seven o'clock. Almost night. Her watch had said it was just after one o'clock when she had gone off to hunt mushrooms.

Her face scrunched as she tried to think. She'd been hunting off the trail, very near to the steep forest slope. The trail had been muddy from the early morning rain, slippery. She remembered tripping over a log and losing her footing and sliding into a kind of gully, a dry place, deep, and then stopping there to rest. She might have fallen asleep, she wasn't sure. When she woke she'd had to walk a long way to get back up and out, even turning around twice to not get too far away. In the end she'd found the right path and made it back to camp.

But maybe other things had happened to her, things she didn't remember. Maybe she had hit her head against a tree or a rock when she fell. That would explain why her head hurt. Maybe she'd been asleep for longer than she thought, tucked in a hidden place that her parents could miss when she didn't answer their calls. Maybe all of it had taken far, far longer than she thought.

But if her parents were still out looking for her their backpacks would be in the camp, wouldn't they? She wasn't sure. Maybe not, if they hadn't been sure how long they'd be away. Or—she closed her eyes tightly—if someone bad had taken them.

Callie felt the tears starting to come. She sat down on a stump and let them flow.

Minutes passed before she stopped. When she did, she told herself to breathe slowly, to think what her parents would expect. She remembered what her mother had said to do if she was ever separated from the family—stay where you are, ask a safe-looking grownup for help if you can. Try not to be afraid.

"We will always, always find you, Callie," her mother had promised, hugging her close.

She would do as she'd been told. With nighttime coming and no safe grownup to ask she would stay right here at the camp and wait for her parents to come back—or until another camper came to help her.

She wiped the wetness from her face with the sleeve of her t-shirt. Her backpack, which she could use as a pillow if she needed to, held things that would help her get through the night: her silver astronaut blanket, her stand-up flashlight with four extra batteries, her water bottle, three energy bars—and Flying Girl.

The tarp had been strung in a clump of trees not far from the fire pit. The trees made a good backrest and with the tarp around her Callie felt safer. She would just have to sit up all night, watching and waiting, with Flying Girl to keep her company. She clutched the book to her chest and laid her flashlight beside her, ready for the darkness.

When her eyes opened with the sun, the book was still on her chest. She had stayed awake long into the night, until, without her agreement, her eyes had closed. No campers had come to the campsite, and her parents had not returned.

But she had dreamed of Flying Girl. Now she knew what she needed to do.

When Flying Girl wanted a wish to come true she would go to the high places outside her village. There she would make a gift of respect—stones, leaves, branches, and one special thing she treasured—and perform a lifting dance to help the wish fly up to the spirits of the great heavens—the sky, the stars, the wind. Callie would do the same. She would make her way to the top of the mountain and send out her wishes—that her family be together again, that her mother and father be safe.

She would follow the trail they had been on, the trail that led upward. In their mountain hikes, they had always found places where the trees opened and they could see the peaks and valleys around them. That would help keep her going upward. Her mother had said they'd been going toward something called the Dome, the highest place on the mountain. They might think she would go there now. Or at least she might find a safe grownup at the top, because people who liked mountains liked to stay up high.

She tried to remove the tarp from the rope to take it with her but the knots were tight and wouldn't give. She would have to leave it. The three pairs of shorts that had been left drying were another matter. She stuffed those in her pack.

Then she set off again on the muddy trail that wound ever upward.

She was very hungry—she had eaten all three of her energy bars the night before—but she would think about that later.

* * * *

Now Callie huddled in her rock shelter and listened for the bear. It had been many minutes since she'd heard any thrashing—in fact, now that she thought about it, she hadn't heard any animal sounds at all, not even the chirping of birds or the strange gargling noises that squirrels often made.

If not for worrying about the bear, she would be fine in this shelter. She had walked a long way since leaving the camp this morning, it felt good to rest. She thought there must be a bad storm coming—she could see that the sky beyond the forest was growing dark, though her watch said it was only two o'clock, still afternoon. She was glad she had a plastic poncho in her pack for rain. When the bear went away, she would put it on.

She had to know more about the storm. Since she'd heard no sounds of the bear, she decided to take a chance. She scooted on her bottom to the ledge opening to better hear the woods, see the sky. She felt colder when she did. The world around her was truly darkening, a deep, scary blackness, as if day were suddenly being turned to night by an angry magician. The storm that was coming must be very great indeed.

She risked crawling out farther, beyond the opening, just for a moment. It was puzzling. The great thunder clouds that she had expected—clouds black enough to turn day to night—were not there. But she did see a star in the darkening sky—a star, in the daytime? Of this Callie could make no sense. Did bears look for shelter in a storm? She didn't know. She only hoped they wouldn't look in *her* shelter.

Then she heard again the sound that brought such fear—a great branch cracking in two like the shot of a gun in a movie. Then another, then a third. Some big animal, maybe afraid of the darkness, was running through the forest. She couldn't tell how close or exactly where. But near enough.

She darted back into the shelter and froze. She had been so brave, so hopeful. Now she felt the pressure of a hard fist in her chest. She could not run, not fight. She could only sit. And wait. If the bear saw her, there was nothing she could do.

She crouched against the rock wall and squeezed her eyes tight. Her lips moved in a whisper, a wish, a prayer. "Help me, Flying Girl, don't let the bear find me. Please, please don't let him find me."

She drew her knees to her chest and buried her face in her arms.

She didn't how long she'd stayed that way. She was only aware of a different feeling in the air, like something had changed in the forest. Something for the better.

She raised her head slowly and stared out beyond the opening. She saw—or was it felt?—the day growing lighter. It was still much too dark for daytime—the sun must still be buried behind thick clouds that let in little light—but there was a grayness that had not been there before. Maybe the day was not moving towards night after all. Maybe the sun would come back.

Callie looked at her watch. Three o'clock. One whole hour she had been in the shelter. She decided she would stay where she was until the sun returned and all the sounds of the forest were safe. For now she heard only the wind moving through the trees.

Then, softly, there it was: a bird's call, then another. Not far behind that, the clack-clack-clack of a squirrel. No cracking of branches, nothing crashing through woods.

As she watched, the day grew brighter. Her heart rose up like one of Flying Girl's wishes. There was a new spirit to the forest, as if an evil curse had been lifted. Callie could feel the world around her coming back to life. She had come through the night, and she had come through the storm.

The bear, she knew in the same moment, was gone. She didn't know how she knew this, but she did. Her sureness of it grew stronger with the sun, wrapping around her like her mother's hugs after a bad dream. Somehow her heart was certain. She was safe.

She crept out from under her rock and stood, turning her face upward to the now blue sky. "Thank you, thank you," she said, opening her arms wide, letting happy tears spill from her eyes.

She was ready to start again.

* * * *

She'd been on the trail for a good while when she first heard the laughter. Was she imagining things? No, there it was again, what sounded like many voices. A murmuring jumble of voices, almost like the buzzing of a great hive of bees. But these were not bees, these were human noises.

She craned her neck to listen. The sounds were off to her right, but there was only empty forest in that direction. Could there be a campground out there somewhere beyond what she could see? A campground with safe-looking grownups?

To look for it she would have to go off the trail and hike through the woods. The idea was scary. If she wandered off the trail she might never find it again. She could lose the campground and never reach the mountain top. No, for now she would stay on the path she knew. She would walk farther on, see if the bees buzzed louder or softer as she went. Then she would make up her mind.

She did not have to go far. The trail branched suddenly to the right and came to an end at a paved roadway. And there, just beyond the tree line, were people. Hundreds of people. Maybe even thousands of people. Families and children, and a great, winding sidewalk to a high lookout point at what had to be the very tippity-top of the mountain.

This had to be the Dome. She had found it.

She began to run.

One of the first safe-looking grownups she saw was a park ranger. A woman. Callie knew about park rangers, they were there to help. They could help her find her parents.

The ranger was talking to a man and pointing, like giving him directions to somewhere. Callie moved nearer. The ranger's badge said "Lib Sutton." Callie liked that name: Ranger Sutton.

As she came close, Ranger Sutton saw her and stopped talking.

"I lost my parents," Callie blurted. "I need to find them."

The ranger bent to one knee. She took a picture from her shirt pocket and looked at it, then at Callie. "Your name wouldn't happen to be Callie Scott Randolph, would it?" she asked gently.

Callie nodded, then burst into tears and threw her arms around the ranger's neck.

Ranger Sutton held her tightly and let her cry. When her sobs quieted, the ranger said softly, "Let me look at you."

She took Callie's hands from her neck and held her at arm's length. She brushed back her hair and looked at her scrapes and bruises. Callie realized how dirty she must be.

"I fell," she said. "I don't know what happened to my mother and father."

"Come," the ranger said.

She took Callie by the hand and sat her in the shade of a tree. Then she walked a short distance away and spoke into her radio. Callie heard the words "okay," "scared," "ambulance."

The ranger ended her call, sat down next to Callie, and smiled. "Everyone's been out looking for you. Your mom and dad are with the rescue team. We'll take you down to the visitor center and get you some food and clean up those cuts and scrapes. Your folks will meet us there. We'll want to hear all about where you've been and what happened to you."

Callie closed her eyes. Her mother and father were safe. They hadn't been taken by Jacket Man. And she was safe and not eaten by a bear. Soon she and her family would be together again and everything would be fine. Half of her wanted to cry, the other to leap, leap, leap.

"I came back to the camp and no one was there. I had to reach the top of the mountain to send out my wishes for my family."

Callie liked Ranger Sutton's face. It was kind. Warm. "Everyone was looking hard for you, but we couldn't find you," the ranger said. "Your parents had to run back down the trail in the dark to get help."

"They leave their phones in the car. They said phones don't always work in the mountains. A bear was after me."

Ranger Sutton's smile got even bigger. "You're a very brave, very smart mountain girl, Miss Callie, and I'm very, very proud of you."

Callie looked down at the ground at the word "brave." She didn't feel brave. "Is an ambulance coming?"

Ranger Sutton patted her arm. "Just to have a look at you, make sure everything's fine."

Callie didn't like that but she knew her parents would want it. She pointed to all the people. "Is this the Dome?"

"Yes."

"Why are all these people here?"

"They came for the solar eclipse."

Callie looked at her.

"An eclipse is when the moon moves in front of the sun during the day and hides it for a while. It gets like night in the middle of the afternoon. It doesn't happen often, so when it does it's very exciting."

"The moon hides the sun and makes it look like night?"

"Uh huh. But only for about two minutes. Then the sun comes back again. This was a good place to see it."

"I thought a storm was coming."

The ranger's radio crackled. "Be right back." She walked some steps away.

Callie thought about the ranger's words and in an instant she knew what had really happened—why there had been no thunder clouds, no storm, and why, for no good reason, she had been so certain that the bear had finally gone away. It was all because Flying Girl had heard her wish and had called the sun and the moon to bring darkness to the Earth so the bear could not find Callie huddled in her shelter.

Should she try to explain this to Ranger Sutton? No, probably not. And probably not to her mother and father either. Grownups didn't believe those kinds of things.

She sighed happily and clutched her backpack, hugging Flying Girl closer to her heart.

Toni Goodyear is a former journalist, winner of the North Carolina Press Association Award. Other past careers include ghostbusting (yes, really). Her short stories have appeared in the Anthony Award-winning anthology *Murder Under the Oaks*, *The Killer Wore Cranberry: Room for Thirds*, *Kings River Life Magazine*, *Carolina Crimes: 19 Tales of Lust, Love, and Longing*, and *Fish or Cut Bait*. A member of Sisters in Crime, she holds a Ph.D. in Psychology from the University of North Carolina at Chapel Hill.

TO THE MOON AND BACK

KRISTIN KISSKA

Don't worry, Katelynn sweetheart. That was our last pit stop. Next time we stop, we'll be in South Carolina. I promise! Are you comfortable back there? Seatbelt buckled? I know you prefer riding in the front seat, but you should rest. We have a long drive tonight, but it'll be worth it.

Aren't road trips exciting? It's been a few years, but we had such fun exploring when you were little. The beach. Hiking trails. Museums. Especially the planetarium.

August 21st has been my favorite day of the year, ever since you came into my life. I can hardly believe you're turning thirteen in a few short hours. Oh, these years have flown by much too quickly! Mama's taking you someplace exciting for your birthday tomorrow. You'll see.

I hope you like this car. Did you notice it's blue? Just like your eyes, maybe a shade or two darker. Blue has always been your favorite color. Even as a toddler, you insisted on wearing blue every day. Your hair was so short I fashioned a big blue bow headband to ensure no one would mistake you for a little boy. Such independence! I always loved that about you. I've cherished every moment in my heart. How you would decorate any frosted-over window with your hand print and finger drawings—I framed a picture of the infinity sign you once left on my car window. How you would mimic me applying makeup and perfume at my vanity. How you would help me make dinner by stirring the ingredients with your very own spatula. Blue, of course.

The crowbar? Oh, don't mind that. I should've left it behind, silly me. Let's not bicker, not on our special adventure.

Check out that beautiful moon. It's following us, you know.

You were probably too little to remember, but when you were a preschooler, you used to sit on my lap every night, and we'd read bedtime stories in the rocking chair. We'd rock back and forth, back and forth. But no matter how many books we read, you always saved our favorite story for last. The one about the bunny arguing with its parent about who loves the other more. After turning the last page, you'd snuggle into my neck and repeat the last line, "I love you to the moon and back, Mama." Do you remember that, sweet Katelynn?

Even in kindergarten, you insisted I read that board book aloud to your class when it was my turn to be the parent *book buddy*. Those were good days. Good memories. Weren't they?

Trust me, you had your sour moments. You could throw a tantrum with the best of them. I left many a half-full grocery cart inside the store so that you could work through your meltdown without shattering the eardrums of the other shoppers. And I'll never forget that time we transitioned from bottles to sippy cups. Lordy, you had lungs! Sometimes I worried the neighbors would alert social services.

Goodness me, my fingernails are in tatters. How did I let them become so chipped and dirty? You don't mind, do you, sweetheart? You never minded any of my little faults. We've always had a bond.

Oh, I never regretted not going back to work after you were born. Not for a minute. No one could've pried my little Miss *Katelynn Anne Jameson* from my arms, thank you very much. And I certainly wouldn't have paid someone for the privilege of watching you when that's exactly what I wanted to be doing. We'd endured way too many years of fertility treatments and miscarriages before you came along. You were my miracle baby. From the moment my obstetrician first amplified your heartbeat, you were mine. All mine. No one could've cared for you as well as I could. I craved every precious moment I spent with you, holding you, inhaling your fresh newborn scent, memorizing your fingers, your toes, the dimple in your left cheek, the exact shade of your gray-blue eyes with flecks of sea green.

You're not saying much, sweetheart. That's okay. Tired? Why don't you lie down and rest while I drive? Almost-thirteen-year-olds need their sleep. Especially you. Don't you worry about a thing. Mama's got a plan. We're going to drive straight through the night and get to Greenville by lunchtime tomorrow. We should arrive with time to spare.

I just love that gorgeous moon—*La Bella Luna!*

She's got a big show for us tomorrow. On your birthday! The total solar eclipse will be visible from our old South Carolina home just after two p.m. I've been waiting to take you back there for a while now, but I wanted to surprise you. The lunar shadow will completely cover us as the moon passes in front of the sun. At that moment, heaven will touch Earth. Everything will be okay again. Like magic. You'll be just like you used to be.

Remember your long, wavy hair? I have a picture of you right here in my wallet. Oh, my word! I must have forgotten my purse back in

Virginia. Silly me. Not to worry, Mama's got it all under control. Anyway, back to your hair. So golden. And thick. And shiny. I used to brush it for hours.

Forgive me, I shouldn't have brought up your hair. Thoughtless mistake. Believe me, it crushed me when we had to cut it off, too. But, you see, it started falling out. What else could we do? Watch fistfuls of strands fall out every day? No. We had to nip the problem in the bud. Even at ten years old, you were strong. Thinking of others before yourself. You insisted on donating your beautiful locks so some other child who'd lost their hair could have a wig. The hairdresser came into your hospital room and snipped off those two precious ponytails while you sobbed into your pillow.

It was blue, your pillow. I made sure the hospital room was decorated for my Katelynn Anne. Everything had to be cozy, cheerful, and blue. Blankets. Window curtains. Stuffed animals. Pictures. A display of handmade "Katelynn Strong" get well cards and posters from your school classmates and ballet friends covered every inch of wall space. I draped light blue organza fabric over the privacy curtain separating you from your roommate. I even knit matching downy soft blue caps for you and me to wear to protect our bald heads from the cold.

Oh yes, I cut my hair off, too. The same day you did. Do you remember that? As long as you couldn't have hair, I wouldn't either. I couldn't let my baby girl suffer alone. I kept my promise. I still haven't grown back my hair, although sometimes I have a hard time finding scissors these days to keep it that way.

Why is my neck so itchy?

I wear blue every day. Just for you.

Because I love you to the moon and back, sweetheart!

Not like those doctors. They lied. All of them. Even my doctor. *Especially* my doctor. After all this time, I thought she—also a mother—understood me. Lies.

Who would've thought your silly little headaches could be such a problem? A dose of pain reliever always cleared it up. Your dad and I shouldn't have waited to take you in to see someone. But your first seizure—watching you writhe and thrash on the floor—well, my world collapsed in that moment. Second, third, fourth opinions. What good were they? Every last specialist we consulted said your tumor was inoperable. But chemotherapy? Overkill. I didn't believe them then, and I certainly don't now. There *had* to be some other way. You can't tell me it's reasonable to drip poison through the veins of a child for months on end, and she'll recover. Oh, hell no.

Poison is poison is poison.

Did it stop the doctors? No.

I will never forget that day. Your father and I stood by your bed as you napped. The doctor handed your father the clipboard before retreating from your hospital room like ... like the coward he was. It hovered between us, that death sentence. I couldn't read the forms through my tears, but I knew what they said. Authorization for chemotherapy treatment.

How could I sign that form? As you lay sleeping next to me, your skin was so smooth, your breathing so sweet, your face so angelic. So peaceful, so precious. It was my responsibility as your parent—your mother—to advocate for you in any way I could.

So I snatched that clipboard away from your father and ran out into the hallway.

Give it to me. That's all your father said. Again and again like some warped recording on repeat. Give it to me.

Instead, I ripped the papers into confetti and threw the pieces in the air. They fluttered to the ground silently. Do you remember that snowfall when I woke you up to come outside and see the flakes? Just like those! It was a magical moment.

But when I handed your father the empty clipboard, he slapped me. For trying to protect you!

Your goddamned father believed those doctors and signed a fresh set of papers. I never forgave him, you know. I tried to stop them. I even sued the hospital, but it didn't work. Amazing that the judge ruled that *not* treating a child with chemotherapy is considered endangerment. I'm not sure I ever shared that with you. I only wanted you to feel our love.

So the doctors prescribed their cocktail of poison. And it corroded you from the inside out.

What did those oncologists care? It wasn't their child lost among the tangle of tubes connected to her. They never watched their daughter's body wither away into a skeleton covered in orange-tinted skin. They never had to push the IV stand twice daily behind their daughter as she exercised by using a walker to hobble down the hospital hallway, the same daughter who only months before had *grand jetéd* and *pirouetted en pointe* at her spring ballet recital. They never sat next to a hospital bed begging their child to eat just one more spoonful of broth and then hold a bucket for her to vomit her dinner. They never sat up night after night crying and bargaining with God to let them have cancer in lieu of their child.

God didn't listen to me.

But you've never suffered alone, sweetheart. I moved into the hospital with you. I never had an uninterrupted night of sleep either. Any time a nurse jabbed you with a needle, I stuck myself with a safety pin. I made myself throw up anytime you did. I even scraped the underside of my nose until I had the same chafing you did from your oxygen tube.

Jeez, I wish my arm would stop itching. Oh, wait—where did this blood come from? Am I bleeding? I must've scratched too much.

Never mind.

Don't you worry, Katelynn. Your pain is all in the past. Like I said before, Mama has a plan. The total solar eclipse will make everything right again. I promise. We're making a pilgrimage. God owes it to us. You'll get healthy. Maybe we'll even move back to South Carolina someday soon. Just you and me, Katelynn Anne. You'll see. We'll be just like we were before your diagnosis. Happy, healthy, and carefree.

Do you like the color of the car I borrowed? Oh, I forgot. I asked you that before. It's a nice one with leather seats. The only trouble is my dress. Did you notice the flowers on it are also blue? For you. Always for you! But the ties in the back of the gown don't help over much with coverage. My legs keep sticking to the seat in all this humidity. That's the only problem with August in the south. The humidity is unbearable. But for your birthday road trip, we can endure anything, right? Even the noise in the trunk.

Oh no! We're getting low on gas. Why couldn't she have filled the tank before I left? So inconsiderate. Not to worry. I'll figure something out. We'll still make it to Greenville by lunchtime, plenty of time before the eclipse happens. We must. I'm sticking to the back roads, rather than the interstate highway because there's less traffic. And I'm not turning on my headlights so that we can see the full moon better. *La Bella Luna* casts all the light we need.

Trust me, sweetheart. Mama will take care of everything.

I can't wait to see the look on those doctors' faces when I prove to them that my treatment plan for you worked, while their poison didn't. Doctors used to take an oath to uphold ethical standards. To try to *help* their patients. Times have changed! Nowadays, a medical degree, a white lab coat, and a stethoscope amount to a license to kill.

But Dr. Moretti was different. She convinced me that she understood me.

Yesterday, my therapy session started just like any other. And we've had hundreds! As usual, Dr. Moretti sat behind her pristine desk and took notes. She nodded with her sympathetic smile and asked me warm, thoughtful questions about you. I trusted her. But when I noticed the framed photo of her two little children—it was the only personal decoration in the entire office!—I knew we had a connection.

Motherhood.

I thought I'd finally found someone who could intervene on our behalf. So I told her my plan. I'd never told another soul. Did I mention that already?

I mean, how often does a total solar eclipse happen? Almost never. And this one will occur on August 21st, your birthday. In our old hometown. It's more than a coincidence. It's a sign to us from God. It was all meant to be. Heaven will touch Earth, and God will make everything all better again. Normal. His gift to us. His apology for ignoring my prayers before. But then Dr. Moretti called for an orderly. She tricked me.

All lies.

She was no better than any of the other doctors. We won't ever have to depend on the likes of those monsters again. Not after this trip. Not to worry.

And as for your goddamned father? I've asked for—no, demanded—a divorce so many times, I've lost count. I'm so sorry to share that news, sweetheart. Especially on your birthday. But trust me, it's for the best. Your cancer came from *his* blood line, not mine. No one told me about his family's medical history until after you were diagnosed. I never would've knowingly put your life at risk. You believe me, right sweetheart? But even after discovering he was the source of your cancer, he should've scoured the world for alternative treatments, but no! He subscribed to the whole poison plan and thwarted my every attempt to protect you. If I'd have known back then ... well, I would have started with a better gene pool.

Blue!

Can you see the blue lights out the back window, Katelynn? How pretty! They remind me of the string of blinking blue lights decorating the mini Christmas tree next to your hospital bed. It was one of the rare times when your face relaxed in pure delight at the hospital. You were able to be an innocent, pain-free child again, for a few blissful moments. Do you remember that?

I just wish these flashing blue lights weren't quite so bright in my rear view mirror. The glare makes it hard to see the lines on the road.

Oh, look! It's the police. They must be here to escort us to see the total eclipse, just like that time the fire department paraded you home after one of your long hospital stays. Do you remember? All our neighbors lined the streets waving their "Welcome home, Katelynn" posters. A police escort is lovely, but they really shouldn't have bothered. We're doing just fine by ourselves. Aren't we? Now don't get concerned, sweetheart. You lie down and rest. Not much longer to Greenville. Let Mama take care of everything.

My, my, my, we are really getting the royal treatment. Two police patrol cars. One just passed us and maneuvered in front of us. The other is behind us. With the lights flashing, people might mistake us as part of the president's motorcade. But why are they slowing down?

No, don't slow down! That's not part of my plan. We have to get to Greenville in time to see the eclipse. We'll never make it if we slow down. If they're going to escort us, they should speed up.

It's getting a bit hot in here. Are you over-warm, sweetheart?

Flashing red lights, too? An ambulance is racing up behind us with its sirens blaring. Oh, I get it. The police are slowing so it can pass us quickly. We don't want to be in their way. Someone must be in trouble. Emergency victims need a quick response. You know, we had to call 9-1-1 for you when you had your first seizure. You had just gotten home from school when you fell and started convulsing on the kitchen floor. The EMTs took you straight to the emergency room. Do you remember riding in the ambulance? They let me ride in the back with you. I held your hand the entire way to the hospital, which wasn't easy because the paramedics had strapped your head and hands to the gurney in case you convulsed again. Your dad met us at the ER. I was terrified for you, assuming the worst case scenario was that you might have diabetes. In retrospect, that would have been a blessing! I had no idea what we were in store for at the time. They took a scan of your head. That's when we first found out you had a tumor.

Why are the police cars stopping? This isn't right. Keep going! The ambulance can fly by us while we're driving.

Wait a minute, one of the troopers just stepped out of the patrol car and is coming toward us, talking into his walkie-talkie. Was I speeding? I forgot my purse, so I don't have my license. Damn, that won't help get us out of here fast, but not to worry. Mama will take care of everything.

Oh, no. Why isn't the ambulance passing us? It's stopping, too, blocking our car. Don't wedge us into a corner. Move it, people! You're in our way. We'll never make the eclipse if we don't go.

Don't be scared, Katelynn. Just lie down and rest. I don't want you to fret and get sick again. Not when we're so close to making you all better.

I can't seem to stop scratching my leg.

We don't have time for this! We can't miss the eclipse. It's my plan. It's how I'm going to save my Katelynn.

Please move the police car out of the way. We need to go. Now! Don't make us miss the eclipse. Please. I'm begging. I thought the police were going to escort us.

Officer, could you please turn those sirens off! They're hurting my daughter's ears, and I can't hear you.

Thank you.

No, I won't get out of my car. Here, I'll crack the window, but I'm keeping our doors locked. Driver's license? Well, um, I accidentally left my purse at home, so I don't have it. The registration must be in the glove compartment somewhere. Give me a moment to look.

Blood? What blood? Oh, that's nothing. That's just from my skin. You see, I've been scratching.

Stop! You can't just haul me out of the car like that! I have rights. I haven't done anything wrong. I'll report you!

Wait, how do you know my name? Did my husband send you? Tell him to go to hell and then call my divorce lawyer.

Take these handcuffs off me!

Under arrest? For what? I don't care a whit what my rights are. I didn't steal Dr. Moretti's car. I *borrowed* it. She gave me the keys. See? They're right here! It's not a crime to take my daughter for a drive.

Yes, my *daughter*. She's in the back seat of the car. We're driving to South Carolina to see the total eclipse at 2:38 p.m. tomorrow. Now if you don't mind, we still have a long way to go.

Stay away from my daughter! Don't lay a hand on her. I'm her mother. If you touch her, I'll sue for child endangerment. Abuse. She's in my custody, and she's getting better. Leave my daughter alone. You'll scare her!

No, the back seat is *not* empty. I know you can see her, plain as day.

Passed away? You're lying!

Don't listen to them, Katelynn. They're lying to us. Big, ugly lies.

Why does everyone try to convince me that Katelynn is dead? My daughter did *not* die two years ago! See how peacefully she's resting in the back seat? How content she is? Look, she's wearing her favorite light blue sundress and the cap I knitted for her.

The crowbar? I brought it along for protection. Two women traveling alone in a car aren't safe. What if we were stopped by an axe murderer?

I already told you. The blood is from my neck, my arms.

A stretcher—is that really necessary? No one here needs a stretcher. Everyone's fine. And if we can get to Greenville, then by this time to-morrow, Katelynn will be in the moon's shadow. She'll recover, and everything will return to normal. She'll be cured.

Don't take me away from my daughter! I can't leave my child alone in a car.

Stop!

Don't open the trunk!

No, Katelynn is lying down on the *back seat*, not the trunk. Get away from the trunk—

Oh, God.

Wait. What?

A woman's head?

It's not what you think. You don't understand.

You see, I … I didn't … I didn't mean to … it's wasn't my fault … it's just that Dr. Moretti wouldn't listen … and I thought she was one of the good ones. She made me believe we had a connection. Mother-to-mother.

Killing her wasn't part of my plan!

But Dr. Moretti was going to stop me from saving my daughter … I told her my plan to see the eclipse … I'd organized the whole trip so carefully … but she tried to lock me back up in that psych ward … if I was admitted to the hospital, how could I get Katelynn to the eclipse? It was Dr. Moretti's fault, not mine. I had to save my daughter. What choice did I have? Any mother would do as much to save her child! I failed my daughter once, I couldn't fail her again.

The rest of Dr. Moretti's body? I don't remember. Virginia. North Carolina. Different places. My last stop was about half an hour ago.

No! Not a syringe. No more needles. We're done with all the poison! Get these restraints off of me. We have to go. We're running out of time. The needles will make me too drowsy to drive.

No!

I'm so sorry, Katelynn Anne.

I ruined your birthday. We almost made it to the eclipse. Please forgive me, sweetheart. There won't be another total solar eclipse for seven years. But not to worry. We'll make you better. Somehow! We'll be together again. Soon. Mama will figure something else out.

I love you to the moon and back.

Kristin Kisska used to be a finance geek, complete with MBA and Wall Street pedigree, but now Kristin is a self-proclaimed *fictionista*. Kristin contributed short mystery stories to the Anthony Award winning anthology, *Murder Under the Oaks* (2015), *Virginia is for Mysteries*—Volume II (2016), and *Fifty Shades of Cabernet* (2017). When not writing suspense novels and historical thrillers, she can be found on her website—KristinKisska.com, on Facebook at facebook.com/KristinKisskaAuthor, and Tweeting @KKMHOO. Kristin lives in Virginia with her husband and three children.

RAYS OF HOPE

HARRIETTE SACKLER

Julie Spencer sat on a cliff overlooking the ocean. It was the special place she came to when she sought peace. The slap of waves against the shore and the cry of gulls overhead were so soothing that she often would fall into a dreamless sleep, free of the images that haunted her both day and night.

Julie lived a solitary existence by choice. It wasn't that she disliked the company of others. Julie was just loath to burden them with her deep-seated issues that originated from an unresolved childhood trauma.

Graduating with honors from the University of Pennsylvania with a doctorate in American literature, Julie enjoyed a successful career as a book critic and reviewer. She spent her days alone in the confines of her large isolated home on the New England coast, rarely leaving the estate that her grandparents had gifted her. Several trusted employees tended to her needs and, on the rare occasions Julie ventured into town, she did so quickly, in sunglasses and a wide-brimmed hat, anonymous and unrecognizable. In her thirty-five years on Earth, Julie had never encouraged friendships or intimacy. She wanted to be left alone.

* * * *

"Good night, my darling. Sweet dreams." Julie's mother gently kissed her on the forehead and pulled the comforter up to the five-year-old's chin.

"Night, Mommy. I love you."

"I love you, too, sweet girl. See you in the morning."

Julie hugged Teddy, her favorite stuffed animal, and almost at once drifted off to sleep.

* * * *

Julie was awakened by the sound of angry voices. Mommy and Daddy are fighting again, she thought. That happened a lot. Mommy didn't like Daddy to work so hard. But they always made up, so Julie wasn't frightened. She snuggled under the covers and fell back to sleep.

Helga, the Spencer's housekeeper, kissed Julie awake. The elderly woman's eyes were red and wet with tears as she hugged the little girl.

"*Liebchen*, you must get up now. There is a gentleman here who needs to talk to you."

Julie rubbed her eyes and looked at Helga.

"Who is he?"

"Darling, he is a policeman. Something happened last night that he needs to talk to you about. Let me help you dress and then we can go downstairs. He's waiting for you in the kitchen."

They used the back stairs that led directly into the kitchen. Mommy never let Julie go that way without a grown up with her. The stairs were steep and uncarpeted and could be dangerous for a little girl.

When they reached the kitchen, a big man was sitting at the table, drinking a cup of coffee. He looked up and smiled when Julie walked into the room.

"Good morning, Julie. My name is Detective Cochran, and I'd like to talk to you for a few minutes."

"Okay. Are we going to talk about strangers?"

"Strangers?" The detective looked puzzled.

"A policeman came to my school and told us not to talk to strangers. He brought us coloring books, too."

"That policeman was right for sure. But, I'm here to talk to you about something else. Is that okay?"

"Sure," Julie sat across the table and began eating the pancakes Helga had put in front of her.

"Julie, can you tell me about what you did after dinner last night?" The policeman spoke in a soft voice, and Julie decided that she liked him.

"Umm. After dinner, I played Barbies with Mommy. Then she gave me my bath, helped me put on my pajamas, and read me a book."

"Anything else you remember?"

Julie thought for a minute and then said, "She put me to bed with Teddy and kissed me goodnight. Then I went to sleep."

"Sweetheart, did you wake up at all after that?"

Julie frowned and bowed her head. "I woke up because I heard Mommy and Daddy fighting. Then I went back to sleep."

"Did you get out of bed at all and leave your room?"

"No. I was sleepy. When Mommy and Daddy fight, I just go back to sleep."

"Do Mommy and Daddy fight a lot?"

"I guess so, but then they make up."

"Do you know why they fight?"

"Daddy works very hard and Mommy doesn't like that very much."

"Julie, are you sure it was Daddy you heard last night?"

"Who else could it be?"

The nice policeman thanked Julie for talking to him and left the kitchen. When she finished her breakfast, Helga took her back to her room to get her dressed. She told Julie that she was going to be visiting with Nanny and Papa Sloan, Mommy's parents, for a while, and that she was going to have a wonderful time.

"Will Mommy and Daddy go with me?"

Helga wiped her eyes and said, "No, little one, they had to go somewhere today. They told me to tell you that they love you very much."

Julie nodded, then began gathering her dolls and toys for the trip.

* * * *

And so, Julie's life was changed forever in one tragic night. When Helga had arrived for work at the Spencer home that morning, she had found Mrs. Spencer's tangled body in the front foyer at the bottom of the main staircase. After checking for life, she immediately called the police who responded in a matter of minutes. Paramedics pronounced that Mrs. Spencer was indeed deceased, and the medical examiner and crime scene unit were called in. It was possible that the death had been an accident, but until that was verified, it had to be treated as a homicide.

When Julie left her home with her grandparents, they did their best to shield her from the sight of the commotion in front of the house. They told her that Mommy had been badly hurt from a fall down the stairs, but it was weeks before they disclosed that Mommy had gone to Heaven to live with God. The little girl was inconsolable and only wanted to see her Daddy.

Julie wouldn't learn for years that her father had been arrested for his wife's murder. An autopsy revealed that Elaine Spencer had been forcibly pushed down the stairs, there was no indication of a break-in. Arthur Spencer had returned from his business trip earlier in the evening. Although he vehemently insisted he had gone straight to his office and slept on the couch there, no one was available to confirm his alibi. Nanny and Papa told Julie that her Daddy had to go on a very long business trip.

Through her childhood, Julie missed her parents terribly. But at her tender age, it would have been impossible for her to understand what had really happened. Her family wanted to protect her. She enjoyed her life, living with Nanny and Papa in their spacious apartment on Manhattan's West Side. She went to a private school, learned to play the piano, and took classes in ballet, tennis and anything else she fancied. Her Uncle Freddy, Mommy's brother, came by to take Julie to the movies, the zoo, and museums. She spent her summers at Grandma and Grandpa Spencer's big house in New England. She swam in their pool and learned to ride on Truffles, her very own horse. And, as time went on, the memory of her parents slowly faded.

On her fifteenth birthday, the joy of her childhood ended. It was then that Nanny and Papa sat Julie down and recounted the circumstances of her mother's death. She was told that her father was incarcerated for murder.

"Why didn't you tell me this before?" Julie's face was a bloodless white and wet with tears.

"You were too young to understand, sweetheart. We wanted to let you have a good childhood. The Spencers felt the same way. Why burden you at such an early age?" Papa wiped his eyes with a trembling hand.

"Where is Daddy? Is he still alive?"

"Yes, he's alive at the prison in Ossining. The Spencers visit him several times a year, and they say he's in good health and always asks about you. He's written to you often and we've saved the letters for you."

"Well, I want to see him. I can't believe he killed Mommy. I can't. Maybe that night I was wrong. Maybe it wasn't Daddy who was fighting with Mommy."

* * * *

Several days letter, Uncle Freddy accompanied Julie for a visit with her father. She'd read all his letters, in which he assured her that he had loved her mother and would never have harmed her in any way. He said he had indeed stayed at his office the night she died so he could be at an early meeting the next day. He heard of his wife's death only when the police came to his office. Julie wanted to believe him.

Sing Sing, the infamous prison, was located upstate in Ossining, New York. It was an awful looking place, and it made Julie's skin crawl. Freddy waited in the car, telling Julie she and her father needed time to be alone.

Her first sight of Daddy brought back a flood of memories. His smiling face and soft kisses on her cheek. His strong shoulders as he carried her piggyback around the house. The loving look in his eyes as he tucked her into bed. The way he and Mommy laughed together at silly things.

It surprised Julie that she recognized her father right away. After all, she hadn't seen him in ten years and she was such a little girl when he left. He looked bigger and stronger. His hair was cut short, and there were frown lines etched in his face. But his eyes sparkled when he saw her, and a big smile brightened his face.

"Oh, Jules, I've waited for this day so long. What a beautiful young woman you've become. But I'm not surprised. You were always special."

"Oh, Daddy. I just found out what happened. I would have come earlier."

"I know, baby, the family wanted to protect you, and I can't blame them."

"Daddy, did you kill Mommy?"

"Honey, I swear on all that's holy, I would never hurt your mother. If her death wasn't an accident, then there's someone out there who took my wife from me. And, I can tell you, I'd like to find out who."

"I don't remember much about that night. I was very young and woke up to hear an argument downstairs. I thought it was you and Mommy, but maybe I was wrong. Can that be?"

Arthur Spencer thoughtfully looked at his daughter.

"Of course. Because I wasn't there. Are you sure it was a man you heard?"

"It would have had to be, since I thought it was you."

"Well, maybe one day, you'll remember. But for now, I just want to look at you and enjoy our time together. By the way, who drove you here? You certainly didn't come here alone."

"No, I didn't. Uncle Freddy is waiting outside for me."

"Ah, Freddy. How's he doing? He hasn't come to visit in a few months."

"He comes by often and spends time with me. He lives downtown in Greenwich Village, in a cool apartment. Sometimes he brings a girl-friend to Nanny and Papa's house. None of them like to go to museums or bookstore or do the things I like."

"Well, I'm not surprised," said Daddy. "Freddy always was the play-boy. And, not anything like your mother."

"Daddy, aside from Uncle Freddy, does anyone else come to visit?"

"A few people, sweetheart. My parents. My attorney. My former business partner, Tommy Cole. Do you remember him? We used to get together a lot with his family. Remember his kids, Kim and Zach? You used to love to play with them."

"Yes, I sure do. Kim and I are still friends. We go to the same school."

"That's good," said Daddy. "They're good people."

When it was time to leave, Julie told her dad that she would visit him often. She assured him that she'd try hard to remember that night. Whose voice had she heard fighting with Mommy?

* * * *

It was then that Julie's life took a dramatic turn. She became focused on a way to uncover the memory that could set her father free. She became obsessed. Much of her time was spent reading and researching psychological, spiritual, and mystical strategies that could help her. Luckily, she was a very bright and intelligent young lady who was able to tend to other areas of her life simultaneously.

Julie kept up with her studies, first in high school and later in college and graduate school, but she refused to squander her time on unnecessary activities. She had no social life, refused to join a sorority or join sports teams, or do any of the things that young women were anxious to do. Her every spare minute was spent in pursuit of one memory.

Julie's two sets of grandparents looked on helplessly. They had found that their interventions were not welcomed by their granddaughter. No amount of pleading or cajoling could affect the course her life was taking. Feeling saddened and defeated, Julie's Spencer grandparents decided it was their time to move to a warmer climate and enjoy their senior years in a new environment. So many of their friends and acquaintances had relocated to the coasts of Florida, and they wished to do the same.

Since they were blessed with abundant resources, they turned over their New England home to Julie, who had always loved being there. Fortified by her promise to visit them, and assured that her Nanny and Papa Sloan would keep a close watch on her, they moved south.

In seclusion, Julie was able to pursue her obsession without much interference. She meditated, underwent regression therapy and hypnosis, consulted psychics, and even visited a fortune teller. But nothing unlocked that long lost memory.

* * * *

One cold, blustery winter day Julie sat at her desk reading a novel that had been sent to her to review. The author had used a solar eclipse as background for an intriguing story of truth and redemption in the early days of civilization. Julie was mesmerized and couldn't stop reading. This topic, which she had known nothing about, inspired her to research the spiritual interpretations of the impact of such an eclipse on the lives of humans. Most sources cited its negative and evil repercussions. Punishment for bad deeds. A portent of difficult times. Destruction. But one source offered a different interpretation. A Judaic scholar citing the Talmud, the vast Hebrew compendium of laws and traditions, spoke of the light that emanated from the borders of an eclipse as "rays of hope." These "rays of hope" represented enlightenment and truth: signs that God has not deserted the people of Earth. Julie continued her research. Could this provide a way to unlock her memory?

The next solar eclipse would occur over the summer, six months away. Its course would make it visible in New England. Julie would be watching. But before then, there were preparations she needed to make. She'd visit her father, Nanny and Papa in New York, and Grandma and Grandpa Spencer in Palm Beach. Maybe her life would change after the eclipse, and then she'd have good news for them. But for now, she wanted to see them all. None of them were getting younger, and she loved them all dearly. And the visits would take her mind off the eclipse.

* * * *

Julie's first glimpse of her Dad was upsetting. He'd aged so. His hair, or what was left of it, was completely gray. His shoulders were stooped, and he seemed shrunken. His blue eyes had dulled.

"Oh, Daddy, you don't look well. Are you sick? Have you seen the prison doctor?"

"No, honey, it's just that life in here has taken its toll. The boredom, the need to be vigilante every minute day or night, the noise. It's wearing me down. If it wasn't for you, I don't think I'd be able to keep going."

Her father's hopelessness alarmed Julie. He was defeated. She wondered how long it would be before he gave up completely.

"Please, Daddy, try to keep your spirits up. For me. For Grandma and Grandpa. We love you and need you. Please."

"Oh, I'll do my best, sweetheart. But I'm tired. The years in here have worn me down."

When the visiting hour was over, Julie left the prison in tears. She knew in her heart that she was going to lose her father if he was forced to remain in prison. And, she couldn't even blame him.

* * * *

The days she spent with Nanny and Papa in the city were upsetting also. Her mother's parents were deep into their senior years, and Papa wasn't in the best of health. The tragic death of their daughter had taken a terrible toll on them, and their ability to put on brave faces had diminished over the years. Papa's doctor had suggested that they seriously consider relocating to a warmer and drier climate to alleviate Papa's pulmonary issues. They were planning to take a trip out to Phoenix and adjacent Arizona environs to look at senior communities out there. Julie heartily agreed and assured them she would visit often.

While she was in the city, July spent time with her Uncle Freddy. She'd remained close to him through the years, and he came north to visit with her whenever he could get away from his demanding public relations job. They shared a deep concern for Nanny and Papa and agreed that Papa's health requirements warranted an immediate move to a more hospitable climate. Freddy was very disturbed about the news of Julie's dad and said he'd make it a point to travel to Ossining to see his brother-in-law.

Julie told him about her plans to view the eclipse. He asked if he could come up to New England and view it with her.

"By all means," said Julie enthusiastically. "Why don't you plan on spending your summer vacation with me? We can enjoy some serious beach time and maybe visit some museums and galleries in Boston. You know, I don't get out much and try my best to avoid people. But you're different. You're my favorite uncle. As a matter of fact, you're my only uncle!"

"It's a deal," Freddy laughed. "It'll be a great way to spend a vacation. And I need a good seafood fix, too."

Julie hadn't told Uncle Freddy the underlying reason why she was anxious to view the eclipse. She was almost certain he would think she had completely lost her mind. But, in truth, it wasn't a bad idea to have someone with her. Just in case.

* * * *

Julie was heartened by her visit with her Spencer grandparents in Florida. They looked well and lived an active life. No idleness for them. They belonged to various special interest groups and did volunteer work with a number of local nonprofits. Grandpa was playing an active role with a prison reform movement. Their hearts were broken by their son's incarceration for a crime they adamantly denied he was capable of committing, and flew north to visit with him often and wrote encouraging letters daily. They chose to devote their energies in a proactive way. She left them feeling uplifted.

* * * *

The day of the eclipse arrived. Armed with beach chairs, a basket filled with cheese, fruit, a bottle of wine, and eye protectors. Julie and Freddy settled themselves on the rocky cliff overlooking the ocean. Julie's stomach was in knots, and her heart beat so fast it felt like it would pop out of her chest. Freddy, unaware of his niece's anxiety, was in a jovial mood.

As the time of the eclipse drew near, Julie did her best to relax. If this phenomenon didn't unlock that deep memory that had consumed her, she didn't know where to turn. This seemed to be her very last option.

The sky began to darken. A bright, sunny day, slowly turned into night. With their eye protectors in place, both Julie and Freddy looked up to the sky. An excruciatingly bright aura appeared along the edges of the moon-blocked sun. Rays of hope.

* * * *

Julie didn't know why or for how long she'd lost consciousness. The day was once again bright and the sun was shining. The eclipse had passed. It didn't seem that any great revelation had come to her. Julie was shattered. Unbidden, tears of frustration streamed down her face.

Julie turned to look at her uncle Freddie. His hands covered his face and his shoulders shook with silent sobs. Alarmed, Julie reached out to him.

"Freddy, what's wrong? Were your eyes injured by the eclipse? Please tell me, what's wrong."

After several moments, Freddy's hands fell to his sides. Bloodshot eyes looked towards Julie.

"During the eclipse, I realized I had to make things right," he said haltingly. "Julie, I've done terrible things, and I'm gonna burn in hell. It was me. I did it. I killed my sister. All these years, I've kept quiet to save my own ass. I destroyed the lives of your father, my parents, and the Spencers. And you."

Julie felt as though she was caught in a nightmare. It was hard to process what she was hearing.

"Why did you kill my mother?" Julie's asked in a low monotone.

"I gambled. I was in the hole for a lot of money I didn't have. I needed my sister to help me out, just like she always did. But she said no."

"But why did you have to kill her?"

"God knows I didn't mean to. I just got so angry. She told me to get out, then turned and went up the stairs. I followed her and begged, pleaded with her to help me out. She said she'd never give me another dime ever again. It was time for me to grow up. Take care of myself."

Freddy stopped talking for a moment and covered his face with his hands. He appeared to be in a great deal of pain. But certainly not as much as those whose hearts he'd broken.

"She wouldn't change her mind," he continued. "Here her husband was swimming in dough, and she wouldn't help out her brother. I saw red."

He paused again, seeming to try to gather up the courage to continue on.

"She had her back to the stairway. I just lost it. I shoved her, and she went down the stairs. I froze, realizing what I'd done. I ran down to the foyer to help her. She lay there, broken. My sister was broken. I ran out of the house, got in my car and left."

There was silence for several moments. And then, Julie rose to her feet. Her back was rigid and her face was expressionless. The eclipse had indeed resulted in enlightenment, but certainly not in the way she'd anticipated.

"We have to go back to the house," she commanded Freddy. "There are calls to be made."

Freddy got to his feet and wordlessly followed his niece.

After the police came to take Freddie away, Julie would speak to her grandparents. The Spencers, she knew, would rejoice, to the extent they were able. She would give the news to Nanny and Papa in person, fearful of the consequences. But before heading for New York City, she'd make the trip to Sing Sing. She'd tell her father he was coming home.

Harriette Sackler can barely remember a time when she wasn't on the Malice Domestic Board of Directors. As Grants Chair, she has a unique opportunity to encourage and support writers on the road to publication. Harriette is a twice-nominated Agatha Award nominee for Best Short Story. She is one of three Dames of Detection, who are the co-publishers and editors of Level Best Books. She and husband live in the D.C. suburbs with their two Yorkie terriers. The loves of their lives are their four little grandchildren. Harriette is an animal advocate and volunteers with two pet rescues. Visit her website at: harriettesackler.com

WOMEN'S WORK

KB INGLEE

The District of Columbia, September 29, 1875

Charles Lawrence had cajoled Emily into coming along to observe the eclipse with a team of scientists.

"It will be fun," he had said. "We have little enough of that these days. You will lean something, as well."

Charles Peirce had sent the invitation two weeks earlier. Emily Lawrence was surprised when her husband accepted it. The two Charleses had become friends at Harvard when Charles Lawrence had taken a course from Peirce's father. Emily had known Mrs. Peirce, Zina, since their school days.

There had been little contact between the two couples after they moved to Washington, Peirce for a job with the Coastal Survey, and Emily and Charles to set up their detective agency. Emily believed that Peirce had issued the invitation because the Lawrences could arrange a convenient location, open land within the District, but outside of Washington City.

The sun was just rising as Emily settled onto the blanket that covered the stubble at the edge of the newly harvested hayfield. Zina Peirce was nurturing a small campfire in the road near Emily's blanket. Their husbands stood head to head, deep in some esoteric discussion. Two others, who had been introduced as Robert Brewer and Alvin Goss, were busy setting up the equipment for the observations.

Emily had little idea of what she was looking at. A three-sided tent sheltered an odd device that looked like a telescope bolted to a buggy wheel and secured at the top of a four-legged metal stand. There were two other hand-held telescopes, and three cameras on tripods with boxes of prepared glass plates. On a table next to the tent were weights, graded from a few ounces to several pounds, and two brass chronometers. Emily counted five mirrors on a second table along with a jar of carefully sharpened pencils and a stack of unused journals. A tiny young woman neatened the piles and took her seat behind the table.

Emily was quite sure she wanted no one to try to explain how this all worked.

"This is only a partial or annular eclipse," commented Zina hanging a coffee pot over the fire. "Charles is using it to train his assistants."

Emily had been several years behind Zina at school. It was no surprise when she married the son of a prominent Harvard family. Emily had been expected to do the same. Zina was an intellectual in her own right and had published several radical articles on women's subjects using her maiden name, and one using the name Zero, at her husband's request. Emily suspected Peirce's disregard for women had more to do with his self-absorption than with any real dislike.

"You will need to protect your eyes when you look at the sun," said Zina. "Charles has glasses for the men. We will have to be content with a pinhole camera." There was some bitterness in the comment. A woman like Zina should be up with the scientists, not entertaining a guest.

Zina described what everyone was doing. Emily realized Zina was well acquainted with the process. She had gone to Europe with the party of astronomers sent to observe the eclipse in 1871.

Gross and Brewer were making sightings and calling out readings to the young woman. No one had bothered to mention her name.

Mr. Stuben strolled into the midst of the company, as he had every right to do, since he owned the land. He went up to the two Charleses as they stood by the unwieldy telescope.

Emily took the cup of coffee Zina offered and asked her about the housekeeping cooperative she had set up in Cambridge. "I read your article on it. How did it actually work? Have you tried to set one up in Washington, as well? I could surely use one here. Running an office and trying to keep a home is quite impossible."

Zina chatted on about her cherished work until the moon had crept up on the sun so that each were in proper position for the scientists to begin their work. Then she turned the tables on Emily. "And what does a lady detective do? Do you carry a gun? Do you have it with you now?"

Emily pulled her tiny Merwin Hulbert out of her purse.

"Women's work. Not only do you get less pay, you get a smaller gun," joked Zina.

Emily described the life of a detective, accentuating the lurid bits and ignoring the tedium of most of it. Nor did she mention that she took no pay at all, only an occasional outlay from petty cash.

As the sun rose higher, the men working at the equipment picked up the pace to be ready when the eclipse started.

"It isn't so different from being a scientist," Emily said, inclining her head toward the men. "You develop an hypothesis and then test it. You keep doing it until you have found the real answer."

"But isn't it dangerous?" asked Mrs. Peirce.

"Sometimes, but not often."

The sky began to darken, and the birds began their evening song. Emily thought the flock must be very confused since the dawn chorus had been only a few hours earlier. She watched as they flew, one by one, to a large oak tree to settle in for a nap.

The crew seemed to be having trouble with one of the big cameras, and Zina went to help with it. Emily turned back to watch the birds.

A puff of smoke rose from the other side of the corn field that lay between them and the oak tree. The sound of the shot reached Emily as the first bird rose from the sanctuary, followed by the rest of the flock in a mad dash for safety. It seemed they were not to be the only poachers on Stuben's land today.

Stuben and Emily's husband glanced in the direction of the shot and put their heads together briefly. The scientists seemed too engrossed in the experiment to notice. Emily leapt up and made for the cornfield.

She wrestled her way through the corn that was taller than she was, and reached a spot near the oak tree where the shot had been fired. The sun was disappearing slowly as the moon crept up on it. There was plenty of light to see by, but it felt like early evening.

A man lay face down in the wagon track between the corn field and what looked like a pumpkin patch. Had he been running away? There was no sign of the shooter, but an aged Winchester rifle leaned against the oak tree.

Emily went to the victim. He was indeed without a pulse. Whoever had fired the shot was either well trained or very lucky.

Standing near his feet, she turned in a complete circle for a good look at the surroundings. There were two paths through the cornfield, places where the corn stalks had been flattened. The downed stalks of both paths pointed toward the oak tree. The one to the right was her own. The other was twenty feet or so to the left of hers. They both must lead back to the hay field where everyone should still be watching the sun.

As she combed the spot under the tree where the shooter must have stood, Charles and Stuben appeared. She held up the shell casing she had found so Charles could see it.

"Do you know who this poor man is?" asked Emily, putting the shell casing in Charles's hand.

"I do," said the farmer. "His name is Henry Singleton. He came to us two weeks ago, looking for a room. We sent him to a boarding house closer to Washington City. He said he needed something he could afford as close to the city as possible. He had a fast horse, so it wouldn't have taken him long to get to work from here. Haven't seen him since."

Charles put his hand on Stuben's arm. "Keep the others away, will you? If they ask you anything, just tell them that you know nothing. Oh, and you'd better send your son for the police."

"Go round by the road, not the short cut through the field." Emily indicated the drying corn almost ready for harvest. "We don't want to tread on any evidence, and it would be a good idea to preserve as much as we can for your harvest."

Charles watched the farmer walk away, then, indicating the left hand path, said, "Shall we see where it leads?" It was clear to both of them that it led straight to the pavilion where everyone was absorbed in the work. Emily sighed, thinking that none of them would have noticed a thing out of the ordinary.

They moved slowly up the path, inspecting it inch by inch. There was a partial footprint near a small puddle, but not enough to be able to identify the maker.

"Charles, which one do you think it could be? Zina had just gone to help with the camera, and you and Stuben were standing by the pavilion."

Charles added his list. "I was watching Peirce. That leaves the two assistants or someone from the outside."

"The trail through the corn points to someone here."

By the time they emerged from the cornfield, Peirce and his assistants were deep into the observations. The moon had covered the sun partially and Emily had to remind herself not to look at it. The eclipse was as full as it was going to get.

"Scientists are good observers. Maybe someone saw something we missed," said Emily to Charles as they strolled along the edge of the field.

"Don't count on it. They are also very good at concentrating on their subject. All eyes would have been on the equipment and the sun."

"We'd better tell them. We can't keep them in suspense until the police get here." Charles headed toward Peirce.

"What's happened, Emily?" asked Zina as she hung a stew pot over the fire.

"There's been a murder on the other side of the cornfield."

Zina seemed neither shocked nor frightened. "Is that why you took off in such a hurry? Well, none of us did it. We were all in plain sight of each other, and intent on our jobs."

Emily was not the least surprised at this reaction. Zina really did have the cool detachment of a scientist.

"Did you hear the shot?" asked Emily.

"Yes, I thought someone was birding. That flock flew out of the tree when the gun went off."

Emily watched as Charles broke the news to Peirce, who seemed not at all interested. He shrugged and went back to work. Once they saw the body, if they did, it would become real for them. But for now, their task was more important.

Zina beckoned to the young woman, whose name Emily still didn't know. The two women set out willow pattern plates and highly polished silverware on the table by the fire. Everything was more elegant than Emily would have expected for such and outing.

"I'll bet no one appreciates this but us," whispered Zina to Emily.

"I'm sure," she replied. But her mind was on the murder.

As the three women set out the food, Emily pulled the young woman to one side.

"No one has told me your name. I assume you have one."

The woman laughed as Emily hoped she would. "I'm Lucy Chambers. I'm not sure anyone here except Mrs. Peirce actually knows my name."

Zina picked up where Lucy left off. "She had been sitting at the table taking dictation from the men working the equipment. She does it well, hence my husband's inability to remember her name. If she was poor at it he would learn her name as he fired her."

Ah, thought Emily, remembering the bitterness in Zina's comment, *women's work*, when Emily had shown her gun.

The men broke away from their tasks to eat. It was nearly two in the afternoon and no one had eaten since dawn.

"Let's go see if you know the victim," said Charles putting his hand on Peirce's shoulder. It could have been a friendly move, or a way of getting his attention. In spite of Charles's announcement, everyone still seemed blissfully ignorant of the murder hidden from them by the tall corn. Emily hoped they could solve the case before the police arrived and devastated the field looking for clues.

A few minutes later, Charles appeared at Emily's shoulder. "Peirce verified Stuben's identification of the victim as Henry Singleton. Peirce says he had just hired him to be part of the field team. He came down from Baltimore last week. He had not been introduced to the rest of the team, but that doesn't mean none of them knew him."

"So it is likely that someone from the team knew he was joining them and had a reason to want him out of the way," Emily said.

Charles nodded. "Well, we know who didn't do it. Do you have any thought on who did?"

Emily shrugged. "Odd that the murderer left the gun leaning against the tree. Why didn't they take it away or hide it?"

"Mmm," Charles said, "maybe they thought we couldn't identify it. It's a pretty ordinary Winchester. Old and well loved."

"Maybe it was important to them and they planned to come back for it. Or maybe what they had done frightened them, and they weren't thinking."

"I am going back to wait for Stuben and the police. You stay here and keep the gang under control." Charles kissed her on the cheek and ducked back into the cornfield.

Peirce was sitting in a lawn chair, looking content with the world as though no dead man had marred his outing. As Emily approached, he stood up.

Emily took the opportunity to grill him about his assistants. The two young men had worked for him for several years. Robert Brewer was a gifted scientist and good with the paper work, which made him invaluable. It was well known that Peirce was easily distractible and seldom finished any project. The other, Alvin Goss, was newer but showed promise. Though Peirce didn't say it directly, it was clear that Goss was deferential to his boss, and flattered him unmercifully.

"Why would anyone kill my new assistant? It isn't like either of them were being forced out."

"What about Miss Chambers?" Emily asked.

"Lucy? She's a girl."

"She is a woman, and quite as capable of murder as any of us." Had she actually just defended a woman's right to be a murderer? Well, in the few years they had been in Washington she had met a few.

"You sound like my wife."

He turned away from her abruptly and made for the food.

As Brewer and Goss began packing up the equipment, Lucy was stacking the papers and slipping them into a leather case. As she grabbed for a handful of pencils, she scattered them into the hay stubble. Emily went to her assistance.

"I'm not usually this clumsy," Lucy said.

"You seem nervous," said Emily. "Are you afraid someone will recognize the gun?"

Lucy gaped at Emily. "What makes you think I did it?"

"Well, I'm not entirely sure, so I thought I would ask you. The path into the corn field starts right behind your chair. Either you made it, or saw who did. Since you haven't been forthcoming, I suspect you made it. Of all the people except myself and Mrs. Peirce, you are short enough to be hidden completely by the corn. If you carried the rifle with you, someone would have noticed. You must have come earlier and stashed it. Oh, yes, and I see there is some mud on your shoes. Will your foot match the footprint we found?"

A quick succession of emotions ran across Lucy's face. Emily didn't try to identify them, except that the first was fear and the last resignation.

"I brought my father's gun in with the equipment. It was easy to slip it into the sack for the tripod of the big camera," Lucy said. "I think I left it at the tree by mistake. I've never shot at anyone before. I wish I hadn't, but I was so angry."

Lucy began to shake. Emily took her hand to soothe her. This would never do if she planned to get any more information out of her.

Lucy went on, her voice trembling with the realization of what she had done. "I suppose I really should have shot Peirce himself, instead. He is the one who refuses to see who I am or what I do. He thinks the son of a friend with no training can do what I have done now for several years. Well, he can't hire him now."

When the police had come and gone, Emily joined Zina in cleaning up the picnic area.

Zina said, "It is too bad for the poor young man. And Charles will find someone else to do the job, but not for the pittance he paid Lucy."

Award winning short story author KB Inglee's work is set between the early colonial period and the late 19th century. Her day job is as an historical interpreter, which helps her get the details right. If you like this Emily Lawrence story, you can read more in *The Case Book of Emily Lawrence*, also by Wildside Press. She lives in Delaware with her family and too many pets.

OPEN HOUSE

BRIDGES DELPONTE

Like most things, it started small. A Red Sox beer coozi. A fancy desk pen. A Provincetown fridge magnet. Trinkets from his favorite Sunday ritual. Open houses. To Keefe, it wasn't stealing, just collecting. In lousy real estate markets, open houses bloomed like spring wildflowers. Desperate owners didn't mind him walking on their carpets, sitting on their beds or eyeing their bathrooms. So why care about a missing mug or placemat? Less to pack up in the end, he thought. But that was before the curse, and that psychic.

This weekend, he treasure-hunted in Waltham, a community hemmed in by highways and corporate office parks, with its mix of ramshackle duplexes and upscale McMansions. He headed for an open house in Piety Corner. Parking his Honda, he pulled on a blue sports jacket from a Belmont open house. Clipboard in hand, he pretended to jot down notes as he sized up a modest brick ranch. Noticing him, a bottle blond realtor brushed off two terminal renters with lousy credit and little hope of buying.

"Come on in. It's great inside."

"John Walker," he said smiling. "No relation to the scotch."

The realtor laughed, a little too hard.

"Donna Smeals, Sunset Realty."

On her sign-in sheet, he scrawled this week's alias and his ex-girlfriend Melanie's cell number. Let Donna pester his ex with follow-up calls. Handing him a listing, she droned on about granite counter tops and stainless steel appliances. He glanced around for his prize. Slim pickings.

"Any idea why they are selling?" Keefe asked.

He noticed Donna's momentary lip twitch. "Not sure. Maybe downsizing."

Polite real estate speak for owners one step ahead of foreclosure, Keefe thought.

"Chocolate chip cookie?"

Munching a cookie, he spun his usual tale about a job transfer. He mentioned his wife, Amber, and their two kids, Cody and Madison, plus their golden retriever, Charlie. None of it true. But he liked this story of normalcy that eluded him in real life.

"You'll love the backyard. Perfect for your kids. And Charlie." She winked and slid open glass doors to a brick patio and fenced yard.

Keefe saw a black mutt furiously digging a hole.

Donna clapped her hands. "Get out of there. That damn neighbor's dog. Tunneling to China."

She rushed out and seized its collar. The dog growled and clenched a plastic doll between his teeth. As he got closer, Keefe noticed a robed statue. She tried to pull it out of his mouth, but he wouldn't release it.

"This oughtta work." Keefe waved a stick in the air and flung it over a hedge.

The excited pooch raced after it, dropping the statue. Donna hurriedly kicked dirt over the hole. Keefe picked up the statue. Some kind of saint. Dirt clung to its pale bearded features and the red folds of its robe.

"What's this?" he asked.

"Saint Joseph. Blessing their happy home."

More like a superstition meant to answer their miserable prayers to unload this albatross. Keefe had read about it online. Bury him upside down in your backyard and your home sells fast. Then dig him out and display him in your next home. If you don't follow through, it's bad luck, damnation or both if you believe this stuff. Donna's cell phone chimed out a silly ringtone.

"Excuse me." She whipped out her phone and headed inside.

Keefe secreted the statue away in his jacket pocket and left for his next open house.

* * * *

Late Sunday afternoon, Keefe pulled into the driveway next to his landlady Evelyn Murphy's Somerville home. He rented a second floor studio in her aging carriage house. Trudging up a narrow staircase, his portly frame brushed against both walls. At the landing, he took a hit from his inhaler. His asthma seemed to be getting worse. Maybe this new inhaler would work better. He breathed in deeply and dumped his haul on his kitchen counter. A brass card case. An oak picture frame. A paisley tie. And that Saint Joseph statue. He neatly flattened each house flyer, laying a trinket on each one for later cataloging.

In his studio's sloped eaves, he had attached rows of shelves crammed with hundreds of knick-knacks from three years of open houses. His most prized possessions were displayed on a wooden mantel above a fireplace, including a silver cocktail shaker engraved, "With love and kisses, Suzie," from an oversized Tudor in Newton with an awful harvest gold kitchen. Suzie held a privileged spot on his mantel, next to a picture of Albert, his deceased pet guinea pig.

Keefe heard a dog barking. Peeking out his window, he spied a twenty-something girl in tight jeans. Purple highlights streaked her jet black hair. She tugged the leash on a brown-and-white cocker spaniel and pored over a rental listing taped to Murphy's mailbox. She marched up to Murphy's house and banged on her door. He knew Murphy wasn't home, skipping church to play slots at a Connecticut casino.

Getting no answer, she pulled her dog up a gravel driveway to the carriage house. She pressed her nose against a window to the downstairs studio. He watched as she turned to leave, hoping she wouldn't come back. He liked a quiet downstairs. Who needs a mangy pooch barking all night or crapping in his yard?

His eyes followed her as she walked back to the street. Turning at the last minute, she caught him staring at her. He darted away from his window. A moment later, his doorbell buzzed. He ignored it, but she kept leaning on it. A rattle of gravel striking his window startled him. Seconds later another spray of gravel bounced off the glass. Keefe grimaced. She better not break his window. He lumbered downstairs and cracked open his door.

"What the hell are you doing?"

"Getting you to open door," she said with a thick, Russian-sounding accent. Her dark brows jutted above her green eyes. A silver nose ring and eyebrow studs sprouted from her porcelain skin. Probably some druggie who hung out in sketchy Teele Square.

"Why you hide?"

"Not hiding. I live here."

"Why you no answer?"

"I'm busy."

"Doing what?"

"None of your business." Before slamming his door shut, her dog bolted upstairs. Keefe raced after it, fearing the worst.

"Niko," she yelled.

Keefe panted as he reached his upstairs landing, bracing himself for doggie destruction. Instead Niko lounged on his battered futon.

"Get off that," he said.

Niko didn't budge.

The girl appeared and sternly uttered a string of foreign words. Niko sheepishly returned to her side. She stared at Keefe's curios lining his apartment shelves. She picked up a tiny ceramic thimble and popped it on her index finger.

"My Baba, my grandmother, collects. In Ukraine. What you call?"

"Thimble." Keefe snatched it from her.

A token from that white Cape Cod in Watertown. Never going to sell at its asking price, with its tiny master and telephone booth bathroom.

"Why you have?"

"I'm a collector," he said.

She examined his tchotchkes, each arranged on a rumpled open house flier. Picking up the statue, she said, "You steal Jesus."

"Saint Joseph." He yanked it away. "I'm no thief."

She laughed. "You liar, too."

"Take your dog and get out."

"I need apartment." She shook Murphy's rental leaflet in his face.

"No druggies. Only people with jobs."

"I have job," she said.

She dug into her jeans pocket and pulled out a business card. Keefe glimpsed at it, "Madame Irina. Psychic Healer. Parties. Counseling. Davis Square."

"If you're really a psychic, you'd know my landlady's not home. So find another place." He flung her card on the floor.

"I want apartment, thief," she shouted.

"Stop calling me that. Go away. She's not home."

"Then wait here for her." Irina flopped down on his couch.

"Get lost or I'm calling 9-1-1."

"Go ahead, Jesus thief," she said, pointing to his collection. "Tell them you steal from me. My Baba's favorite statute from Ukraine."

"Statue, not statute."

"Maybe you try rape me." She pulled the neck of her t-shirt collar off her right shoulder.

Keefe sighed. He didn't need tongues wagging about a cop car out front. "All right. I know where she hides a spare key. I'll show you."

He tramped downstairs with Irina and Niko on his heels.

"Wait here while I get it."

In the rear yard, he grabbed a garden hose. Keefe returned to find Irina flipping through mail overflowing in the empty studio's box.

Keefe grinned as squeezed his garden hose full blast on her and Niko. "Go to hell, crack whore."

As Niko whined, she started swearing. She spit out angry words in Ukrainian "You be sorry. Curse you." Irina gave him the finger as she hurried off with Niko.

Back in his apartment, his heart pounded and Keefe mopped his brow with a pale blue handkerchief from that gray Greek Revival in Cambridge with icky popcorn ceilings. He sucked on his inhaler and breathed more easily.

Calmed, Keefe again cataloged his treasures. Gathering up the statue, he scrubbed off dirt under his faucet. He saw several dog bite marks. Chuckling, he placed it between a Darth Vader bobblehead and a nude centerfold shot glass on a bottom shelf. He set his Hello Kitty alarm from a Dutch colonial in Saugus for his early shift at Moon's Quikstop. The cashier job bored him, but it paid his bills. And Moonsavi was a decent boss, a hard-working Pakistani, with three successful gas marts.

Before closing his eyes, he smiled at his mantel treasures. "Good night, Albert. Sweet dreams, Suzie."

* * * *

In a deep sleep, a sudden bang nearly threw him out of bed. Another loud whack followed. Keefe sauntered over to his window and squinted into the darkness looking for any clues. He saw nothing. Probably squirrels racing around the roof. He crawled back into bed.

As he nodded off, his studio shook with ferocious whacking of hammers beating against its roof. With each mighty bash, his trinkets popped up in the air and tumbled off their shelves. Keefe jumped out of bed as his entire studio shook with incessant hammer thwacks. The ceiling cracked open and plaster fell around Keefe's shoulders. He clutched Suzie and Albert's photo and fled downstairs.

Pushing open the door, Keefe felt something soft and squishy. The stench hit him as he stepped into a pile of dog crap. "That bitch," he said.

He staggered into his driveway in his underwear. Gasping for breath, he expected to see his neighbors fleeing their homes. But all was quiet. He stumbled over to Murphy's front porch and peered inside. Bathed in blue TV light, she snored loudly in her recliner. Keefe felt his chest tightening. Having forgotten his inhaler, Keefe stumbled up his apartment stairs. When he flicked on a light, his knick-knacks remained tidily on their shelves. The ceiling appeared smooth and intact.

"Some nightmare," he mumbled.

He put down Suzie and Albert's photo. Squeezing his inhaler, he gulped a lungful of spray. Surveying his studio, he shuddered before lurching back to his bed.

"Ow!"

Looking down, he stepped on his shattered nudie shot glass, cutting his foot. He cleaned and bandaged his gash. Keefe swept up broken shards before finally laying down. Listening to his fan's hum, he tried to shake off this bad dream.

Yet he never fell back asleep that night or the next five nights. The same delusion repeated itself, the hammering getting louder and the shaking growing more intense. For once, Keefe actually looked forward to work. His waking hours at Moon's became his only refuge from his recurring nightmare.

* * * *

"You look like hell, Keefe," said Moonsavi, examining last night's receipts.

"Haven't slept much."

"Finally got yourself a woman." Grinning, Moonsavi's dark moustache curled above his upper lip.

Keefe shrugged. No woman since Melanie dumped him four years ago. "You ever have a nightmare over and over that feels real?"

"Yeah, my mother-in-law," said Moonsavi.

"No, I'm serious. The past five nights, my whole apartment's shaking. Like an earthquake."

"It's Somerville, Keefe."

"I know, but it's so real. Keep thinking I'm gonna die."

"It's an old house. Probably settling."

"Maybe it's haunted," remarked an elderly customer. She thumbed through tabloids in a magazine rack. "Lived in a house in Maine, once. Ghosts bumping around all hours." She plunked down twenty dollars and pointed to a roll of lottery tickets.

"I've lived there for six years, ma'am. Not a sound until this week." Keefe tore ten tickets off and handed them to her.

"Maybe you pissed them off." She wagged her finger. "Better tell 'em you're sorry or else."

Moonsavi watched her waddle out the door. "Okay, are you doing drugs or something, Keefe?"

"No. Nothing like that. But I got a new inhaler."

"Could be a bad reaction. Call your doctor. Something like that might kill you." Moonsavi motioned with his finger as if slitting his throat.

Tired of walking around like a zombie, Keefe contacted his doctor for another prescription. At lunch, he dropped it off at CVS and then drove home for a short nap. He nodded off to Judge Judy reruns.

A sharp jab to his stomach roused him. He held his stomach as his spasms intensified. His heart thumped wildly as his stomach swelled like a beach ball. Buttons popped off his shirt and shot across his room. Waves of excruciating pain rippled over him. Keefe groaned in agony and gasped for air. Suddenly his pants' crotch seams tore open and murky water gushed out.

In searing pain, he caught sight of a bloody crown of a baby's head cresting between his legs. Screaming in horror, he clenched his bed pillows in distress. A howling baby sprang out and quickly turned dark blue, its umbilical cord wrapped around its neck. Choking, its high-pitched shrieks echoed in Keefe's apartment. He tried to free the baby from its noose. Doubling over, he fell off his bed and smacked against cold floor tiles. His eyeglasses flew off his face.

Wheezing, he hungrily sucked in blasts from his inhaler. He coughed and shuddered as the baby kept screeching. Keefe squeezed his eyes shut and rocked back and forth. His buzzing cell phone alarm startled him. He leaned against his bedside, breathing slowly and deliberately. The dying baby was gone. His stomach pains ebbed, his heart rate steadied. He rubbed his sore jaw and felt a wiggling broken tooth.

"Shit." Crawling across his floor, he snatched up his cracked eyeglasses. "Damn it!"

His pants were drenched with sweat, but were neither torn nor bloody.

"What the hell?"

Not another bad dream. He examined the inhaler and threw it across his room. Checking his watch, it was time to go back to work. He changed into fresh clothes before heading to Moon's.

* * * *

"Chrissakes, what happened to you?" asked Moonsavi.

"Fell on a loose step."

He didn't dare tell Moonsavi he thought he gave birth to a blue baby.

"Take these." Moonsavi handed him a pair of readers from a display. Keefe reluctantly put them on.

Moonsavi looked squarely at him. "You sure you're not?" He pantomimed tipping back a liquor bottle.

"No. I'm just having a bad week." A soft whistle escaped from his loose tooth.

"Sounds like a regular kazoo, Keefe."

"Think I busted a tooth when I fell." He showed Moonsavi his damaged tooth.

"You gotta get that fixed. Might get an infection."

"I don't have a dentist," he said, whistling "s" once more.

"You do now. My brother runs a dental clinic in Davis Square."

"I don't have that kind of money." Another low whistle seeped out.

"I'm his big brother. Paid for his schooling. You can work it off on extra shifts."

* * * *

After waiting three hours, Keefe got a temporary cap. Plodding back to his Honda, he grabbed a $100 ticket stuck to its windshield. Keefe angrily stuffed it into his pocket.

On his way home, he picked up pain killers, a new inhaler, and an ice pack. The wipers slapped his windshield as torrents of rain swept across his car. He drove to his apartment and reached for a green, duck-handle umbrella, a souvenir from a weathered farmhouse in Wayland. The umbrella stubbornly refused to open. Rain soaked him as he bolted for his front door. He stepped into another load of dog crap. Tossing down his broken umbrella, he kicked off his soiled sneakers and peeled off his drenched clothes. Keefe stomped upstairs naked. Collapsing on his couch, he cradled an ice pack against his cheek and spied Irina's business card on his cocktail table.

Looking around, he found an air horn he collected from a Medford bungalow near Tufts with a gigantic foosball table in its dining room. He dialed her number and got her answering machine. Pressing his air horn up against the receiver, he let it blast for about 30 seconds.

"Two can play this game, bitch!" He let loose another long blast.

His ears ringing, he stretched out on his couch and noticed his Darth Vader bobble head crushed under his cocktail table. He gathered up smashed remnants of its black plastic helmet. Another victim of his terrible birthing delusion, he figured. He glanced at his lower shelf where that Saint Joseph statue now stood alone.

"Watch your step, Joe," he said, glaring at it. "I've got my eye on you."

He washed down two painkillers and passed out on his bed.

* * * *

Around midnight, his mouth dry and sticky, Keefe wandered over to his fridge. He guzzled orange juice from the carton. In the glow of his fridge light, Keefe noticed the Saint Joseph statue standing on his mantel. He walked toward it and discovered Suzie and Albert's photo lying in the sooty fireplace. Snatching up the statue, Keefe decided to toss it into his trash. Suddenly, the sound of hammering rang out again and shook his entire apartment. As Keefe headed for his trash bin, the screeching baby reappeared, clinging to his leg. The floor started pitching violently back and forth, like the deck of a storm-tossed ship. The roar of pounding waves grew deafening.

Keefe dodged his couch sliding past him as his studio lurched wildly from side-to-side. All his kitchen cabinets squeaked open and closed several times before dancing off their hinges. Cabinet doors crashed around him as he frantically latched on to his kitchen counter. A huge saltwater wave washed over him. His double bed and cocktail table floated past him as sea water steadily rose around him. Scrambling on to his counter, he cried out as his collected objects skated off their shelves into saltwater whirlpools. Momentarily, he thought about wading in to rescue his treasures, but deep swells overcame him. Booming surf, infant wails, and thunderous hammer smacks cascaded over him. Suffocating, he felt his lungs collapse.

The next thing he remembered was waking up on his kitchen floor. His face rested in a puddle of orange juice. He dragged himself up. His apartment appeared orderly and dry with Suzie and Albert back on his mantel. Keefe glanced at the statue sitting on its lower shelf. He convinced himself that his hallucinations were lingering side effects from his old inhaler mixed with painkillers. He refused to let some dumb superstition or nutty Ukrainian curse keep messing with him.

* * * *

At work the following morning, Keefe churned the week's mishaps over and over in his mind. When Moonsavi stepped out, Keefe jumped on the office computer searching for Ukrainian curses, finding little. He reluctantly typed "Saint Joseph." He discovered this saint was a busy guy outside of fielding prayers about house sales. Saint Joe protected carpenters, pregnant women, overseas immigrants, and cabinet makers, too. By lunch, he decided to get rid of him. Racing home, he stepped over Niko's daily poop drop and dashed upstairs. He marched over and grabbed the statue from its shelf.

"You're toast, Joe," said Keefe.

He tossed it in his kitchen trash can and yanked out the liner. Keefe dumped the bag on the curb for morning pick-up.

Back inside, Keefe plucked a cold soda from his fridge and plopped on his couch to watch TV. A local newscaster suddenly interrupted the sports news.

"Frank Chapel, live on location, with this breaking story. A horrific murder-suicide has rocked this quiet family neighborhood. A Waltham man, Gregory Hazakian, has allegedly shot his wife and smothered his newborn daughter, before turning his gun on himself. Neighbors indicated that Hazakian's carpeting business recently fell into bankruptcy and their family home faced foreclosure. Now it's the scene of this terrible family tragedy."

A camera zoomed in on a brick ranch house with a "for sale" sign out front.

"Oh my God," whispered Keefe.

His soda can slipped from his fingertips. It was that Piety Corner home from Sunday's open house. Trembling, his mind flooded with thoughts of that statue. Keefe raced outside and stuffed the trash bag into his car trunk. He drove around looking for a home under renovation. He found a large blue dumpster outside a Queen Anne Victorian in Arlington. He threw the bag in and listened for its clang against the dumpster's walls before speeding away.

When he got back home, Keefe quivered and dissolved into tears when he found Saint Joe back on his mantle, his beloved Albert photo smashed to pieces and Suzie flattened like a corn tortilla. Fearing another night of agony, he packed a duffle bag for an impromptu trip to visit Mom in Worcester. Dealing with her incessant carping would be heaven compared to another hellish moment with Saint Joe. When he picked up his phone to leave Moonsavi a message, he glimpsed Irina's card lying on his cocktail table.

* * * *

New Age flute music and patchouli incense floated outside Sacred Space, a Davis Square shop for natural therapies and supernatural beliefs. Keefe wandered past displays of homeopathic remedies, Tibetan chimes, and Native American Talking Sticks. Spiritual books with titles like, "Your Inner Yogi" and "The Path of Enlightenment" crowded the shelves.

"Hi, I'm Sunflower," said a young woman. She wore a batik kaftan and a long brown braid hung down to her waist. "Anything to soothe your chi?"

"Looking for Irina."

"This way."

Sunflower led him along a narrow hall before parting a beaded curtain. Keefe observed two bean bag chairs around a low plastic table. A worn deck of tarot cards was stacked next to a brass tray with three fresh incense cones and a half-burned red pillar candle.

"Have a seat," she said, smiling. "I'll let her know she has a guest."

Keefe dropped down into a bean bag. He hated being there, but he'd run out of ideas. Irina entered her reading room with a frown on her face, her hands on her hips.

"My curse not work yet. You still alive, Jesus thief."

"Stop leaving dog shit at my doorstep."

"You psychic now, too?" She grabbed her tarot cards and shuffled them. "Why you here?"

"Gotta problem."

"Twenty-five dollars, first fifteen minutes."

"That's a rip-off," blurted Keefe.

"You no like. You keep problem," said Irina, turning to leave.

"No, wait."

Keefe pulled out a cheap steel money clip, a reminder of that mildew-ridden condo in Revere above a seedy pizza joint. Irina sat down and scooped up his money. She lit her candle and incense, closing her eyes as she inhaled deeply. Then she abruptly placed a plastic kitchen timer on her table.

"Fifteen minutes. Go," she said.

As the timer ticked, Irina showed no emotion as Keefe relayed his open house ritual, his collecting of the statue, the strange visions, and all the harms that had befallen him. He explained his effort to dispose of Saint Joe and its reappearance in his studio.

"You bring with you?"

"No way. You gotta tell me how to get rid of it."

Irina shut her eyes and seemed to fall into a stupor, humming quietly. She murmured a few words in Ukrainian and then popped her eyes open as her timer rang.

"Twenty-five dollars, fifteen more minutes."

Keefe reluctantly slapped down more money. Irina reset her timer and once again fell into a daze. Swaying back and forth, she suddenly stopped and stared at Keefe.

"You steal saint. You return."

"I can't."

"Why not?" she demanded.

"The owners aren't ..." Keefe fidgeted in his seat. "Aren't around anymore."

She stared at him, appearing to look right through him.

"Okay. They're dead."

Irina crossed her arms and raised her left eyebrow in disdain. He told her the sordid news story. Shaking her head, Irina put her fingertips to her temples and rubbed them, her eyes snapped shut. At one point, Keefe wondered if she fell asleep. About to wake her, she suddenly stirred.

"You do penance," she said, her eyes still closed. "No more open houses. Sell everything you stole. Garage sale, every Sunday. Until everything gone. Then put statue back in hole. Start tomorrow. But finish before solar eclipse or curse stay forever."

"I can't do that," stammered Keefe.

"You must do."

"I only want to get rid of Saint Joe."

She opened her eyes wide. "You do or no break curse."

"But how does selling everything help?"

"You pay for sins. Maybe saint forgive you. And keep you busy Sundays. So no more stealing."

"What should I do with the money?"

"Every Monday, you come here. Give to me for charity." From under the table, she pulled out a blue ceramic jar marked "Ashes of Problem Clients."

"Why do I have to give it to you?"

"Keep you honest, thief. Every dollar to charity."

"Who's going to keep you honest?"

"You go with me to donate when done." Before he could protest further, the timer buzzed.

"Twenty-five dollars, fifteen more minutes."

He couldn't afford to plunk down any more money so he promised to obey her instructions.

* * * *

That evening, under Joe's watchful eye, Keefe stayed up all night putting price stickers on every item. In a sleepy daze, he tacked up garage sale flyers in the early morning hours. It pained him to arrange his collection on two long folding tables in his driveway.

Under a hot July sun, Keefe sweated as voracious bargain hunters groped his favorite souvenirs and haggled over every price. Within the first hour, it was sheer agony to hand Suzie over to an unshaven man wearing a loud Hawaiian shirt. Keefe felt an incredible urge to chase after Suzie, but he decided to stick with Irina's plan to escape Saint Joe's vengeance.

He sold about a third of his collection during his first Sunday sale and for the first time in a week, Keefe enjoyed a peaceful night's sleep. On Monday, during his lunch hour, he dutifully handed over $300 to Irina. As five more Sundays rolled by, he filled Irina's jar with cash totaling $932.37. With each passing week, his bizarre dreams slowly ebbed and then evaporated.

On the sixth Sunday, he sold his last three items, the day before the solar eclipse. Keefe felt strangely liberated.

* * * *

That Monday, Keefe took early lunch to drop off his final deposit of $1.65 to Irina with Saint Joe in his passenger seat. When he arrived, Sunflower sat dejected in a tie dye sundress at her counter.

"Is Irina in?"

"No, she's gone. Last night, she cleaned out my cash register and took her ...."

Before Sunflower finished, Keefe rushed to the back of her shop, his heart ready to explode.

"I feel so stupid," continued Sunflower. "Irina was good for business. Brought lots of people in for readings."

Her reading room was empty. No bean bag chairs, no table, no candles or incense, and definitely no blue jar.

"The cops told me she's a seasoned con artist. Been shaking people down for years. Always one step ahead of police up and down the East Coast."

The cold slap of humiliation smacked Keefe across his face. He fell to his knees and wanted to cry. No tears would flow. Opening his mouth to scream, no words escaped his lips, only a pained groan.

"You okay back there?"

Keefe heard Sunflower scuff toward him in her hemp sandals.

She lightly touched his shoulder. "Want some chamomile tea?"

Shaking his head no, Keefe let Sunflower help him to his feet. He handed her the final $1.65 and sauntered out. Driving aimlessly around, Keefe furiously plotted his revenge on Irina, even though he knew he'd never see her again. Momentarily, the idea of rebuilding his collection flashed across his mind. Yet he felt Saint Joe's eyes boring into him.

Hoping to beat the eclipse, he raced to Piety Corner. Broken yellow police tape fluttered in the wind from stakes planted around the lawn. As the moon started to roll across the sun, undulating strips of light streaked across the deserted house. Gripping Saint Joe, Keefe marched to the backyard. As the sky darkened and the world around him fell silent, he burrowed into the black loam with his bare hands. He placed the statue, head first, into the hole. Keefe dared not look up at the eclipse for fear of being struck blind as he covered the grave with fresh earth. He ran back to his car and collapsed with fear and exhaustion.

* * * *

For the next month, he found himself routinely driving by the Hazakian house as a succession of different "For Sale" signs appeared. Soon, he noticed new signs no longer appeared on the property as weeds consumed it.

One Sunday, he drove to Piety Corner with borrowed yard tools from Mrs. Murphy. He mowed the home's grass, clipped its hedges, and swept its front steps. From then on, Keefe toiled to keep the property up every weekend. He raked leaves in fall and shoveled snow in winter. As months stretched toward a year, he wondered how much longer it would take for Saint Joe to relent. But Keefe kept going to Piety Corner every week, hoping the saint might one day grant that miracle.

Bridges DelPonte has published three non-fiction books, two novels, several fantasy, mystery and science fiction short stories, and numerous articles in the legal, travel, and business fields. Her mystery, *Deadly Sacrifices —A Marguerite Montez Mystery*, won a Royal Palm Literary Award (2d place) for Florida writers. Her paranormal contemporary fantasy, *Bridles of Poseidon—The Last Emissary Series*, was a finalist for a Royal Palm Literary Award. When not writing, she teaches law courses, creates educational game apps, and lives happily in sunny central Florida. To learn more about Bridges and her writing, please visit her web site: bridgesdelponte.com

RELATIVELY ANNOYING

JOHN CLARK

"Dammit Ezra!" I surveyed the disaster that used to be my prized terrarium. Shards of glass were scattered across my bedroom floor, mixed with the remains of plants and the hideaway for the white rat who hosted my science experiment. I knew exactly what had happened while I was doing chores in the barn.

Ever since my aunt, uncle, and cousin had moved to Freeman, Maine, from just outside Boston, I'd had to be on my toes 24/7. Ostensibly, they had moved here to find a slower, more healthy lifestyle, but I knew better. Cousin Ezra Evans was trouble. Big, noisy, determined trouble.

While Mom and Dad hadn't come right out and said it, I'd overheard enough snippets of hushed conversations to know that moving here had been as much to keep him out of jail or some other secure environment as anything. Ez was wicked smart, but had the impulse control and social skills of a deranged hamster. He'd lasted less than a week at Freeman High before being expelled. Now he was home schooled.

At first, I'd been thrilled to have a relative nearby who was near my age. Then I'd started bearing the brunt of his obsessions and overbearing attitude. You see, Ez thought he knew everything about anything and his ears only picked up what agreed with him, never anything he didn't like or that sounded like a question he couldn't answer.

Today's disaster was a perfect example. He'd been ranting about the terrible consequences of the upcoming total solar eclipse for weeks. Almost everything coming out of his mouth implied that this one was not only unique, but was going to be the downfall of mankind. No wonder nobody wanted to be around him. It was coming next Monday, August twenty-first, but we were well north of the best viewing path, so I couldn't figure out why he was so wound up. How could anything bad happen during an eclipse anyhow? We'd been having them since the dawn of time and I couldn't recall anything in my history classes about them affecting humanity. Sure, there were accounts of early hysteria, but that was due to superstition and unfamiliarity, not anything real. Even so, Ez had been wound up tighter than a teddy bear, so much so that my father had banned him from the house until after the eclipse.

My shattered terrarium was clear proof that he'd defied the ban and in the process ruined my chance at making it to the state science fair, not to mention the loss of more than a hundred bucks of hard-earned money I'd spent setting it up.

You see, it wasn't just the white rat that was missing, it was also a breeding pair of Mongolian Camel Ticks that were gone. I'd had a devil of a time jumping through more hoops than a trained circus animal in order to get permission to buy them. It had taken calls and letters to both of our senators, the US representative for our district and the Maine Fish and Wildlife office in Augusta as well as an import permit. The whole process had taken four months and more writing than my English literature class, but it had been worth the effort. With the help of my mentor, Dr. Alonzo Burke, professor of entomology at the local college, I'd designed an awesome science experiment, one that had a real shot at winning the state science fair. And now my idiot cousin had ruined it.

As I tried to calm down and clean up the mess, I thought about what Ez had been so agitated about the last time we'd been together. It was something about the eclipse altering the upper layers of the atmosphere and allowing strong bursts of radiation through that might affect certain species. For whatever reason, he'd gotten fixated on it being a certainty and not a possibility, seguing from there to being convinced that my imported ticks were among the species that would be altered.

When I'd pressed him on why he believed it, he'd stopped talking to me and walked off. If he hadn't, I think I would have broken his face. At the time, I figured that would be the end of his foolishness and I'd concentrated on school, helping around the farm and polishing the written part of my experiment.

I gave myself the rest of the day to cool off, figuring that Ez had gone into hiding and his parents were likely to stonewall me if I went to confront him. Instead, I used Google Earth to scout the area around their house to see if anything jumped out at me as a likely spot for him to let the rat loose.

I knew his thinking wasn't as sharp as he wanted everyone to believe, not to mention the fact that I doubted he'd bothered to do any real exploring of the area. After all, he was a city kid, and arrogant to boot, so I was sure he hadn't thought through what to do after stealing the rat. I had a momentary wish that he'd get distracted and the ticks might start feeding on him, but squelched it. What I really needed was to find the rat ASAP and hope the ticks were still attached. Without them, my experiment was toast, and likely any chance at an out-of-state scholarship when I graduated a year from now.

Nobody answered the Evans's door when I knocked on it shortly after breakfast the next morning. I went out back and peered in the side window of their garage. Their Subaru wagon wasn't there, leading me to believe Ez had badgered his parents into taking a road trip to avoid dealing with me. That was going to make finding my science experiment even more difficult.

We were fortunate to have a decent hardware store in Freeman and I'd been Fred Pratt's lawn guy since eighth grade, so he was happy to let me go down in the basement to see what size live catch traps he had in stock.

"I'll give you a good deal on whatever you find. Hardly anyone has any interest in them now that those electronic pest repellers are so cheap and easy to use." Fred gave me a flashlight so I could look in the part that wasn't wired.

The downstairs of Pratt's Emporium was the kind of place any self-respecting teen boy would get lost in. The store had been in Fred's family for four generations and it was likely that some of the stuff in willy-nilly piles had been there for almost as long as the place had been in operation. I got distracted by some of the pinup girl calendars going back to before my dad had been born. There were some real lookers on them, fly specks and all.

Three hours later, I was covered in oily sweat and filthy cobwebs, but had managed to find six traps small enough to be useful. I packed them in a cardboard box with reinforced handle holes in each end and headed back upstairs.

Even after getting a discount, buying the traps left my wallet so thin I'd have to borrow money from Dad if I wanted to take Sara Jane to the county fair this weekend, but I knew two things. The traps were a necessary gamble and I needed the distraction that being with my sweetie on Saturday night would provide. We fit together like a romantic jigsaw puzzle. Half the time we didn't need to talk because we were on the same wavelength. As soon as I got the traps set, I was going to call her so she could help me settle my head.

After parking Dad's pickup on the road past my cousin's place, I unfolded the printout of the area and checked to see where I'd planned on setting the first trap. It was a good thing I'd been hunting since I turned ten. Both my dad and my grandfather had spent hours on end teaching me how to move silently and read terrain. I was pretty sure I had marked the most likely spots where Ez might have turned the rat loose, now I had to translate the map into on-the-ground reality.

I was even dirtier and sweatier by the time the last trap had been set and I was cussing myself out for not thinking to bring bug spray with me. Sure, the black flies were long gone, but there were swarms of deer flies and every swampy spot unleashed a fresh horde of ravenous mosquitoes. I used lots of anti-itch cream after my shower.

Mom must have known I'd be teetering on the edge of angry because she had my favorite August meal waiting when I came downstairs. There's nothing better than monster cheeseburgers, home-cut fries, and wild blueberry pie with home-made vanilla ice cream to take the edge off a sour mood. I leaned back and groaned happily after seconds on dessert.

"How you doing?" My dad looked over at me from his rocker on the front porch.

"I'm holding it together, I guess. Good thing Ez beat feet. I'm not sure what I'd do if he'd been stupid enough to stick around. I just hope I get lucky. I don't have time or money enough to replicate my experiment or come up with something as good." Heck, I lucked out by getting to test whether or not a foreign species could carry Lyme Disease and whether I could find a way to turn off the carrier gene. Even a halfway decent report on my experiment would probably land one of the top scholarships. Without something like that, I'll be lucky to go instate and not graduate with a ton of debt.

"Sure wish I could help you more, but things are pretty hectic at work right now and I don't dare ask for time off." Dad sighed and stared out at the growing twilight.

I kept my mouth shut, Dad's woods smarts would be help in my needle-in-a-haystack search, but he was right. As supervisor at the canning plant in town, this was his busiest season what with corn, blueberries, and green beans arriving by the truckload every day. I understood, but that didn't mean I was happy.

I wasn't too mad or too tired to skip seeing Sara Jane. Heck she's so amazing even rocks would drag themselves across the road if it meant spending time in her presence. She's smart, curvy in the best places, and has a neat sense of humor along with green eyes and strawberry blonde hair that hangs halfway down her back. She could care less about being popular, playing violin in the school orchestra instead of cheering, but put her on the basketball court or soccer field and she'll school you every time.

I'd called her right after finding the broken aquarium, so we didn't need to talk about it. Instead, we helped her mother cut and ready beans for canning. That might sound like a pretty hokey date, but I liked the smooth rhythm the three of us created while sitting together on the front porch, working to the sounds of local bluegrass music from the nearby radio station in Skowhegan.

Between Sara Jane therapy and sheer tiredness, I managed to sleep until ten the next morning. I made my lawn mowing and garden weeding rounds before giving in to the urge to check my traps. I took Dad's spare truck, even though the inspection sticker was two months past due. We had no local police force and the county sheriff's patrols didn't bother coming around other than weekends unless there was a complaint. My chances of avoiding a citation were pretty good.

I tossed a couple gallon jars with holes punched through the lids behind the seat and headed off praying I'd get lucky.

Three hours later, I was marveling at my luck, all of it bad, but interesting. Who knew so many different creatures liked peanut butter on a celery stick. All six traps had been sprung. Unfortunately, I'd captured two skunks, a snake, a weasel, a red squirrel and a baby porcupine, but not my rat. I had one heck of a time releasing the skunks. With my hopes a bit dimmer, I reset each trap and headed for home.

Thursday and Friday went pretty much the same. I made my rounds, cutting lawns and weeding gardens. I had a reputation for doing a careful job and showing up regularly, so even with mowing most places every other week now that the grass had slowed in the summer dry season, I still had more than fifty property owners relying on me, plus another dozen or so who had hired me to keep weeds at bay in their flower and vegetable gardens.

As soon as I was done, I went back to check my traps. The first day three had critters in them, but no rat. The next day four were full, but still no luck. I was beginning to realize how much my quest resembled looking for a needle in a haystack.

I said to heck with checking them on Saturday. It was the next to last day for the Somerset County Fair, an event that Sara Jane and I looked forward to all year. We liked the rides, but we liked people watching even more, delighting in making up fantastic stories about some of the more colorful folks who wandered along the midway. We were certain that some of them came from other planets to visit the fair because we never saw their like any other time of year.

I was tied up again on Sunday morning, but for a different and very pleasant reason. My grandfather and I had a ritual every Sunday from the first of June through Labor Day. We hopped in his jeep and went up to camp. Until his health started to deteriorate, my grandfather lived at the family camp on Carrabasset Lake, about fifteen miles north of town. Who could blame him? He could watch every kind of wildlife native to Maine, catch trout and salmon and fry them up on the deck while loons serenaded him. I knew getting out there was the thing that kept him going and I loved being out there just as much.

It was overcast and drizzly when he dropped me and half a dozen pan sized trout off late that afternoon. I debated skipping the traps, but guilt over leaving anything in such a small space for another night made me hop in the truck and drive off.

The fox kit was cute and wicked feisty, obviously unhappy about not being able to escape the suddenly cold rain. I wasn't too thrilled either and as soon as she ran free, I hurried to check the last trap before heading home to get dried off. I was beginning to dance around the fact that I wasn't likely to find either the rat or my prize ticks. The more I thought about it, the worse the queasy feeling in my stomach got.

It rained all day Monday and the only sign there was anything different about the sun was a half hour where it got really dim, but we'd had summer storms that acted like that in the past. There was no way I'd mow lawns today, so I had the eclipse coverage on television and alternated between listening to the commentators and skimming one of the books assigned for summer reading.

I must have dozed off because I woke from a really bizarre dream about monsters and cosmic rays to hear an excited commentator interviewing someone from NASA about the unexpected and unprecedented barrage of cosmic rays hitting the northern hemisphere.

"We've never seen the unique convergence of giant solar flares and a total eclipse simultaneously. Apparently the dimming from the eclipse acted on our upper atmosphere in such a way that there was, for lack of a better description, a paralysis of the layer that blocks most of the intense solar radiation."

I leaned forward to watch, the sick feeling returning in waves. Had my crazy cousin been ahead of the curve after all? If so, why did he believe stealing my experiment was going to be a good thing? The scientist was still answering questions, so I concentrated on getting as much information as possible.

"No, we have no idea what the consequences of such a radiation barrage might be, nor how soon we might notice any changes. The one thing we do know is that the strongest rays hit along the 45th parallel in the northern hemisphere, with the most affected area hitting approximately fifty miles on either side of that line from the eastern border of Vermont to the Atlantic Ocean just north of Eastport, Maine."

I shut my book, then turned off the TV. Holy hell, we were right in that path. I sure hoped this was like so many other alarmist pieces of news. Heck, every time there was any kind of inclement weather, the newscasters tried to make it sound like the world was ending. We'd had school canceled several times last winter based on ominous predictions that fizzled, making the superintendent look foolish. I sure hoped this was that sort of event.

By Wednesday, the frenzy surrounding the radiation scare had subsided, knocked aside by another mass shooting and a volcanic eruption in Mexico. I couldn't help but marvel at how short attention spans had become in the age of instant everything. With the eclipse over and feeling like there was no hope of finding my science experiment, I returned to mowing lawns and weeding with a vengeance.

My cousin was still among the missing, as were his parents. Dad said something about an email letting him know that they had gone on an unplanned vacation to New Mexico. After briefly hoping Ez got bitten by a large rattlesnake, I dismissed him from my mind. If he never showed his face in Freeman again, I'd be perfectly happy.

My life settled into a routine. School would start in a couple weeks, so I tried to make every moment count. If I wasn't working or fishing with my grandfather, I was enjoying Sara Jane's company.

It was four days before school resumed when I realized I'd left the traps in the woods. Guilt washed over me big time and I hated to think my getting distracted by the radiation scare might have resulted in any animals suffering. I jumped in the truck and headed out.

The guilt got worse and worse. I found a dead skunk in the first one and then a dead rabbit in the next. Fortunately the others were empty. I was about to pick up the last trap and carry it to the truck when I smelled something. It had a faintly rotten odor, but there was something unusual as well. After setting the trap down, I followed the scent, making sure to move slowly and check my surroundings after every step. I didn't know why, but I could feel the hair on the back of my neck standing up.

The smell grew stronger as I neared a small brook that flowed from Dingman Pond to the Carrabasset River. I remembered my grandfather saying something about there being coyote dens nearby.

I stopped when I spotted several misshapen carcasses on the bank just above a small waterfall. The creepy feeling intensified the closer I got. There was definitely something amiss here. I stopped just outside an area surrounding the dead animals where the ground had been torn up like nothing I'd ever seen. Whether they'd done it during their death struggles or was caused by what killed them wasn't clear.

After I got my nerves under control, I moved closer, kneeling by one of the carcasses. What I was looking at had been a large male coyote, but was now not much more than a ragged hide over bones. Whatever had come after it and the others had sucked almost everything out, leaving just enough organic matter to create the smell I'd followed. All told there were five adults and three pups, each one nearly mummified like the one in front of me. I snapped a few pictures with my cellphone and ran like hell.

After showing my parents the photos, I called the local game warden and reported what I'd found. I could tell he was skeptical by the tone in his voice, but he asked me to email him copies of the photos and said he'd stop by tomorrow.

Ten minutes after I emailed him the pictures, he called back, saying he was on his way and not to tell anyone else what I'd found.

His warning made me even more unsettled, so I went online and searched for any recent reports of dead animals in Maine. After reading three reports of people finding dead deer, moose and coyotes and noticing that in each case the animals were almost mummified when found, I was ready to have a nervous breakdown.

My nerves were in even worse shape an hour later. Warden Barry Maxwell was a pretty scary guy. Just the way he looked at me had me feeling like I should be confessing to some violation of the fish and game laws. When he said he wanted me to show him the dead coyotes, I realized it was the last thing I wanted to do.

Thankfully Dad offered to come with us and suggested it might be wise to take firearms along. Warden Maxwell agreed. I grabbed my Remington 1100 shotgun and a handful of #4 buckshot shells while Dad went to get his 30-06 bolt action. Having that much firepower might seem like overkill to anyone else, but remembering what awaited us by the stream, made it seem more like not enough protection.

Maxwell had a powerful flashlight in his hand as soon as we stopped his truck. I noticed he'd unhooked the safety strap on his holster as well. He motioned me to lead the way and I did after an audible gulp.

The dead animals were as I'd left them. Dad and I stood together while the warden examined each one. I couldn't stop glancing nervously into the surrounding darkness, certain I was hearing numerous unnamed creatures stalking us. I kept telling myself to man up, but there was something out there that wasn't normal, I was sure of it.

Maxwell completed his examination, taking samples of hide around some of the wounds as well as snapping a bunch of photos with a fancy camera while I held the light. We were about to leave when he froze, shining his flashlight up the stream. Two pairs of reddish eyes reflected light back at us. From where I stood, it looked like whatever was watching us must be at least four feet tall. I couldn't think of any creature native to Maine that was that size and had reddish eyes.

My father flicked the safety off and raised his rifle at Maxwell's quiet command. I readied my shotgun even though it wasn't likely to be effective at the distance these things were from us.

The creature on the left started toward us, moving at a speed that seemed faster than anything I'd ever seen move in the wild. Dad fired and ejected the spent shell, slamming the bolt down and tracking the thing, firing another round seconds later. I heard the bullet ricochet as a high pitched whine came from whatever was heading toward us. What kind of animal had an exterior so tough that a 300 grain hollow point bounced off it?

I didn't have time to ponder the answer. Whatever was attacking was now within range, so I aimed and pulled the trigger as fast as I could, pumping more than 100 lead balls at the thing. The sound of five shots so close together was deafening, but that was the least of my worries. I scrambled to reload while both my father and Warden Maxwell continued firing. By the time I was ready to fire again, the creature had turned, bounding after the one that hadn't attacked.

"You must have hit it in the eye," Dad said, "because I saw it flinch just before you had to reload. Christ, I've never seen anything like that. I swear I saw four or five rounds bounce off it. What kind of creature is bulletproof?"

"I don't know, but I'm sure going to do my best to find out." Maxwell looked grim as he shined the light around. There was a faint trail of fresh blood running in the direction the thing had taken as it left. He pulled a disposable glove from a belt pouch, followed by what must be an evidence bag, slipping the glove over one hand and walking forward until he could grab some of the blood and a few leaves under it.

There were several more reports, all quickly suppressed, about similar creatures preying on wildlife, as well as one report of a truck being severely damaged when it hit an animal crossing the road about twenty miles north. Then for the rest of the time before school started, it was as though we'd imagined everything.

On the first day of our senior year, Sara Jane and I arrived early to get preferred lockers as well as good seats in our home room. We were excited about starting what we hoped was the best year of our school career. Not even the sting of losing my science project could dampen my good feelings today.

Twenty minutes later, I was summoned to the principal's office. The secretary had a strange look on her face as she handed me the phone. I recognized Warden Maxwell's voice immediately and pulled a chair over to sit in before my legs gave out. Somehow, I knew he wasn't calling to wish me a successful senior year.

"The forensic lab in Augusta analyzed the blood sample and I need to ask you a question. Can you account for the ticks you were approved to import?"

At first, I wasn't able to make any connection, then as realization hit me, my body went ice cold. In addition to being larger than most other tick species, the ones I'd imported were known for having a voracious appetite and being pretty aggressive. God, what had I done? More accurately, what had my idiot cousin done?

I quickly explained how Ez had stolen them along with their host, how I'd done everything possible to recover them and what Ez thought was going to happen during the eclipse.

There was a long pause. "I guess your cousin was more on target than anyone could imagine. The analysis showed the blood contained DNA from both insects and animals. The head of the lab said his best guess was that whatever sucked the coyotes dry must have been able to assimilate some of their genetic characteristics, creating the mother of all parasites. He said if he were a betting man, he'd say we're dealing with a tick that's bigger than a full grown wolf, able to run faster than a bear and has an exoskeleton that's stronger than half-inch steel. In other words, the mother of all wildlife nightmares. Hold on, I have another call coming in."

The wait until he came back on the line was just long enough for me to flash through guilt, white hot anger and sheer terror as I remembered the way the creature had come at us in the woods.

"Things are worse that I imagined. The state police just got a call from the Freeman Elementary School. Those things have been breeding far faster than anyone could imagine and they have the school surrounded. I have to go."

I found myself babbling into a dial tone and as my trembling hand placed the phone back on the counter, I realized life was never going to be the same again.

John Clark is a retired Maine librarian with a checkered past. After 27 years in mental health, he worked as a systems librarian and a public library director. Now sober he uses his experiences from the dark times as fuel for books and stories. He reads avidly, mostly YA fiction, and is a reviewer for several print and online venues. When not reading or writing, he wins stuff and has amazing gardens.

ASCENSION INTO DARKNESS

CHRISTINE HAMMAR

Helena McGregor stood in her beige blouse, short red leather skirt, and high heels on the steps of the house she used to live in as a child. She squinted at the scorching sun. The August heat wave had sat over Southern Finland for days and it was hot like in an oven. Not even a breeze in the air.

Although she'd woken up at three a.m. and driven to the TV studio for make-up and to record nine new episodes of her TV show, she looked impeccable. At noon, she'd left for her childhood village, Larvala, where her old house stood waiting for a vacationer. Driving along the motorway she'd suddenly felt terribly tired. She desperately needed the vacation.

The bangs of her short hair glued to her forehead and she felt a trickle of sweat starting to run down her temple. Carefully she patted her temple dry with her fingertips. Wrinkling her nose, she cast her eyes over the overgrown garden. It certainly didn't look like a garden anymore. She glanced at the time on her telephone. Just past two. What to do for the rest of the day, or come to think of it, for the rest of the two-week holiday? Cutting grass in this heat didn't tempt her, so she decided to pick some of her favorite flowers, daylilies. They had spread and there was now a huge patch of them in the garden. Upon her arrival she'd opened all windows, but the air in the old house still smelled stale and needed refreshing.

Going out she was about to lock the door, but remembered that in this peaceful village it wasn't necessary to lock doors even for the night. She walked to where the lilies bloomed in abundance, inhaled their lovely scent and sighed with contentment. A couple of leaves and a big bunch of flowers, she thought, and started cutting.

* * * *

Emma lifted the grocery bags and the beer packs into the back of her car in the scorching hot parking lot of the Larvala S-Market. It was already late in the afternoon, but the sun still shone bright and hot. The plastic bag containing three bottles of whisky she'd bought for her partner, Tapani, keeled over and she hastily grabbed and straightened it.

Her day had not gone well. She'd forgotten to compile the monthly Sales Report for the company's Sales Director. When he sent her an email reminding her, she'd panicked and gathered the numbers. As her telephone beeped, she clicked Send and the report was on its way. She picked up her phone. Tapani.

—Don't forget to buy me more whisky and beer, if you don't want to look like an aging, bruised Barbie tomorrow, he'd said.

Emma had felt like spitting.

—Calm down. I'm going shopping on my way home.

—And bring me a couple of thick steaks. I'm not eating any fucking poor peoples' shit! Tapani had added before cutting off.

Before she left for home, Emma went to the nearby department store and bought herself a new bottle of perfume. She'd sprayed some on her neck and wrists and inhaled. The lovely fragrance of Daylily had filled her nostrils.

She slammed the tailgate door shut wishing Tapani's neck had been between the door and the chassis and stood, keys in hand, squinting at the sky. Luckily her Volvo, as well as her place of work, had air conditioning. She could seldom wear light summer clothes. She had to wear high collar jumpers with long sleeves and trousers to conceal her bruises. Her life had been an endless string of stress, panic, bruises and blood for too long.

* * * *

Helena put the bunch of daylilies in a big vase and carried it onto the living room table. Arranging the flowers, she heard a cough behind her back, startled and turned around.

—What are you doing here?

—Came to welcome you home, Tapani said handing her the bunch of daylilies he'd hidden behind his back.

Helena looked at Tapani's swollen face and red-rimmed eyes. Am I never going to get rid of that abomination of a man, she thought. Although he was dressed in tidy, clean blue trousers and a clean white pique shirt, she could smell the old alcohol and the sweat. She'd made a big mistake spending a couple of hot nights with him years ago on a camping trip. After that he'd followed her in school, and even after they graduated, like a dog. When she'd left for Scotland to study, Tapani had moved to live with their classmate Emma after squandering the meager inheritance his parents had left him on booze and gambling. She'd heard their coexistence wasn't very happy.

—Thank you, but I already cut some.

Tapani took a step closer and she felt herself stiffen.

—Surely these will fit somewhere, he said and smiled.

She had no intention of taking the flowers. She knew from bitter experience that it wasn't healthy to go too close to a smiling Tapani.

—Put them on the table there beside the chair, she said and gestured towards the window. —I'll put them in water later. It was nice seeing you, but now I must start cleaning. Thanks for the flowers.

Tapani didn't move. Instead he sat himself on the sofa.

—Great house you have here. Roomy. Nice furniture, too.

Helena shook with disgust. The man was eyeing the room as if he owned the house. How in hell am I going to get him out, she thought and reached for the vacuum cleaner in the cleaning cupboard, glancing into the living room. Tapani had raised both arms to rest on the back of the sofa and crossed his legs on the table. He didn't look like leaving anytime soon. She dragged the vacuum cleaner into the living room and plugged it in. Then she walked to stand in front of Tapani and handed him a can of Pledge and a dust rag.

—If you're going to delight me with your presence for a while longer, be useful. Dust.

Tapani got up and stepped in front of Helena. She backed a couple of steps.

—Big mistake. I won't have anything to do with any wives' chores. I'll come back when your cleaning frenzy is over, he said. —Must be the time of the month, he added and grinned.

Helena sighed a sigh of relief when he left. She locked both the front and back doors and went into the kitchen. Poor Emma, she thought and poured herself a glass of sparkling wine.

* * * *

When Emma came home she found the house in its usual chaotic state. The sound of the television filled the living room, there were empty beer cans, a couple of used glasses and an empty whisky bottle on the table. She wondered why Tapani's clothes were strewn everywhere. Tapani himself lay on the sofa in his underpants white as a dead body, holding the remote. She wanted to tell him to put his clothes away and to clean the table, but she knew what would happen if she did: Tapani would have a blind fit of rage and she more bruises.

Emma returned to the kitchen and unloaded the groceries. She put the whisky bottles and the beers on the kitchen table. Then she dug out her new perfume from her handbag and walked over to Tapani.

—Did you bring the booze?

—Yes, yes. Everything's on the kitchen table.

She looked around in the room.

—This place needs cleaning.

—What's this cleaning frenzy going on in this village, Tapani grumbled, shook his beer can and finding it empty, dropped it to the floor.

Emma stretched out her hand and sprayed some perfume in the air.

—Have a sniff, it's Daylily! Bought it today.

Tapani sprang up and grabbed Emma's hand holding the perfume bottle. He squeezed her wrist so hard, she had to let the bottle fall. Tapani grabbed the tiny bottle before it hit the floor and threw it against the wall.

A suffocating smell spread into the room. Emma froze. Then she barged out covering her nose and mouth with her hand. The delicate fragrance had become an overwhelming stench. Outside she breathed deeply. She heard Tapani's commanding voice, but didn't care. She had to get away! She remembered that Helena would have come home for her vacation and dug the car keys from her pocket.

When she closed the car door, Tapani came staggering out on the porch. His mouth was moving, but she could only hear a faint mumble, although he probably shouted at the top of his lungs. The whole village probably heard, but so what? Everyone was accustomed to his yelling. No one would pay attention anymore. She turned the radio louder and backed the car from the yard slinging gravel up on the porch.

* * * *

She stepped on the brake in front of Helena's house almost causing herself whiplash and stopped the car by the side of Helena's red Lexus.

—Helena! she called out as she ran up the stairs to the door.

The house looked eerily quiet. She pulled at the door handle, but the door was locked. She knocked. No answer. She ran back down, took Helena's spare key from under the steps and opened the door.

—Helena! Are you at home?

No answer.

Emma walked to the living room. Helena was lying on the sofa, deep in sleep, her arm hanging over the edge. An empty bottle of sparkling wine was on the table with an empty glass rimmed with lipstick.

Emma started gently shaking Helena. She inhaled and smelled the scent of the daylilies lingering from the vase on the table. Helena opened he eyes.

—Morning, Emma said and sat herself down. —Started your holiday with a bang, did you?

Helena got up to sit and smoothed her hair.

—I cleaned this bloody house and needed refreshment.

—Oh, right, Emma said and nodded.

She picked up the empty bottle.

—No wonder you passed out. By the way, why is your front door locked?

Helena told Emma about Tapani's visit.

—So that's why his clothes were strewn all over the house. I almost believed he'd run a fashion show for his drunkard friends, Emma said and started giggling.

—This is no laughing matter, Emma! The man is crazy, Helena said.

—You've got to get rid of him! she added and stood.

Emma's giggling morphed into sobs.

—I know, but how? she whispered. —He never leaves the house.

—We'll find a way, don't you worry.

When she returned home, Emma opened the door, careful not to make any noise. The stench of the perfume had dissolved to bearable. She heard fitful snoring from the living room. One bottle of whisky had disappeared from the kitchen table and the beer box had been ripped open. She moved the remaining two bottles of whisky onto the draining board and squatted to put the beers in the drawer in the fridge. Then she sat down and started to ponder Helena's suggestion. A garden party for the three of them started to sound better and better by the minute. All Helena's neighbors would be gone and the icing on the cake was that there would be a Lunar Eclipse, although a partial one. It would start around seven in the evening and for five hours it would be very dark. The candles would look nice in the dark garden.

Emma crawled into bed in a hopeful mind, sighed and closed her eyes. Everything would work out just fine.

* * * *

The next morning Helena got up early. After breakfast, she began to plan the menu for the party.

She spent the best part of the morning surfing the net looking for recipes for entrées, main dishes, salads and desserts. Finding some, she printed them out. She wrote the grocery list and continued surfing the web, this time looking for cocktail recipes. There was going to be lots of alcohol! Stirred drinks, shaken drinks, plain drinks and beer. Tapani would have the time of his life! And then, later, drinks with her own secret ingredient.

When she'd found everything she needed, she closed the web browser and rested her chin on her palm. She'd have a week to sort out the garden. The long grass needed to be scythed and mown. Two new flowerbeds had to be dug and she'd have to visit a nursery for new rose bushes for the both of them.

* * * *

Emma sat quiet at the breakfast table. She looked at Tapani, who'd gotten up amazingly early and dragged himself to breakfast. He sat opposite her half asleep munching on his toast. Something stirred inside her as she looked at him. She remembered the beginning of their romance. She'd been so in love! Then Tapani had moved in with her. When he hadn't found any work, everything started to slide downhill. She squeezed her eyes shut and opened them. This was not the man she'd been so madly in love with. This man was a stranger.

—Tapani, she began. —Helena is arranging a garden party next Saturday. We're invited.

Tapani raised his eyes, looked at Emma and burst into laughter. Breadcrumbs flew out of his mouth. Emma looked at his yellow teeth covered in white stuff. He started coughing and coughed for some time.

—Are you invited, too, he asked having caught his breath.

Emma crossed her fingers in her lap so hard she feared they would dislocate.

—Us. Me and you.

Tapani squinted at Emma.

—How'd you know?

—I went to see Helena yesterday.

Tapani observed Emma from behind his half shut eyelids. What had Helena told Emma? That he had brought her lilies? Most importantly: what had Emma told Helena?

—So that's where you took off. Did you go to whine over your broken perfume?

Emma didn't answer. She stood and started to clean the table. Tapani jumped up and swept his coffee cup and saucer to the floor.

—What have you told Helena? he yelled.

Emma braced herself. Must keep calm now, she thought and started to put the dishes into the dishwasher. No police now, come what may.

—I didn't get a word in edgewise. She was all about her TV show, she started blabbering and closed the dishwasher. —You know how full of herself she is. Can't talk about anything but herself. She told me that in all the next instalments there'd be a celebrity guest. She was so excited about it, she didn't talk of anything else.

Emma walked to the cleaning cupboard trying to act as cool as a cucumber, but listened for the sounds behind her and waiting for Tapani to grab her. Nothing happened. She took out the brush and dustpan making sure she didn't make too much noise and returned to the kitchen.

Tapani had sat down at the table. She swept the shards and put them into the bin as Tapani got up. He took a glass from the cupboard and filled it with whisky from the bottle on the draining board and downed it.

—Yeah, she's always pretended to be so bloody elegant and important. Even her boyfriends had to be some bloody engineer saplings.

Emma let out a quiet sigh of relief.

—I'll start cleaning now.

—I'll take a nap, Tapani said and walked into the living room carrying the bottle of whisky.

On the threshold he glanced at Emma over his shoulder.

—Don't even think of vacuuming while I sleep.

Emma rolled up her sleeves, fetched a pair of rubber gloves, a dust rag, detergent and a bucket from the cleaning cupboard. She'd have time to vacuum after Tapani had left for the pub.

She gathered all Tapani's clothes and dropped them in a heap in front of the washing machine. She'd only recently ironed a couple of his cotton and pique shirts and two pairs of trousers and now he'd thrown them all over the house. He must have tried really hard to make an effort to dress nicely for Helena. Emma shook her head. He was and had always been obsessed with Helena.

She started emptying his trouser pockets. A lighter, Spraymint mouth freshener, keys. He'd not seen a dentist in years, didn't even wash his teeth. No wonder he had to use mouth spray. Luckily she didn't have to kiss him. The mere thought made her shiver. The only thing Tapani ever kissed was the mouth of the whisky bottle. She filled the washing machine, added detergent and clicked the on button. Why had the man she once loved turned into such a monster, she wondered staring at the wall as the machine started gushing.

* * * *

On the morning of the garden party Emma woke to thunder and lightning. On her way to the kitchen she glanced into the living room. Tapani was still asleep on the sofa. Outside the rain pelted the ground sideways and occasionally hit the window sounding like fistfuls of sand. Hopefully the weather would settle by evening, otherwise the party would have to be cancelled, she thought breaking eggs into the frying pan. She'd gone through the whole party plan with Helena: the food, the drinks, the setting and decorations, even the timetable. Helena had bought everything needed and she'd given her share of money for the expenses.

* * * *

Helena bustled in her kitchen, occasionally looking out the window. If the weather wouldn't let up, the plan had to be changed and the party moved inside. It could cause some minor difficulties, but nothing that couldn't be fixed. The previous day she'd picked big bunches of daylilies and a couple of fistful of their bulbs. The whole house smelled wonderful again.

The big pot on the stove bubbled merrily. She opened the cover and peeked at the boiling bulbs and leaves in the pot and nodded. Even though the concoction smelled worse than fermenting nettles in water, the end product would turn out superb.

—This is going to be good, if not first class, she mumbled to herself.

Humming to herself, she took a bottle of brandy and a bottle of banana liqueur and started preparing a cocktail. She'd found the recipe on-line. According to the writer of the recipe the mix tasted good, but was deceptive. She smiled. Her version of the drink would be that, too. Tapani would get a real kick. They'd only drink wine with Emma. If all went as planned, they would later pop a bottle of bubbly to celebrate.

* * * *

The weather cleared by noon and the sun came out. As Emma and Tapani walked over to Helena's house the soaked ground fumed as the dampness evaporated.

—Welcome, Helena said and hugged Emma, but shook Tapani's hand only briefly.

—Where are the others? Tapani asked looking around.

—There's not going to be anyone else. This is our party to celebrate our long friendship, Helena said. —We've been friends for over 30 years! That's something to celebrate!

—Fine, Tapani said. —When's the party starting?

—Welcoming drinks first, Helena answered and went inside.

—Weird party.

—Well, there aren't so many of our classmates living in Larvala anymore.

—She could've invited somebody else, too.

—The idea popped into Helena's mind such a short time ago. There was no time. I'm sure we'll have fun.

Emma sniffed the air loudly.

—Smells delicious! The grill is on!

Tapani turned to look at the table and the three plates on it.

—Looks like it's going to be one dull party. I'm going to the pub.

Helena had come out and stood behind Tapani's back. She placed the drinks tray on the table.

—Doesn't pay to leave now, she said. —Let's have a welcoming toast.

Helena grabbed a tall glass filled with a brownish liquid and handed it to Tapani. She then handed Emma a glass of wine and took her own.

—Welcome once more!

—Thanks for the invite, Emma said and took a sip.

Tapani downed the drink and gacked for a moment.

—You sure can mix a drink, he said and wiped his mouth with his hand.

Helena smiled and glanced at Emma.

They sat talking for a while and Helena topped up Tapani's drink a couple of times. Then she stood and went over to the grill to fetch the cooked meat.

—Dig in, she said stacking Tapani's plate with grilled pork, salad and dressing.

—I'm not going to put any rabbit food into my mouth, Tapani said and pushed the salad aside.

—Didn't you know that veggies are pure medicine for sexual potency? Helena asked. —The salad dressing is an old family recipe. You can't decline, unless you want the wrath of the past generations upon yourself.

Tapani looked at the salad swimming in a brownish dressing and grinned.

—Medicine for sexual potency, eh? So, you got plans?

Helena cringed. Tapani looked at her from under his eyelids. She realized his eyes looked like a lizard's. She felt like an insect going to be snatched in a second. She steadied herself and topped up Tapani's drink.

—Just in case the pork is too salty. Emma and myself will have wine.

The bigger part of the moon had disappeared and Helena lit the candles on the table. She glanced up. It would be pitch dark very soon.

Emma sat content and stared into the candlelight. Surprisingly the evening had gone quite amicably. Tapani had eaten and drunk without grumbling about everything Helena had put in front of him.

Suddenly Tapani got up and clutched his stomach.

—I feel sick.

Helena looked over the rim of her glass at Tapani swaying beside the table.

—No wonder, considering the amount of alcohol you've drunk, she said and took a sip of wine. —You probably have alcohol poisoning.

—Call an ambulance then! Tapani cried out, vomited and collapsed to the ground.

Helena and Emma listened to his groaning.

—I can't stand that sound, Emma whispered with tears in her eyes.

—Hang on there. We just have to wait.

An hour later Tapani fell silent. The stench of feces floated towards the two women.

—He's shit his pants, Emma whispered.

—Part of the disease, Helena said.

She rose and walked holding her nose to where Tapani lay and bent to look at him.

—Won't be long now, she said returning to the table. —Let's go and pop a bottle of bubbly. It smells much better inside.

* * * *

After they finished the bubbly, they went out to collect the dishes. The candles had burnt out and it was pitch dark in the garden. The moon was hidden and everything was quiet. After washing the dishes, they returned to the garden wearing disposable gloves and headlamps and undressed Tapani.

—Will the neighbors see these lights? Emma asked touching her headlamp.

Helena shook her head the light of her headlamp bouncing off black trees.

—No fear. The Hannikainens left to visit their parents for the weekend and the Toropainens are in Rhodes. No-one anywhere nearby.

They buried Tapani in the other big flowerbed Helena had dug and planted all the rose bushes on both.

Helena threw Tapani's clothes into an empty rainwater barrel, poured a bottle of charcoal lighter fluid on top, and threw a burning matchstick into the barrel.

Emma opened the second bottle of bubbly and they toasted, staring in the dark at the flying sparks and smoke bursting from the burning barrel.

—And so he left you without a trace. As if he'd ascended into darkness, Helena said when the fire had died out.

Ms. Christine Hammar is a Native Finn and Finnish speaker, but also speaks Swedish and English, in which language she also writes. She has been writing since the time she learned how to and has written several articles for Finnish magazines (in Finnish). Ms. Hammar chaired the Finnish Writers Association, Uudenmaan Kirjoittajat ry, from 2005 to 2009 and is currently a member of the board, Treasurer, and Membership Roster Officer as well as the Association's Web-Maven. She is also the Treasurer of Lions Club Nurmijärvi/Rock. Ms. Hammar is currently writing a cozy mystery set in Finland.

CPSIA information can be obtained
at www.ICGtesting.com
Printed in the USA
BVHW02s1215261117
501262BV00002B/191/P